THE TASTE
OF BATTLE

THE TASTE

FRONT LINE ACTION 1914–1991

OF BATTLE

BRYAN PERRETT

CASSELL&CO

Cassell Military Paperbacks

Cassell & Co
Wellington House, 125 Strand
London WC2R 0BB

Copyright © Bryan Perrett 2000

First published by Cassell & Co 2000
This Cassell Military Paperbacks edition 2001

A CIP catalogue record for this book is available from the British Library

ISBN 0-304-35863-0

Printed and bound in Great Britain by
Cox & Wyman Ltd., Reading, Berks.

CONTENTS

7

INTRODUCTION

9

OLD CONTEMPTIBLE

Sergeant John Brodrick, Platoon Sergeant,
Royal Barset Rifles, Mons, August 1914

27

MAJOR ROBIN THORNE

Company Commander,
Royal Barset Rifles, The Somme,
November 1916

47

CORPORAL JACK HAYNES

Tank Corps, Cambrai, 20 November 1917

67

CAPTAIN EWALD BREIHAUPT

Storm Troop Company Commander, France,
21–28 March 1918

89

LIEUTENANT BRUNO VON RAVENSTHAL

25th Panzer Regiment, Belgium and France,
May 1940

115
SECOND LIEUTENANT ANDREW BRODRICK
Royal Artillery, Cyrenaica, November 1941

137
PRIVATE AL HOGAN
US Marine Corps, Betio Island, Tarawa Atoll,
20–23 November 1943

157
LANCE-CORPORAL TOM WOOD
7th Royal Barset Rifles, Normandy, July 1944

179
CORPORAL KEN BURMAN
Armoured Car Commander, Cavalry Reconnaissance,
The Ardennes, 15–17 December 1944

203
RIFLEMAN JAMES WOOD
Royal Barset Rifles, Malaya, 1956

221
PRIVATE JOE LUBNIK
US Artillery, Vietnam, 1968–1969

237
CORPORAL GARY SHANKLAND
Light Infantry attached Cumberland Fusiliers,
Saudi Arabia and Kuwait, February 1991

INTRODUCTION

Having been asked to produce a book on how some of the major battles of the 20th century might have looked to the soldiers participating in them, I found myself confronted with a dilemma on how to proceed, largely because the soldier's view is naturally restricted to what is going on in his immediate vicinity and he has little or no knowledge of what is taking place elsewhere. It would, of course, have been very easy for me to quote directly from the accounts left by survivors, but many of these were written with hindsight and tell us very little about their authors.

The fact is that these men were not two-dimensional figures existing solely in the time span of the evidence they have left us. They all had a background, a life after the events they described, and their own differing personalities. Their hopes, fears and ambitions were the same as everyone else's, and sometimes their motivation was influenced by factors beyond the battlefield. There was also a continuity in military life, both at the personal and regimental levels. If a man had fought in the First World War, his son might have fought in the Second, and his grandson may have fought as a conscript in one of the conflicts of the 1950s or 1960s; the chances are that, in the British Army at least, they will all have served in the same regiment.

My problem therefore was how to combine the factual experience of survivors with narratives that tell the reader how their battles must have looked to the individuals concerned. The solution seemed to lie in what has become known as 'faction', that is, the placing of fictitious characters in an historical setting and making them think and act as men of their own time. This would enable me to include episodes which actually took place in the various battles and, where appropriate, words that were spoken at the time.

Because I was dealing with war at the lowest level, where facts known to the generals are not available, none of the protagonists in

these stories holds a position higher than that of company commander; the rest are subalterns, sergeants, corporals and privates. Some
are professional soldiers, others are volunteers or conscripts. As with
any such representative group of men, their backgrounds and personalities are very different; what they have in common is the need to
overcome their fear, endure hardship and fight for their own survival
and that of their comrades. To emphasise continuity, some characters
also play a minor role in subsequent narratives.

Some of the battles I have chosen will already be familiar to many
readers. They cover several infantry actions in various forms, includ-
ing Mons, the Somme, the US Marine Corps' bitter struggle for Betio
Island in Tarawa Atoll, Normandy, the Malayan Emergency and the
Gulf; the experiences of a tank driver at Cambrai, a junior officer in
Rommel's 7th Panzer Division during the German Army's 1940
blitzkrieg drive across western Europe, and an armoured car commander thrown entirely on his own resources during the Battle of the
Bulge; artillery actions include that of a field regiment attacked by the
Afrika Korps' panzers, and the defence of a fire base in Vietnam.
None of the protagonists are particularly heroic, and indeed some are
very unwilling participants, but in their different ways they cope with
the pressures imposed on them and perform their various tasks to the
best of their abilities.

Several months elapsed between my writing the stories of Sergeant
John Brodrick at Mons and Corporal Gary Shankland in the Gulf. No
connection existed between the two in my mind, yet the thought
struck me that if they somehow met they would both feel at home in
each other's company, despite their actions being separated by eighty
years in time and the immense social and technological changes of the
intervening period. Perhaps this was an unconscious projection of the
thought that the best armies are strong in the kind of virtues that
propagate themselves. Should ever the fads and fancies of so-called
'political correctness' be permitted to poison the process, decadence
will become a fact and we shall deserve its consequences.

OLD CONTEMPTIBLE

Sergeant John Brodrick, Platoon Sergeant,
Royal Barset Rifles, Mons, August 1914

A mounted staff officer detached himself from the group containing the brigade commander and signalled the column to halt.

"A COMPANY – HALT! FALL OUT!"

As the company, leading the 1st Battalion Royal Barset Rifles, broke ranks to sprawl beside the road, Lieutenant-Colonel Aindow trotted past to join the brigadier. Sergeant John Brodrick strolled down the line to join his old friend Sergeant Dick Platt, with whom he had shared sixteen years' service in the battalion. Platt, wiping the sweat from inside his cap, was clearly unimpressed by his surroundings.

"What a miserable bleedin' dump! If this is Belgium, Fritz can have it for all I care."

"This is the worst part," replied Brodrick. "The rest of it's alright, so they say. Point is, Fritz says he wants it, we say he's not having it, so that's that."

"Yeah, alright. State my feet are in, just let the bastard cross my sights an' I'll show 'im what 'e can an' can't 'ave! Where the 'ell are we, anyway?"

"Saw a signpost backaways – reckon we're just south-west of Mons."

It was the afternoon of Saturday, 22 August 1914. Some days earlier the battalion had landed at Boulogne to the cheers of the population for whom, apparently, nothing was too good for *les braves Anglais*. Since then it had been transported by train some distance inland, travelling in cattle wagons the sides of which bore the chalked legend '*Chevaux 8 Hommes 40*', and then commenced its apparently endless march to the north.

The countryside was dull, the poplar-lined roads straight and monotonous, the cobbles of the French *pavé* hard and unforgiving, and the summer heat tremendous. Some of the recalled Reservists, now nearing middle age and badly out of condition, were unable to keep up and had straggled into camp each night red and perspiring under the weight of their Field Service Marching Order, receiving little or no sympathy from anyone.

"Didn't straggle like that on the Frontier, did ya, Metcalfe? Knew what the Afridi bints'd do to yer privates, dincha? Be fizzin' in the fryin' pan by now, like as not, wouldn't they? Drop out again termorrer an' yer'll get a dose of field punishment, understand? So sort yerself out, lad!"

Pack straps began to rub, knee-joints to ache from the steady pounding, and blisters to rise on burning feet. The younger soldiers were warned not to remove their boots or they would never get them on again. Most men, with the tacit approval of officers and NCOs, had undone the top button of their tunics. Yet, it was not all bad. Marching at ease, they had swung along in fours, laughing and joking as the miles passed. In the villages, the people had rushed out to cheer, pressing wine, cakes and cigarettes on the marching men. In the towns, although Colonel Aindow had called the column to attention and rifles were unslung and brought to the trail, it was the same, with ranks being jostled by crowds of well-wishers. There had been similar scenes before the battalion left England. Its members basked in their new-found role as heroes, willing to forget that in time of peace many of these same civilians looked on Mr Thomas Atkins as a brutal, drunken lecher, pointedly excluding him from the best pubs and confining him to the pit in some music-halls. Suddenly, he was the man of the hour, his hand shaken, his back slapped, his beer bought for him.

It helped relieve fatigue, too, when the band struck up every so often. The men also sang a lot, usually soldiers' songs the words of which happily meant nothing to the smiling, waving men and women they swung past. Recently, they had been told that the first enemy troops they would encounter were commanded by a General Alexander von Kluck. Inevitably, some wag had composed a derogatory rhyme about him, which they cheerfully bawled to the tune of 'The Girl I Left Behind Me':

Oh, we don't give a **** for old von Kluck,
An' all his ******' army!

The battalion had crossed the Belgian frontier that morning. It soon encountered the first refugees it had seen, a steady trickle of families hurrying in the opposite direction. Many had loaded their most treasured possessions on to perambulators, handcarts and farm wagons. They were harried and confused and did not respond to the men's sympathetic shouts that they would soon be back home again. From the east came a distant but steady thumping rumble which became louder as the morning wore on. When, during one of the hourly halts, they were told that it was the guns of a French army already in action on their right, a sense of anticipation ran through the ranks.

At first, the Belgian landscape was little different from the French, but gradually the open farmland was left behind and the column entered a dismal area dominated by slag-heaps, colliery winding gear and chimneys. Between them, railways wound their way along low embankments and there were clusters of miners' single-storey cottages. Here and there a church spire broke the skyline. Some of the slag-heaps gave off wisps of sulphurous smoke, but in an attempt to break up the harsh industrial scene the summits of the larger, older mounds had been planted with dwarf firs. Not even the bright sunlight could dispel the depressing nature of the view and it was this which had brought forth Platt's comment.

A guide detached himself from the group surrounding the Brigadier-General and exchanged salutes with Major Carlton, A Company's commander.

"If you'll follow me, Major, I'll take you up to what looks like being tomorrow's firing line."

"Very well. How close are the Germans?"

"Difficult to say," replied the staff officer. "Our own cavalry's a mile or two out in front, of course, and some of them seem to be in contact with Fritz's, so his infantry may be anywhere between five and ten miles off."

Their route took them between two slag-heaps to a straight stretch of canal running along a shallow valley through flat, marshy fields. The canal was about 70 feet wide and was spanned by frequent bridges. Beyond, the ground rose slightly in the distance and there appeared to be some woodland.

"You're to dig in here, Major," said the guide. "I'll bring up B Company on your left. Your C and D Companies will be digging in behind you near those slag-heaps – give you a bit of depth. Someone from another brigade will be coming in on your right. Good luck."

He saluted and rode back to where B Company were emerging from between the slag-heaps.

Packs off and tunics removed, the men began to dig steadily with their entrenching tools. By later standards, the trench was shallow, but it provided protection to chest height, the spoil being heaped on the enemy side and shaped into a parapet with embrasures. It was extended to the right by a battalion of the Cumberland Fusiliers as they came up. Colonel Aindow arrived with one of the Barsets' two medium machine-guns, which he instructed Carlton to emplace on his right so that its fire intersected that of the machine-gun on B Company's left, some 600 yards in front of the battalion's position. He also ordered an outpost to be set up in a house 50 yards beyond a bridge carrying a track to the far bank of the canal. Carlton detailed a corporal named Slater and a dozen men for the task, additionally ordering them to set up unobtrusive range markers at 600 and 800 yards from the bank, using strips of four-by-two rifle cleaning cloth attached to sticks stuck in the ground.

It was dusk by the time everything had been completed to Carlton's satisfaction. Grateful that the sun had set at last, Brodrick sat on the edge of the trench and allowed his body to cool in the comparative calm of the evening. His father had been a joiner and hoped that he would follow in his footsteps, but even as a boy he had never imagined wanting to be anything other than a soldier and in 1898, aged 18, he had, much against his parents' wishes, enlisted for a period of 22 years. Since then, he had seen active service against the Boers in South Africa and against tribesmen on the North West Frontier of India. Viewed by his superiors as steady and reliable if unimaginative, and by his subordinates as firm but fair, he had reached the rank which he believed constituted the Army's backbone and, all things being equal, he hoped to retire with a Company Sergeant Major's pension in six years' time. Meanwhile, he was content to go where he was sent and fight whoever presented a threat to his country. If he had a philosophy, its canon consisted of the four precepts drummed into him as a young soldier at the Regimental Depot all those years ago – fear God, honour the Queen (as it had been then), shoot straight and keep clean.

They were simple enough rules to follow and he had found them to be a useful guide through life.

Dick Platt dropped down beside him.

"Gasper?"

Brodrick handed him a cigarette and the two smoked in silence for a while. Platt, eldest son of a farm-hand, had left school early to ease the burden on his over-large family, working with a travelling fair during the summer and taking whatever casual work he could get in winter. In the end, sheer necessity had driven him into the Army and, finding that the security and comradeship suited him, he had decided to make it his career.

"How d'you think they'll shape up?" he asked.

Brodrick looked along the line of the trench. There were still numerous South Africa and India General Service medals to be seen on the tunics of the senior NCOs and older hands, and some of the recalled reservists even sported Sudan medals, so there was plenty of experience there. When the time came, these men would act as a steadying influence on the younger soldiers, who were an average mix of good material, men down on their luck and last-chancers.

"They'll be alright, Dick. At least they're better trained than we were the first time."

"Yeah, they can shoot straight an' fast an' they know 'ow to take up a concealed fire position. We've Brother Boer to thank for that, if nothing else. Remember Colenso? Gawd, what a shambles!"

"Remember it? You wouldn't believe the Angel Gabriel himself if he told you what went on there! Guns lost, officers down and some kid of a bugler still sounding the bleedin' *Advance!* into a bend of the river surrounded by crack-shot Boers! Bullets comin' in from all angles!"

"Yeah, we was lucky to get out o' that one. What was 'is name, that bugler? Dunn, wasn't it? Civvies carried 'im shoulder 'igh when 'e got back to London. Thought 'e was some kind of an 'ero. Should 'ave 'ad 'is arse kicked, more like!"

"That's civvies for you, Dick. Still, we learned fast after that – once they gave us some decent generals. Tough customer, though, Brother Boer – never knew when to pack it in."

"Reckon Kaiser Bill's boys'll give us much of a scrap?"

"Nah." Brodrick took off his cap and scratched his head thoughtfully. "There's a lot of 'em but they're mostly bleedin' conscripts –

doubt if there's one in a hundred o' their regulars seen what you'd call proper service. Alright, they've been bummin' their chat since they gave the French a good hidin' forty years back, but it's all wind and piss. No experience, do it all by the book."

"Wonder if the book says anything about sixteen aimed rounds a minute!"

They both laughed. Since the Boer War the British Army's standard of musketry had reached unequalled levels of speed and accuracy.

"They'll learn, just like we did – those that are still on their feet tomorrow night!" said Brodrick.

His eyes wandered along the darkening length of the canal to the right where, in the distance, it swung in a loop around the north of the huddle of lights that marked the town of Mons.

"If old von Kluck is coming down from the north-east like they say, then the blokes in that salient will catch it first, I reckon."

"Mebbe. Can't count on anythin' in this game, though."

Their discussion was interrupted by the arrival of Colour-Sergeant Doyle and his ration party with clattering dixies of tea and stew.

"Char up! Come an' get it, me lucky lads!"

With the party was Company Sergeant-Major Wood, erect as always and carrying his pace-stick beneath his left arm at the regulation angle. Through the gloom he spotted Brodrick and Platt.

"Ah, you two Sarn'ts! Just the men I want to see! The Major's back from seein' the Colonel and he says we're in for a heavy day of it tomorrow, so when your blokes have been fed I want ten men from each of you. They'll go back with the Colour Sarn't an' bring up extra ammunition – another fifty rounds per man an' six belts for the machine-gun, got it?"

"Yes, Sarn't Major."

"Right, then. An' as from now, the rest are on stag until stand to – two hours on an' four off. An' they'll keep a sharp look out while they're doin' it, right?"

"Right, Sarn't Major."

The night passed without incident. One hour before first light the battalion stood to, lining its trenches and staring silently towards the north. When dawn came, it was one of mist and thin drizzle. Birds began to sing, causing Brodrick to wonder, as he had on similar occasions in the past, that Nature always got on with its own business, whatever Man was doing. After stand-down, Colour-Sergeant Doyle reappeared with his tea dixies, sliced bread and tins of jam.

At about 0600 there came the sound of firing from the salient around Mons. It amounted to nothing more than a rattle of rifle fire, but this was quickly followed by the deeper banging of guns. Shells could be seen bursting around the perimeter of the salient. Then, quite suddenly, there was a crescendo of rifle fire lasting for several minutes, accompanied by the prolonged stutter of machine-guns. This died away but was repeated at regular intervals, while the volume of German artillery increased steadily.

Major Carlton took up a central position behind A Company's trench. "STAND TO! WITH TEN ROUNDS, LOAD!"

Along the line, rifle bolts slid smoothly open, the first five rounds were pressed down into the magazine with the right thumb and the clip was knocked away with the heel of the hand; the second five followed, the bolt pushing the top round into the chamber and simultaneously knocking out the clip with a thin metallic click.

"SAFETY CATCHES ON! WATCH YOUR FRONT!"

As the minutes passed in silence the drizzle ceased, the mist started to lift and the clouds began to break up, promising another hot day. Colonel Aindow had come forward and stood beside Carlton.

"Cavalry patrol, about ten strong, straight ahead, about twelve hundred yards," said Carlton, lowering his binoculars. "Got 'em, Colonel?"

"Yes, I've got 'em. My guess is that Fritz has stubbed his toe badly on the Mons salient and now he's trying to work round the flank. Judging from the speed they're coming on, this particular bunch haven't the slightest idea we're here."

"I agree, Colonel. If we make ourselves less visible I think we may have some prisoners for you in a few minutes' time."

The two dropped into the trench beside Brodrick.

After giving orders that there would be no firing upon pain of court-martial, Carlton continued to observe the patrol through an embrasure. The light had begun to glitter on the enemy lance points. Carlton knew that all branches of the German cavalry carried lances but, as the patrol came closer at a smart trot, it was apparent from the flat mortar-boards topping their skull-caps that this particular patrol really were lancers. As far as he could make out there was an officer and about ten

15

troopers, heading down the track past the outpost towards the bridge.

"With luck, we'll bag the lot, Colonel," he said to Aindow. "I spoke to Corporal Slater in the outpost last night, and he knows just what's required."

The patrol halted to observe the house from a distance, then, satisfied that it was apparently deserted, came on, heading towards the bridge. When they were just thirty yards away, every window and door spluttered fire. Troopers were shot from their saddles, horses went down and within seconds the patrol had ceased to exist. Two survivors, evidently wounded, tried to escape by lying along their galloping horses' necks, but neither covered 100 yards.

Slater and two of his men emerged from the door of the house at a run. The German officer, struggling to free himself from beneath his dead horse, seemed to be reaching for a pistol. Slater, who played rugby football for the battalion, landed on top of him with all his bulk, then disarmed him and yanked him upright by the collar. None of the other surviving lancers, including two wounded men supported by three unhorsed comrades, seemed inclined to argue. To the cheers of the rest of the company, Slater and his two escorts marched the captives across the bridge.

"Visitor for you, sir," he said, shoving the officer hard in Carlton's direction, "Doesn't say much, but he's tricky so watch him – tried to pull this on me!" He brandished the prisoner's Luger automatic.

"Well done, Corporal Slater!" said Carlton. "Bloody good effort, and make sure you tell everyone I said so. Keep the pistol for your trouble – never know when it might come in handy."

"Thank you, sir."

"And you," said Carlton, turning to the badly winded German, "can take off that sword. You won't be needing it where you're going!"

The young officer, slowly recovering his breath as he watched his men being marched away, did as he was bidden. He suddenly seemed to realise that Aindow was the senior officer. Awkwardly, he struggled to salute, bow from the waist and click his heels simultaneously.

"I am Leutnant Rupprecht von Hentzau – at your service, Herr Oberstleutnant!"

"Are you, now?" said Aindow dryly. "Met your grandfather while I was with the Military Attaché's office in Berlin. Taste for married ladies and meddling in Balkan politics. Complete cad if ever I saw one."

"In the German Army we do not take so serious a view of these episodes, Herr Oberstleutnant!"

"Really? I'm sending you back to Brigade where they'll want to ask you a few questions. Tell me, Mister Hentzau, before you go, did your Kaiser really call us 'A Contemptible Little Army'?"

An expression of surprise flickered across the young officer's face, but his self-confidence was clearly returning.

"I have not heard this and I think it is most unlikely. Yet, we are disappointed in you!"

"Why?"

"Because, when you have such smart red uniforms, you choose to go to war in a brown golf suit, Herr Oberstleutnant!"

"Just as you wear grey instead of blue, Mister Hentzau. Get rid of this pup, Carlton – he's too cocky for his own good."

After Aindow had returned to his headquarters, A Company continued to watch its front. Brodrick's platoon commander, Second Lieutenant Piers Allan, moved in beside the sergeant. Fresh-faced and enthusiastic, Allan had just left Sandhurst. Brodrick thought him a likeable lad although, like many another young officer who had served with the platoon over the years, he needed fathering until he was professionally capable of standing on his own feet. More enemy cavalry patrols appeared in the distance, observing the line of the canal cautiously. From Mons itself, the sound of battle had intensified and seemed to be moving further south. To the rear, church bells could be heard ringing for morning service.

"They must know where we are by now, Sergeant," said Allan.

"They're not quite sure, sir. Anyway, they'll want to work us over a bit with their artillery before they start anything."

Ten minutes later the first shells began to arrive. Brodrick was surprised that the enemy had so many guns at his disposal, but he was correct in his assumption that the gunners were unsure of their target. The shells, a mix of high-explosive and shrapnel, exploded and burst over a wide area stretching from the far bank of the canal to the slagheaps behind. As far as A Company was concerned, the bombardment caused neither casualties nor damage during its brief duration.

"Here they come!" shouted someone.

Emerging from the trees in the far distance were heavy grey masses. They seemed to consist of companies ranked four deep in successive lines, led by officers whose swords flashed in the sunlight. They came on at a steady walk, like a crowd going to a football match. Already shells from the British artillery were bursting among them and shrapnel had begun to carve swathes through the ranks, but still they continued to advance. None of A Company's Boer War and Frontier veterans had ever been presented with such a target before. A buzz of incredulous comment filled the trench.

"Gawd, will yer look at that! Load a bleedin' amateurs!"

"Right, Fritz, me ole pal – yer askin' for it an' yer friggin' well gonna get it!"

Allan expressed what he hoped was a more professional view to his sergeant.

"We were told at Sandhurst that they rely on mass and weight for their attacks!"

"That a fact, sir? Well, we'll soon see how much good it does 'em!" said Brodrick.

"Stop jabberin' like a cartload o' monkeys! Now wait for the word o' command!"

The Sergeant-Major's bellowed reprimand reached the full length of the Company's line.

Carlton watched the advancing grey mass until it was about 1,000 yards distant, then his voice rang out.

"A COMPANY! FIX – SWORDS!"

The Rifle tradition was firmly upheld within the Regiment. With a steely slither bayonets were withdrawn from their scabbards and latched into place. Allan climbed from the trench and stood behind it, drawing his sword. Brodrick glanced up at him, sympathetically aware that the young officer was doing his best to set an example yet knowing that it belonged to another age.

"Put it away, sir, before you do someone an injury!"

"But ..."

"Best save it for close quarters, sir – not that it'll come to that this time. Now jump back in – you don't want to give our position away, now, do you?"

Allan slid down into the trench, looking foolish and a little hurt. Brodrick decided to mollify him.

"Besides, sir, you're more use to us alive than dead!"

The platoon commander grinned ruefully.

"If you say so, Sergeant. You're usually right."

Carlton watched the leading German ranks pass the unobtrusive 800-yard range marker.

"A COMPANY – AT SIX HUNDRED YARDS ..."

The riflemen adjusted their leaf backsights, adopting their firing position while, in low voices, the old hands offered advice.

"Check your safety catch is off ... mark your target ... aim at the belt buckle ... wait for the word of command!"

"RAPID INDEPENDENT ... FIRE!"

The front of the company erupted in a sudden blast of flame. Staying in the aim, the riflemen worked their bolts with practised efficiency, firing at the steady rate of one round in less than four seconds. Soon the floor of the trench was littered with empty brass cases. On the flanks the machine-guns were stuttering steadily as belts snaked their way into the breeches.

The leading German companies staggered as if hit between the eyes, their dense formation ensuring that each bullet found two billets. Within a minute they had collapsed in a sprawl of grey heaps. Waving their swords, the officers of the second wave led their men on, breaking into a run in the desperate hope of crossing the bullet-swept killing ground as quickly as possible. Their formation now ragged, the Germans surged forward with suicidal courage.

"Sights down, sir?" Brodrick suggested to Allan.

"Yes. SIGHTS – FOUR HUNDRED! CARRY ON FIRING!"

The last few scattered groups whose will had carried them through the murderous artillery, musketry and machine-gun fire collapsed 100 yards short of Corporal Slater's outpost.

"CEASE FIRING! PLATOON MARKSMEN ONLY – FIRE AT WILL!"

"Another little trick we learned from Brother Boer, sir," explained Brodrick. "They're not all dead and wounded out there, not by a long chalk, so we'll tickle up anyone likely to cause trouble."

He detailed the platoon's First Class Shots for the task.

"Corporal Gibson, Lance-Corporal Cooper, Riflemen Shaw, Hughes and Gordon. You're after officers, NCOs, blokes showing a bit of initiative and anyone who wants to carry on scrapping – got it?"

Some of the Germans had begun shooting from among the bodies of their comrades. Most of their fire went high and they were the first to die at the marksmen's hands. Next, a steady toll was taken of officers and NCOs until all among the fallen grey ranks had learned to lie still.

For over an hour nothing further happened. The sun climbed towards noon as the Riflemen squatted in the trench, slaking their thirst from their water-bottles and swapping stories. Brodrick smiled inwardly, observing that, as always, the younger soldiers were the most voluble. Their morale was understandably high, but he could not let it turn to dangerous over-confidence.

"Alright, alright, that's enough – all you've done is earn your pay! So stop twitterin' like big soft girls an' make sure you've got a full magazine for the next lot!"

A steady drone announced the approach of a strange-looking monoplane from the direction of the enemy. It was flying several hundred feet high but the black crosses painted on the underside of its wings were clearly visible and the sun glinted on the pilot's goggles as he leaned over the side of the cockpit. The sight generated interest among the Riflemen, some of whom had never seen an aircraft before. On reaching the canal the pilot turned along it in the direction of Mons, then headed back towards his own lines.

"Now we're in for it, sir!" commented Brodrick. "He'll tell his pals in the artillery just where we are an' they'll have our range to the yard."

The bombardment, when it started thirty minutes later, was heavier than anything even the veterans had experienced. While medium shells exploded uselessly on the slag-heaps, the enemy's field gunners were clearly concentrating on the trench lines. Most of their high-explosive rounds impacted in the canal or just beyond the trench, in the bottom of which the Riflemen huddled. Shrapnel, however, began to cause casualties as it slashed downwards. In Brodrick's platoon one man was killed instantly by a splinter through his skull and three more sustained wounds to the head and shoulders. Broderick told them to apply field dressings and make for the regimental aid post when the bombardment lifted. Behind him a sudden explosion was followed by screams. A high-explosive shell had at last found the trench and exploded within, bringing down part of its walls. It had fallen between two men and simply blown them apart. Those nearest the impact and the surrounding areas were plastered with blood and fragments of flesh. One man was screaming, another vomiting and the rest were staring in a state of numbed shock. To his surprise he saw Allan working his way towards the scene. As the lieutenant began tossing the larger remains over the parapet the screaming stopped and the men fell silent as they watched. The grisly task finished, he picked up an entrenching tool.

"Listen," he said quietly. "No two shells fired from the same gun are ever quite the same – if they were, they'd keep landing in the same hole, wouldn't they? So where I'm standing has to be one of the safest places in the world, hasn't it? Now, I want some help to repair this damage."

Without speaking, those nearest began shovelling the earth back into place, the work taking their minds off the horror they had just witnessed. The task was almost complete when Carlton's whistle shrilled. This time the Germans had continued their shelling long enough for their second attack to form up and advance approximately halfway to the canal.

"Here they come again!"

Brodrick took his place beside Allan. The youngster's set face, clenched jaw and rapid swallowing all indicated that the shock of the past few minutes had begun to sink in.

"You handled that well, if you don't mind me saying so, sir."

"Frankly, I just want to throw up! You hear about people being blown apart, but no one tells you what it actually looks like, do they?"

Brodrick glanced at him, knowing that the boy was being torn out of the man, and that it was hurting.

"No, they don't tell you any of that, sir. I've never got used to it, either, but it's part of job. Look at it like this – they never knew what hit 'em."

Allan continued to stare stonily ahead. Brodrick picked up one of the casualties' rifles and handed it to him.

"You'll be okay, sir. We can use an extra hand just now, so why not grab a *bunduk* and take it out on Fritz?"

"Good idea." Allan pulled himself together with an almost physical effort. A fierce anger seemed to boil up inside him, allied to the knowledge that he must reinforce his new-found authority over the men.

"Now listen to me, No 1 Platoon! I've seen the cooks shoot better than some of you! This time you shoot to kill, or I'll send you back to join 'em!"

A day earlier they would have reacted sullenly to such a comment from a new officer, but now it was different and they knew that Allan was simply goading them to further effort.

"You heard the officer!" shouted Brodrick. "Magpies don't count, inners don't count, only bulls score!"

"A COMPANY! – AT SIX HUNDRED YARDS ... RAPID INDEPENDENT FIRE!"

Once again, the firing line erupted in its terrible 'mad minute', and, once again, the enemy's leading ranks crumpled. The Germans, however, had learned something from their earlier experience. As soon as they came under rifle fire they went to ground, then began advancing by alternate platoon rushes, covering thirty yards at a time. In this way they began to make some headway, although as the range shortened and the sequence became predictable each platoon began to take casualties. To some extent these were offset as those who had been pinned down during the earlier attack now joined the advance. Those platoons not advancing directed a spluttering rifle fire at the trench, but it was the shooting of breathless, heavily burdened men and most of it went high or thudded into the canal bank. Soon, the details of their spiked helmets, each with a regimental number on its cover, became visible. Finally, firing from the hip, stepping or stumbling over their fallen comrades, the remnant of the attackers sank to the ground just fifty yards short of the canal and not even their officers' frenzied shouts of '*Vorwärts!*' could get them moving again.

Carlton appeared at Allan's elbow.

"They're getting too close for comfort, Piers. I want your platoon to clear the immediate area beyond the bridge. It'll give the Sappers a chance to put their demolition charges in place, and at the same time we'll pull in Corporal Slater and his chaps from the outpost. You'll get covering fire from the rest of the Company. Brigade have asked the Gunners to put down a barrage for you in five minutes' time, so be ready to move."

"Yes, sir." Allan gave his orders and Brodrick chased the men out of the trench to the limited shelter provided by the bridge approach.

"Come on, you horrible lot! Time for some cold steel – just the chance you've been waiting for!"

Also crouched below the bridge approach were a Royal Engineer lieutenant, a sergeant and two sappers with their demolition charges.

"Wouldn't have your job for a big clock!" said Brodrick to his opposite number. "Don't you go blowing that thing until we're all back on this side!"

"Don't worry, chum, we'll keep an eye on you!"

A sound similar to tearing cloth marked the start of the artillery barrage. A line of shell bursts erupted some 300 yards beyond the bridge, tossing some of the prone Germans about.

Allan had already drawn his sword and revolver.

"COME ON, NUMBER ONE PLATOON!"

Across the bridge the platoon shook out into an extended line.

"CHARGE!"

Yelling and with bayonets levelled, they ran at the enemy. Some of the Germans threw up their hands in surrender and were thumbed to the rear; others bolted and were shot down. There was no resistance and Allan halted the attack 100 yards beyond the bridge, forming a firing line among the enemy dead and wounded. Brodrick ran back to the house, in the garden of which a number of the enemy lay sprawled in the abandoned attitudes of death. Slater appeared at a smashed window.

"Get out of there!" shouted Brodrick. "Get your blokes back across the canal! And take the prisoners with you!"

It was taking the Germans some time to digest what had happened. They were clearly reluctant to open fire for fear of hitting their own men and during the interval the sappers' heads could be seen bobbing about under the bridge. At length Carlton appeared above them, blowing three long blasts on his whistle.

"That's the recall!" said Allan. "Back you go!"

Bullets cracked past their heads as they raced for the bridge. Breathless, they dropped into the trench. During the counter-attack two men had been wounded, neither seriously, and they were sent back to the regimental aid post. Brodrick overheard a snatch of conversation between Carlton and a captured German officer, evidently a major. The man's bloodstained right arm was hanging uselessly, his face was smeared with earth, one of the points of his carefully waxed moustache was awry and his monocle was cracked.

"For two years I train my battalion until it was the best in the regiment," he was complaining, "and now you have destroyed it! It was madness to send us against your massed machine-guns!"

"Actually, we only have two-machine guns per battalion, old chap," said Carlton equably. "We tend to rely more on good shooting by our riflemen."

The German's monocle dropped as he regarded the occupants of the trench.

"*Ach, du lieber Gott!* It is fortunate for Germany that your army is so small – but not so fortunate for those of us who have to fight you!"

Once again the German artillery opened up, presaging another attack. This time the gunners also bombarded the house which had contained the company's outpost, quickly reducing it to a blazing ruin. The attack, when it came, was evidently delivered by the opposing commander's last reserves. The attackers were fewer in number and did not press their assault with anything like the vigour displayed earlier in the day. Soon they had been driven to ground, too far off to present any immediate threat.

"PLATOON COMMANDERS!" shouted Carlton.

"Take over, Sergeant," said Allan as he left for the orders group.

"Sir!" Brodrick pulled out his watch. It said twenty-past-four and he was surprised, as he always was in action, how quickly the day had passed. Allan was soon back with fresh orders.

"Right, Number One Platoon, pay attention! We've been told to pull back!"

There was an immediate chorus of protest which Brodrick could hear echoed in other platoons.

"What the bleedin' 'ell for, sir? They're licked!"

"Yeah! See the way they ran when we went out after 'em? We can 'old that lot till Christmas if we 'ave to!"

"Shut up and listen!" said Brodrick. "You might learn something!"

"The French on our right are continuing to retreat," continued Allan. "That means our blokes in Mons are in danger of being surrounded, so they've got to pull back too; and it stands to reason that when they go, we've got to go as well."

"Trust the bleedin' French!" said someone.

"We'll move by platoons and pass through C and D Companies. Then we'll be directed to a new defence line which we'll hold until everyone else has passed through."

On the right, the Cumberland Fusiliers had already begun thinning out. The Royal Engineer officer shouted a warning and the bridge suddenly went up with a roar, scattering shattered timber and girders across a wide area. The platoon began assembling their kit. As the company were leaving the trench the sound of a distant bugle call, repeated several times, floated across the canal. Someone had provided a temporary sling for the German officer's wounded arm, and for this he seemed grateful.

"They are sounding the signal to cease firing," he said. "The battle is over!"

"Move now," said Carlton to Allan.

As they passed between the slag-heaps they caught up with No 2 Platoon, being shepherded along by a craggy-faced, broken-nosed corporal named Johnson who had joined the Regiment at the same time as Brodrick. Had he not been so free with his fists, Johnson could have been wearing sergeant's stripes by now, but he had been broken several times for brawling and was once again climbing the promotion ladder. A chill spasm of dread ran down Brodrick's spine.

"Where's Sergeant Platt, Johnno?" he called.

Johnson turned and walked slowly towards him.

"Cob o' shrapnel 'ad 'is number on it, Sarge. Took 'im in the 'ead. 'E was dead before we could get to 'im. I'm actin' platoon sergeant."

A succession of images flashed across Brodrick's consciousness. He and Dick knocking back beer in a dozen places around the world. Himself as Best Man at Dick's wedding and Godfather at the christening of his two children. Dick's joy when he finally got his Army Certificate of Education and when he put up his third stripe, as though he'd conquered the world. Dick talking about his ambition to run a tobacconist's shop when his engagement expired. Simple pleasures of a simple man, now reduced to a huddle under a groundsheet in an abandoned trench. Brodrick looked back across the canal where the numerous German wounded were supporting each other, hobbling or crawling towards their own lines.

Unexpectedly, Johnson, the hard case, shook his hand.

"I'm really sorry, chum. I mean it."

"I know, Johnno, I know," said Brodrick. "Who'd be a friggin' soldier? Come on, the pair of us have got work to do!"

By later standards, the Battle of Mons was a mere skirmish. The British sustained about 1,500 casualties, the Germans twice as many.

Its effect was to delay von Kluck's advance by a day, but not halt it. The retreat of the British Expeditionary Force from Mons was an epic of endurance during which von Kluck was checked again at Le Cateau on 26 August with much heavier loss on both sides. Following the Battle of the Marne, in which the German invasion plans were finally defeated, the BEF was moved to the Ypres sector at the northern end of the Allied line. There, between 18 October and 30 November, the terrible rifle fire of its infantry battalions and dismounted cavalry regiments defeated every attempt to dislodge them. The Germans' newly raised Reserve Corps were formed from young, idealistic but inexperienced recruits, including a high proportion of university students, and because of the horrific casualties these sustained, they referred to the battle as 'The Massacre of the Innocents'. Conversely, on 11 November the rout of several regiments of the Prussian Guard, the élite of the Imperial German Army, provided convincing proof of the BEF's quality. By the end of the battle, however, most British units had been reduced to a fraction of their original strength and, in modern terms, the BEF had simply been 'used up'. Many of its original members, especially wounded men returning to duty, were posted as instructors to the new armies that were taking the field.

Many of the incidents I have described actually took place during the Battle of Mons and the words used by prisoners are based on those spoken at the time. The Kaiser subsequently denied that he had ever called the BEF 'A Contemptible Little Army'. On the other hand, while giving vent to an hysterical outburst prompted by his generals' failure to capture Ypres, he did describe its members as 'trash and feeble adversaries, unworthy of the steel of the German soldier'. With a perverse irony, those who served with the original BEF chose to call themselves The Old Contemptibles for the rest of their lives, taking immense and entirely justified pride in the fact.

MAJOR ROBIN THORNE

Company Commander, Royal Barset Rifles,
The Somme, November 1916

An hour before first light on 13 November 1916, Major Robin Thorne left B Company headquarters dugout and joined his men for the pre-dawn stand-to. They were silently lining the trench at regular intervals with one or two peering through slits in the sandbags. Every so often their expressionless faces were lit by a flare drifting over No Man's Land. To the north the horizon flashed and rumbled with distant gunfire, while from the south there came the prolonged stutter of machine-gun fire. These things were of no concern, for they belonged to someone else's battle.

The 10th Battalion The Royal Barset Rifles was a 'Pals' battalion, raised during the heady days of 1914 when Lord Kitchener had urged groups of friends and workmates to form units in which they could serve together. So, too, were the Regiment's 11th and 12th Battalions which, together with the 10th, formed the 519th (Barchester) Brigade. The fourth unit in the brigade was the Regiment's regular 2nd Battalion, recently returned from India. At first, it had clearly not welcomed having to serve alongside the volunteer Pals, but over the previous four-and-a-half months' fighting on the Somme its attitude had undergone a complete change. The brigade had been spared the terrible débâcle of 1 July, when in the space of an hour or two the Army had sustained nearly 60,000 casualties. There had, however, been plenty of fighting since so that of the original members of all four battalions almost half had either been killed or were now in hospital recovering from wounds of varying severity. In their place had come a steady stream of men from the replacement depots who, though they might have their origins in Barsetshire and wear the same badges, had still to earn their place in the close comradeship which existed among the older hands.

Thorne's family were corn merchants and, after graduating from Oxford, he was to have joined the business. Instead, when war had broken out in August 1914, he had enlisted in the 10th Battalion and been accepted for officer training, being commissioned shortly after. The battalion's officers had then included a number of regulars and recalled reservists who occupied the senior positions, middle ranking Territorials and numerous volunteer subalterns like himself. Most senior officers, too old or unfit for active service, had been replaced by experienced men who, in the main, had been wounded during the early battles on the Western Front. However, since the brigade had first been committed to action in mid July 1916, heavy casualties among the officers had ensured rapid promotion. Thorne remained a substantive lieutenant but had been appointed acting captain days after reaching the front and temporary major just two weeks since. He was painfully conscious that his unexpected rise resulted from the death or wounding of many close friends whose absence he keenly felt, and the burden of additional responsibility weighed heavily on his shoulders. The shallow but now permanent furrow between his brows and the downward lines created by a jaw held tight too long revealed that the burden was beginning to etch itself on his features. These, together with the moustache he had grown on joining the Army, made him look far older than his 24 years.

Something ran across his boot. Instinctively, he knew it was a rat and kicked out hard, the resulting thud and squeal giving him great satisfaction. Rats in their tens of thousands, sleek, fat and self-confident, were a fact of life in trench warfare and he held them in deep loathing, particularly the manner of their feeding.

He reached the centre of the Company line. He was conscious of the dim shape of Company Sergeant-Major Brodrick looming out of the darkness and returned his salute.

"Listening post back?"

"Yessir. Came in ten minutes ago. Nothing to report."

They spoke in little more than a whisper. Brodrick was the consummate professional. As a sergeant he had fought at Mons, Le Cateau and Ypres, where he had been awarded the Distinguished Conduct Medal and earned his wound stripe. On recovery he had been posted to the 10th Battalion with a handful of similarly experienced regular NCOs, being promoted to warrant rank shortly after. Steely-eyed, erect, immaculate despite the mud in which they all lived, he always seemed in complete control of every situation and was a shrewd judge of character.

The long silence continued with every sense attuned to what might be taking place in the blackness beyond the parapet. Tiny sounds assumed immense importance until they could be interpreted. No one spoke. A line of pale grey began to show in the sky above the enemy position, 150 yards away.

A relative had recently sent Thorne a parcel, thoughtfully enclosing an oblong trench periscope. The illustration on the box had shown a clean-cut, determined-looking officer peering through the instrument while his equally clean-cut, determined men waited in a dry, beautifully revetted trench below. It was a far cry from the muddy duckboards and battered walls of his own position, which occupied a former German trench. He climbed on to the firestep and raised the periscope above the sandbag parapet.

Nothing moved. In the distance was the German wire with, beyond, some fragments of wall marked on his map as Dupont's Farm, surrounded by the shattered trunks of trees. There had been one small change since the previous evening. A German body had been hanging upside down in the company wire. Now all that remained was a leg, the boot trapped fast between tangled strands. The rest had apparently been blown apart by shellfire during the 'evening hate'. Elsewhere, the ground was pitted with craters in which lay more bodies, British and German. Why, he asked himself, did they always seem to lie in such carefree attitudes? Was it because their troubles were over? Some would be covered by shellfire, others unearthed. In death their skins soon assumed grey, yellow, blue or green tinges, then they began to swell internally until, sometimes, their buttons burst. First to be gnawed or pecked would be their hands and faces. No longer of this world, they were ignored, but one could not ignore the sweet, sickly smell of their decomposition which seemed to be everywhere. Thorne could tolerate all the other stinks of trench life, the unwashed bodies, the latrine buckets and the expended cordite, but he had never got used to this. He wished for a wind to cleanse the air and was glad that the summer flies had gone.

Suddenly, the periscope was twitched out of his hand to land with a clatter on the duckboards. Only afterwards was he conscious of the crack of the shot. The periscope had a hole drilled through it and one of the mirrors was cracked. Brodrick handed it up to him with a hint of disapproval.

"Short and sharp, sir – that's the trick! Fritz doesn't like to be stared at!"

"Och, yon kiddie's nae more than an amateur!" The Highland lilt belonged to Rifleman Jock Mackay, one of the company's two snipers, lying with his eye to a loophole. Mackay, a ghillie, had married the maid of one of his employer's visitors and moved south to become a gamekeeper. "Ye could see his muzzle flash for miles – d'ye spot him, Tommy?"

Twenty yards to the right Rifleman Thomas Rose, another former gamekeeper, was also peering through a loophole.

"I've got him, Jock. He's under that bit of corrugated iron, about eleven o'clock, just in front of their wire, right?"

"Right enough. Let's gie him a wee surprise! Sir, would ye mind hauldin' yon gadget above the parapet a while longer?"

Thorne did as he was asked, carefully watching the iron sheet. Two shots cracked out simultaneously, the sheet jumped and a jackbooted leg appeared, twitched briefly and lay still.

"We'll no be hearin' frae him again," said Mackay.

Almost at once a German machine-gun opened up, sending earth flying from the sandbags. Hardly had the gunner finished his burst than the air was filled with the sound of tearing cloth. The 'morning hate' had begun. Everyone took what cover they could as the shells landed. Fountains of earth erupted on either side of the trench, splattering those below with soil. The British guns replied, causing similar eruptions in the German lines. The hate lasted just five minutes then subsided. It was now fully light and clearly neither side was going to make a move.

"Right, Sarn't Major, they can stand down. Orders in fifteen minutes."

"Very good, sir."

Thorne walked back towards his dugout. At one point the hate had brought down part of the trench's rear wall, exposing a skeletal hand, the wrist enclosed in a rotting sleeve. Inevitably, Rifleman Haynes, a tiresome combination of barrack-room lawyer and funny man, had hung his equipment on it.

Thorne paused, pointing.

"Haynes, get rid of it!"

"Why, sir? He's doin' a useful job!"

"I SAID GET RID OF IT!" Thorne could feel an unjustifiable fury rising as he glared into Haynes' truculent face.

"Whatever you say, sir!" Haynes picked up an entrenching tool, lopped off the hand and flung it over the parapet. "Anything to oblige a gentleman, sir!"

Haynes always played it to the limit. Most of the time he was a liability. The problem was that in action he settled down and displayed real powers of leadership although, on principle, he always refused the offer of promotion.

The same shell had ripped away most of the sacking curtain over an alcove housing a latrine. Within, Corporal Metcalfe could be seen upon a makeshift seat, immersed in the *Daily Mirror*.

"Good morning, Corporal! Thunderbox a bit breezy this morning?"

"Ah, good morning, sir! 'scuse me if I don't get up!"

"Don't even think about it!" There were roars of laughter from those nearby. "What's the news?"

"Can't rightly say, sir," said Metcalfe, pointing to the newspaper's dateline. "This is last week's. They reckon we're winning, though!"

"Well, if it's in the paper it must be right, mustn't it?"

Rounding a traverse Thorne was temporarily halted by a carrying party with tea dixies and hayboxes, led by Colour-Sergeant Renshall. They exchanged salutes and Renshall paused while his men dispensed breakfast. He was below average height, a pre-war Territorial who had worked for a wholesale grocer and had slotted easily into the all-knowing, slightly conspiratorial world of quartermasters and their assistants.

"Now then, Colour, what have you brought us today?"

"There's gunfire, sir, but no rum as it didn't rain enough last night – accordin' to the MO, that is, even if it is the middle of November! Then there's burgoo, o' course, there's barkers an' beans but no bread, 'cos by the time it reaches us from the field bakery it's mildewed. Plenty o' hardtack, though, an' bags o' butter an' jam."

"What kind of jam?"

"Plum an' apple, sir."

"Plum and apple – for breakfast?"

"Yessir. Nothin' else available. By the way, sir, I picked up your ammunition indent for tomorrow on the way past."

"Well?"

Renshall lowered his voice, tapping the side of his nose as he spoke: "A word to the wise, sir." The Colour-Sergeant's expression had become so confidential that Thorne half expected a secret handshake. "I'll be bringin' you up plenty o' extra ammo durin' the day – an' two days' iron rations!"

Renshall winked as the implications sank in. "Dare say you'll know the rest before too long, sir."

So that was it. The battalion would be going over the top next day and, as usual, it was the Quartermaster's department which had got first wind of it. Thorne entered his dugout just as Marshall, the company clerk, was replacing the handset of the field telephone.

"CO's conference at ten ack emma, sir."

"Thank you, Marshall."

Woodruff, his batman, brought him his breakfast, which he had done his best to keep warm on the dugout's little internal combustion stove. No sooner had he finished than the members of his own orders group began crowding into the confined space. They included his Second in Command, Lieutenant Adam Black, Second Lieutenant Malcolm Emerson, commanding No 5 Platoon, three sergeants temporarily commanding Nos 6, 7 and 8 Platoons, CSM Brodrick and Colour-Sergeant Renshall. Thus far, he could tell them nothing, concentrating instead on the routine business of strength returns, sick reports, working and fatigue parties, ordering an additional weapons inspection during the afternoon. There were no disciplinary cases or request men to hear so that when the group dispersed he began strolling towards Battalion HQ, encountering Harry Ellis, commanding A Company, as he entered the communication trench leading back to the reserve line. Ellis could be good company, but experience had left him with a sharp edge to his humour. If he liked you, well and good; if he didn't, you were soon aware of the fact.

"Something's up, isn't it?"

"Looks that way. Phase lines all the way to Berlin, I expect," said Ellis. They both laughed. Overhead a stray shell whimpered and somewhere a machine-gun fired a long burst. These were everyday sounds on a quiet day and not worth comment.

At the entrance to the Battalion HQ dugout a captain wearing staff officer's red tabs emerged, colliding with Ellis. He was tall, thin, had a large Adam's apple and displayed prominent teeth in an insincere smile.

"Sorry!" he said.

"Ezra Slope," said Ellis, regarding him with obvious distaste. "What brings you so close to the Hun?"

"I've just dropped off some air recce photos for you – hope they're useful," replied Slope with oily charm. "I do envy you chaps, you know, in the thick of it and all that."

"I'm short of officers," said Thorne, feeling his anger beginning to rise again. "I'll give you a try if that's the way you feel."

Slope spread his hands in a deprecating gesture. "Thanks awfully, but I know I'll be needed back at Brigade."

"Can't think why," said Ellis. "Piss off, Slope!"

"Er, yes – and good luck to you both."

"Related to the Bishop," said Thorne, staring after the staff officer's retreating back. "Has to be seen to be doing his bit, but the Brigadier's been told to look after him. Old clerical family, you know."

"Makes you sick, doesn't it?" said Ellis tartly. "I hate all bolos, but he's the worst of the lot."

The dugout was jammed with the battalion staff, company commanders and attached artillery and signals officers, all trying to study their maps and take coherent notes. Lieutenant-Colonel Adrian Grantly looked what he was, a regular officer who had been on the point of retiring when the war broke out but had stayed on. Thus far, he had borne up remarkably well, but the strain of the past four months was now visibly taking its toll. His eyes had a permanently tired look and his hair, iron grey when he took command, was now white. He cleared his throat.

"Gentlemen, let us get on. We've been given a job and not much time to prepare for it. First, information. The enemy opposite belong to a Bavarian regiment. They may be less enthusiastic than our Prussian friends but you can't take anything for granted. For our part we shall be employing the whole brigade. You're all familiar with the terrain and the adjutant will be handing out air recce photos showing the details as at last light yesterday. Second, intention. This battalion will capture Dupont's Farm and wood. Third, method. A and B Companies will capture the farm itself in Phase One; C and D Companies will pass through and secure the wood in Phase Two. Fourth, liaison. To prevent a narrow salient being formed, our Eleventh Battalion will also advance on the left and our Twelfth on the right. Once the objective has been secured, our Second Battalion will relieve us and we shall go into brigade reserve. Fifth, timings. A barrage will be fired from 0650 until 0710. Our startline will be our forward trenches and we shall cross it at 0705."

More detailed briefings on specific aspects of the operation were given by the battalion's intelligence, signals and medical officers, the quartermaster and the artillery's forward observation officer.

Grantly brought the conference to a close. "Gentlemen, as usual, brigade have prepared full and complete orders for us, allowing for every possible contingency." There was ironic laughter as he held up a sheaf of papers. "I should like to add two things. The first is that we have all seen the results of rigid adherence to plans and timings. These orders are to be obeyed with intelligence and flexibility. The second is that we all know the value of firepower at the sharp end when the counter-attacks come in, as we know they will. It may or may not be possible to get the Vickers machine-guns up to you. For that reason, you will ensure that the maximum possible number of Lewis guns are with you at all times. I shall be round to wish you all luck later in the day."

Thorne spent the next few hours preparing the company plan of attack and issuing his own orders. Since the horrific casualties of 1 July it had been mandatory to detail a Left Out Of Battle Party so that decimated units could be re-formed on an existing nucleus. This time it would consist of Adam Black, his Second in Command, CSM Brodrick and a dozen men, including one or two who were beginning to show symptoms of shell-shock. This phenomenon had not manifested itself in earlier wars, he reflected, because battles had only been fought at intervals, whereas now the troops were exposed to the enemy's fire more or less continuously, imposing an intolerable burden of stress on some of them. Authority, fearing an epidemic of shirking, was far from sympathetic; the result was that by the time medical officers consented to the evacuation of the worst cases serious psychological damage had been caused. Thorne saw both sides of the argument but foresaw little respite until the present offensive was over.

When stalemate had set in at the end of 1914 the higher ground on this sector of the front had remained in possession of the Germans. The purpose of the offensive had been to drive them off it and in so doing tie down troops that would otherwise have been employed in the blood bath they were inflicting on the French at Verdun. Much of the shallow ridge had already been taken at fearful cost but the enemy was still fighting tenaciously for every foot of the remainder. Thorne calculated that the battle had already lasted about 140 days and doubted whether the task could be completed before the winter rains turned the battlefield into a quagmire. Secretly, he had welcomed the first frosts and heavy showers, knowing that soon deteriorating conditions would put an end to the fighting.

Colonel Grantly's encouragement of initiative had resulted in Thorne and Ellis adopting a common plan for the opening attack. Both companies would leave their trenches under cover of darkness while the bombardment was in progress. They would take up a position in No Man's Land within 100 yards of the enemy's wire, then rush his forward trenches as soon as the barrage began rolling forward towards his support line. Anticipating the inevitable counter-attack, both company commanders had ordered the issue of additional grenades.

After the evening stand-to Thorne strove to catch a few hours' rest. He was desperately tired but unable to detach his mind from the morrow. When, eventually, sleep did come, it was shallow and troubled. In no time at all, it seemed, Woodruff was shaking his shoulder.

"Gunfire, sir. Plenty o' rum in it today."

"Thanks. What's it like out there?"

"Cold, sir. No moon, but a fair bit o' frost."

That was bad, as movement could easily be detected against the whitened ground. Thorne shaved quickly then, leaving his service dress hanging on the wall of the dugout, pulled on a soldier's tunic with his insignia attached to the shoulder-straps. Next, he buckled on webbing equipment and began blackening his hands and face, reflecting that if officers wished to survive these days they had to be indistinguishable from their men. As he did so, the artillery began its thunderous bombardment. Finally, he donned his steel helmet and, slinging a rifle, stepped out into the flickering darkness of the trench.

He visited each of his platoons in turn. They were standing-to in the trench, blackened up and with dulled bayonets, their faces set and expressionless. Here and there a man yawned, a sign which Thorne had learned to recognise as the body's reaction to fear rather than lack of sleep. In pre-war days he had known some of them. Most were decent, hard-working men who, on summer Sundays, had put on their best suits and walked with their girlfriends or young families in the park at Barchester. He had begun to hate what the war was doing to them. On trench raids these same men would arm themselves with nail-studded clubs, vicious knives or spiked knuckle-dusters and he had seen their usually genial, easy-going faces assume expressions of bestial ferocity during the savage bouts of hand-to-hand fighting. He had begun to wonder how many of them he would be taking home with him and the thought depressed him.

He glanced at his watch. The hands were approaching the hour at which he and Ellis had agreed their companies would move forward.

"Over you go – no talking and absolutely no noise!"

The ladders were in place and gaps had already been opened in the wire. He clambered out with them and was conscious of stealthy movement all round him. Shells could be seen bursting in and just short of the German trenches. At length the forward movement ceased and the line lay still, awaiting the moment to attack.

The shelling slackened momentarily, telling Thorne that the gunners were adjusting their sights for the next phase of the rolling barrage. He was worried that the Company, lying dark against the frosted ground, was visible to the enemy who would now be tumbling up from their dugouts. Sure enough, a whistle shrilled and two rockets flashed skywards, the German signal for SOS defensive artillery fire. He could not afford to let them be caught in the counter-barrage and scrambled to his feet.

"COME ON, B COMPANY – CHARGE!"

A breathless, yelling run brought them to the enemy wire. A machine-gun began to stutter. A volley of grenades was hurled at the German trench beyond, to be answered by several stick grenades and rifle fire, punctuated by explosions and screams on both sides. Some of the wire had been gapped by the shelling but there was still plenty of work for the men with wire-cutters. Then the Company was flowing like a tidal wave down into the trench. Coal-scuttle helmets could be seen bobbing along the communication trench to the rear, while those Germans who remained surrendered at once.

"CLEAR THE DUGOUTS!" shouted Thorne.

During the early days of the battle serious casualties had been sustained by advancing units which left uncleared dugouts behind them. Nothing could be left to chance and when repeated shouts of *'Raus!'* brought no response grenades were tossed inside. Meanwhile, the rest of the Company worked frantically to turn the captured trench round, shifting sandbags to create a parapet on what was now the enemy side.

As the light strengthened, a sudden prolonged howling overhead announced the arrival of the enemy's defensive barrage. To his horror, Thorne observed the dense line of shell bursts erupting not only among the battalion's advancing C and D Companies but also among the two flanking battalions. The lines halted, went to ground, and finally began drifting back towards their own trenches, taking their casualties with them.

Suddenly, Thorne felt terribly alone. A and B Companies had taken Dupont's Farm, but that amounted to little as the farm buildings had long since been reduced to brick dust that stained the surrounding chalk and only a few fragments of wall remained above ground. The shattered wood beyond the farm contained the enemy's reserve line and was still in German hands. Sooner rather than later the enemy would counter-attack in the hope of recovering the lost ground. Taking stock of the situation, he calculated that excluding wounded and those guarding prisoners, he had about 80 riflemen and three Lewis guns available to meet the attack. Two German machine-guns had been captured but the breech block of one had been removed by the gunner when he made his escape and the water jacket of the other had been holed by fragments of the grenade which had killed its crew. A runner arrived from Ellis to tell him that A Company, with 70 men and two Lewis guns, was also consolidating its position but was somewhat overlooked by a slight rise to its left.

The German bombardment, which included trench mortars as well as artillery, began at 0800 and continued for fifteen minutes, during which several men were killed or injured and a Lewis gun and its team were eliminated by a direct hit. Thorne was directing the walking cases into a dugout when a wall of field-grey, topped by coal-scuttle helmets, rose from the enemy's reserve trench and began charging across the intervening space.

Orders were not necessary. Riflemen and Lewis gunners opened fire at once. Some of the Germans dropped but the rest came on. There was a pause while Mills bombs crossed with stick grenades in the air, then the enemy made their final rush, led by a tall officer blazing away with a Luger pistol. Thorne shot him as he reached the sandbag parapet. He toppled into the trench head-first, landing on his helmet, and lay still. Half a dozen more Germans leapt into the trench, only to be shot or bayoneted in vicious little mêlées. Those attackers still on their feet could be seen bolting towards their own lines.

A sudden outburst of firing and grenade explosions to the left attracted Thorne's attention. A number of A Company's men were running from their trench into his own, covered by one of their Lewis gunners and a small grenade party. When the last of them had passed, one of his own sergeants pulled a barbed wire rest out of a recess in the trench wall and dropped it, so forming a barrier in the angle of a traverse.

A very young subaltern, face streaming with blood, reported to Thorne. He was wild-eyed and rattled out his words so quickly that they were unintelligible.

"Slow down, boy. What's your name?"

"Boyd, sir. Andrew Boyd."

"All right, Andrew, tell me what happened. Where's Major Ellis?"

"I think he's dead, sir – he was hit when they broke into the trench. One platoon was pinned down by fire from those slopes on our left. Then the rest of us were swamped – there were just too many of them, you see. Some of the chaps got away into No Man's Land – they're probably still hiding in the craters out there. My platoon was on the right, and I thought we'd stand a better chance with you, sir."

"Quite right." Thorne examined the jagged gash across the boy's cheek. The wound was not as bad as it looked, although it would leave an ugly scar. "Nasty cut you've got there. How d'you come by it?"

"Bayonet, sir. Could have been worse."

"And what happened to the man responsible?"

The subaltern frowned at the revolver he was holding, then replaced it in its holster.

"I killed him, sir."

"Didn't have much choice, did you? This your first time in?"

"Yes, sir."

Thorne handed him his flask.

"Take a good pull on this and then distribute your men among our platoons – and get yourself patched up."

A few moments later a call was passed along the trench that a German officer had appeared at the barrier with a flag of truce and a request for a parley. Thorne reached the traverse and was confronted by a genial, cigar-smoking captain and a soldier with a white rag tied to his bayonet.

"Ah, Major, so there you are!" said the German, as though he were greeting a long-awaited guest. "Perhaps you would care for cigar while we talk?"

"No thanks, I'll stick to my pipe if it's all the same to you," said Thorne. He seated himself on an upturned ammunition box and filled the bowl methodically while he regarded the other through the wire of the knife-edge barrier. "From Bavaria, aren't you?"

"*Aus Bayern, ja*. Before the war we have many English visitors to our beautiful homeland. When all this is finished maybe you will come and see us – we will give you a much friendlier welcome than we did this morning!"

Thorne applied a match to the pipe, puffing steadily until it was drawing nicely. "What do you want?" he said.

"Major, you have few men left and can expect no help from your own lines. It must have occurred to you that your position is hopeless. So, if you were to surrender now it would prevent further pointless loss of life – you and your men will be well treated, I promise you. If you do not surrender within one hour you will simply be wiped out to no purpose. The decision is yours."

Thorne had expected neither more nor less but was determined to give nothing away. "I'll think it over," he said, standing up. The German saluted and disappeared behind the traverse.

"Wants us to pack it in, does he, sir?" asked Corporal Metcalfe as Thorne walked past. "I reckon we've got him worried."

"Could be," said Thorne. The facts of the matter were, however, as the German had stated them. Since the survivors of A Company had joined he had about 90 men and three Lewis guns with which to defend a single trench lacking wire on its exposed side. Sooner or later they would be overwhelmed. One alternative was to retire to their own lines, but that was impossible in daylight and by sunset the probability was that his Company would have ceased to exist if they remained where they were. So what was he to do? The unexpected, said a voice in his head – you do the unexpected. And what was that? Why, attack, of course! He took out the detailed air reconnaissance photographs he had been given and studied them. From the trench he was holding two parallel communication trenches ran back to the reserve trench which remained in the enemy's possession and lay just beyond the shattered copse. If he could take the reserve trench the communication trenches could be incorporated in a scheme of all-round defence. The men would be stretched very thin but against this it would make accurate shooting by the German artillery very difficult and disperse its effect across a much wider area. Short of surrender, there was no real alternative. He called in his platoon commanders and explained the plan to them, adding a few important details.

"There will be no shooting until we reach the objective, no grenades will be thrown, and there will be no yelling until we are within ten yards of the trench. We simply run like hell and get stuck in with the bayonet. The time is now eleven twenty-five – we shall attack at eleven-thirty-five. Now go and brief your men."

The wall of running khaki was halfway between the two trenches before the Germans reacted. A few scattered shots rang out and an alarm whistle shrilled but it was too late. Those manning the trench surrendered or bolted as the yelling riflemen poured over the parapet. Many of the Germans were still below in their dugouts. Grenades in hand, men were already shouting for them to come up.

"*Raus! Raus mit Hände hoch!*"

The occupants filed out with their hands raised. Grenades were then flung down the stairways and parties descended into the smoking interiors to collect the enemy's weapons and ammunition. A wounded sergeant seemed to be the senior rank present and from him Thorne learned that the company's only officer had been killed during the morning's counter-attack. He was surprised to discover that there were less than forty prisoners, most of whom seemed to welcome captivity. That suggested the German threat of extermination had been a bluff, but what was the reason for it? The enemy was obviously not going to mount a major attack on the main British line, but he might be planning a limited withdrawal and in such circumstances the close proximity of Thorne's Company would be far from welcome. If that were the case, their presence was now an even greater menace to the German plans and there was bound to be a vigorous reaction.

A dozen tasks demanded his immediate attention. The Bavarians had to be herded back into the dugouts and, despite their evidently low morale, guards had to be placed at the entrances. The captured trench had to be turned round, the communication trenches manned and put into a defensible state, Lewis guns sited and ammunition allocated. Some of the German rifles were issued with orders that they should be kept loaded and used in an emergency. Looking round, he suddenly realised why Dupont's Farm and its wood were so important to the enemy. They were situated on an imperceptible rise that provided an overview of the trench systems to the north and south. He also noticed that the Germans had prepared a layback position on a low, gently rolling feature some hundreds of yards to the east, so they were evidently prepared for the loss of the farm.

Taking two of the aerial photographs from his map case, Thorne marked the company's position carefully and handed one each to Woodruff, who doubled as his runner in action, and Andrew Boyd.

"I want you to take this back to Colonel Grantly. Tell him we've taken the Phase Two objective and show him where we are. Tell him we may be able to hold on until last light if he can lay on a box barrage whenever we're attacked. After that, however, we may have to pull out unless we're reinforced. Got it?"

"Yes, sir."

"Good. Make sure you take different routes – it will reduce the risk. Best of luck to you both."

As they set off down a communication trench Thorne was inclined to put his money on Woodruff, who had a strange knack of darting unpredictably between the craters, his quick movements providing only the briefest of sightings for the enemy's snipers. On the other hand, Boyd fully understood the importance of the message and would do everything in his power to deliver it. It mattered little, as long as one of them got through. Choosing a new runner from one of the platoons, Thorne set up a command post in a crater among the broken trees, taking care that he could see every point of the little salient he had created. It was strange that the Germans had not reacted yet. Against this, they had been confronted with a totally unpredictable situation and would wish their response to be effective. What would he do in the German commander's shoes? The traditional way of eliminating a salient was to pinch it out from the flanks, so the probability was that simultaneous counter-attacks would come in from north and south. His thoughts were disturbed by a shout from Sergeant O'Rorke, the beefy Irishman commanding No 7 Platoon.

"Sor! Haynes has done a bunk! Not that Oi'll miss the flappin' gob on him, but he's taken three o' the blokes with him!"

"Damn him! If anyone else tries it I'll blow his bloody head off!"

Haynes might be objectionable, but he had never behaved like this in action before. Was morale in the Company crumbling? Had the men been pushed too hard for too long, and was this the start of the rot? As the hands of his watch marked the passing minutes, Thorne was suddenly conscious of cold and an infinite weariness. For some reason Haynes' apparent desertion had also engendered a sense of depressing isolation. Knowing that he must shake this off, he toured the platoons. They seemed glad to see him and appreciative of his concern.

Shortly after he had returned to the makeshift command post the first shells began to fall. As he had anticipated, they were distributed across the entire area and caused few casualties. To the left and right he could see the enemy infantry clambering out of their own communication trenches to mount converging attacks on the salient. He blew his whistle hard but the platoons had already opened fire, the rattle of their rifles mingling with the short bursts of the Lewis guns. CSM Brodrick always maintained that their musketry did not measure up to the standards of the Old Army, but they weren't doing badly and plenty of Germans seemed to be going down. Even so, the defenders' lines were terribly thin and the enemy, moving rapidly between shell-holes, kept coming on. Thorne knew that within minutes the trenches would be overrun and it would all be over. There was a thud of running boots behind him.

"Where d'you want this, Boss?"

It was Haynes, cradling one of the German machine-guns captured earlier in the day. Behind him, another man was labouring along with the mounting and two more were carrying ammunition boxes.

"There!" Thorne pointed to his crater. "And for God's sake stop that crowd on the right!"

The mounting was set down, levelled, the gun slotted on to it, and a belt fed in the breech. Haynes settled himself behind it, satisfied himself as to the range, pulled the cocking handle twice and opened fire, traversing slowly but steadily along the German line. The attack wilted and died.

"Now the other lot!" shouted Thorne.

The gun was swung round and began cutting its way through the attackers on the left. As it did so a line of shellbursts mushroomed among them, matched almost immediately by one on the right flank and another across the front of the salient. It was the box barrage Thorne had requested and it meant that at least one of his messengers had got through. Soon the Germans could be seen running for their own trenches. It would be some time before they could mount another attack.

"I, er, think we owe you an apology, Haynes. We thought you'd cleared off. Some of us would have been in real trouble if you hadn't arrived when you did."

Haynes knuckled his forehead in mock gratitude. "Thank, 'ee, Squire, that makes it all worth while then, doesn't it! An' whatever you think o' me, I don't let me mates down."

"As I said, you're owed an apology. Motor mechanic before the war, weren't you? How did you manage to get that gun into working order again?"

"It's called cannibalisation, sir, but I wouldn't 'ave expected a gentleman like you to know anything about that. Just took the breech block from the smashed gun an' fitted it to this one – bit fiddly like, but we managed it in the end. Bin back sooner, but we stopped for a fag."

For once, Haynes was occupying the high ground in the troubled relationship with his company commander, and was clearly enjoying every minute of it.

"I'm going to offer you a Lance-Corporal's stripe again," said Thorne. "You've earned it."

"No thanks. Nothin' in the rules says I 'ave to accept promotion is there, sir?"

"No. Tell me, are you walking out with anyone special at home?"

Haynes, taken aback, assumed his customary look of truculent suspicion.

"Easy come, easy go, that's me. What's this about?"

"Whoever it was, she'd be proud to walk down Barchester High Street with a man wearing the Military Medal ribbon, wouldn't she?"

A variety of emotions flitted across Haynes' face.

"Yeah, well. Wasn't just me, y'know, sir," he said, indicating the others who worked on the machine-gun.

"I know. No one will be forgotten, I promise you."

"Thanks. An' while you're in a good mood, sir, there's one more thing."

"Well?"

"Well, I made a mistake joinin' up with the infantry. I'm a bit of a square peg in a round 'ole, as you might say. I'd be better doin' what I know best, so I'd like a transfer to the Tanks. An' as you an' I 'ave never got on, that'd suit the pair of us, sir."

Thorne debated whether he should let an experienced infantryman go, but decided that in the overall context the rapidly expanding Tank Corps could make better use of Haynes' skill.

"All right, I'll support your application. Now get that gun properly dug in."

Haynes lingered for a moment, looking conciliatory.

"Yes?"

"Er, the Company did well today, didn't we? I mean, all of us."

It was as much of an olive branch as Haynes was likely to offer.

"I think so."

Half an hour later Thorne was eating bully beef and some black bread found in a German dugout when Woodruff arrived back.

"Colonel Grantly's compliments, sir, and the Second Battalion will be relieving us at 2000. After that, we're going into brigade reserve, 'cos C and D Companies got cut up by that barrage early on. There's talk Jerry'll pull out during the night – something about new gun positions further back."

The 'evening hate', when it came, was of unusual severity and length. It was, in fact, Thorne reflected, just the sort of bombardment the enemy usually put down to cover a withdrawal to new positions. At 2000 hours men of the 2nd Battalion, looking incredibly spruce and clean, began taking over the position. With the prisoners supporting the wounded, Thorne's men began filing through the Company checkpoint.

It took about an hour to complete the handover. Thorne took his leave of the Second's commanding officer in the dugout selected by the latter as his headquarters. He found the colonel, a dapper, fierce little man, speaking on a recently installed field telephone.

"... Yes, Brigadier. Patrol commanders report the trenches on both flanks are deserted. Yes, sir. In about an hour? I'll pass the word they're expected, then. Goodbye, sir."

He turned to Thorne, smiling. "Well now, young feller, you've had quite a day of it, by all accounts. Look a bit done in, so why not join me in a sniftah before you go?"

Thorne had long since finished the contents of his own flask and was grateful for the fiery liquid burning its way into his stomach.

"Hun's hopped it, y'know," continued the colonel. "Last straw, for him, you and your chaps. The Eleventh and Twelfth Battalions are on their way forward right now. By the way, the Brigadier wants a word before you turn in – pat on the back, shouldn't wonder."

Scattered flakes of snow were falling as Thorne made his way back across the old No Man's Land. From the checkpoint figures he calculated that he had brought back some seventy fit men. Seventy from the 140 that had constituted two companies only that morning. Seventy who would be available next time, whenever that was. A week? Ten days? A month? And how many next times would there be?

The Battle of the Somme lasted from 1 July until 18 November 1916. The British sustained some 418,000 casualties, the French 194,000 and the Germans 650,000. The Allies gained a strip of territory approximately 20 miles long and up to seven miles deep. During February 1917 the Germans abandoned their remaining positions and withdrew to the stronger defences of the Hindenburg Line.

On the first day of the battle British losses amounted to 19,240 killed, 35,493 wounded, 2,152 missing and 585 captured, a total of 57,470 representing the highest casualty rate in the Army's history. On 15 September the British committed a handful of tanks to battle for the first time: they achieved local successes out of all proportion to the numbers employed and showed something of the shape of things to come. During the battle the Victoria Cross was awarded to no less than 50 individuals ranging in rank from private to lieutenant-colonel. The fictitious incident I have described is, therefore, typical of the many minor actions that made up the battle. Nevertheless, the terrible sacrifices demanded on the Somme, particularly from Pals battalions like that in our story, marked a turning-point in national history, for never again would the British place quite such confidence in their military and political leaders.

General Erich von Falkenhayn, the German Army's Chief of General Staff, had decreed that lost ground must be recovered 'by immediate counter-attack, even to the use of the last man'. As a result of this German casualties quickly exceeded those of the Allies. When Falkenhayn was succeeded by Hindenburg and Ludendorff at the end of August this doctrine was replaced by one of defence in depth with fewer troops holding the front line. Even so, losses continued to mount and the best of the professional junior officers and NCOs were killed in incessant fighting which bled formations white. It is, perhaps, wrong to place too much emphasis on the contemporary comment of one German staff officer that the Somme marked 'the muddy grave of the German field army', for that army remained capable of some very hard fighting indeed. It would, however, be appropriate to regard the Battle of the Somme as a major factor in the progressive weakening of the German Army that led to its collapse two years later.

Very probably, the point would have meant nothing to the men manning the trenches in late November 1916, for although the fighting had ceased their horizons still consisted of a few hundred yards of mud and barbed wire, shared throughout the winter ahead with the ever-present rats and intrusive lice.

CORPORAL JACK HAYNES

Tank Corps, Cambrai, 20 November 1917

In the grey pre-dawn light Corporal Jack Haynes allowed the big engine to idle as he let the tank creep forward into line with those on either side. Outside, machine-guns could be heard firing to mask the sound of hundreds of such engines, yet in this mode they made remarkably little noise. He switched off and the entire crew scrambled out for the last smoke and taste of cool, fresh air they would have for many hours. He glanced up at the huge fascine mounted above the front of the tank, then clambered on to the roof to check its release gear. The sooner he could dispose of it the better, he thought. It made the vehicle nose-heavy and sluggish.

It had been just over a year since he had been in action. Then, he been an infantryman, fighting on the Somme. As soon as the battle was over he had requested a transfer to tanks, which meant the Heavy Branch of the Machine Gun Corps. The transfer had taken several weeks to come through and during that time the divisional commander had ceremonially presented him with the Military Medal he had won during his last action. In due course he had been told to report to the field headquarters of the Heavy Branch, located at Bermicourt, a small village near St-Pol. There, he had been interviewed by a captain who, while impressed by his civilian qualification as a motor mechanic, declined to post him to an active unit.

"You're not much use to us as you are," he had said. "You need training. After that, as we are expanding at such a rate, we may make use of you as an instructor. I'm going to send you to our depot at Bovington in Dorset. If you're lucky, they'll grant you some disembarkation leave."

Evidently, his disappointment had shown, for the captain had continued:

"I've been looking through your records. There's good and there's bad. It seems you've got a chip on your shoulder. Take my advice and get rid of it. We don't like it."

That wasn't the way Haynes had seen it. His opinions were usually right, so why shouldn't he say so? Anyway, if people laughed when he took the rise out of officers and NCOs, where was the harm in that? Kept everyone cheerful, didn't it? And as for promotion, he knew a lot better than to be running round doing the officers' dirty work for them, didn't he? Nevertheless, on this occasion he kept silent.

During his leave he had met Mary. At school he had paid her little attention, but she had grown into a strikingly attractive young woman with a mind of her own. She had seemed pleased to see him and they had walked out together for several nights. Striving to impress, he had consciously made much of himself to her. Some of his stories made her laugh but others, notably concerning his successful clashes with authority, did not, much to his surprise. He was, he admitted to himself, badly smitten, and at length told her so. Her response hit him like a blow in the solar plexus.

"Now you listen to me, Jack Haynes! You're a nice enough lad underneath, but you're your own worst enemy. You go round gettin' people's backs up for no cause, an' what for – a few laughs with your pals? I want a bloke who'll make somethin' of himself. Alright, your medal's a start, but you can do better. So, just for now, I'll write to you, an' that's all! The rest is up to you."

Knowing that Mary could have her pick of Barchester, he had returned to Bovington considerably chastened. Soon, however, other matters began to demand his attention. Fascinated, he watched as the huge lozenge-shaped tanks, including the early Mark I he had seen on the Somme and the new Mark IV, crawled across the already scarred heathland. The Heavy Branch Machine Gun Corps also provided a number of surprises in itself. Like the rest of the other ranks, he was required to change his cap badge for the Corps' crossed machine-guns surmounted by a crown, although the officers continued to wear the service dress of their parent regiments. Instinctively, he sought grounds for offence in this but could find none, especially as everyone seemed to wear a tank arm badge on their right arm. Furthermore, when there was heavy work to be done on a tank, such as repairing a track or removing a sponson, everyone, officers and men alike, joined in, with orders spoken quietly by the most experienced member of the crew, whatever his rank. Suddenly he began to realise that manning a tank was a team effort in which everyone depended on everyone else. It was a challenge, but one he welcomed.

Not that he was allowed anywhere near a tank for a while. The first stage of his driver training course involved classroom study of the Daimler 6-cylinder sleeve-valve 105hp engine that powered the Mark IV. This was simply a much larger version of a Daimler 5hp engine he had worked on for one of his employer's customers before the war. He therefore had something of an advantage over the rest of the class and allowed his cockiness to re-assert itself, thereby incurring the wrath of the staff-sergeant instructor.

"Alright, Mister Clever Dick Haynes, you're not God's Gift to the Heavy Branch! Just wait till we get to transmission, steering and tracks – then we'll see how good you are!"

As he had no experience whatever of tracked vehicles, these were indeed complex areas in which he had as little knowledge as everyone else. He made mistakes but, loving machinery, he learned quickly and asked intelligent questions.

Having completed their theoretical training, the class was then introduced to the Tank Mark IV. They learned that it weighed approximately 28 tons and that there were two types known as male and female. The male was armed with two naval 6-pounder guns firing either high-explosive shell or case shot, plus two Hotchkiss and four Lewis machine-guns; the female was armed with six Lewis machine-guns. It was easy to tell them apart because the male had much larger sponsons. The crew of both consisted of a commander and driver, four gunners and two secondary gearsmen, a total of eight men. The training intake's gunners were presently on a course at the Royal Naval Gunnery School, during which they would spend some time at sea, firing the 6-pounder from the bucking deck of a destroyer at a target towed by another warship, this being considered the best way of simulating the type of firing on the move that would be needed at the front.

For driver training, the sponsons were removed to increase ventilation, giving a deceptively light and airy feel to the interior. The engine and transmission filled much of the available space; the crank handle for starting the engine, at which there was room for four men, was located behind the engine. To Haynes' surprise, the bench on which he and the tank commander sat was upholstered in red leather and stuffed with horsehair, providing a luxurious contrast with the rest of the stark interior. He had the usual driver's controls, but the tank commander had two brake levers, one for each track. He learned that to change direction he held up his left or right hand, depending on which way he intended to turn. The secondary gearsmen, who sat on leather bicycle saddles on either side of the crank casing, would then react according to his further signals. To turn left, he would point downwards with two fingers and the gearsman would disengage the drive to the left track. For a gentler turn, he would point upwards with one finger, the gearsman would drop from second to first gear and the vehicle commander might apply his brake to the left track; to return to straight running, he would hold up two fingers, the gearsman would select second gear and both tracks would turn at the same speed. Tight turns at low speed were practised endlessly to avoid the prospect everyone dreaded, namely crushing any of their own wounded infantrymen who lay in the tank's path.

Obstacle crossing presented its own hazards. The tank was set at various types of trench. Some it simply reached across without apparent effort, but at the wider trenches the nose would drop steadily until it struck the far wall. The driver would gun the engine while the tracks scrabbled for purchase and slowly the huge machine would claw its way upwards at a steep angle until the far side was reached. To this end, drivers were required to demonstrate their skill by balancing their tank on a large knife-edged ramp. The vehicle would climb steadily with nothing but sky in the forward vision slits. If the driver under-estimated how far he had to go and eased the throttle too soon, the vehicle simply rolled backwards; on the other hand, if he maintained the level of power too long after the nose had begun to fall, the vehicle would crash down the reverse slope with the prospect of causing severe bruising and contusions for those within. The mental effort was intense, but Haynes, palms sweating, managed to sit his tank on the knife-edge, nose and tail gently rocking, at the first attempt.

"Well done," said the staff-sergeant instructor beside him. "Maybe you got a knack for this after all."

Drained, he was unable to reply or even boast about it afterwards. He had already reached the conclusion that life in tanks presented its own discomforts and dangers. With the engine at high revolutions and the tracks clattering around the hull, the noise level within was appalling. The unsprung rollers of the suspension faithfully followed every pitch and roll of the ground, flinging the crew around in a series of unpredictable jolts and lurches; to save themselves, they would grab the nearest hand-hold available and burns were frequent. When, for realism, the sponsons were fitted, the temperature soon rose well above 100 degrees and the airless heat was compounded by the smell of hot oil and machinery.

"You should try it when the guns are in action!" remarked a Welsh veteran of one of the early tank actions during a lecture. "Place fills with cordite fumes and you can't breathe. What with that and the heat, you slow down so much you can't think straight after a while – not enough oxygen getting to the brain, you see. Turns some people real funny, too. So take my advice and get as much fresh air into the vehicle and yourselves while you've got the chance."

These lectures emphasised the good and the dark side of fighting in tanks. The Mark IV was not only proof against rifle and machine-gun fire, shell splinters and blast, but also against the German K anti-embrasure ammunition which had been able to penetrate the old Mark I. Against this, no real counter had been found to 'bullet splash', the spurts of molten metal that forced their way through vision slits and joints in the armour to inflict minor if painful wounds on exposed skin, and sometimes to blind; nor against 'flaking', which had similar effects and was caused by small, red-hot fragments thrown off the inner face of the armour by the impact of bullets outside. Crews had been issued with slotted metal goggles and chainmail visors to protect their faces, but these were generally discarded because of the intense heat inside the vehicle, as was an issue of leather crash-helmets. Once, an officer with a badly burned face had spoken to them about the recent tank actions in Flanders and Haynes had asked him about the dangers presented by the enemy's artillery.

"During the early stages of an attack you'll have plenty of near misses, but they won't give you much trouble," said the officer. "Once you've crossed Jerry's trenches, that's another matter, because that's when you'll run into his field guns. Normally, you can expect our infantry to deal with them, but some will want to take you on over open sights, and if you want to survive you'll get them before they get you."

The officer paused, recalling painful memories.

"A direct hit may just blow a hole in the armour and cause some casualties. You may even be able to keep fighting. But remember, you'll have nearly a hundred gallons of petrol, two hundred rounds of six pounder and thousands of rounds of small-arms ammunition aboard, so if you're penetrated there's a real chance of fire followed by explosion. If a fire starts, you've only got seconds to get yourself and your pals outside and as far away from the vehicle as possible. Use 'em well."

When the course ended, Haynes was shocked to read in the postings orders that everyone save him had been allocated to battalions already serving in France. Instead, he was ordered to report to the company office. There, the company commander tossed a pair of lance-corporal's stripes across the desk at him.

"You've done well, Haynes, and we want you as an instructor here. Sew these on right away."

"Thank you, sir, but I'd sooner get on back to France with the lads. Not really interested in tapes – just want to get on with my job, sir."

He had spoken more from habit than conviction and a trickle of fear ran down his back as he tried to visualise Mary's reaction. Furthermore, the major's pale eyes were boring uncomfortably through his own into the back of his skull.

"This is your job," said the major coldly, the edge on his voice akin to ice cracking on a pond. "You will do it, and you will do it well. If you do not, you can clear off back to wherever it was you came from, because we have no use for prima donnas here. Now, let us all get on with some work!"

"Yessir!" said Haynes, saluting smartly as he picked up the stripes.

His task was to instruct successive classes on the workings of the Daimler engine. To his surprise, he found that he enjoyed it. His ability to make the class laugh made willing students of them and this, coupled with an unsuspected capacity to impart information, produced excellent results. Six weeks later he was promoted to full corporal. On 29 July 1917 the Heavy Branch became the Tank Corps, its members changing their cap badges for one showing a tank enclosed in a crowned laurel wreath with the legend TANK CORPS enscrolled across it. Haynes felt that the Corps was already earning a permanent place in the Army and, with a surge of pride, thoroughly approved of this recognition of its independence. He did not approve of being dragged away from his class to provide demonstrations for the endless stream of politicians and minor European royalty who visited Bovington to see the new wonder weapon for themselves. His old resentment of authority began to simmer beneath the surface, kept in check by giving his passengers a rough ride and an oily handshake at the end of it. It was, however, this aspect of his work that made him feel guilty about his easy life at the Depot. He made up his mind that he wanted to return to France.

During a weekend leave he put his plans for the future to Mary.

"I've been thinking what to do when this is over. Working for someone else isn't for me. Reckon I'd do better as my own boss."

"I think you're right, Jack."

"Got my eye on a little place on the Plumstead Road. Make a good little garage, it would. We could start doing repairs, then get some petrol pumps, and when we get bigger we can sell cars. Could be a little gold mine."

"And who's this 'we' you're talking about?"

"Well, I hope we'll get married. I'd do a lot better with you keepin' me on the straight an' narrow!"

She had laughed and said she'd think about it.

"Tell you the truth, Mary, I'm thinking of going back to France, and I'd like us to marry before I go."

Her angry reaction took him completely aback.

"You stupid man, Jack Haynes – you've already done your bit! Can't you see I want to be your wife, not your widow? Plenty o' girls got married 'cos their blokes were goin' to France, an' now they're wearin' black! If they send you, I'll wait for you, but if you volunteer you'll just have to take your chances!"

And with that she had burst into floods of tears. No one had ever cried for him before and, beyond mumbling a promise not to volunteer, he knew not what to say or do.

The whole matter, in fact, was out of his hands. The underlying current of talk at the Depot was that in France the generals persisted in employing tanks on shell-torn, waterlogged sectors of the front. When, as they often did, the tanks bogged down in the atrocious going, they were blamed for the subsequent failure of an attack. If the process continued, the future of the Corps seemed uncertain, but there were also rumours that its senior officers had demanded the chance to show what it could achieve with a concentrated attack delivered over ground of their own choosing. Nothing was said officially, but in mid-October the junior instructors from the Depot suddenly received orders to report to the huge tank complex that had been established at Erin in France.

Haynes found himself serving with H Battalion, where he was not only allocated a tank of his own to drive but also required to bring several drivers in his company up to scratch. Much of the time was spent putting together large, tightly bound bundles of brushwood. Seventy-five such bundles were then assembled into a huge fascine around which chains were passed and hauled taut by two tanks pulling in opposite directions. When finished, the fascine was ten feet wide, nearly five feet in diameter and weighed over a ton.

The purpose of the fascines was explained at a subsequent briefing. The Corps was to attack a sector of the famed Hindenburg Line, which the enemy considered to be impregnable. This was fronted by deep belts of barbed wire that were impenetrable by infantry and its trenches had been dug sufficiently wide and deep that tanks would be unable to cross them. To solve the problem the Corps had devised a drill using fascines. Within companies, three-strong sections would advance in arrowhead formation. The leading tank would crush its way through the enemy wire and turn left on reaching the first trench, engaging the defenders with its starboard guns. Of the two tanks following behind, that on the left would release its fascine into the trench, cross it and also turn left, opening fire with its port guns. The third tank would cross the same fascine and head for the support trench, into which it would drop its own fascine then cross and turn left. Finally, the lead tank would retrace its path, cross the front trench by the first fascine and, with the second tank, cross the support trench by the second fascine. This would leave the entire section beyond the support line with one fascine in reserve and the supporting infantry closing up behind.

Some training was carried out, during which Haynes noticed that a few tanks had been fitted with chains and grapnels. These, he deduced, would be used to pull large sections of wire out of the infantry's path. Much of the time, however, was spent in getting the tanks into a battleworthy condition. Ammunition lorries arrived in each section's maintenance area, the males each stowing 184 high-explosive shells and 20 rounds of case shot for their 6-pounders, plus 5,640 rounds for their machine-guns, while each of the females stowed 12,972 rounds of machine-gun ammunition. Finally, the huge fascines were hoisted aboard, secured and their release mechanism checked.

During the third week of November units began leaving Erin for the front. As the company drove its Mark IV tanks up the ramp on to the line of waiting railway flats, Haynes could see several more fully loaded tank trains on parallel sidings. Clearly, the coming attack would involve several hundred tanks. Their loads carefully sheeted under tarpaulins, the trains left as soon as it was dark and long before dawn had reached their destinations. Once unloaded, the tanks were led on foot by their commanders into lying-up areas in ruined villages and woods, then carefully camouflaged. No fires or lights were permitted, nor was wandering away from the vehicle in daylight.

It was clear to Haynes that they would be going in soon. His intestines began to ravel as the old familiar knots of fear took hold. More than ever, he wanted to survive, uninjured, because now he had someone very special of his own at home. Experience had taught him that waiting was the worst part, sometimes worse than the reality. Keeping busy helped, as it distracted the mind from fear and even loved ones. He polished the various parts of the engine until they gleamed, then did it again.

The tank commander was a young Scottish officer, Second Lieutenant Sandy Dunbar, who still continued to sport his Glengarry. During the afternoon of 19 November he received a duplicated sheet which he read to the crew.

"It's from the Corps Commander," he explained. "It's a Special Order of the Day and it contains the following points:

1. Tomorrow the Tank Corps will have the chance for which it has been waiting for many months, to operate on good going in the van of the battle.

2. All that hard work and ingenuity can achieve has been done in the way of preparation.

3. It remains for unit commanders and tank crews to complete the work by judgement and pluck in the battle itself.

4. In the light of past experience I leave the good name of the Corps with great confidence in their hands.

5. I propose leading the attack of the centre division.
"It's signed, Hugh Elles, Brigadier-General, Commanding Tank Corps."

There was a murmur of general approval among the men. Once, Haynes would have ridiculed the idea of a general's promise to lead an attack, but this was the Tank Corps, where things were done differently. He felt a surge of pride. Later that afternoon the entire company's crews were called together, maps were distributed and the detailed plan of attack was explained. Shortly after dusk the Quartermaster-Sergeant's lorry arrived with rations for each tank, including sixteen loaves, 30 assorted tins of food and containers of fresh water.

Towards midnight the crews mounted and the tanks were guided forward very slowly along white tapes to the point where they would cross their own lines. The final stages of the approach were not completed until 0500. When he dismounted, Haynes received the impression of an apparently endless line of tanks on either side. The minutes ticked away as the crew smoked, exchanging desultory conversation. At 0600, as the light was beginning to strengthen, Dunbar gave a startled exclamation.

"Here's the General! Crew – 'shun!"

"Stand easy, please, and carry on smoking."

Brigadier-General Hugh Elles was a tall, angular figure with a strong, intelligent face that featured a hawklike nose and a determined chin. A glowing pipe was clenched between his teeth and his ash walking-stick seemed to be wrapped in some sort of coloured cloth. He moved past Dunbar to talk to the crew.

"Morning to you – tank in good order, is it?"

"Yessir!"

"Glad to hear it. In twenty years' time you can tell your grandchildren what we did today. Good luck to you all!"

The General passed on up the line. "He's getting aboard *Hilda*," said Dunbar, glancing at his watch. "Time we got mounted ourselves. Start up."

Zero hour was at 0620. At 0610 the tanks moved forward sufficiently to allow the infantry to deploy behind them, and took up their own attack formation. Haynes could see his section leader's tank some distance in front and, even further ahead and to the left, the dark shape of another tank which he guessed must be *Hilda*. Movement ceased and the crew waited the last few minutes in tense silence.

To preserve the element of surprise, and to keep the battlefield as free from craters as possible, there had been no preliminary bombardment, but at zero hour itself 1,000 guns were to open fire on the enemy trenches to neutralise the defenders. When they did so, it was with an immense flash and a concussion of sound that seemed to reverberate off the steel walls.

"Driver – advance!" said Dunbar.

Haynes signalled the secondary gearsmen to engage first gear and let in the clutch. The male began to move forward, slowly gathering speed. He signalled second gear, double-declutched expertly as he went up the primary box and opened the throttle wide with his right hand. The going, as predicted, was superb, consisting of smooth grassland over hard chalk as yet unspoiled by shellfire. They were rolling down a gentle slope and this, coupled with certain adjustments he had made to the engine, meant that they were moving at a speed well above the maximum 3.7mph quoted in the handbook; his impression was that they were doing 5mph, and perhaps a little more.

"Slow down!" shouted Dunbar into his ear. "We're catching up the section leader!"

"Safest place is as close to our barrage as we can get, sir!" replied Haynes. "Believe me, I've tried it!"

Dunbar thought for a moment, then nodded. Haynes could see the bombardment erupting along the German trench, with occasional smoke shells intended to blind the machine-gun posts. Everywhere the enemy was sending up streams of SOS rockets. Shells began to burst here and there among the tanks, their splinters rattling off the boilerplate sides. The ground suddenly fountained ahead of Haynes. Fragments of chalky soil were blasted through the visor into his face but he kept going, rolling in and out of the shallow, smoking crater. Beside him, Dunbar was yelling orders to the sponson gunners, Lance-Corporals Paddy Byrne and Mike Dexter manning the port and starboard 6-pounders, and their respective machine-gunners, Privates Dai Evans and Jim Roberts. The constant tonking sound of rifle bullets striking the armour was suddenly supplemented by a sustained metallic hammering as the German machine-guns came into action. A spark of hot metal flew off the inside of the cab, embedding itself in the back of Haynes' right hand. Angrily, he pulled it out. The wound, though small, was painful and it bled copiously. He was conscious of the 6-pounders banging away and the rattle of their own machine-guns. He hoped they were shooting fast and low, as they had been taught. A movement to the left caught his attention.

"My God, sir, will you look at that!"

It was *Hilda*, far ahead of her sisters, grinding her way forward through the 50-yard-deep belt of German wire, crushing it beneath her tracks and scattering its stakes. But that was not all. From the hatch in the centre of the roof Elles was holding aloft his walking-stick, flying a brown, red and green flag. It was the most inspiring sight Haynes had ever seen, quickening his blood and evoking in him a primitive fighting madness. He opened the throttle as far as it would go.

"Halt!" shouted Dunbar sharply. "I SAID HALT!! We've got to let the section leader and Number Two through first!"

Haynes did as he was bid, the gearsmen went into neutral and Dunbar applied the brakes. The section leader's tank crawled through the wire, crabbed round to the left and began engaging the defenders below with its starboard guns. Their No 2 tank, a female on the left of the section arrowhead, followed as far as the edge of the trench. Haynes knew that the fascine's release gear had been pulled but the huge bundle refused to move. The driver gave his vehicle a sharp nudge and the fascine toppled into the trench. The tank slid down on to it, machine-guns spitting fire, slowly crawled out of the excavation and turned left.

"They've had enough, sir!" shouted Byrne. "They're giving in! Comin' out in droves, they are!"

Once again, the sight was beyond Haynes' experience. Everywhere along the front shaken, bewildered grey figures were emerging from the trench, casting aside their weapons and helmets and walking forward with their hands raised.

"Advance!" said Dunbar.

Haynes drove through the cleared lane towards the fascine crossing. There was no sign of the fascine itself and he knew that it must be embedded deep within the trench. He was seized by a wild fear that if he botched the job, blocking the crossing with a ditched tank, he would never live down the shame of it. He caused the gearsmen some annoyance as he took time to line up the vehicle exactly on the female's track marks. Locking the differential, he eased the hand throttle open until the engine was just above idling speed, then moved very slowly forward to the edge of the trench. Still no sign of the fascine, but it had to be there.

"Hang on!" he shouted.

The vehicle passed the point of balance and the nose began to fall. He felt their own fascine shift, pulling them down faster than he intended. He had never before seen a trench so wide or so deep. With his left hand he steadied himself against the lip of the visor. Behind, the rest of the crew clung to their hand-holds for dear life. The near-vertical descent seemed endless though it lasted just a second or two. Then the nose struck something spongy.

Now! he thought, Give it everything you've got!

He opened the hand throttle to its widest extent. The nose began to level and the tank shifted uneasily as the fascine below was further compressed by its weight. As the track horns struck the far wall of the trench he could see the scars made by the female in its passing. The tracks scrabbled for a hold, dislodging loose chalk, then bit as they reached the firmer soil below. Very slowly the nose began to rise until sky appeared. He dared not show mercy to the roaring engine behind, especially as he felt his own fascine shift again, its inertia now striving to drag the tank back into the trench. When, at last, the ground came into view as the vehicle returned ponderously to an even keel, he felt such a sense of relief and achievement that he laughed aloud.

"Enjoy that, did you?" said Dunbar, with dour Scottish humour. "Well, you can do it again in a wee while. Straight ahead!"

The interior of the vehicle had become unbearably hot and as resistance had virtually ceased they risked opening the visors a little. Haynes could see that some of the No 3 tanks from other sections were already tackling the enemy's support trench, from which prisoners were straggling in their direction. To his surprise, Elles appeared, striding briskly back towards them, followed tamely by several groups of helmetless Germans. The Corps Commander had all the appearance of being a very contented man. Puffing at his pipe, he gave them a cheery wave and pointed at the support line with his stick, around which the now-tattered flag was once again furled.

"Now there's a proper general!" said Haynes. "If we'd more like him we'd have finished Jerry off long since!"

"He'll be glad of your approval," said Dunbar dryly. "Now speed up and let's get across that bloody trench."

They ploughed through the wire without incident, halting at the edge of the support trench. It was deep but not as wide as the front line. Haynes released the fascine, which tumbled cleanly into the gap to wedge itself between the lower walls. Both sets of gunners prepared to rake the trench as they crossed, but the defenders had long since either fled or surrendered. The crossing itself was much easier than before and, having been freed of its cumbrous burden, the tank seemed to take it easily in its stride.

Once across, Dunbar halted the tank and allowed the crew out for some air while the rest of the section caught up. Haynes borrowed the officer's binoculars and surveyed the battlefield. It was a scene of movement amid which widely separated shells burst periodically. Tanks and infantry were moving forward from the old enemy front line, passing droves of prisoners trudging in the opposite direction. Here and there a ditched Mark IV, nose or tail up, protruded from a trench. There were, too, a few scattered tanks, evidently halted because of battle damage, crew casualties or mechanical breakdown. The wire-cutting tanks were busy heaving away whole sections of the entanglements with their grapnels. In the middle distance the crew of a Mark IV had taken to the roof to extinguish a burning fascine, probably set ablaze by red-hot shell splinters. He wondered why they didn't dump it, then reached the conclusion that they couldn't because the release gear had also been damaged.

Whenever a crowd of infantry passed by they cheered and waved their helmets. One of their officers told Dunbar they had expected to be decimated but had taken their objectives almost without loss. Haynes and the rest of the crew lost count of the times their hands were shaken or grinning faces said something like "Thanks, chum, you done us proud!" Most of the crew knew from personal experience the sort of ordeal the infantry usually underwent and could only reply, "It's been a pleasure, mate!"

Their other tanks arrived and the section leader, Captain Robson, allowed their crews a breather. The company commander galloped up and all tank commanders were summoned to a briefing. As communication between tanks in action was almost impossible, section leaders sometimes controlled their movements on foot; company commanders, who had more ground to cover, controlled their sections on horseback. Haynes thought that their chances of survival were short term at best, but they never seemed to shirk the job. Dunbar returned to the tank with his map and briefed them in turn.

"Things are going much better than expected, so there's been a slight change of plan. We're going to exploit the breakthrough with a reserve infantry battalion. Our objective is a hamlet called Pleincourt, about a mile further on. It's marked as an artillery area, so keep your eyes peeled."

"Once we were pleased with ourselves if we advanced a few hundred yards," thought Haynes. "Now, we're talking in miles!"

As soon as the infantry arrived they moved off again. During the pause the Germans had scraped together parties of riflemen and machine-gun teams in the hope of delaying the advance until they could establish a new defence line. The machine-gunners kept firing until they were overrun or shot down by the 6-pounders. The riflemen stood no chance at all and simply added to the number of prisoners sent to the rear under escort. In their desperation the enemy also despatched waves of aircraft to attack the tanks. These had little effect. One or two were shot down by the infantry's Lewis gunners and the rest were chased off when they were bounced by British aircraft.

The advance was proceeding up a shallow downland slope when Dunbar glanced up from his map, commenting that Pleincourt lay just beyond the brow of the hill. Haynes could see that the section on their right was some way ahead and that its leading tank was crossing the crest. Even as he watched a brilliant orange flash blossomed against the front of the vehicle and it lurched to a standstill. A second flash and it began to belch grey smoke from every aperture. A sponson door was flung open and two figures appeared, running hard down the slope. A third followed from the far side. The interior erupted into a roaring inferno. A fourth figure, its uniform and hair aflame, appeared in the sponson doorway, fell to the ground, rolled over once or twice and lay still. A second later the stricken vehicle seemed to heave internally and was blown apart.

Haynes was struck dumb with horror and fear of whatever it was that lay beyond the skyline.

"Take her over very gently," said Dunbar. "Let's see what we're about."

He dropped into bottom gear and eased the tank over the crest. The few houses forming the hamlet were about 100 yards away. Between the tank and the hamlet was a German field battery. The guns had been withdrawn from their pits and, having limbered up, were hooking on to their horse teams, save for two which were covering the withdrawal of the rest. The crew of one was swinging round the trail so that the muzzle of the gun was pointing directly at the tank. Dunbar seized the forward machine-gun. It stuttered a few rounds, then jammed.

"Christ!" His voice rose as he screamed at Dexter, the starboard 6-pounder gunner. "Case shot! Field gun at two o'clock! Get it before it gets us!"

Case shot was a horrible weapon. It consisted of hundreds of small iron balls strung together with wire and it ripped apart anyone it touched. After what he had just seen, however, Haynes had no reservations about its use. The 6-pounder banged.

He had the briefest impression of the German gunners being cut to ribbons just as their weapon spat a dagger of flame. Then everything seemed to happen at once. The tank staggered under a tremendous blow. Simultaneously there was a flash, a concussive explosion and a scream of pain from Dunbar. Choking fumes and smoke caught in his throat. When they cleared he saw that the port visor had been torn off and was aware that the tank was starting to crab to the left. Through the gap the port horn was visible, badly buckled and ripped open, the broken track tumbling like a chain over the shattered idler assembly. The 6-pounder banged again as he brought the vehicle to a standstill. Dunbar, a shard of metal protruding from his left thigh, his left cheek ripped open to expose the teeth and with part of his ear missing, was white as a sheet, staring straight ahead but still pulling on the starboard steering brake.

"Got to ... straighten up," he muttered.

"It's alright, sir," said Haynes. "We got the bastards. Lost a track, though, so the rest is up to someone else."

"Better ... get everyone out, then."

"Come on, lads – give me a hand with him."

With difficulty they heaved the officer through the sponson door. The battle had passed them by and the infantry, cheering, were storming the hamlet with fixed bayonets. The two field guns were silent now, their crews sprawled around them. A third, its horses dead in their traces, was some way beyond, the gunners standing with their hands raised. Dunbar was bleeding heavily and drifting into shock.

"He needs hot, sweet tea," said Haynes as they applied field dressings to the wounds. One of the crew disappeared inside, re-started the engine and placed a can against the exhaust manifold. When the brew was ready Haynes supported the officer as he drank. Some of the fluid escaped through the gash in his cheek. As pain began to assert itself he gave Dunbar a morphia tablet, then slipped a tourniquet around the upper part of the injured thigh. A medical orderly and two stretcher-bearers from the infantry came over.

"Thanks to you, there's not been too much for us to do today," said the orderly as he changed the dressings after examining the wound. Dunbar was now semi-comatose.

"You're a lucky man, sir." The orderly sounded cheerful and encouraging. "As far as I can see, your thigh bone's not been touched, but you've still got a Blighty one. Take a while, but we'll have you back on your feet. Right, boys, take him down to the aid post."

"What's the score?" asked Haynes when the officer had been carried out of earshot.

"He'll walk, in time, with a limp and a stick. Pity about the face, though – he's a good-looking lad."

Haynes had been subconsciously aware that the orderly was wearing the black buttons and badges of the Royal Barset Rifles.

"Which battalion?" he asked.

"Tenth, Corp."

"That a fact? I was with the Tenth right through to December last year, when I transferred."

Their conversation was interrupted by Captain Robson, who had walked back from the hamlet. Haynes explained what had happened and they examined the damage together. The German shell had exploded against the inner face of the horn, close to the track tensioner.

"We've a few spare links, sir, so the track's no problem – but the idler wheel's dished, the stub axle is out of true and the tensioner's had it. Looks like a job for workshops."

"I agree," said Robson. "See that your blokes are fed, then send one of them back to battalion HQ with your exact position. They'll arrange for you to be towed out, but you may have a bit of a wait."

"Very good, sir."

Tins of meat and vegetables, mopped up with bread and washed down with tea, provided them with a very welcome meal. A large infantry carrying party with ammunition, reels of barbed wire and other consolidation stores, began filing past them towards the hamlet. Beside them strode the immaculate figure of a regimental sergeant-major. Haynes recognised him at once and jumped to his feet.

"Mr Brodrick, sir!"

The RSM turned towards him.

"Yes, Corporal – what is it?"

"Remember me, sir – Haynes?"

"Oh yes, I remember you – the King's Hard Bargain, you were! And now they've given you two tapes – what's the world coming to?"

The crew had begun shuffling to their feet. The approach of an RSM, wherever he came from, was a serious matter and could spell trouble.

"Get on with your dinner, lads," said Brodrick equably. "You may be the scruffiest, oiliest bunch o' soldiers I ever did see, but today you've done wonders, and don't you ever let anyone tell you different!"

"You've been promoted, sir," said Haynes. "Don't suppose there's many of the old B Company crowd left, are there? Major Thorne still with you?"

Brodrick shook his head.

"Passchendaele. Remember Woodruff, his batman? Got hit out in No Man's Land. The Major went out after him. Sniper did for them both."

Haynes felt a sudden and unexpected sense of sadness.

"That's bad, sir. Always did look out for his blokes, not that we all deserved it. He was a good officer."

Brodrick regarded him shrewdly. Haynes had grown up and, surprisingly, something useful had been made of him.

"Who tamed you, lad?"

Haynes grinned diffidently. "That would be telling, sir!"

Brodrick laughed.

"Sounds like a good 'un. Better marry her before someone else does! Good luck!"

During the first day of the Battle of Cambrai the mighty Hindenburg Line was breached on a seven-mile front to a maximum depth of $5\frac{1}{2}$ miles. This was achieved in less than twelve hours. In the past it had taken three months and a quarter of a million casualties to achieve a similar penetration. British casualties during the first two days of the battle were fewer than 6,000. Of the 474 tanks which took part in the battle, losses on 20 November amounted to 65 destroyed or put out of action by direct hits, 71 breakdowns and 43 ditched. Their crews, consisting of some 690 officers and 3,500 men, sustained ten per cent casualties.

On 21 November, for the only time during the war, church bells in cities, towns and villages across the United Kingdom rang out in celebration of a great victory. The Tank Corps' plan of attack had worked perfectly, save on one sector where the local infantry commander chose to vary it. Cambrai changed the face of warfare and broke the crippling power of the defence. Sadly, senior commanders did not exploit the victory and on 30 November, after the tanks had been withdrawn, the Germans counter-attacked, recovering much of the ground they had lost.

Those crewmen who fought at Cambrai were honoured for the rest of their lives by the Tank Corps and its lineal successors, the Royal Tank Corps and the Royal Tank Regiment. Haynes has been loosely based on a real individual who served as a tank driving instructor both at Bovington and in France. The rest of the narrative has been drawn from survivors' recollections of what took place on 20 November. As is sometimes the case with great battles, their common experience leaves an impression that the severity of the fighting was exceeded on many lesser occasions. The brown, red and green flag flown by General Elles was symbolic in that it signified that the Tank Corps' purpose was to lead the Army out of the squalid mud and blood of trench warfare to the clean green fields beyond the enemy's line. These colours were adopted by the Tank Corps and its successors, together with the unofficial motto, 'Through Mud and Blood to the Green Fields Beyond'. Today, when an Old Comrade dies, the Regimental journal records his passing as being to the Green Fields.

CAPTAIN EWALD BREIHAUPT

Storm Troop Company Commander,
France, 21–28 March 1918

It had been the idea of Major von Kolb, commander of the Storm Troop battalion, to hold a dinner for his officers before they moved up to the front for what they had been promised would be the final offensive of the war, already called the Kaiser's Battle in anticipation. The dinner itself, consisting of vegetable soup, a goulash and local cheese, reflected their poor rations, but the cooks had done their best with it and someone had produced a few bottles of excellent hock in which the toasts to His Imperial Majesty and to victory had been drunk. Now, the chairs were pushed back, cigars, admittedly of poor quality, had been lit, and, as was usual in a German mess, the general conversation had become a light-hearted discussion of female conquests.

It was at this stage of the evening that Captain Ewald Breihaupt decided that he really did not care for one of his company's subalterns, Acting Lieutenant Horst Meisel. Nor was he alone in this, for Meisel had a humourless, intense personality and a very large chip on his shoulder. Like many idealists, he had joined the Army straight from university, where he had read philosophy, seeing most of his friends shot down by the terrible British rifle fire during the First Battle of Ypres, better known in Germany as 'The Massacre of the Innocents'. Wounded himself, he had been posted to the Eastern Front on his recovery. There, he had displayed aggression, initiative and courage on more than one occasion, being awarded the Iron Cross First Class. He had risen to the rank of sergeant in a remarkably short space of time and in comparatively recent months had been granted a temporary commission. When the Army was combed for the fittest and best soldiers with which to form its new Storm Troop battalions, his commanding officer had had no hesitation in recommending him.

Meisel was undeniably good at his job, but his prickly resentments made him a difficult companion. On the one hand, as the son of a post master in a small town, he was proud to have become an officer in the Army, even suggesting that the scar on his cheek was the result of a duel rather than the grenade fragment that had actually caused the damage. On the other, he felt unjustly excluded by the battalion's regular officers and was jealous of the camaraderie engendered by the Spartan cadet academies in which they had spent their youth. Soon after his arrival he had made a number of tactless pronouncements on the obsolescence of social privilege within the officer corps, yet when he was addressed as *Herr* Meisel he clearly resented it as a reflection on his origins and his status as a temporary gentleman.

What people disliked about him most, however, was the pomposity with which he expressed extreme opinions, many of them clearly dating from his student days, on every conceivable subject. The French, like all Latin nations, he decreed, were decadent and would long since have been dealt with had it not been for the intervention of the treacherous British. Likewise, the Russians were shaven-headed savages, the Turks steeped in oriental corruption, the Austrians prisoners of their own habitual inefficiency. His special hatred, however, was reserved for the British, whom he described as traitors to the German strain in their bloodline, caring only for the wealth created by their maritime empire; a merciless race whose blockade was deliberately starving Germany's women and children. Just now he was holding forth to his fellow subalterns in a voice that penetrated the length of the table.

"You will, I am sure, be familiar with the prophetic work of General Friedrich von Bernhardi regarding the present war. In it the General emphasises that Germany's spiritual and intellectual vigour in itself creates an historical mission to assume leadership of the civilised world or perish in the attempt. In such circumstances, he continues, war is not only justified but becomes a biological necessity for the survival of the race!"

"My dear Meisel," said Kolb sharply from the head of the table, "Your conversation is a little too serious for the occasion. We should all like to know you better, so why not tell us an amusing story from your past?"

"Sir, I regret I have no such stories to tell," replied Meisel loftily. "My past has been devoted first to my studies, and then to the performance of my duty to the Fatherland."

"Very commendable," said Breihaupt equably. "No women?"

Meisel coloured and shook his head. There were chuckles.

"I wonder why?" someone asked.

Breihaupt was startled by the venom in Meisel's quick, angry glance down the table. The talk became general again until someone opened the inn's piano and a sing-song began. By degrees, the officers drifted away to their beds, knowing that an early start was required for their march up to the front.

Sleep eluded Breihaupt for a while, as it always did the night before he went into action. He had begun the war as a dragoon, screening the march of the armies during their great wheel through Belgium and northern France. Thereafter, there was no use for cavalry on the Western Front. His regiment considered itself lucky to be sent east, where there were still opportunities for mounted action against the Russians, rather than serve in the trenches as infantry. The short campaign in Romania during 1916 had given the cavalry a last opportunity to distinguish itself, but after the overthrow of the Tsarist regime the following spring the Eastern Front had remained relatively quiet save for one last short-lived attempt by the now demoralised and undisciplined Russian Army to regain the initiative.

As the autumn of 1917 turned to winter he began to hear more and more about what were being called the Hutier tactics, which had apparently been used with great success to capture Riga in September, to inflict a crushing defeat on the Italians at Caporetto in October, and to recover much of the ground lost during the great British tank attack at Cambrai in November. The essence of these tactics, he learned, involved Storm Troop detachments moving in groups, their chosen weapons being the grenade, of which each man carried at least one bag, the Bergmann light machine-gun and submachine-gun, and the man-pack flame-thrower. They advanced at a run, rifles slung, taking advantage of every scrap of cover, and if they encountered opposition they worked their way round it, leaving it to be dealt with by more conventional infantry units following behind. Continual movement was the essence of their tactics, their aim being to overrun the enemy's artillery batteries and, if possible, penetrate his command and administrative areas. So successful were some attacks that the Storm Troopers had actually been delayed by their own supporting artillery fire, so a system of flare signals was evolved to tell the gunners when to lift their fire on to the next target. Furthermore, at the higher levels, commanders were instructed to commit their reserves only in support of successful penetrations instead of, as formerly, against the strongest resistance encountered.

At last it seemed that someone had found a way of breaking the dreadful trench deadlock. The British, Breihaupt knew, had placed their faith in the tank but the German method seemed to produce more permanent results. Employed on a large scale, he believed that it could bring the war to a swift and dramatic conclusion. When the call went out for volunteers to form Storm Troop battalions, therefore, he had submitted his name without hesitation.

At the training centre near Sedan it was emphasised that only fit men of proven ability would be selected. He had few reservations about his fitness but was worried that his cavalry background would render him unsuitable. He was told that it would not because his experience of more mobile warfare on the Eastern Front was of greater value than that of some who would be unable to shed the ingrained methods of trench warfare, although his abilities would be carefully monitored.

The training was carried out on dummy trench systems containing strongpoints, machine-gun posts, dugouts and all the usual obstacles. The emphasis was on speed in achieving a local penetration with grenades and flame-throwers, then exploiting this with a penetration beyond the trench lines as quickly as possible. Breihaupt experienced no difficulty with this and was impressed by the enthusiasm, initiative and intelligence displayed by the volunteers under his command, many of whom had been awarded decorations during their earlier service.

Gradually, the larger picture began to unfold. The Storm Troop battalions were to spearhead a major offensive for which the Army's leading artillery experts were preparing the most devastating bombardment of the war. This would include a high proportion of the new gas shells, capable of delivering their deadly contents with pinpoint accuracy, unlike the old gas release cylinders which became a two-edged weapon when the wind shifted. The sector chosen for the attack would be saturated with high-explosive, cloaked in smoke and drenched with gas shells, leaving the already stunned defenders groping in a dense fog, choking and blinded.

Furthermore, once the Storm Troops had broken through, they would receive immediate close support from Battle Flights formed by the Imperial Army Air Service. Each of these consisted of six Hannover CL or Halberstadt aircraft manned by specialists in ground strafing. Attacking from a height of 200 feet, their task was to break up groups of enemy troops in the path of the Storm Troops.

Nor was this all. After Cambrai the Army had decided that it would, after all, form a tank arm of its own. As yet small in size, it was equipped with captured British vehicles plus a few of its own design. At this stage its function was to assist the specially trained Battle Groups in their task of reducing the strongpoints by-passed by the Storm Troops. In turn, the Battle Groups would be followed by the mass of the infantry divisions, which would eliminate the last pockets of resistance on the captured ground. To Breihaupt, it seemed as though the whole system resembled a gigantic snake in that once the tail had caught up, the head, formed by the Storm Troopers, would shoot off again.

The final stages of training were conducted with live ammunition. Inevitably, over-enthusiasm led to mistakes which resulted in accidents, some of them fatal, but this was considered to be an acceptable price if the new methods were to be honed to perfection. As usual, Meisel was grandiloquent on the subject:

"To have created a new warrior who dares to advance into the teeth of the enemy's immense firepower is a proud achievement for the German infantry. Our efforts will result in a victory crowned with glory, passing on to the new generation a spiritual legacy, namely the science and teaching of the new man. In pursuit of such ideals the lives of individuals are of little importance."

Although Breihaupt tended to disregard most of what the subaltern said, he too was affected by the general climate of optimism. The coming offensive, he learned, was to be mounted against the British. If they were beaten and sued for peace, reasoned the High Command, the French would do likewise, whereas the reverse was not the case. In addition, the overall intelligence picture suggested that the British were suffering from a number of difficulties. Their politicians, it seemed, were sensitive on the subject of casualties incurred during the previous year's battles in Flanders and were deliberately withholding reinforcements in England so that the generals could not mount another such offensive. As a result, the British had been unusually quiet since Cambrai. They had recently taken over more of the French line but such was their manpower shortage that brigades had been reduced from four to three battalions, all well below strength. They had also restructured their system of defence which now contained three elements: a Forward Zone, consisting of a series of strongpoints that were little more than fortified outposts; a Battle Zone trench system manned by about one-third of the defenders, some two or three miles behind; and a Rear Zone trench system housing the reserves, some four to eight miles beyond. The evidence provided by air reconnaissance, patrols and prisoners confirmed that every aspect favoured the coming German offensive. The Forward Zone provided the Storm Troops with ample opportunity to infiltrate; the Battle Zone was within range of the German artillery yet lacked dugouts in which the troops could shelter during bombardment; and in places the Rear Zone trenches were either incomplete or had not even been started.

As the briefings continued, the full scope of the offensive became clear. Its objective was the communications centre of Amiens, beyond which lay the Somme estuary and the sea. Once the sea had been reached, the Western Front would have been torn apart and the British armies would be confined to a coastal enclave, fighting for their own survival rather than victory.

Early on the morning after the dinner the battalion entrained for the journey to their designated sector of the front. Arriving after dusk they marched for several miles into the attack assembly area. Their fly-fronted tunics were not conducive to smartness, especially when slung about with grenade bags, but the men were conscious that they were the Army's élite and swung along with a confident air, their tramping feet marking the cadence of their marching songs. There was an atmosphere of unseen bustle and activity all around them. They passed one artillery battery after another, containing more guns of every size and calibre than Breihaupt had ever seen concentrated together. He later learned that every battery had already pre-registered its targets, not with ranging rounds, but by precise mathematical survey.

His sharpened sense of anticipation was, however, somewhat dulled when they entered the trenches from which their attack was to be launched. There, a high proportion of the infantrymen whose sector they took over were middle-aged men and boys, the majority wearing expressions of resigned disinterest, providing a sharp contrast to his own fit and eager young soldiers. For the first time doubts stirred uneasily in his mind. Had it been right to cream off the Army's best men into the Storm Troop battalions, thereby reducing the quality of the whole? How would the rest react if the promised victory did not come quickly, or the storm troopers were decimated? He forced himself to shake off such thoughts. Everything possible had been done to ensure that victory would be won. Success would in itself inspire the battle-weary soldiers of the Western Front to fresh and decisive efforts. It would also ease the situation at home, where conditions were every bit as bad as Meisel had suggested they were. There were acute shortages of food and domestic fuel, inflation had reduced the value of the Mark, there were strikes in support of political reform and Bolshevik elements were at work among the disaffected, seeking to provoke civil unrest. Thus, victory had to be won, and won quickly, before the fresh American armies now forming could reach Europe and tilt the scales irrevocably against Germany and her allies. There could be no turning back; for good or ill, the die was cast.

The next day was spent in final briefings. Officers and NCOs carefully verified the enemy's positions and plotted their routes forward, then checked their men's equipment, paying particular attention to gas masks. The medical orderlies made up the contents of their satchels, supplementing their supplies of antiseptics and absorbent paper dressings; good quality lint was but a memory now. After the evening stand-to a meal of sausage stew arrived in containers, accompanied by black bread and haversack rations for the next few days. It then became possible to snatch a few hours' rest, though such was the sense of anticipation that few slept. The front lapsed into its routine of night activity, both sides sending up periodic flares and engaging in sporadic artillery fire. At about 0200 a dense fog descended, restricting vision to a few yards. Breihaupt felt a deep sense of satisfaction. Even the Almighty seemed to be on Germany's side, providing as he had a cloak of invisibility for the Storm Troopers when they would need it most. Nevertheless, the fog would create problems of its own, particularly when it came to maintaining the correct direction of the advance and preserving contact with flanking units.

At 0440 the entire landscape seemed to rock as the massed artillery opened fire with a vivid simultaneous flash. This was followed by a long sustained roar but the air itself was too disturbed by continuous shock waves to convey more than an impression of sound. Breihaupt knew that the British guns were replying because bursting shells showered those below with flying earth. Most of his men, however, remained secure in their dugouts and, after a while, the fire of the enemy artillery slackened appreciably. The combination of darkness, fog and drifting smoke prevented him from seeing the damage done to the opposing outposts, but he doubted whether anyone would be left alive in them. He could only imagine the carnage and destruction that was taking place in the British lines beyond, the command posts and communications centres torn apart, the wrecked batteries, the wretched infantry seeking what cover they could in their incomplete trench systems and bivouac areas. To those present, he thought, the sights, sounds and sheer terror of the experience must resemble the *Götterdämmerung*, the Twilight of the Gods, from which there was no escape.

At 0640 the guns ceased firing as suddenly as they had begun. So far, Breihaupt knew that only the opening phase of the bombardment had been fired, the pause being necessary to rest the sweating gunners. Thirty minutes later the guns thundered out again. With the dawn a watery sun had risen behind the German lines, a pale orb lacking the warmth to burn off the fog although as it climbed it would be of assistance in maintaining direction. The trench periscope revealed little save swirling grey, punctuated here and there by the diffused red, yellow, violet and green flashes of exploding shells.

From 0900 onwards the bombardment rose to a crescendo. According to the briefing its pattern had now changed to a rolling barrage that would eliminate what remained of the enemy's Forward Zone with a deluge of high-explosive, gas and smoke, then lift 300 metres, remain static for three minutes, lift again, and so on.

Breihaupt ordered the men out of their dugouts. Their set faces were those of men about to go into action, but there was also an underlying eagerness which gratified him. The air was already tainted with drifting gas. At his command their familiar faces disappeared behind masks which gave a fearsome impression of ruthless anonymity. The hands of his watch moved on. At 0940 he gave the signal to advance. The platoons scrambled out of the trench and quickly disappeared into the fog at a run. He followed with the small group of runners he needed to control the company's progress.

After a few minutes he realised that he must have veered too far to the left for he came upon the wreckage of what had once been a British outpost. All that remained was a jumble of tossed sandbags, smashed weapons, bodies, torn limbs and bloodied scraps of khaki uniform.

He hurried on, correcting his direction. Already distress rockets, fired in the vain hope of relief, were soaring skywards from those outposts still holding out. Ahead, too, were the distinctive rocket signals from his own platoons, now moving so quickly that they were requesting further lifts in the rolling barrage. The going, consisting as much of it did of overlapping craters, demanded hard physical effort. Breihaupt found himself perspiring so heavily that the eye-pieces of his respirator kept misting over.

The sound of heavy firing came from directly ahead and they dived into a shellhole as bullets cracked past. The fog was suddenly lit by the orange glare of flame-throwers. Evidently they had reached the forward edge of the enemy's Battle Zone. Aware that he could not exercise proper command while wearing his respirator, Breihaupt cautiously removed it. Although the air was still heavily tainted, he decided that he must take the risk for short periods.

"Find out what's happening," he said to a runner.

The man had been gone for several minutes when one of their own rocket signals went up some distance to the right, confirming that the first line of trenches had been crossed. The runner dropped into the crater, panting as he removed his respirator to deliver his message.

"Sir, Lieutenant Hundt reports that he has encountered determined opposition and sustained casualties. Lieutenant Sichart and his men are moving up to support him."

"No, no, that won't do," said Breihaupt. "Inform both officers that they are to break contact immediately, retire into the fog and try again three hundred metres to their right, where they will find a gap in the enemy line!"

His group headed in the same direction to find that the bombardment had not only torn the British wire apart but also blown in whole sections of the trench beyond. One of Meisel's sections was holding the flanks with grenades and flame-throwers while the rest of the company streamed across and disappeared again into the grey mist. As he jumped the trench Breihaupt had an impression of dead and wounded Tommies lying on the duckboards below.

Some way beyond they came across the emplacements of a field battery which had been almost obliterated by the bombardment. Smashed guns and limbers, dead gunners and horses lay everywhere. The survivors, limbering up their one remaining gun, were taken completely by surprise and surrendered when the team leaders were shot dead in their traces. Their expressions varied according to the individual; a few showed relief, but the most common emotions were clearly bewilderment, resentment and resignation.

Leaving two lightly wounded men to guard the prisoners until they could be escorted to the rear, Breihaupt urged his officers to greater efforts, emphasising that, if possible, he wanted the company to be through the Battle Zone before the mist lifted.

Shortly after, they came across a second trench line from which a heavy fire was opened. This time, no convenient breach had been blasted for them by the artillery. Finding a communication trench, Breihaupt concentrated several flame-throwers to keep the nearest of the defenders' heads down, then pushed a group of submachine-gunners along it. Grenade explosions were followed by screams and the rattle of Bergmanns. Having taken the immediate vicinity of the trench junction, the rest of the company passed up the communication trench and scrambled out on to the open ground beyond to continue their advance. The affair had cost valuable time and casualties, including several men killed, all of which Breihaupt regretted but considered to be a necessary sacrifice.

The fog had been thinning for some time. At about 1300 it lifted abruptly, revealing the Battle Zone's third trench line some 400 metres away. The Storm Troopers came under immediate fire, supplemented by that of a nearby field battery, and for the first time found themselves completely pinned down. This was just the sort of situation for which the Battle Flights had been designed, but so far they had been grounded by the mist, leaving Breihaupt with no alternative other than await their arrival. When they and their escort did appear, however, their effectiveness was sharply reduced by the intervention of swarms of British fighters. The sky above became filled with brawling aircraft, the Germans having marginally the better of it. On the other hand, such of the Battle Flights as were able to break through strafed from the approved height of 200 feet, whereas the British came in with a real killer instinct to machine-gun at what Breihaupt believed to be little more than head height. This unsettled his men, for although it caused fewer casualties than might have been expected, the sheer sound and fury of the attacks was terrifying at close quarters, especially when there was so little cover available. Nevertheless, the German air effort must also have been effective, for during the late afternoon the battery pulled out, leaving two of its guns behind for want of teams. Shortly afterwards, the infantry left their trench, their withdrawal being covered by smoke shells.

The Storm Troopers immediately occupied the abandoned position. The trench formed the rear edge of the enemy's Battle Zone and was the final objective for the day. Breihaupt strolled over to the battery position to examine the abandoned guns; their breech blocks and sights had been removed but they would still make a useful addition to the company's tally. He was aware of the sound of continued heavy fighting from the positions they had by-passed. It seemed as though the British, having recovered from the shock of the bombardment, were offering stubborn resistance to the Battle Groups and others. Although he had never fought against them before, he was aware of their reputation for obstinacy in defence and, allowing for this, concluded that the Battle Groups would be later than anticipated in catching them up. He therefore deployed the platoons to cover an enemy approach from every angle, using the captured trench and craters.

The night was full of unseen movement which he took to be the remnants of British units retreating past them. Several times fire was exchanged with shadowy groups which swerved away into the darkness. Individuals, often supporting wounded comrades, were allowed to enter the little perimeter and promptly taken prisoner. At midnight their supporting Battle Group began to arrive, accompanied by a carrying-party with additional ammunition and a further day's rations. One of the officers told Breihaupt that, more often than not, the British had fought on until overwhelmed, inflicting higher casualties than had been anticipated. Kolb appeared shortly after, confirming that the next day's advance was to take them through the enemy's Rear Zone.

"Everything is going according to plan," he said confidently. "I have received reports that the entire enemy front has collapsed – all the indications are that we have taken thousands of prisoners and large quantities of artillery and machine-guns."

Breihaupt passed on the good news to his men, who were further encouraged when the dense fog descended again before dawn. The bombardment, though formidable, was not as intense as the previous day's, nor was it as prolonged. Once more the platoons vanished into the mist and Breihaupt followed with his runners. He glanced at the abandoned battery as he passed. To his astonishment the two remaining guns and their limbers had gone. An examination of the ground revealed that during the night the enemy had brought up teams, muffling the sound by padding the horses' hooves with cloth. He chuckled to himself at their cheek.

In less than an hour they reached the British Rear Zone, which on this sector ran along the crest of a gradual slope. At first resistance was fierce but gradually the defenders' fire slackened and finally ceased altogether. The platoons surged forward, working their way past a ruined cottage and down the reverse slope in pursuit of a few running khaki figures. When Breihaupt reached the crest he saw that the position consisted of a single half-completed trench, lacking wire and revetments, and that in places even this meagre protection had been obliterated by the bombardment. The trench contained numerous casualties and the twisted metal of what had been a Vickers medium machine-gun.

One of the runners drew his attention to the cottage. Someone was waving a piece of white cloth from the doorway. He stood up, signalling the occupants to come out. There were about ten of them, an ill-assorted lot both as to age and size. The curious thing was that while they were equipped as infantrymen, their uniforms were too spick-and-span for front-line troops. It was important to know whether the British were bringing up reserve formations. As he walked towards them two grizzled lance-corporals, the senior ranks present, stiffened to attention and saluted on seeing his shoulder-straps. Their campaign ribbons and bearing clearly indicated that they were old soldiers.

"You are reinforcements?" he asked. "When did your regiment reach the front?"

"Our regiment's already at the front, sir."

"Then why are you not with it, corporal?"

"Can't say, sir. We're a mixed bunch – I'm the regimental tailor, Tom here's the regimental barber, the rest are clerks, drivers, mess waiters, batmen and cooks. When the word came the regiment was pulling back, they told us to grab our rifles, gave us fifty rounds apiece and said we were to hold you up till the ammo ran out. Well, it just has."

"How many of you were there?"

"Can't say, sir. Our officer and sergeant were killed during the shelling. So were a lot of other lads. A good few seemed to get away, though, so you'll be seeing them again."

"We'd have held you till the cows came home if it hadn't been for that shelling, sir," said his companion. For all the man's years Breihaupt saw in his face the same bewilderment, defiant pride and resentment the prisoners had shown yesterday.

"You have done your duty," he said, not unkindly. "Now, the war is over for you. Be glad you have survived it, as you have your other wars."

It was good that the British were having to resort to combing out their regimental rear areas to plug the gaps in their crumbling line, yet disconcerting to know that some of these men at least would obey their orders and fight to the last round. Hardly had the prisoners been despatched to the rear when a runner arrived from Kolb. The company was to remain where it was until an awkward salient had been eliminated. Breihaupt chafed at the delay but appreciated the dangers that lay in getting too far ahead of the main advance. By evening the difficulty had been resolved and they were joined again by their Battle Group, which had been diverted off their axis during the day. Once more the company spent a restless night, sensing rather than seeing the British filtering back from their broken Battle Zone, albeit in smaller numbers.

There was no mist the following morning. Breihaupt's first objective was a canal bridge, but every mile of the company's approach to it was bitterly contested by parties of riflemen, Lewis gun teams and snipers concealed in cover. In these circumstances the Battle Flights were of little help as they were often unable to identify their targets, whereas the British aircraft were under no such handicap.

Nevertheless, the storm troopers' drive, energy and aggression finally brought them to the canal bank. To Breihaupt's surprise the bridge was still standing. One of Meisel's squads tried to take it at a run, but this was clearly what the enemy engineers had been waiting for and it went up under them, blasting girders, decking and bodies high into the air. The demolition, however, was not quite complete and by concentrating his light machine-guns into a fire base that suppressed the dwindling opposition on the far bank, Breihaupt was able to pass the company across in single file.

They were now entering the tormented landscape of the old Somme battlefield. Nature had tried to re-assert herself so that, superficially, it had begun to resemble chalky heathland, but it was also riven by old trench systems that, while they presented ample opportunity for infiltration, also provided the enemy with excellent cover from which to delay the advance. It was an infinitely depressing place of rusting wire entanglements, flooded craters, smashed equipment and skeletal human remains.

Breihaupt suspected that Meisel had begun shooting his prisoners. He could not be certain, nor could he be everywhere at once, but on one occasion he came across a Lewis gun team that had obviously fought to the last; nearby, four weaponless Tommies were lying in a line, their numerous wounds indicating that they had been cut down by a single burst of submachine-gun fire, delivered at close quarters. When he tackled Meisel on the subject the latter merely shrugged.

"Those who surrender after firing at us until the last moment will receive no mercy from angry men who have just lost comrades," he said flatly. "In the hot blood of battle the restraining influences of civilisation no longer apply."

There was some truth in the argument, but Breihaupt was far from satisfied.

"Killing in cold blood is another matter, Herr Meisel, and will not be permitted while I command! I trust that you understand and will make your men fully aware of this!"

"Of course I understand, Captain – but I also understand that it is important to teach the enemy that their futile resistance will be crushed with inexorable and total ruthlessness!"

There was a gleam of fanaticism in Meisel's eye and a silky impertinence in his voice. Breihaupt felt his face suffuse with fury.

"Who, pray, is to teach the enemy this valuable lesson – the Tommies you have just killed? And what would be the consequences of such an education? Would they not fight the harder, knowing what awaited them? Such methods have always been counter-productive and will not be tolerated – do I make myself clear?"

There was no repetition of the incident. It took a further two days for the storm troopers to cross the old battlefield and during that time Breihaupt's belief in victory slowly drained away. He had been confronted with a variety of tactical problems, all of which had been overcome, but the cost in casualties had been high. Of his platoon commanders, Hundt had been killed and Sichart severely wounded. He reorganised the company into two platoons, one commanded by Meisel and the other by Sergeant-Major Lindner. The heavy flamethrowers were discarded when their fuel ran out. Breihaupt was not sorry to lose them. They were always the enemy's first targets and, such was the toll among their operators that, in the absence of volunteers, men had to be detailed to carry them. What worried him most, however, was that while the British were admittedly still retreating, he was only just keeping pace with them. They were now much quicker at getting their guns away and in general their artillery support was growing stronger. The German batteries, on the other hand, seemed to become less effective with every day that passed. As for the brigade and divisional headquarters it had been hoped to overrun, they remained obstinately beyond reach, yet his men were being pushed to their physical limits. Ammunition was beginning to run short, too. Small quantities came up at night, but they barely equalled daily expenditure. Equally serious was the complete lack of rations. The men had eaten what they were carrying and were becoming increasingly hungry. Breihaupt appreciated that without food, they would be unable to maintain the present pace for much longer. Furthermore, they had been drinking the green, stagnant water in craters and some had already lost control of their bowels. Tired, depressed by the loss of comrades and dispirited by their surroundings, they were obviously losing their edge.

During the evening of the fifth day Breihaupt discussed his difficulties with Kolb, knowing that the major had direct access to higher command headquarters. Kolb was sympathetic but could offer no immediate relief.

"It seems, my dear Breihaupt, that we have become the victims of our own success," he said. "Severe problems are being experienced in getting the artillery across the devastated zone created by our preliminary bombardment. Again, as you well know, the former Somme battlefield presents similar difficulties. Naturally, the same considerations apply to the transportation of supplies. You should have received rations, but I suspect that they have somehow been 'diverted' along the way."

"So, those who deserve most receive least," replied Breihaupt bitterly. Kolb shrugged.

"That, we are both aware, is the way of the world. Encourage your men with the thought that they have not much further to go and that the supply situation will improve steadily."

"I hope you are correct – they will not be grateful for promises we are unable to keep."

"I hope so, too. Strictly between ourselves, I am inclined to the view that insufficient attention was paid to the planning of this aspect of the battle. I find this surprising as we already know that the British experienced identical difficulties during their own offensives."

During the next two days they left the dismal Somme battlefield behind and began to advance across country that had not been fought over. It was apparent that villages, farms and houses had only recently been abandoned by their occupants, but there was little or no food to be found and all the livestock had been driven off. Nevertheless, the unspoiled landscape in itself raised their spirits a little.

At one stage they were held up by three tanks. Breihaupt had never encountered tanks before and regarded the distant lozenge shapes with interest. He was surprised by the volume of machine-gun fire they produced, supplemented from time to time by high-explosive shells. Checked frontally and with no means of dealing with the armoured monsters, he was forced to dribble small parties past them, but as soon as the tank commanders realised what was happening they simply withdrew very slowly to new fire positions. Hours went by without the storm troopers being able to make any real progress.

At length, towards dusk, two of the tanks disappeared behind a line of poplars. The third seemed to have developed mechanical trouble. Only the left track was turning, causing it to veer to the right, and finally it stopped. After a few minutes the doors opened and several figures, some of them carrying Lewis guns, scrambled out and ran for the safety of the trees. Most escaped the storm troopers' fire, although one man was bowled over.

Breihaupt followed Meisel's platoon as it ran hard for the abandoned vehicle. Meisel had reached an open door when the tank was shaken by an internal explosion. A blast of flame flung him on to his back. He arose, visibly shaken, his eyebrows burned off and his uniform scorched. In a fury, he advanced on the wounded tank crewman, who was tying a field dressing around his thigh.

"You – where have the other tanks gone? And how many more are there in this area?"

The man, a sergeant, lit a cigarette and subjected him to a level gaze.

"That's for me to know and you to guess, mate," he said, exhaling a plume of smoke. Meisel's already broiled face became empurpled with rage.

"You are insolent! Stand up when you speak to a German officer!"

"Alright – gimme a wooden leg an' I'll do me Long John Silver impersonation for you!"

Meisel kicked him hard on his wounded thigh. The man screamed as he rolled in agony.

"That is enough!" said Breihaupt sharply. He took Meisel to one side, unable to conceal the dislike in his lowered voice.

"Herr Meisel, if you wish to receive the respect due to a German officer, I suggest you start behaving like one! Now, perhaps you and your men will continue the advance – we have already been delayed long enough."

As Meisel, humiliated and angrier than ever, stalked wordlessly away, Breihaupt returned to the prisoner. The man was white but his pain was subsiding.

"That should never have happened, Sergeant, and you will be correctly treated from now on. Meanwhile, I should be glad of an answer to the question you were asked."

"You can have my number, my rank you know, and my name's Haynes, sir. You know I can't say more than that."

"Perhaps not. Will you tell me what happened to your tank?"

"Drive sprocket stripped, sir. Nothin' for it but to set the demolition charge an' scarper. Don't want you blokes usin' it, do we, even if they knew how to fix it?"

Breihaupt formed the opinion that the prisoner was a rogue but a good soldier for all that. He chuckled and turned away.

By the morning of the next day his men were clearly nearing the end of their physical resources. Their hunger had begun to affect them to the extent that they were unable to maintain the severe pace demanded. At about noon one of Kolb's runners arrived on a captured motor-cycle with urgent orders. It seemed that a message had been dropped by a reconnaissance aircraft, the pilot of which had flown over Albert, the town lying directly in their path, to the effect that the area between it and their goal of Amiens was clear of enemy troops. Albert, therefore, must be seized as quickly as possible while a Marine division was rushed forward to exploit this unexpected good fortune.

By encouraging the men with the likely prospect of food, Breihaupt extracted additional effort from them. When they entered the town they encountered a number of British troops, few of whom seemed inclined to give any trouble. Some were stragglers belonging to units that had already passed through, but others were looters or deserters, many of whom were drunk. They willingly told the storm troopers that ample food and drink was to be had for the taking, guiding them to a supply depot located in sheds near the railway yard.

The depot was like Aladdin's cave. Stacked high were huge stocks of every kind of liquor, tinned goods and other food, millions of cigarettes, and many, many items which, because of the blockade, had become but a memory in Germany. Ravenously the men gorged themselves upon whatever they came across, washing it down with beer, wine and raw spirits. The effect of alcohol on empty stomachs rapidly produced an inebriate bedlam in which all reason and order were lost. Breihaupt came across men looting tablets of soap, only to discard them as they tore open boxes containing razor blades, writing paper or toothbrushes, all being trampled under foot in the frenzy to make the next discovery. One man he saw was delightedly using both hands to rub polish into his cracked boots.

The men were completely out of hand, deaf to orders, reason or threats. As more troops reached the depot the wild scenes became yet more chaotic. Having satisfied his own immediate hunger, Breihaupt returned to the main street where he met Kolb and told him what was happening. The major, close to despair, could offer no solution.

"This could not have been foreseen. The advance has come to a standstill at the most critical time. It is as bad as if the British had laid a trap for us. What would happen if they were to counter-attack us now?"

Soon the streets were full of drunken, staggering storm troopers and Marine infantry, free to loot wherever they pleased. One man, waving a bottle, paraded up and down in a top hat; another wandered by with an empty gilt picture frame; more appeared, garbed in female underwear, hats and feather boas. At length Sergeant-Major Lindner appeared. Somehow, he had managed to cajole most of the company into following him to a basement cafe, bringing their bottles with them. Breihaupt decided to verify their condition for himself.

As he approached he could hear the discordant sounds of a drinking song, bellowed laughter and raised voices. From the top of the steps he looked across a sea of sweating, inebriate faces beneath a hanging fog of tobacco smoke. Some men, lying on the floor or across tables, were already in an alcoholic stupor. The sight of Meisel, tunic open and arms round the shoulders of two soldiers, disgusted him. The standards to which he had been brought up demanded that one lead the men, share their hardships, look after every aspect of their welfare and maintain a friendly but intentionally distant relationship with them; what one did not do was get blind, stinking drunk with them at any time, let alone during a period of intense operations. The noise level abated somewhat as they became aware of his presence. Meisel stood up, swaying a little as he waved a bottle.

"Comrades, here is our gallant leader at last! Join us in a toast to victory, Captain!"

"We have not yet won the victory, Herr Meisel. In fact, at this precise moment we are in serious danger of a defeat, so you will end this celebration at once!"

His words were disregarded.

"Come on, Captain, have a drink! Join in the fun!"

"OUTSIDE, ALL OF YOU – THAT IS AN ORDER!"

No one moved. There were defiant looks and angry murmurings.

"We're staying where we are, you miserable bastard!" shouted a voice. "The lads have bust a gut for you and you won't even have a drink with us! Get lost!"

Breihaupt reached for his pistol holster, feeling Lindner's restraining hand on his arm. There was a long, tense silence.

"Easy, sir – this could end in bloodshed," said the Sergeant-Major. "They've had it rough and lost a lot of friends. They're alright but they need to blow off some steam. Besides, at the moment they're useless – just look at 'em!"

Lindner was right, of course. Breihaupt smiled and the tension ebbed away.

"Very well, you will have a party to remember, I hope. So good, in fact, that Herr Meisel will shoot dead anyone who tries to leave the building!"

The men were grinning again. Suddenly, he pulled out his pistol and fired at the ornamental ceiling rose, bringing down chunks of plaster on Meisel and those nearest to him.

"And that is my contribution!" he said cheerfully as his victims strove to dust themselves off amid gales of laughter. At least, he thought to himself as he and Lindner set off to find beds for themselves in an abandoned house, he would know where to find them in the morning.

During the night the *Feldgendarmerie* established some sort of order and troops were pushed through the town to continue the advance. They barely cleared its outskirts before being mown down as they approached a railway embankment. When Kolb's battalion was ordered to mount a fresh attack, Breihaupt expressed his bewilderment.

"According to the air intelligence report received yesterday, there were no enemy troops between here and Amiens!"

"That may have been correct at the time the report was made," said Kolb flatly. "However, we must remember that the enemy's lines of communication are now much shorter than our own. He has evidently used the delay caused by yesterday's unfortunate episodes to insert reinforcements into the gap. Unless the momentum of our offensive can be restored I fear that it is finished."

Breihaupt explained to his Company what was required, then led them through the back street to the point from which the attack was to be delivered. The men, hung-over and sheepish, followed quietly, but after a short preliminary bombardment they attacked with their usual zeal. They began to fall under a withering fire at once. Breihaupt saw Meisel go down, his legs apparently swept from under him. The brief scream of approaching shells was followed by explosions everywhere. Then he was flying through the air and the world disappeared into a black void.

Time ceased to have any meaning. He retained blurred impressions of voices, of being handled and carried in jolting vehicles, an unspeakable agony that returned him to blessed unconsciousness, and faces bending over him. When he finally came to it was in the clean bed of a base hospital located in a convent. Nuns, German and British doctors and orderlies were working among the casualties of both sides. His left arm had been removed above the elbow and his side was heavily bandaged where shell splinters had been removed.

After a few days he was told that he was being evacuated to a convalescent hospital in Germany. A cheerful, pipe-smoking British doctor sat him on a bench in the courtyard while the ambulance was being refuelled. A strident voice reached them through the open window of a nearby ward.

"I intend to devote myself single-mindedly to politics. The existing parties hold no interest for me. I envisage an entirely new, dynamic force ..."

"Good, God, it's Meisel!" said Breihaupt.

"Friend of yours?" asked the doctor.

"Not by any stretch of the imagination, Major!"

"Pain in the neck – annoys your chaps as much as ours. Took a bullet through the ankle. Won't walk properly again so he's looking forward to his discharge."

"... it will be necessary to purge our national life of those elements who have proved indifferent or hostile to a German victory. I refer, of course, to the international conspiracy of Jewish financiers, to trade union agitators, Bolsheviks, gipsies, and ...."

"Shouldn't care to live in Germany if he and his pals ever come to power!" said the doctor.

"There's not much chance of that," replied Breihaupt. "We're not all idiots, you know!"

They both laughed.

Altogether, Ludendorff mounted four major offensives on the Western Front during the spring and summer of 1918, of which that described was the first. When they failed to produce the hoped-for results, it was apparent that a German victory was no longer a possibility. As the Allies returned to the offensive the German armies were forced to abandon all the gains they had made and were still retreating when the Armistice was signed in November.

The creaming off of the Army's best men into the Storm Troop Battalions proved to be a serious mistake. Once the storm troopers were dead much of what remained was of lesser quality; latterly, reinforcements marching up to the front were hailed as 'blacklegs', 'scabs' and 'warmongers'.

The collapse of the drive through Albert to Amiens occurred much as I have described it. An oft-quoted primary source in this connection is the diary of a German officer, Rudolf Binding (*A Fatalist at War*, Allen & Unwin, 1929), who witnessed these scenes at first hand. Binding gives their date as being 28 March, although German troops actually reached Albert the previous day.

I have attempted to make Ewald Breihaupt fairly typical of the contemporary German regular officer corps at the regimental level. He is a professional, an essentially decent man, anxious to preserve standards; unfortunately, he does not fully understand a world that is changing, and his limited imagination prevents him seeing far beyond the Army.

Even in the midst of a world war the regular officer corps, keen to preserve its élite status, maintained strictures on recruiting to its ranks. Middle-class reserve officers did not possess quite the same standing, although their numbers were greater. Officer casualties were heavy, but rather than grant commissions to men from the ranks, the Army created a new category of appointment for promising NCOs. Thus, while I have described Meisel as possessing a temporary commission, his precise rank was that of *Offizierstellvertreter* (Officer Substitute), according him the responsibilities of a subaltern but not the status. His ideas, however, were widely held in Germany at the time; in fact, he quotes from General von Bernhardi's book *Germany and the Next War*, which was first published in 1911 and ran to several popular editions. Many such ideas formed the basis of the Nazi ethos and in this context the considerable support provided by Ludendorff himself for Hitler during the latter's early political years should not be forgotten.

LIEUTENANT BRUNO VON RAVENSTHAL

25th Panzer Regiment, Belgium and France, May 1940

Although Bruno von Ravensthal had witnessed history in the making, events at the time had followed so quickly one upon another that they had melded into a continuous experience the memory of which had been further blurred by the more protracted experience of later campaigns in North Africa, Russia and western Europe. In his later years, when journalists and historians asked him to recall the lightning campaign of 1940 which had not only destroyed the armies of France, Belgium and Holland but also sent the British scuttling back to their island, he had difficulty in placing the incidents of which they spoke in their precise context, although a few still retained a vivid clarity of detail. Of course, as a lieutenant commanding a single platoon of tanks he had been but a small cog in a huge machine and hardly privy to the decisions made by his dynamic divisional commander, the future Field Marshal Erwin Rommel. What he remembered most was what he could describe least, namely the mounting fatigue that made him long for sleep as days and nights of constant movement followed each other, and short but intense periods of mortal terror compounded by the fear that he would betray himself. Unless those who sought his memories could comprehend such things, they would never understand how, gradually, the fatigue and the fear had been suppressed by the sheer ease with which the victory over odds had been won and the consequent increase in the chances of survival.

As his family's interests had centred on farming and forestry they had survived the worst effects of the inter-war years when roaring inflation followed by depression had all but destroyed Germany's economy. When the Nazi Party had come to power, quite legitimately, they had little direct contact with the new Establishment, which they tended to despise.

"Riff raff and guttersnipes!" Bruno's grandfather, a *Junker* of the old school, had said. "Unemployable elsewhere, so they turn to politics – that's where democracy gets you!"

As the younger son, Bruno would not inherit the estate and some consideration had to be given as to how he would earn his living. The professions, commerce and industry did not interest him, nor did an academic career, although he was serious-minded and studious by nature. During a visit to Berlin with his father he had read a curious inscription on the little Temple of Victory in the Unter den Linden:

'GERMAN WAR IS AN AFFAIR OF THE INTELLECT – THE INTELLECT IS STRONGER THAN ANY OTHER FORCE'

"What does this mean?" he had asked.

"It means creating the conditions for a decisive victory before the first shot is fired," replied his father, a former General Staff officer.

"But we were defeated during the last war."

"Yes, because insufficient consideration was given to certain factors in our early plans. Had it been otherwise, our recent history would have been very different."

Interested, Bruno began reading military history, becoming particularly absorbed in the influence of new weapons on tactics. The choice of the Army as a career followed naturally and, in fact, merely extended a family tradition. As a cadet his earnest approach to life earned him some ribbing, but he took it in good part and even acquired a degree of popularity, acquiring for himself the nickname of Professor.

During the 1939 campaign in Poland, Lieutenant Ravensthal had commanded a six-strong platoon of Pz Kpfw Is and IIs. The Poles, having little armour, were not equipped for a modern war and, already surrounded on three sides by German territory as they were, they had been unable to withstand the concentric onslaught of tanks supported by overwhelming air power. Yet it had not been quite the walkover Dr Goebbels had suggested. The enemy had often fought with suicidal bravery, manning their anti-tank and field guns until shot down around them. Despite the fact that no tank battles had been fought the German tank strength had been reduced by one fifth during the single month the campaign had lasted, a figure the good doctor had striven to conceal with constructive accounting. Those who had actually done the fighting suspected the truth; Ravensthal's platoon, for example, had sustained the loss of one tank destroyed outright, one with battle damage requiring heavy repair in Germany, and two were unfit for further service and needed a complete mechanical overhaul.

In those days the formation had been known as the 2nd Light Division. It had been raised from former cavalry units and consisted of one light tank battalion, two motorised infantry regiments, a reconnaissance regiment, artillery and supporting units. The success of the armour in Poland had evidently pleased the Führer so much that the strength of the four Light divisions was augmented by expanding their tank element to regimental size. Other additions were to follow and on 18 October 1939 the 2nd Light became the 7th Panzer Division. During the first week of February 1940 its popular commander, Lieutenant-General Georg Stumme, who had led it in Poland, was replaced by Major-General Erwin Rommel.

Having become used to Stumme's way of doing things, Ravensthal found the new arrival somewhat unsettling at first. A small, spare man, he radiated nervous energy. From his throat dangled Imperial Germany's highest decoration, the *Pour le Mérite*, awarded for the ruthless drive he had shown at Caporetto, resulting in the capture of over 9,000 Italians and 80 guns. Although he was not a Nazi, Rommel was on excellent terms with the Führer and until recently had commanded the latter's Escort Battalion. He promptly embarked upon an exhaustive training programme, pushing units and their commanders to the limit. His treatment of those who failed to measure up to his standards was fair but sometimes harsh; for example, one of the battalion commanders in Ravensthal's own regiment was sacked on the spot. Nevertheless, while he was, on occasion, prepared to make his senior officers' lives hell, he also ensured that he was known personally to all the troops, with whom he established an amiable relationship, even posing for photographs from time to time. Once, he had travelled aboard Ravensthal's tank during an exercise. He had been friendly enough, but Ravensthal had sensed the pent-up energy and impatience, likening it to a volcano about to erupt, and decided to maintain a low profile. One of the general's aides, Lieutenant Joachim Most, was a pleasant fellow, but the other, Lieutenant Karl Hanke, was a fanatical Nazi whose self-importance and high-handed ways quickly made him unpopular.

The problem for Ravensthal was that Hanke was on close terms with a Waffen SS officer, Obersturmführer Detlef Meisel, whom he often invited to the mess. Meisel's father was a high-ranking Party official whose opinions were greatly valued by Heinrich Himmler. The image he liked to cultivate was that of the hero who had been seriously injured during the last year of the Kaiser's War and he walked with a pronounced limp. It was true that he had served in the Storm Troop company commanded by Ravensthal's Uncle Ewald, and had been wounded in the same engagement that had cost the latter his arm. However, Uncle Ewald knew of several episodes that did not reflect much credit on Meisel Senior as an individual, and in recent times he had received a visit from the Gestapo who told him to keep his mouth shut or suffer the consequences. Ewald retorted that in the event of such 'consequences' a Swiss lawyer had been given authorisation to release details of the incidents in question to the world's press. There the matter had rested, but Ravensthal knew that his uncle was being watched and as he had no wish to prejudice the situation by revealing the family connection in casual conversation with Hanke or Meisel Junior, he avoided them as much as possible.

Since Poland, the division's armoured regiment had been substantially re-equipped. It still possessed about one hundred of the old Pz Kpfw Is and IIs, armed respectively with machine-guns and a 20mm cannon, but its principal strength lay in approximately the same number of Czech-built Pz Kpfw 38(t)s which, being armed with a 37mm gun and two machine-guns, provided a substitute for the German Pz Kpfw IIIs issued to the majority of the panzer divisions; in addition, there were thirty-six Pz Kpfw IVs, armed with a short 75mm howitzer, which would serve in the battalions' heavy companies.

The Polish campaign had proved the validity of the German concept of armoured warfare as well as reinforcing the self-confidence of the armoured troops themselves. There were, nevertheless, many officers, Ravensthal included, who had strong reservations about tackling the British and French, and these gave rise to very serious doubts when it seemed probable that Belgium and Holland would be invaded as well. It was true that the Belgian and Dutch Armies possessed very little in the way of armour, and that what there was consisted of light tanks and armoured cars. True also that while the British had invented armoured warfare, years of deliberate political neglect had left their army so bereft of equipment that even now, months after the war had begun, all they had in France was one under-strength tank brigade plus a few light armoured reconnaissance regiments. What worried most German officers was the size of the French tank fleet, estimated to number 3,000 vehicles, outnumbering the Germans by three to two; worse still, the Pz Kpfw Is and IIs would be useless in a tank battle and if they were excluded the German gun tanks would be facing odds of three to one. Furthermore, while some of the French designs were indifferent, others were better protected than and out-gunned every German tank in service, and although some officers sought comfort in the fact that the French preference for one-man turrets tended to reduce efficiency, others felt that this was a minor point given the overall strength of their opponents. Again, geography was not working in Germany's favour, as it had in Poland. Because of the formidable defences of the Maginot Line along the Franco-German frontier, the only way for the panzer divisions to penetrate France was through Belgium. To Ravensthal and others this seemed ominously like a repetition of the strategy which had failed in 1914. If the German armour was fought to a standstill the result would, once again, be a stalemate followed by a long war of attrition for which Germany was simply not prepared.

Against this, there were signs that the French, who were the dominant opponent on land, had little stomach for a fight. It would have been easy for them to have made a move while the bulk of the German Army was engaged in the Polish campaign, but they had not done so. Nor did they react when, in April, Denmark and Norway had been overrun in rapid succession – further proof, Hanke said, that the Führer had perfected new and invincible methods of waging war that would restore Germany to her rightful place as world leader. Instead, the level of activity along the Western Front remained as it had been since the outbreak of war, restricted to minor patrol clashes and sporadic shelling. Intelligence sources suggested that, for a variety of reasons, the French, increasingly troubled by demoralisation and desertion, would not offer serious resistance. Ravensthal was not alone in taking the contrary view that being attacked might be the one thing the enemy needed to pull himself together. Taking all these factors into account, he was less than enthusiastic about the offensive in the west for which the Führer was clearly preparing.

Early in May the division assembled close to the Belgian frontier. During the afternoon of the 9th the regiment was placed on short notice to move. As there had been similar alerts in recent days, Ravensthal was not unduly alarmed, but at about midnight the battalion adjutant, Lieutenant Geiger, pushed his head through the bivouac flap.

"Bruni, it's on! Orders in ten minutes!"

At the orders groups there were maps to be marked and incredibly detailed movement schedules to be studied. Ravensthal saw that their route forward would take them across the frontier into the Ardennes, through St-Vith and on to the Meuse. The roads were reserved for the division's mass of vehicles while the neighbouring infantry formations were confined to cross-country routes. Each phase of the advance was intended to conform with the schedule's complex timing, a projection which Ravensthal felt would depend entirely on the degree of opposition encountered.

For some reason, perhaps because it marked the beginning of so decisive a series of events, the sound he always associated with that first morning of the offensive was the rising hum of the tanks' inertia starters. They were, of course, fitted with electric self-starters but the company commander had a bee in his bonnet about preserving battery life and insisted that they only be used as a matter of operational necessity. Brandt, Ravensthal's driver, was already in his seat and had turned on the ignition while Ahrens, the 37mm loader, and Greise, the tank's radio operator and hull machine-gunner, inserted the long handle through the stern plate and began cranking. Inside the engine compartment the system's flywheel began turning, slowly at first, then faster and faster until it tripped across to engage the engine. Brandt was an expert mechanic and it fired at once. For a few moments longer the company remained in its harbour area as final checks were made on the radio net, then began moving off by platoons.

Ravensthal learned later that the division had crossed the frontier at 0530. In the lead, as usual, was the armoured reconnaissance battalion with its armoured cars and motor-cycle troops, followed by the divisional advance guard. His own battalion remained with the main body of the armoured regiment and entered Belgian territory a little later, followed by the motor rifle regiments, artillery, pioneers and the many other units which formed the division, covering many miles of road.

In the light of subsequent events, Ravensthal remembered the first days of the offensive as being rather dull. For the first few hours the prospect of imminent action sharpened the senses, but little of note happened. They drove past an abandoned frontier post and entered the rolling, wooded hills of the Ardennes. Overhead, the incessant Luftwaffe activity provided impenetrable air cover. To his surprise, Ravensthal found himself exchanging cheerful waves with happy families lining the roadside, then realised that they were of German extraction. Only a few miles beyond the frontier, however, all the invaders received from the civilian population were cold, sullen stares. They rolled into St-Vith to find that three of the town's four bridges had been captured intact. Beside them were small groups of men in Belgian uniforms who shouted encouragement to the troops as they drove past. Later, he learned that they belonged to a special operations unit and were known as Brandenburgers, their task being to prevent, by fair means or foul, the enemy demolishing bridges the loss of which would delay the early phases of the advance; once again, he had to admit to himself, Hitler's new order of things had left nothing to chance.

Beyond St-Vith they continued along winding wooded valleys between rolling hills. Progress became slower and from time to time the column came to a standstill. Sometimes the distant sound of firing came from ahead, although it was always brief. They began to encounter barricades and deep craters blown in the road. These delayed them further, but none of them were covered by fire as he would have expected; indeed, he began to wonder why the Belgians had evidently decided not to fight anything more than brief delaying actions in country which was so suited to anti-tank defence. Some wounded prisoners belonging to the *Chasseurs Ardennais* were brought in, but they simply shrugged when interrogated. In the event, none of the obstacles caused a protracted hold-up as detachments from the reconnaissance battalion were generally waiting to lead the column on diversionary routes along farm tracks or secondary roads, and where no such routes existed the pioneers were quickly called forward to deal with the obstruction.

Ravensthal could recall little of the second day's advance save that at about noon they crossed the Ourthe and that the French appeared to have entered the battle, for during the afternoon they came across several dead horses and the bodies of their riders, indicating that one of their patrols had clashed unsuccessfully with the reconnaissance battalion's armoured cars. A mile or two beyond the scene of the encounter they came across an abandoned French light tank which he would like to have examined, had time permitted.

During the afternoon of 12 May sounds of fighting reached the column as it closed up to the Meuse at Dinant. At about 1630 the tanks reached the river at various points only to see the bridges erupt as the enemy fired their demolition charges. The French, entrenched on the far bank, were offering fierce resistance despite having to endure air attacks. After several tanks had been knocked out the remainder sought cover wherever possible. The situation remained unaltered during the night. There was talk at one stage that the dismounted troops of the divisional motor-cycle battalion had used an ancient weir to secure, first, a wooded island in mid-stream, and then a small bridgehead on the enemy bank, but their hold was said to be tenuous.

Next morning a further attempt at crossing was made in rubber assault boats, screened by smoke from burning houses beside the river. It was shot to tatters, leaving boats drifting downstream to sink with wounded aboard. Ravensthal began to think that the division had a serious problem on its hands until, in mid-morning, things began to happen. The regiment's heavy companies were ordered to move their Pz Kpfw IVs to the northern outskirts of the town to provide fire support at a new crossing site the divisional commander had selected, and for good measure Ravensthal's company was despatched as well.

The slopes above the enemy bank were being shelled, but they were still spitting fire from innumerable positions in houses, rocks and woodland. Bullets clattered off Ravensthal's armour and shells burst nearby. The tanks trundled slowly along the river road, their turrets traversed towards the enemy, engaging every target which revealed its presence. General Rommel seemed to be everywhere at once. Within the space of several minutes Ravensthal saw him clambering aboard a Pz Kpfw IV to indicate targets to its commander; organising machine-guns, mortars and 20mm anti-aircraft guns into fire bases; and rushing here and there in his command armoured car.

Gradually the French fire began to slacken although when the first wave of assault boats was rushed to the water's edge the surface of the river was still being flayed by automatic weapon, mortar and artillery fire. Some of the flimsy craft were ripped apart by direct hits or near misses but the rest continued to land their riflemen on the far shore, where the latter immediately began fighting their way up the slopes beyond. As the tanks continued to give covering fire Ravensthal noticed that Rommel himself was aboard one of the assault boats.

While the crossing continued the whole area became a scene of intense activity as the pioneers brought their pontoons and bridging equipment forward. Rommel, having encouraged the riflemen by his personal example, had now returned and Ravensthal could hear him applying the spur to the captain of a pioneer company that was assembling 8-ton pontoons:

"No, no, those are useless! Everything depends on getting tanks and anti-tank guns rafted across in case the enemy counter-attack while the bridge is being constructed! Use the 16-ton pontoons – speed is what counts now. I'm relying on you!"

While the pioneers worked like fiends to assemble the bigger pontoons, the General walked along the bank to where the rest of the engineers had begun launching the floating bridge. At one stage Ravensthal saw him jump into the water to lend a hand. He wondered where the man's energy came from.

Although direct fire from the opposite bank had been suppressed, the German intention was now obvious to the French, who began hammering the crossing site with their artillery. Casualties among the pioneers were heavy but they worked on. At length the cable ferry was ready and Rommel's eight-wheel command armoured car was driven aboard. As Ravensthal watched its slow progress across the 120 yards of fast-flowing water, Captain Heilmann, his company commander, scrambled up beside him.

"We're going next, Bruni," he said. "We've got a better anti-tank capability than the Fours, so they want us up front as soon as we can be got across. I'll go first, followed by company headquarters, then you follow with your platoon."

Watching the shell bursts fountain around the armoured car, now in mid-stream, Ravensthal felt the icy hand of terror tighten around his intestines. As a very small boy he had once fallen into a deep, fast-flowing stream and only been rescued with difficulty by some of the estate workers. Since then he had been afraid of water and never learned to swim. The ferry reached the far bank, unloaded its burden and was slowly winched back. Heilmann's tank crawled aboard and the process was repeated. Each leg of the journey took so long that Ravensthal estimated that it would be well into the night before the entire company was across, even if all went well.

It did not. The next tank, commanded by Sergeant-Major Seebach, was halfway over when a shell exploded beside the ferry, which quickly took on a sharp list as water poured into the ruptured pontoon. Seebach's tank began to slide sideways, its weight increasing the angle of the list until, to Ravensthal's horror, the vehicle toppled into the river with a tremendous splash. Huge bubbles rose to the surface but, so far as he could see, none of the crew managed to get clear. The tank had been closed down and there was little chance any of its hatches could have been opened before it became embedded, belly up, in the river's muddy bottom. Ravensthal could imagine the desperate, hopeless scramble for survival in the darkness as the water rushed in through every crack and joint. He swallowed hard, wiping the cold sweat from his face. Freed from its burden, the ferry assumed a more even keel. It was gingerly hauled to the bank where the pioneers replaced the damaged pontoon. This took time, so that it was not until the light was fading that Ravensthal was called forward. He made the crew dismount as soon as the tank was aboard; they were unhappy but accepted his point that the risks posed by the shelling were preferable to drowning. As, for good measure, the pioneers had also loaded an anti-tank gun, its crew and some ammunition, the deck of the raft was very crowded and the freeboard dangerously low. The proximity of the water and their agonisingly slow progress conspired to make Ravensthal perspire with cold fear; furthermore, the motion of the ferry, though slight, brought him to the edge of vomiting. From time to time they were drenched by spray as shells exploded nearby. After what seemed an age the raft came to a standstill in the shallows and the pioneers ran to lower the ramps.

As they drove ashore Ravensthal reflected that, however hard and unpredictably bumpy the 38(t)'s suspension might be, it was infinitely preferable to the motion of anything afloat. In the fading twilight he followed Heilmann's tracks and found the company commander near the top of the ridge. From ahead and on either flank came the sound of small-arms fire and the thud of grenades.

"So far, so good," said Heilmann. "The infantry are coming over in such numbers now that they've been able to expand the bridgehead. There's not much we can do in the dark, but we can be sure the French will counter-attack in the morning so we'll get another crack at them then. Let's hope there are a few more of us around to deal with them."

During the short summer night another tank joined them on average every half-hour so that by dawn there were fifteen in the bridgehead. The first of several weak counter-attacks began shortly after. Ravensthal had been expecting a hard fight but on the sector to which his platoon was directed the French gave up easily. They were using little Hotchkiss H39 tanks but were unsupported by infantry, and the German artillery, firing across the river under the control of an unseen observer, put down a barrage which separated their first and second waves. Ravensthal's tanks opened fire at 500 yards from the cover of a wood, bringing three of their opponents to a standstill. Simultaneously, the riflemen, wishing to conceal their shortage of anti-tank guns, began firing signal flares at the enemy in the hope that these would be mistaken for the tracers of armour-piercing shot. Evidently the ruse worked for the French began backing away.

Satisfied that they were no longer in any real danger, the infantry began to expand the bridgehead. As the day wore on, a constant stream of tanks appeared, indicating that the pioneers had completed their bridge. By evening the division had captured Onhaye, three miles west of Dinant, and there its armoured regiment assembled in preparation for the breakout on the morrow. Leaving his sergeant to complete the replenishment details, Ravensthal attended the battalion orders group, where the mood was optimistic. The 5th Panzer Division, their running mate in General Hoth's XV Panzer Corps, had begun crossing the river; further upstream, XLI Panzer Corps had secured a bridgehead at Monthermé and XIX Panzer Corps was across at Sedan; the Luftwaffe retained complete air superiority over all the bridgeheads; best of all, the French were reported to be withdrawing; the object, therefore, was to break right through them

before they could establish a new defence line; as usual, the reconnaissance battalion would be probing ahead, but as they were now in
open country the tanks would lead the divisional advance in their
usual tactical wedge.

When, shortly after 0900, the regiment moved out of its harbour
areas near Onhaye, its massed ranks seemed unstoppable. The few
French troops remaining in the area either scattered before it or surrendered and were thumbed to the rear. Ravensthal began to feel that,
perhaps, the worst lay behind them when, having learned from his
map that the next village ahead was named Flavion, the company
breasted a rise and immediately came under fire from a dozen or more
stationary tanks some 800 yards distant across the fields. In the centre of the company, which was positioned on the right flank of the
wedge, Heilmann held up his hand.

"Halt!" said Ravensthal into the intercom.

Brandt applied the brakes sharply and the tank came to a standstill,
rocking on its suspension. Ravensthal's binoculars brought the distant
shapes into focus. Once again, chill fear coursed through his veins like
iced water.

"My God!" he muttered to himself. "They're Char Bs!"

The Char B was the most dangerous French tank in service. Its turret housed a 47mm gun that out-ranged the German F 37mm by a
wide margin; it was additionally armed with a 75mm howitzer in the
bow and had heavy frontal armour. In a stand-up fight the 38(t) was
no match at all for it. Once, in Poland, Ravensthal had looked into the
interior of a tank that had been penetrated by an armour-piercing
round; sickened by what he had seen, he had never done so again.
Now, he felt as vulnerable as if he were standing stark naked in the
open.

While these thoughts raced through his mind a series of gun flashes erupted along the enemy line. To his right Sergeant Kuffner's tank
seemed to lurch, then burst into flames; Kuffner scrambled out, followed by Wutzel, his loader, but no one else. He felt the wind of
something unseen as it flashed over the top of his own turret. He
instinctively ducked inside, cracking his head on the cupola as he did
so; for a moment he saw stars, but the worst of the impact was
absorbed by the padded black beret which he continued to wear in
preference to the more recently issued forage cap.

"Load – armour piercing!"

Ahrens slid a round into the breech, which clicked shut as the block closed behind it. In the 38(t) the commander also acted as his own 37mm gunner and, to Ravensthal's annoyance, the Czech designers had paid too little attention to the ergonomics involved. Thus, having selected as his target the tank on the right of the French line, he seized the traverse handle to his left and began cranking the turret round, conscious that the awkward bending of the wrist involved was costing priceless seconds. Simultaneously, while the gun was equipped with an elevating handwheel, he decided to use the shoulder-piece which, though tiring in the long term, was quicker for getting off a snap shot. He adjusted his lay until the graticule markings on the gunsight telescope were correct for line and range, then squeezed the trigger. The gun banged sharply. The trace flashed across the space between the two tanks. There was the flash of a strike on the enemy's glacis plate, then the round ricocheted high into the air. Ahrens was ready with another round.

"Loaded!"

He fired again, with similar result. He was about to thank God that the enemy's rate of fire was so slow when there was a crash overhead and the turret shuddered. He realised that he had used all the luck he could expect; the immediate priority now was to seek cover.

"Reverse!"

Brandt engaged gear and let in the clutch. The tank rolled back from the crest until it reached dead ground.

"Halt!"

To the left Ravensthal could see that his third tank, commanded by Sergeant Heger, was beginning to conform to his movement when something exploded against the front plate. For the moment, however, he had more immediate concerns on his mind. He had noticed that there were a series of louvres halfway along the left-hand side of the enemy's hull and guessed that they were air intakes. He decided to aim for this precise area and directed Brandt to bring the tank to a hull-down position on the crest some yards to their right, selecting his target with care. His second shot was rewarded with a cloud of steam from the enemy's ruptured radiator, followed by belching black smoke as the round ploughed on through the engine. The French crew tumbled out. Before giving Brandt the order to reverse Ravensthal noticed that the track on another of the enemy tanks had been shot away.

On reaching the bottom of the slope he raised himself into the cupola. The enemy round had struck between the forward vision block housing and the periscope, removing the latter and scarring the metal. The rest of the regiment seemed to be veering away to the south-west, leaving his own battalion to engage the enemy. Several tanks were burning or had clearly been knocked out. Nearby, Sergeant Heger's crew were carefully lifting down one of their number. He dismounted and ran across to them. The unconscious man's black uniform jacket was soaked in blood and he was breathing harshly. Ravensthal recognised the pallid face of Krebs, the vehicle's radio operator.

"Rivet," said Heger laconically. "Shank sheered off when that shell exploded on the head. It's in his chest somewhere. Only a matter of time."

Evidently this was another design fault which should have been rectified. Meanwhile, more urgent matters occupied his mind. Kuffner was senior to Heger and would therefore take over the tank while Wutzel, who he knew had some radio experience, took the place of the dying man.

"Sorry," he said to Heger. "I'll have to leave you here with Krebs. The rest of the division is following on, so you won't have long to wait."

Heger shrugged. Just then, Greise, Ravensthal's own operator, called across.

"Lieutenant, you're wanted! The Captain says right away!"

"Where the hell have you been?" Heilmann's voice was testy in the earphones. "Listen, we're to break contact under cover of an air attack and follow the regiment. Someone else can deal with these people."

Ravensthal acknowledged, only too pleased to be out of a battle the outcome of which seemed dubious. Minutes later a steady droning announced the arrival of the Luftwaffe's dive-bomber squadrons. Peeling off from their formations, the tiny dots quickly materialised into gull-winged Ju 87s as, sirens howling, they bore down on the French tanks. Soon the enemy disappeared amid mushrooming explosions and drifting smoke, yet still the whistling bombs crashed among them. Ravensthal imagined that the French crews had more than enough on their minds for the moment, but tossed out a couple of smoke grenades for good measure.

"Driver, advance! Left – on! Now put your foot down and follow the others!"

About a fifth of the battalion's tanks seemed to have been put out of action, but doubtless some would be repairable and would follow on. Breaking through the retreating army was accomplished without the need for further hard fighting. The tanks simply roared past every likely centre of resistance with their guns blazing and the French, demoralised by incessant air attacks and bewildered by the sudden avalanche of armour which had overtaken them, surrendered in droves. In this way entire infantry units, artillery batteries and even small groups of tanks were captured, the prisoners being simply disarmed and told to march back towards the Meuse. On the outskirts of Philippeville the company replenished its fuel at a civilian garage, disregarding the voluble protests of its angry proprietor. Ravensthal helped himself to some fresh loaves at a nearby baker's and, feeling some sympathy for the frightened woman behind the counter, paid for them with Reichsmark notes, telling her that soon they would come in very useful. Beyond the town the battalion ran head-on into a French motor-cycle battalion trying to reach what it imagined to be the front. On seeing the mass of onrushing tanks the riders pulled up sharply and surrendered. They were told to throw their machines in the ditch and join the march eastwards.

During the night the supply trucks reached their harbour area with an ammunition replenishment. Their journey had been made the more difficult by the roads being jammed with crowds of prisoners. One of the drivers told Ravensthal that his portable radio had just picked up the news that Holland had surrendered. This was officially confirmed later. Once again, Ravensthal reflected, the new way of war had triumphed; and, once again, it seemed, the principal lesson of Poland was being repeated, namely that when an armoured formation had broken through the battle zone its own movement provided the best defence.

The next morning's advance took them across the Franco–Belgian frontier but it was made at a steadier pace. Beyond Sivry they closed up to the Maginot Line Extension. Work on this had only commenced in recent months and as yet it offered nothing like so formidable an obstacle as the Line proper, consisting simply of a series of concrete bunkers and anti-tank barriers linked by a shallow wire entanglement. The regiment approached it on a wide front in extended line. Some of the occupants obviously wanted to give up, but others did not and opened fire. A methodical attack was then developed, the tanks engaging the bunker slits with direct gunfire while, supported by the divisional artillery, the infantry and pioneers worked their way forward to hurl demolition charges through the apertures. By evening the opposition had been suppressed and the pioneers had cleared lanes through the obstacles.

It was at this point that Ravensthal began to lose track of the days. The accepted contemporary wisdom was that tanks did not operate at night. Rommel, however, had other ideas and decided to continue the advance to Avesnes, taking advantage of the bright moonlight. Once more those of the enemy who offered resistance were left shaken and bewildered, their resolve shattered by the onset of massed tanks and concentrated gunfire which smashed through their positions and disappeared to the rear. Some French tanks imposed a temporary check on the outskirts of Avesnes but by dawn their opposition had been suppressed.

Even then Rommel was not satisfied. Ravensthal saw him climb aboard the tank of his own battalion commander and then they were off again with the motor-cycle battalion in their wake, leaving the rest to follow on. They took the Landrecies road, which was clogged with a slow-moving procession of refugees, their personal possessions piled upon perambulators, handcarts, farm wagons and motor vehicles of every kind. Intermingled with them were the remnants of broken French units with their own transport, guns and tanks. Ravensthal was aware from his experience in Poland that such columns had their uses in that they often prevented enemy reinforcements reaching the front, but in the present circumstance it was the German advance which was being delayed. The trudging, dispirited troops surrendered promptly enough, but the civilians, dull-eyed and sunk in their personal misery, seemed deaf to repeated shouts of "Get out of the way!" *"Raus!"* *"A droite!"* Ravensthal could see that the divisional commander, impatient at the best of times, was becoming apoplectic with rage. At length, although ammunition was now in such short supply after its prodigal expenditure during the night that restrictions had been placed on its use, the leading tanks began firing short bursts of machine-gun fire over the heads of the fugitives, who scattered in terror. In a similar manner the crowded streets of Landrecies were cleared. The town's bridge over the Sambre was not defended and the tanks roared across. Beyond lay a barracks into which Rommel despatched his aide, Lieutenant Hanke, and several tanks. Later, Ravensthal heard that the occupants had willingly complied with Hanke's order to abandon their weapons and start marching east.

Ravensthal, now very tired, thought that they might have reached the end of the journey, but Rommel had no intention of stopping. A further eight miles had been covered by the time they halted on some uplands where the signposts indicated they were close to Le Cateau. Mechanical breakdowns had been taking place at an alarming rate so that less than half the battalion and the motor-cyclists had managed to keep up. Ravensthal was worried about the state of his own two vehicles, upon which there had been little opportunity for maintenance. When they dismounted to stretch their legs he asked Brandt how far they had come during the past 24 hours.

"About eighty kilometres, sir," replied the driver, who looked more haggard than any of them. "Can't say I'm sorry to stop – my eyes are starting to play tricks on me."

He kicked the track where it had begun to hang loosely under the rear idler.

"Anyway, we shan't be going much further on these. It's a miracle one of them hasn't shed already."

"How much slack can we take up?"

"None, sir. The tensioner's right up against the stop. We need a link out of each side – better still, two."

"All right, it looks as though we'll be here for a while so we'll start now."

Sergeant Kuffner had similar track problems but his engine had also been misfiring and had had to be nursed for the past few miles.

"Petrol's right down, Lieutenant. Pump's probably been sucking gunge from the bottom of the tank – we'll need to take down the fuel lines and blow 'em through."

Rommel, alarmed that so few of his troops had managed to keep up with him, had already set off back the way they had come to chase up the rest. When Ravensthal suggested to Heilmann that this time they had over-reached themselves, the latter was inclined to agree.

"The division's strung out across God knows how many kilometres of country, and with the roads choked as they are we'll not be seeing anyone else for a while."

"Just as well the French aren't about," said Ravensthal.

"Quite. We're almost out of fuel and ammunition. The best thing we can do is put ourselves back into working order and hope the supply echelon gets through."

While Ravensthal helped his crews with their maintenance tasks his mind turned to the course of the campaign so far. They had continued to head in a westerly direction and were now entering the battlefields of the last war. He had half expected the German armour to swing south in a mechanised re-enactment of the old Schlieffen Plan, pinning the French armies back against their own Maginot Line, or even spearhead a drive on Paris, but the High Command was clearly not interested in either option, and this left him puzzled. These considerations aside, the unexpected pause allowed him to snatch a few hours' sleep and the luxury of a hot meal.

It seemed that some of the French wanted to fight after all, for midway between Landrecies and Le Cateau the rest of the regiment had become involved in a stiff action with some of their armour and, because of fuel and ammunition shortage, only held their own with difficulty. It was not, in fact, until the following day that all the division's fighting elements caught up, and then Rommel set them in motion again, advancing a further fifteen miles to Cambrai. It was here, Ravensthal reflected, that the British had launched the first massed tank attack during the last war. The results had been dramatic but they had not taken the town; now, the mere presence of German armour had induced its surrender.

Ravensthal's engine had begun playing up. That evening, while he and his crew were working on the problem, Rommel drove into the harbour area to confer with the regiment's commander, Colonel Karl von Rothenburg, whose headquarters tanks were nearby. Ravensthal caught a little of what was being said and gathered that another night march was contemplated. At that moment, however, General Hoth's command group arrived. Evidently, the corps commander did not approve of the plan and voices began to rise in anger.

"My dear Rommel," said Hoth, "your division has now advanced further into enemy territory than any other, and that means that the dangers of your being isolated have increased proportionally. Further-more, your troops are on the verge of exhaustion!"

"With respect, General," Rommel retorted angrily, "Most of them have just spent the last twenty hours sitting on their arses!"

Ravensthal shepherded his men out of earshot; one did not risk being caught in the crossfire when senior officers disagreed. As he strolled past one of Hoth's vehicles he was hailed by a familiar voice.

"Bruni! My God, what a scruffy officer you've turned into!"

He found himself shaking hands with Fabian Schlosser, an old friend from his cadet school days, now serving on Hoth's intelligence staff. In contrast with the latter's spruce appearance, he had to admit that his battered beret, black double-breasted jacket and trousers were now so oil-stained and ingrained with dirt that no half-decent hotel would allow him through the door. The two chatted about old times and mutual friends for a while.

"Well, Fabi, how d'you think it's going?" he asked at length.

"Take a look," said the other, producing a marked map board from inside the vehicle. To his amazement Ravensthal could see that the three panzer corps had cut a swathe forty miles wide across northern France and a fourth was coming up on their right. To the south Gud-erian's corps had reached Péronne and was advancing along the Somme towards Amiens and the sea. Suddenly the whole German strategy became clear.

"Of course!" he exclaimed. "Our objective is the Channel coast! That means we shall sever the communications of the British and French armies in Belgium! They will be caught in the trap and forced to surrender!"

"When you have quite finished interrogating my staff, Lieutenant!" said an abrupt voice behind him. He turned to find himself con-fronting Hoth, Rommel and Rothenburg.

"My apologies, General," he said, saluting. "It is just that we seem to have accomplished what the storm troop battalions failed so nar-rowly to do in 1918, that is, cut the Allied armies in two. I think we shall win a brilliant victory!"

"I am gratified that our methods seem to meet with your approval," said Hoth dryly as he climbed aboard. "Nevertheless, kindly maintain a discreet silence about what you have seen until your prediction becomes a fact."

Ravensthal thought that perhaps he had overstepped the mark until he saw that Rommel's face had softened into the hint of a smile.

"The success of even the best plans depends upon the will to win," said the divisional commander. "You have it, Lieutenant, so the victory will belong to you and your men."

After that, Ravensthal would willingly have followed Rommel to the gates of hell. As he had expected, the divisional commander had wrung a concession from Hoth and the advance was resumed that night, a few hours later than intended. It covered less ground than had been anticipated and ended some two miles south of Arras, the reason being that French units trying to escape from the trap had entered the gap between the armoured spearhead and the rest of the division. Much of the next day was therefore spent tidying up the situation.

The morning of 21 May was spent in maintenance, replenishment and allowing stragglers to catch up. Because of breakdowns and other losses Heilmann re-organised the company, allocating three Pz Kpfw IIs to Ravensthal's platoon. Against this, the gear selector on Sergeant Kuffner's tank was now playing up so badly that it was decided to leave the vehicle behind for the recovery section to deal with. As Ravensthal did not welcome the idea of being without Kuffner the sergeant transferred to one of the smaller tanks.

At 1500 the regiment moved off in its wedge formation. The operational plan for the day was to by-pass Arras to the south then isolate the town by swinging north on to the high ground to the west. As usual, Rommel's command vehicles were travelling close to Rothenburg's regimental headquarters tanks. At first, all seemed to go well, then Ravensthal noticed that the panzer regiment seemed to be on its own. Obviously, the rifle regiments and the rest were being slow to follow on, and even that portion of the armoured reconnaissance battalion which formed a link between them and the panzer regiment was not to be seen. Rommel's armoured car abruptly swung out of line and headed back through the tanks. Clearly, the General was intending to chase them up. As the car roared past Ravensthal could see from the thunderous look on his face that someone was in for a verbal flaying. The regiment continued on its way, reached its objective, then halted.

As the afternoon wore on it became apparent that something was very seriously wrong. Not only did the rest of the division fail to arrive, it was apparent that all hell had broken loose to the south of Arras. Columns of smoke were rising, there was heavy firing and a general movement of troops and vehicles southwards, but from so great a distance it was impossible to make out the details.

Many years later, as a retired general of the Bundeswehr, Ravensthal was often asked to describe his own experiences on that dramatic day. He could only answer for his own part, which had taken place in the closing stages of the battle. He freely admitted that such was the confusion that he had little or no idea of what was going on. Asked whether Rothenburg should have intervened earlier on his own initiative, he was inclined to dismiss the suggestion as the wisdom of hindsight, adding that he had responded to the recall signal as soon as it had been received, at about 1900.

The regiment had not gone far when it ran into a cleverly emplaced screen of British anti-tank guns and was counter-attacked by French tanks, including a number of formidable Somuas. It all happened so quickly that he had little time in which to be afraid; one moment, he was driving across the French countryside on a pleasant evening, and the next he was lying face down in the grass while fighting raged round him. The intervening seconds contained horrors that he would never forget. The tank sustained a heavy impact, its engine cut out and it rolled to a standstill. There was an overwhelming stench of fuel. When he ducked into the turret, the reason was immediately apparent. There was a round hole in Brandt's visor. The edges of the hole were a rapidly fading red and there were traces of smoke around them. Brandt's head had been burst apart as the armour-piercing round passed through it; fragmented flesh, bone, brains and hair plastered the interior walls of the vehicle and everything within them. On its way to the engine compartment the round had severed Ahrens' left leg, leaving it hanging by a tendril just below the knee. Beneath the blood pumping from severed arteries Ravensthal could see white bone. Ahrens, eyes bulging, had begun to scream. The priority was to get him out, but in the confined space the only exit was through his own cupola; that meant that, somehow, the injured man would have to be manoeuvred across the cramped interior and lifted bodily. Ravensthal knew that he could not do it unaided. The attempt was never made for in that instant the vehicle was shaken by a second impact.

Roaring flame and unbelievable heat filled the interior, forcing him out through the cupola. As he fell heavily to the ground he caught a brief sight of a well-concealed anti-tank gun some 400 yards away, and British helmets bobbing behind its shield. He sought cover behind the vehicle, where Greise joined him, one of his arms hanging uselessly. The radio operator had been escaping through the forward hatch just as the second round struck and the shockwave transmitted through the armour had caused multiple fractures in the arm he was using to lever himself out. For a few seconds they could hear Ahrens shrieking in agony, then there was a pistol shot and all they could hear were the flames roaring through the cupola like a blowtorch, and the sounds of battle.

"There's nothing you could have done for him, sir," said Greise, reading the young officer's mind.

Ravensthal nodded but did not reply. He tried to make Greise as comfortable as possible by pushing his injured arm inside the man's double-breasted tunic and strapping it in place with his belt.

"Hope you weren't looking for a date tonight, Lieutenant," said Greise. "You don't stand a chance!"

Ravensthal took out his metal shaving mirror. His entire uniform was singed, his face was scorched red and his eyebrows had been burned off. They both began to laugh.

They remained pinned down until dusk put an end to the fighting, unable to form any clear impression of what was taking place save that the regiment seemed to be having the worst of the exchange. Once firing had ceased Kuffner picked them up and the tanks set off in a wide sweep to rejoin the rest of the division. It was apparent that the enemy had begun withdrawing from the battlefield.

Bit by bit, Ravensthal was able to piece together what had happened. It seemed that the main body of the division had not long begun to advance when it was struck in flank by a British force of tanks and infantry, appearing from the direction of Arras. In planning his order of march Rommel had placed the anti-tank battalion to meet the possibility of such an attack, but the armour of the British tanks had proved quite impervious to the fire of its 37mm anti-tank guns. The battalion had been overrun, its guns crushed beneath the tracks and their crews shot down. Next, it was the turn of the motorcycle battalion and the rifle regiments, all of which were forced into a precipitate retreat southwards, sustaining casualties and having their transport shot up as they did so. This, in turn, caused a panic in the neighbouring SS Motorised Division *Totenkopf*, part of which bolted. It was at this juncture that Rommel had returned, and although he had been in such personal danger that his aide, Lieutenant Most, was shot dead beside him, he had personally brought the entire divisional artillery into action, including the powerful 88mm guns of the anti-aircraft battalion. This had finally brought the enemy counter-attack to a standstill and, harried by dive-bombers, the British had begun to withdraw by last light. Even so, in some areas fighting continued well into the night as the rallied rifle regiments strove to force the enemy infantry out of the villages they had occupied during the afternoon.

There could be no denying either that Rommel had been badly shaken by the experience or that the division had been hard hit. It had sustained well over 300 casualties, four times those it had incurred so far in the campaign, and it had lost numerous guns and transport vehicles. Thirty of the panzer regiment's tanks had been destroyed which, given that it was already operating at half-strength, was a serious matter. The surviving anti-tank gunners were already contemptuously referring to their little guns as 'door-knockers'.

At the time, Ravensthal had no idea that the counter-attack would have so great an impact on the collective mind of the High Command. He imagined that much of the following day was intentionally spent reorganising and consolidating the division's position. He had an opportunity to examine some of the knocked-out British tanks, of which there were two types. The first, called Matilda I by prisoners, was a strange little two-man machine armed only with a machine-gun; it resembled the sort of celluloid duck that children floated in their baths, but its armour had remained impenetrable to everything but the big Eighty-Eights. The second, known as Matilda II, was a bigger, more conventional design, armed with a 2pdr gun and coaxial machine-gun, and its armour was even more formidable. Again, the thought entered his mind that in some respects German tank designers were failing to keep abreast of the times.

Ravensthal was not actively engaged during the final days of this phase of the campaign. As the regiment's tank strength fell a surplus of officers resulted in his being given a job collecting groups of repaired stragglers and bringing them forward. The division, in common with most of the German armour, had now swung north to attack the pocket containing the British, the Belgian and the best of the French armies. As the resistance encountered was much stiffer, progress was proportionately slower. When the Belgians surrendered on 27 May many expected that the panzer divisions would be used to crush their way through the evacuation perimeter that the Allies had formed around Dunkirk. The task of eliminating the beachhead, however, was given to the Luftwaffe, which achieved only a modest degree of success. Instead, the panzer divisions were pulled out of the line for a period of rest and reorganisation.

Regarding the second phase of the campaign, during which Ravensthal again commanded a platoon of Pz Kpfw 38(t)s, the journalists and historians who came to see him expressed less interest. This surprised him, as it featured much of professional interest and involved the elimination of the considerable Allied forces remaining in central France, some of whom, despite having already lost so much of their armour, put up a remarkably stiff fight. The division, now known as The Ghost Division because its whereabouts sometimes remained unknown to friend and foe alike, was led by Rommel with his usual dash. Ravensthal remembered its highlights as being the capture of St-Valery-en-Caux, where some 46,000 prisoners were taken, including part of the crack British 51st Highland Division, and that of the great port of Cherbourg. By the time France surrendered the division had penetrated as far south as Bordeaux. Nevertheless, he was willing to concede that the campaign as a whole had been won by the dramatic drive from the Ardennes to the Channel, and that what followed was but a necessary postscript.

The 1940 campaign in western Europe was won by Germany in the planning stage, taking full advantage of the probable Allied reaction to a German invasion of Belgium. Its architect, the future Field Marshal Erich von Manstein, possessed one of the finest strategic minds of the war. Once battle had been joined, everything went according to the German plan. Only the Allied counter-attack at Arras caused anything like serious concern, and that because the German High Command, worried about the possible isolation of its panzer spearheads so far to the west, halted their advance for a day. In the longer term it can be argued that this contributed to the success of the Dunkirk evacuation.

The events in this story all took place during the 7th Panzer Division's advance from the German frontier to Arras. Of the real personalities involved, the subsequent career of the future Field Marshal Rommel requires no repetition here. General Hermann Hoth commanded panzer armies on the Eastern Front; in 1941 his troops advanced to within twelve miles of Moscow, but the following year he was unable to relieve the trapped German Sixth Army at Stalingrad; in 1943 he failed to penetrate the southern shoulder of the Kursk salient and was dismissed by Hitler after the fall of Kiev. General Georg Stumme commanded XL Panzer Corps in the Balkans and Russia; in September 1942 he was posted to North Africa and was commanding *Panzerarmee Afrika* during Rommel's absence when he died of a heart attack shortly after the start of the Second Battle of Alamein. Colonel Karl Rothenburg, like Rommel, had been awarded the *Pour le Mérite* during the First World War; widely regarded as one of the best tank men of his day, he was awarded the Knight's Cross for his services in France during the 1940 campaign; he would undoubtedly have achieved high rank had he not been fatally wounded near Minsk on 28 June 1941. Lieutenant Karl Hanke, the fanatical Nazi, though undoubtedly a capable and energetic officer, became too big for his boots and was dismissed by Rommel; this did no harm to his political career, for he later became the Gauleiter of Silesia; he is known to have escaped from Breslau (Wroclaw) in an aircraft when the city fell to the Soviet Army, but was never seen again.

SECOND LIEUTENANT ANDREW BRODRICK

Royal Artillery, Cyrenaica,
November 1941

They were travelling well south of the escarpment because the two exits from the coastal plain, Halfaya Pass and Sollum, were still in Axis hands. In May and June there had been heavy fighting in these areas during abortive attempts to relieve the embattled fortress of Tobruk, but now it had been decided to by-pass their garrisons and break the siege with the infantry and tanks of XIII Corps while, to the south, the armoured brigades of XXX Corps simultaneously brought the German and Italian armour to battle and destroyed it. At least, that was the theory of the Eighth Army's plan.

To Second Lieutenant Andrew Brodrick the desert was not what he expected at all. It was a dirty grey-brown colour, its surface littered with flattish stones or covered with clumps of low, desiccated scrub; sometimes they crossed a boulder field that threatened to shake the Bedford 15cwt to pieces; and sometimes they ploughed their way through areas of soft sand, digging out the wheels and using their sand mats whenever necessary. He was also surprised at the desert's range of temperatures. At noon, even in November, the men stripped down to shorts, rolled-down socks and boots; as the sun dropped they donned their shirts, adding pullovers and long trousers at dusk; at night it became bitterly cold and, during their turns on guard, they could be found in greatcoats and even balaclavas.

The convoy halted at noon and dusk each day. Tea was brewed and food cooked on old petrol tins containing sand on to which petrol had been poured and set alight. Brodrick first became aware of the flies during the noon halt. They were big, ugly, gorged specimens that came apparently from nowhere in their swarms, settling on everything, even forks that were conveying food to mouths. Brodrick was not really surprised by their presence, given that each day thousands of men from two armies deposited their spoil in the desert. The risk of disease was obvious and taking a spade for a walk was simply an act of common decency towards one's fellow men. One of the nastiest pieces of luck that could befall one, he was told, was to find oneself in an area the previous tenants of which hadn't been too particular about such matters. What did surprise him was the sheer determination of the flies, which were deterred neither by improvised whisks nor tobacco smoke. The onset of the *ghibli*, the sharp desert wind that drove stinging sand into the eyes and between the teeth, brought relief from them, and they were less of a plague when the vehicles were moving. They were also responsible for the desert sore, of which the truck's driver, Lance-Bombardier Hickson, had a painful example on his left shin. Hickson changed the dressing whenever possible, warning that grit had to be removed from any cut or graze as quickly as possible and the wound kept covered; otherwise, he said, it would fester, attract flies and become ulcerated.

Brodrick had arrived in Egypt three weeks earlier, having sailed round the Cape in a mixed convoy from the United Kingdom. Having seen the sights of Cairo, he quickly became bored with life at the transit camp. A week ago the adjutant had told him he would be joining a Territorial unit called the West Anglian Yeomanry. Puzzled, he asked whether there had been some mistake, as the title suggested an armoured regiment and he was a Gunner. The adjutant had laughed.

"So are they, old chap. Used to be cavalry and did very well in Palestine during the last war. They were transferred to the Royal Artillery during the 'Twenties, and now they're a Field Regiment with 25-pounders. They've got a regimental number, of course, but being an independent lot they prefer to use what they consider to be their proper title. Good at their job, though."

Hickson had arrived at the transit camp in due course. He had been sent back to pick up some technical spares, and in the process had collected the regiment's mail. His other passengers included two gunners from the transit camp and a man recently released from hospital. The little 15cwt had therefore been crowded, and during the four-day journey they had got to know each other well. Brodrick soon learned that in this environment rank had few privileges and found himself digging the vehicle out with the others, brewing up while the bivouac was erected, and taking his turn on guard. During the afternoon of the fourth day the convoy halted and the Military Police sorted it into packets destined for formations in the forward area. Nearby was a rusting barbed wire entanglement, gapped in so many places that it no longer constituted a physical obstacle, stretching away to north and south as far as the eye could see. Brodrick suddenly realised that he was looking at the famous Frontier Wire that separated Egypt from Libya. A little way beyond one of the gaps and situated beside a track were the knocked-about ruins of a fortified frontier post which his map told him was Fort San Giovanni; on one of the larger white-washed walls still standing were the letters 'VV RE', presumably scrawled by the Italians when they abandoned the post during the previous year's fighting.

He was aware of a steady rumble to the north-west and knew that this must be the battle which everyone knew was still raging. After dark it became a little quieter but from time to time the horizon in that direction was lit by vivid orange or violet flashes. Shortly after first light the various packets in the convoy began to depart in different directions through gaps in the wire. Brodrick, to whom many of the vehicles and the faces of those manning them had become familiar over the past few days, watched them go, wondering where they were going and what lay in store for them. His own packet, consisting of the 15cwt and two 3-tonners belonging to a neighbouring Rajput battalion, was one of the last to leave as it had only a comparatively short distance left to travel.

Once through the wire, they were in the Eighth Army's Reserve Area. Maintaining the north-westerly heading they had been given, they passed various units, including a busy armoured workshop busily repairing battle-damaged Matildas. After they had covered seven or eight miles Hickson said they were nearly there. Crossing a shallow crest they saw the regiment laid out before them – the batteries' staggered gun lines pointing in the direction of the enemy, their command posts just behind, a small cluster of vehicles indicating regimental headquarters, then the wagon lines, dispersed against the possibility of air attack. Some distance to the right were more vehicles and some weapon pits, marking the position where the Rajputs had dug in. As they drove through the Yeomanry's position Brodrick noticed that many officers, presumably pre-war Territorials, were wearing blue-and-old-gold forage caps with a silver wyvern badge; others, whom he guessed were recent arrivals like himself, wore the standard service dress cap with the Royal Artillery's badge in bronze.

Hickson dropped him outside RHQ. Under a camouflage net beside an office wagon the commanding officer and his adjutant were working at separate trestle tables placed six feet apart to convey the impression that each enjoyed his own office. As protocol demanded, Brodrick approached the adjutant first, handing over his documents. The latter introduced himself as Jeremy Corbett-Johnson, then flicked through the papers. At length he rose, commenting, "I'll take you in to meet the Colonel presently."

Brodrick could hear the two of them muttering together.

"Perhaps you'd come this way?" said Corbett-Johnson suddenly. "Colonel, this is Andrew Brodrick. He's been sent up to join us."

Lieutenant-Colonel Sir Martin Strong was a big, bluff, red-faced countryman whose loves were farming, shooting, hunting and his regiment, in which Brodrick guessed from his medal ribbons he had served in the Great War. His grip left his own hand numb.

"We're always glad to see a new face," said the Colonel. "Mind if I call you Andy?"

"No, Colonel, most people do."

"At The Shop, I see."

"Yes, Colonel. I was on the last passing out parade."

"Damn shame. People shouldn't meddle with things that have been working perfectly well for the past two hundred years. At Larkhill, too, I see."

"Yes, Colonel. I did my technical course there. After that I was a bit of a dogsbody, due to all that was happening after Dunkirk."

"Quite so, bad business all round. Now look here, Andy, there are some clever chaps at Woolwich, and Larkhill, too – damn clever. Come up with some first rate ideas – even adopted some of them myself. But in this regiment if something works we stick with it. So we call our batteries Right Flank, Centre and Left Flank, because that's what our squadrons were called when we were cavalry. That way everyone knows where they stand instead of getting confused with a lot of damn silly numbers. Got it?"

"Yes, Colonel."

"Good. Now, they've sent you out to me as a Gun Position Officer, which you're not as you've no practical experience with a regiment.

Fortunately, we're up to strength in officers, so I'm sending you to Right Flank Battery so that you can learn the ropes under someone experienced."

The colonel paused, eyeing Brodrick's cap, if not with distaste, then with surprise.

"Jeremy, we must get Andy a proper hat – the same goes for some other people, too. I thought all that was in hand."

"It is, Colonel," replied the adjutant. "A tailor in Alexandria has already produced some for us. He's having trouble getting badges from the supplier in England."

"Then write direct to the supplier yourself. We really can't be expected to carry on as we are."

"Yes, Colonel."

With that, Brodrick understood that the interview was at an end. He made his way to Right Flank Battery and introduced himself to its commander, Major Jack Freeman, who passed him on to Lieutenant Ralph Edwards, his senior GPO, whom he would understudy for the foreseeable future. During the next two days Edwards familiarised him with the workings of the battery, which differed only in detail from what he had already learned, and he met the gun detachments. Apart from a few new arrivals like himself, most of the officers were involved in farming or estate management, or were business or professional men in the country towns of the counties forming the regiment's recruiting area. Some were related either by blood or by marriage. Very much at ease with one another, they reminded Brodrick of a younger version of his father's Rotary Club. They treated their new arrivals in the friendliest way possible, albeit rather as long-term visitors than permanent members of their mess. They were unlike any other Gunner officers he had met, yet beneath their studiedly casual air he was conscious of a hard professionalism. On balance, he decided that he liked them.

His own route into the Royal Artillery had not been without some personal difficulty. His father, a long-service infantryman with the Royal Barset Rifles, had served in the South African and Great Wars, rising steadily through the ranks until in 1918 he was awarded a Quartermaster's commission. The following year he met a nursing sister and married her. He had retired with the rank of major soon after Andrew was born and taken up the post of Regimental Secretary.

Since then, he had often expressed the hope that his son would follow him into the Rifles. For his part, while drawn to the Army, Andrew had a gift for mathematics which he felt could be put to better use in the artillery, but he was worried as to how his father would accept the decision and decided to seek advice.

Jack Haynes, the local garage proprietor, had served in the Rifles at one time before transferring to the Tank Corps. He had had the reputation of being something of a lad in his youth, but had become a shrewd businessman with a sharp, if honest, turn of phrase. He had a son who seemed to be following in his footsteps, and two fine-looking daughters, to the eldest of whom Andrew had become very attached. His own father and Haynes could not accurately be described as friends, but they got on well enough and there was evidently considerable respect between them. Andrew resolved to discuss his problem with Haynes.

"Fancy being a long range sniper, do you?" said the latter. "Well, that's a good thing to be, but if you want my opinion a bright lad like you should be thinking about tanks – that's where the future lies, and as it looks like we're in for another war you'd best get in there while the promotion prospects are good."

Mrs Haynes, still a handsome woman in her forties, was clearly the household's voice of authority.

"Fat lot of good it did you, Jack Haynes! Ended up with seven months in a prisoner of war camp, he did – not got the sense he was born with! You're best making your own mind up, Andy."

"The trouble is, I'm not sure how my father will react."

"My advice would be to tell him straight out," said Haynes. "He'll be disappointed, that's only natural, but he's a fair minded man and he'll listen. If he thinks you've made your point, he'll go along with you."

It was as Haynes had predicted and so, several months later, after the necessary formalities had been completed, Gentleman Cadet Brodrick reported to the Royal Military Academy at Woolwich, otherwise known as The Shop, home to his fellows from the Royal Artillery and Royal Engineers.

It was during the afternoon of his second day with the Yeomanry that he glanced up from some gun logs to observe a general's open staff car and two escorting vehicles coming to a standstill outside RHQ.

"Methinks a bird of ill omen," said Edwards. "We're not all that far from Army HQ, but they don't normally bother us. One cannot but suspect trouble when such exalted visitors arrive."

A few minutes later *Officers' Call* was sounded. A truck carrying the Rajputs' British officers was bouncing over the desert towards them as they reached RHQ. With a start, Brodrick recognised the figure engaged in close conversation with the colonel. It was Major-General Piers Allan, DSO, MC, who had served with his father in the Great War and, during his subsequent visits to their home, become a sort of courtesy uncle. In recent years he had commanded a brigade on the North West Frontier. Brodrick did not know what his present appointment was but believed that it was something to do with operational intelligence. The general spotted him and, smiling, came across to shake his hand.

"Hello, Andy – fancy bumping into you out here in the blue! How are you getting on?"

"Well, thank you, General."

"Know this young shaver, do you, General?" asked Colonel Strong.

"Good Lord, yes. His father was my platoon sergeant at Mons. Made me put my sword away in case I injured someone!"

Brodrick had heard the story many times but joined in the dutiful laughter. Now that the officers of both regiments had assembled, however, the general had no further time for pleasantries and came straight to the point.

"Gentlemen, I know you're fed up being tied down here in reserve, but all that could change, and very quickly too.

"First, let me tell you the present state of play. On the credit side, Thirteen Corps are making excellent progress towards Tobruk and the Tobruk garrison are preparing to break out and meet them. Against this, Thirty Corps' advance has been temporarily halted. Seventh Armoured Division has had one hell of a mêlée up near Sidi Rezegh, with some of its brigades attacking and defending simultaneously; it needs time to reorganise. Rommel thinks it's finished, but it isn't. His own armour has had a mauling too, and, for the moment, it's been pulled back to sort itself out.

"So, what will he do next? Well, we can rely on his continuing to fight with his armour concentrated, as so far it has given him numerical superiority at the point of contact. As far as we can see, he has two possible courses of action open. The conventional thing to do would be to strike at Thirteen Corps. However, he's not a conventional general. He's foxy and he's a master of the unexpected. He may, therefore, decide to break this way, towards the frontier, rampage round our rear areas, cut our supply lines and replenish his fuel from his garrisons at Sollum and Halfaya Pass. The disorganisation caused would mean that our operations would have to be suspended until the situation could be restored, a state of affairs which cannot be contemplated at this critical stage.

"I assure you, gentlemen, that the Army Commander is fully aware of the potential for trouble and has prepared his own options. My purpose in visiting you personally is to warn you that if Rommel does break in this direction he must be stopped regardless, I say again regardless, of the cost. At this stage I regret I can tell you nothing more."

As soon as Allan had left, the Yeomanry and the Rajputs began preparations for their mutual defence. The latter's anti-tank platoon had four 2-pounder anti-tank guns and while these had nothing like the hitting power of the 25-pounder they could make a useful contribution at ranges under 600 yards. It was agreed, therefore, that Right Flank Battery and the Rajput anti-tank gunners would engage each others' opponents if an attack were pressed to close quarters. Within the batteries, more slit trenches were dug close to the gun positions, additional armour-piercing ammunition was brought forward from the wagon lines, broken out of its boxes and stacked, cartridges were readied and sights checked. Dusk had long since fallen by the time they were able to settle to a stew in their mess tins.

"From what the general was saying, I rather think we're going to be involved in some open sights work," said Edwards. "Andy, d'you think you can handle our right hand section on your own?"

"Yes, I think so," said Brodrick.

"Good. It's not going to be easy for us, though. Our main worry will be that we can't match their rate of fire. We're using split ammunition and have to load the projectile and charge separately; they're using fixed, one piece-ammunition and in theory can fire several rounds to our one."

"Why d'you say in theory?"

"Well, their gun sights are first rate optical equipment, as you'd expect, but they're a mite fiddly and nervous fingers can lead to mistakes. The Mark Threes, by the way, fire 37 or 50-millimetre armour piercing or high explosive, but the HE hasn't much clout about it. The Mark Fours, on the other hand, are armed with a 75-millimetre howitzer, and as far as we're concerned they're a different proposition – fortunately, they're in the minority. They've both got machine-guns in the hull front and the turret – when they're attacking they like to use the hull gun more or less continuously."

Edwards opened a copy of *The Tatler* from the day's mail delivery and began to read it by torchlight.

"What about the Italians?" asked Brodrick.

"What? Oh, yes they've got some tanks, too. They might turn up, or not, as the case may be. You never can tell."

He might have been describing unreliable riders at a point-to-point. Having lapsed into silence for several minutes he suddenly thrust a full page illustration under Brodrick's nose. It showed a smiling, prettily plump girl wearing pearls.

"Ha! Cornelia Ward's got herself engaged! Isn't that just bloody marvellous?"

Brodrick felt unable to comment either way, but made what he hoped sounded like an interested grunt. It didn't matter, as his companion, chuckling from time to time, had returned to flicking through the pages.

Shaken to take his turn in the command post, Brodrick emerged from his blankets to find a bitterly cold night. The stars, however, were at their brightest and the surrounding desert conveyed an impression of timeless peace, belied by the periodic grumbling growl and gun flashes from the direction of Tobruk. He was, nevertheless, glad when the moment came for the pre-dawn stand-to.

Half-an-hour after the battery had stood down a Marmon-Herrington armoured car was seen approaching the gun line at speed from the west. It drew to standstill in a cloud of dust beside Freeman's command post. Its commander, a South African lieutenant, was red-eyed from lack of sleep and possessed several days' growth of beard. Spotting Freeman, he saluted from the turret.

"Sorry, Major, but I think you and your boys are in for some big trouble," he said in a strong Afrikaans accent. "There's twenty-five, maybe thirty, German tanks heading straight in your direction. Pass the word, will you? My set's diss – can receive but not transmit."

"How long have we got?"

"An hour, maybe. They're keeping their speed down – my guess is they're trying to conserve their petrol."

The South African pointed back the way he had come.

"Tell you what, Major, I'll get back to that low crest about three thousand yards out. Soon as I spot their dust I'll put up a flare."

"Thanks – that will help."

The Marmon-Herrington roared off and, having informed RHQ, Freeman called his own men together.

"Right, everyone, as expected we've got a tank alert. As the enemy are known to be approaching on what is approximately our own zero line, no major redeployment is necessary at this stage. We've a little time in hand, so once the guns have been loaded and set to safe, and once you've checked you've got plenty of AP on hand, you've just got time for a quick breakfast. When the enemy arrives, the regimental plan is for us to remain in our slit trenches until he's reached our eight hundred yard marker, then stop him dead in his tracks. All perfectly straightforward. Just keep your heads down until you get the word."

Breakfast consisted of a sausage sandwich and a mug of tea. Brodrick watched the Rajputs' transport disappear in a south-easterly direction, followed by many of the regiment's own vehicles. Those that remained were widely dispersed and tucked into such hollows as they could find.

"Our visitors have arrived," said Edwards.

A red Very light was dropping over the distant crest. The armoured car could be seen making off to the north, its commander evidently having decided to watch the engagement from a flank. Ten minutes later a line of squat shapes appeared against the skyline. Through his binoculars Brodrick could see their sand-coloured paint with black or red numbers on the sides of some of their turrets. There were five of them, halted 30 yards apart. Their commanders seemed to be surveying the terrain ahead.

"Reminds one of Red Indians, doesn't it?" said Edwards. "Waiting to pounce on the wagon train, and all that."

The tanks had begun to move forward again. A second rank followed, then a third, fourth, fifth and sixth, with 70 yards between ranks, positioned so that they did not interfere with one another's line of fire. Heading directly for the lines of silent guns, they did not appear to have noticed the Rajputs. At 2,000 yards they opened fire, halting periodically to lay their main armament but machine-gunning steadily. At first their fire was largely inaccurate but gradually it focused, the Mark IV's shells bursting in front of or behind the guns while the machine-guns kicked up sand all round them and rattled off the gunshields. Some of the German tank commanders, encouraged by the sight of the apparently deserted guns, began to emerge from their cupolas.

Edwards, watching them pass the white range markers, was aware of a restive stirring among the steel helmets in the trenches a few yards ahead.

"STAY WHERE YOU ARE!" His voice had a hard edge.

"Fifteen hundred," he commented to Brodrick. "Start marking your targets."

A neat, round hole suddenly appeared in one of the gunshields.

"Looks like 50mm," said Edwards. "Mark III must be out of HE so he's switched to AP. He'll try it again in a minute. That's twelve hundred."

A second hole appeared in the gunshield and the sights were smashed off as though by a giant wielding a sledge-hammer. Seconds later there was the sound of a heavy metallic impact. The gun, hit on the left axle, lurched convulsively then tilted to the side, its wheel twisted to the horizontal.

"One thousand – GET READY!"

Brodrick looked at the short space separating the trenches from the guns. The sand was being kicked up everywhere and bursting shells were sending splinters clattering off the trails. He could not see how anyone could attempt to cross that and survive.

"TAKE POST!"

Some of the gunners were hit while scrambling out of their trenches, but in Brodrick's eyes the detachments took their positions as crisply as if they had been giving a demonstration on Salisbury Plain – No 1, a sergeant or bombardier, kneeling on the right side of the trail, No 2 kneeling opposite facing the breech, No 3 in the layer's seat to the left of the gun, No 4 to the detachment commander's left, and Nos 5 and 6 kneeling behind the gun with the next projectile and charge.

Both his section's guns remained serviceable. They lay on the extreme right of the regiment's line, which coincided with the left of the German attack. He detailed one gun to engage a Mark IV on the enemy flank while the other took on the next in line, a Mark III. As he did so, he noticed that streams of sparks were flying off some German turrets and realised that the Rajputs had opened fire with their Vickers medium machine-guns. Most commanders promptly ducked inside, but that of the Mark IV, head and shoulders out as though on a Hitler birthday parade, suddenly clapped his hands to his face and disappeared from view.

"Serve him right – cocky bastard!" said one of the ammunition numbers.

As the tanks reached the 800-yard marker Brodrick gave the order to fire. The guns erupted at once and he watched the traces streak briefly across the desert. A red flash blossomed against the front plating of the Mark IV, which lurched to a standstill. Three men emerged, two from the turret and one from the driver's hatch. The vehicle began to belch oily smoke that drifted across the battlefield.

If his second gun had hit the Mark III, it had not penetrated and there was no obvious vital damage. Moreover, the tank's commander was experienced and canny. He ordered his driver to veer left and right for short periods, halting unexpectedly to fire his main armament, and so upset the gunners' aim and timing. Brodrick instructed one gun to track his moves to the right while the other followed him to the left. Using handspikes the trails were swung round and, with their traverse gear, the layers allowed for the target's movements. After several shots, one took off the enemy's left drive sprocket, severing the track in the process. The remaining heavy links ran off the idlers to clatter like a discarded necklace on to the sand. With commendable speed, the crew abandoned their disabled vehicle to shelter in its lee, one being caught by the Rajput machine-gunners. After two more rounds had been fired into the Mark III's exposed hull it began to burn like a blowtorch.

Brodrick had reached a stage beyond terror. Expecting to die, he concentrated on what his training had taught him to do. Two or three members of his detachments had been hit and had crawled back to the trenches to apply field dressings. The level of noise, a compound of guns firing, shells exploding, machine-gun bullets rattling off the gunshields, shouted orders and screams, seemed to compress his mind, which could only absorb what was taking place in his immediate vicinity. He had taken savage pleasure in hurting the enemy but knew that only the first wave had been dealt with and that there was potentially worse to follow.

The battle raged on, but now that its first fury was spent the enemy was becoming more careful. Smoke from the burning tanks drifted between the combatants and seemed to create a psychological barrier which the Germans were unwilling to penetrate. They halted uncertainly, continuing to direct their fire at already derelict guns. Brodrick engaged shifting targets in the murk but was rarely rewarded with the flash of a strike. An explosion wrecked his right-hand gun and left the detachment sprawled around it. His second detachment sustained further casualties and at one stage he found himself serving as an ammunition number until some of the less seriously wounded rejoined them. He was impressed by the way each member of the detachment understood everyone else's job and could take it over without a word being spoken. He did not know how long this phase of the action lasted but quite suddenly firing stopped. The Germans were reversing and the cloud of dust they raised hid each side from the other's view.

He walked over to the wreckage of his second gun. The wounded members of the detachment had been carried or had crawled their way back to the trenches but there were two dead gunners lying beside the trail. One lay on his back; his stomach had been ripped open and frantic efforts had been made to restrain the intestines by tightening a waist-belt around field dressings, to no avail. The smell and the mess were bad enough, but it was the sight of the battening flies that made him throw up. He obtained a blanket from a trench and covered the man, leaving only his helmet and boots protruding.

"Hello, Andy, how are you getting on?"

Ralph Edwards seemed completely calm and collected.

"Got two of them and a possible. I'm down to one gun, though, and I seem to have lost about half the blokes."

"Same here, but we scored one definite and two probables. Nigel Warner's troop has got three guns left, so the battery still has five out of eight guns, which isn't bad, considering. The bad news is that Nigel was killed early on and Julian Hibbert caught a packet coming forward to replace him, so I've got to take over. That means you'll be responsible for our own troop, all right?"

Edwards wandered off with a cheery wave. A 3-ton truck drew up, disgorging some twenty or thirty men each carrying rounds of AP ammunition and charges. Some of them Brodrick recognised as being RHQ personnel. The Colonel stepped out of the cab and was joined by Freeman. They walked towards him.

"Enjoying yourself, young Andy? Rajputs have been on the wireless. Told me to tell you *Shabash!* Means well done – pass it on to your blokes."

"Yes, Colonel."

"Not over yet, not by a long chalk. Rounded up some spare bodies for you – you look as though you could use 'em. And some ammunition too."

He turned to Freeman.

"Altogether, Jack, we seem to have disposed of eight of Master Rommel's precious panzers, but there are plenty of them left and they'll try again. Last time I think we were too hospitable, letting 'em get to within eight hundred. This time let's try welcoming them at a thousand, shall we?"

The Germans, who had retired to an unsuspected fold in the ground, came on again shortly before noon. There were now fewer ranks but each rank numbered more tanks, and they came on at their best speed. Although the Yeomen loaded and fired as fast as they could, scoring the occasional kill, they could not match the volume of firepower directed at them. Again, casualties began to mount among the detachments, to be replaced immediately by men running from the trenches. Glancing along the battery line, Brodrick caught glimpses of the RHQ personnel in the thick of the fight alongside his gunners. There was Hickson, the driver, heaving on a handspike to swing a trail round; there was little Moffat, the bespectacled orderly-room clerk, ramming with the best of them; and there was the cook-sergeant, stripped to the waist with his helmet pushed back, directing his cooks to bring in the wounded or run forward with ammunition. In Brodrick's eyes these men, like his own detachments, seemed somehow to grow in stature as they worked amid the storm of bullets and shells.

This time it proved very difficult to score a kill. Between their firing pauses, the leading wave of tanks took evasive action and they

ONS

ove: 4th Royal Fusiliers resting in the Grande
ce at Mons the day before the battle. The British
editionary Force of 1914 consisted of long-
vice professionals and recalled reservists. The
at and fatigue after a long march are self-evident.
o members of this battalion, Lieutenant Deare
Private Godley, won the Victoria Cross during
battle. (Imperial War Museum Negative No.
70071)

Below: German infantry on manoeuvres in 1913.
Despite the undoubted brilliance of the Greater
General Staff, the German Army persisted in using
the same dense attack formations which, at
considerable cost, had won the Franco–Prussian
War of 1870, notwithstanding the manifold increase
in defensive firepower. Consequently, many British
bullets fired at Mons, Le Cateau and First Ypres
found more than one billet. (IWM Neg No.
Q.53446)

per left: The incidence of head wounds caused
shrapnel led to the rapid introduction of steel
mets. This unposed photograph shows the
nsport echelon of 1st Middlesex Regiment under
. The man at centre-right has just received a
d wound and blood can be seen streaming
wn his face; the Middlesex also sustained the loss
nine horses killed and a water cart riddled. (IWM
g No. 51489)

ntre left: The Mons–Condé Canal at Jemappes,
st of Mons, showing a pontoon bridge

completed by German engineers. A local
photographer, M. Jude, was required to record the
scene the day after the battle. Note the gutted
house at the end of the bridge. (IWM Neg No.
Q.70073)

SOMME

Above: British infantry attack under fire near
Ginchy. (IWM Neg No. Q.1302)
Below: Soldier's-eye view of the Somme
battlefield. (IWM Neg No. Q.1277)

Top: The second wave of the attack goes in. The drifting dust cloud has been thrown up by the supporting barrage. (IWM Neg No. Q.1306)
Above: Support troops leave their trenches to follow up. (IWM Neg No. Q.1312)

CAMBRAI
Below: Tank crew wearing one-piece overalls; their cap badge is that of the Machine Gun Corps. The tank is a female. (Tank Museum Neg No. 230/E6)

above: The interior of a Tank Mark IV male. The commander is on the left and the driver on the right with a Lewis gun between them. The breech of the port 6-pounder can be seen on the left, across the engine. To the right and centre are 6-pounder ammunition racks. (Tank Museum Neg No. 807/B4)

below: An F Battalion female ploughing through a wire entanglement during training at the Tank Driving School, Wailly, shortly before the battle. Sometimes huge swathes of wire would be accidentally dragged along behind the tanks, a sight which the enemy infantry must have found almost as terrifying as the vehicles themselves. F Battalion used playing-card symbols to identify its companies. (IWM Neg No. Q. 6425)

Above: Male tank 'Hyacinth' of H Battalion, badly ditched in a German second-line trench west of Ribecourt. Because the German trenches were dug so wide and deep fascines were used to cross them, but in this case it is possible that all of those immediately available had been used to break through the front line. The infantry belong to the 1st Battalion The Leicestershire Regiment. (IWM Neg No. Q.6433)

Below: An unidentified Mark IV female passing captured 77mm field guns on the Graincourt sect (IWM Neg No. Q.6336)

STORM TROOPS

Right: Storm troopers training at Sedan. Heavy emphasis was placed on rapid exploitation through any gap between the enemy's strongpoints. Notice the officer on the left, urging his men on. (IWM Neg No. Q.55016)

Centre right: Opposition had to be suppressed quickly. Here, while one man hurls a stick grenade, another cuts his way through a wire entanglement. (IWM Neg No. Q.55020)

Lower right: Having captured a trench, Storm troopers advance beyond it with all possible speed. Creaming off the best men into the storm troop battalions had unfortunate consequences; when they had gone the overall quality of German combat troops declined. (IWM Neg No. Q.55013)

Below: Storm Troop Battalion attack in progress. On 21 March 1918 such attacks were preceded by an extremely heavy bombardment, including gas shells, and fortuitously screened by a dense mist. Consequently, little difficulty was experienced in penetrating the British line. (IWM Neg No. Q.55003)

79

FRANCE 1940
Above: A company of 25th Panzer Regiment's Pz Kpfw 38(t)s deployed for an advance across open country. In the foreground is a member of 7th Panzer Division's motor-cycle battalion. (IWM Neg No. RML 119)*
Right: French Char B knocked out near Le Cateau. These tanks, referred to by the Germans as *Kolosse*, were better armed and armoured than any vehicle in the German inventory. (IWM Neg No. RML 79)*
Below: Pz Kpfw 38(t)s and motor riflemen of 7th Panzer Division advancing across country. (IWM Neg. RML 132)*

ght: Burned-out Sd
263 and Sd Kfz 231
noured cars of 7th
nzer Division's
noured recon-
ssance battalion,
stroyed during the
ed counter-attack at
as, 20 May 1940.
e Sd Kfz 263 was a
lio communications
icle; the frame
ove its turret was a
dstead' type of
ial. (IWM Neg No.
L 125)*

ntre right: Tanks of
h Panzer Regiment
ss a pontoon bridge
structed by
rman engineers over
La Bassé Canal, 27
y 1940. (Neg No.
L 151A)*

ttom right: A tired
Kpfw 38(t) driver of
h Panzer Regiment
es a hard-earned
ak. Given the
nner in which the
n Major-General
mmel drove his
sion, the man's
gue and evident eye
in are under-
idable. The padded
ck beret was worn
armoured troops
ing the Polish and
nch campaigns,
ugh it was being
laced by the forage
during the latter.
nk Museum Neg
. 3052/A4)

hese photographs
ne from Rommel's
sonal collection.
ne were taken by
self or his aides,
ers by official
rman Army
otographers.)

CYRENAICA

Above: A troop of 25-pounder gun-howitzers engaging a distant target in the Western Desert. The staggered gun line was adopted to reduce the effects not only of counter-battery fire but also low-level strafing by enemy aircraft. (IWM Neg No. E.6814)

Below: Another view of the gun position, taken shortly after first light. November nights in the desert could be bitterly cold, yet by midday the temperature was such that the gun crews would stripped to the waist. (IWM Neg No. E.6816)

Left: British tank crewmen examine tv knocked-out Pz Kpfv IV. Armed with a shc 75mm howitzer, this tank presented a greater threat to fiel artillery than other tanks in German or Italian service. (IWM Neg No. E.6735)

TARAWA

Right: Knocked-out amtracs and bodies litter the lagoon as mute testimony to the ferocity of the fighting for the tiny island of Betio. The palm trees were stripped during the preliminary bombardment. (IWM Neg No. EN. 10798)

Right: Marines fight their way over the palm-log sea wall. The photograph, taken from the water's edge, gives some idea of the small area in which, for a while, they were pinned down by Japanese fire. (US Marine Corps)

Right: Close-quarter attack on one of the numerous Japanese bunkers. (IWM Neg No. NYF. 11281)

Above: Even inland, the fighting was at close range. To the right is one of the Japanese concrete command bunkers, carefully camouflaged. (US Marine Corps)
Left: The end of a Japanese counter-attack. All but a tiny handful of Japanese fought to the death. (IWM Neg No. EN 12981)

Left: Amtracs unload 75mm pack howitzers and stores during the final phases of Operation 'Galvanic'. (US Marine Corps)

NORMANDY

Above: Infantrymen of 12 Platoon, B Company, 6th Royal Scots Fusiliers, about to cross their startline as artillery batters the enemy's positions. (IWM Neg No. B. 5950)

Below: The Bren group of a Fusilier section penetrate the churchyard at St Manvieu. (IWM Neg. B 5963)

Above: Churchill tanks and infantry advancing on their objective through a smoke-screen. (IWM Neg No, B. 5955)

Below: Fingers ready on triggers, Fusiliers clear the rear of houses in St. Manvieu. (IWM Neg No. B 5966)

(These photographs, and the those on the previous page, are from a sequence taken by Sergeants Leeson and Connolly, two official photographers,

who accompanied an attack by 44 Brigade of 15t (Scottish) Division and remained with the forwar elements throughout. The objectives of the attac which was very similar to that described in the te were the small villages of St. Manvieu and La Gau south of Norrey-en-Bessin. Sergeant Leeson records that as a result of sniping, mortaring and machine-gun fire, the Fusiliers' B Company sustained 50 per cent casualties.)

Right: Frontal view of M8 armoured car, fully crewed and ready for combat. (Tank Museum Neg No. 621/E4)

Below: Interior of M8 turret showing 37mm breech and spent case collector; 37mm ammunition, gunsight telescope, .30 Browning coaxial machine-gun; turret position indicator scale; seats for commander and gunner. (Tank Museum Neg No. 8/C2)

Above: A captured photograph showing Germans stripping dead US troops of their boots, somewhere in the Ardennes. The censor has obliterated all place names from the signpost. (IWM Neg No. EA. 47965)

Left: This still from a German newsreel shows Waffen SS men in process of looting a captured M8 armoured car. The man on the left sports several weapons, including a dagger, plus a belt of machine-gun ammunition. Both he and the man on the right are equipped with short-handled entrenching tools; with sharpened edges, these could be deadly in hand-to-hand combat. (IWM Neg No. EA 48004)

ove: The crew of an M8 armoured car
erving from the cover of a gutted building. The
's most formidable weapon was its radio. (Tank
seum Neg No. 621/D2)

Below: Counter-attack. Armour and infantry of the
US 75th Division approaching the northern flank of
The Bulge. (IWM Neg No. 49864)

MALAYA

Above: An Iban tracker advises his patrol commander. From the marks in the path the trackers could interpret the size of an enemy party, how long since it passed, and even the sex of its members. (IWM Neg No. BF. 10374)

Below: Patrol taking a short rest. At first some men found the jungle claustrophobic and frightening. (IWM Neg No. MAL. 162)

Above: During lengthy stays in the jungle patrols established bases from which they could operate daily. In such 'basha' areas hammocks were slung between trees. (IWM Neg No. MAL. 309)

Above right: A patrol of The Cameronians (Scottish Rifles) exhibits trophies from the successful elimination of a terrorist camp, including communist flags and headgear; their tracker displays his parang, honed to the finest of edges. (IWM Neg No. MAL. 301)

Right: Most of the men in this patrol are armed with the shorter Lee-Enfield Rifle No 5, which was handier than the standard weapon. Constant pressure even in the most difficult terrain finally eroded the communists' strength and will to resist. (IWM Neg No BF. 10387)

VIETNAM

Above: A battery of M101 105mm howitzers firing from a temporary fire support base in support of 1st Air Cavalry Division operations, August 1969. (US Army Military History Institute)

Below: The recently introduced M102 105mm howitzer was a technically superior weapon to th' older M101, but its users found its lower breech extremely tiring to feed during prolonged fire support engagements. (USAMHI)

Above: An M114 155mm howitzer of Battery G ?h Artillery at full recoil. The breastwork ?rounding the gun position consists of ?munition containers filled with earth and topped ?sandbags. FSBs would provide mutual support ?one another when attacked. (USAMHI)

Below: A Chinook helicopter lifts a gun into a prepared position at an FSB. The gun position incorporates a defensive breastwork, ammunition storage facilities and living accommodation for the crew. (USAMHI)

Above: Signallers talk in a casevac helicopter while a medic attends to a badly injured casualty. (IWM Neg No. CT 166)

Below: A Viet Cong prisoner is escorted past on of his dead comrades. (IWM Neg No. CT 175)

Right: The crew of a Warrior IFV engaged in track replacement. The new track is being hauled forward over the rear idler wheel and will be joined below the drive sprocket. (IWM Neg No. GLF 1418)

Below: Challenger tank of the 14th/20th King's Hussars. (IWM Neg No. GLF 1420)

Above: An infantry section deploys from its Warrior IFV. (IWM Neg No. GLF 1407)
Below: Flying the Jolly Roger, a Spartan APC passes a convoy of wrecked and burning Iraqi transport.

Little serious opposition was encountered during the Coalition army's ground offensive. (IWM Neg No. GLF 1277)

moved quickly, throwing up a curtain of dust that concealed those behind. Brodrick was particularly worried by three tanks that were heading for the extreme right of the gun line, guessing that they intended to sweep round behind it. As the range shortened to 300, then 200 yards, another of his guns was put out of action. Certain that they were about to be overrun, he had begun to swing the trails round to meet the three when several tracers flashed across the desert from the Rajput lines. The leading tank jerked to a halt and began to belch smoke and flames as the crew scrambled out, its commander standing briefly on the engine deck to point out the new danger. The two remaining tanks slowed down and began swinging left to present their thicker frontal armour to the Indian anti-tank gunners. In so doing their vulnerable sides were exposed to the Yeomanry, whom their commanders evidently considered to be no longer of any account. Brodrick seized the opportunity at once.

"NOW'S YOUR CHANCE!"

One of his guns banged. The round entered the German's hull just below the rear of the turret. The tank stopped at once. A second later it was shaken by a violent internal explosion and flames erupted from every opening. One man emerged, his clothes on fire. He began to roll in the sand.

Brodrick was standing behind the second gun. The layer was inexperienced but he was doing his best and chivvying him would achieve nothing. Their target was a Mark III with RO2 painted in red on the turret and a frame radio aerial over the engine deck. Brodrick guessed that it was a command tank. When, at length, the gun fired, it was on for line but too high for a hull shot. Instead, it smashed through the turret escape door. He could not be certain of what happened next, but the tank's gun and mantlet jerked and remained at a drunken angle. It seemed probable that the round had struck the breech of the 50mm and expended its residual energy flying round the confined space. The last command the driver had been given was to steer to the left. This he continued to do until the tank was facing the way it had come then, realising that the turret crew were dead, he tried to accelerate out of trouble. The second wave of German armour, emerging from the dust and seeing their commander heading back towards them, hesitated and came to a standstill.

"See if you can put one up his rump," said Brodrick to the layer.

Before that could happen, however, the Rajputs put several 2-pounder rounds into the command tank. Once again the attackers began reversing out of action. When their dust cleared Brodrick could see six or seven more of their number were burning among the hulks that already littered the regiment's front.

"Nice piece of cross-trumping!" Brodrick looked round to find Freeman standing behind him. "It rather looks as though our friend over there has lost half the tanks he started with. Silly ass! If he'd waited for his infantry and artillery to catch up he could have given us a good hammering, used his tanks against the Rajputs and attacked us with his infantry. It might all have been over by now if he'd not been so darned impatient."

"What d'you think he'll do next?"

"Well, I've been watching those dust clouds beyond the ridge and I suspect that his infantry and guns are coming up now. He might try what I suggested, but I doubt it because between you and the Rajputs this has become a bit of a windy corner for him. I think he'll mount a demonstration against the Rajputs to attract our attention, work round our left flank with the rest of his tanks and attack us with his infantry. I'm afraid we're not too well placed to meet an infantry attack, and with us gone there's not much hope for the Rajputs."

Brodrick digested the implications in silence. He knew that the Rajputs' right was protected by a deep wadi that would inhibit a tank attack, and that the Germans would be unlikely to risk an infantry attack over open ground against the unshaken Indians, so Freeman's appreciation seemed reasonable.

"Just one other thing, Andy," Freeman continued. "Ralph has been hit in the jaw – can't speak, so I've packed him off to the aid post. What happens in Right Flank Battery now is up to the two of us."

The shelling started at about 1530. Brodrick got his detachments into the slit trenches which were crowded despite the fact that many of the less seriously wounded had made their own way or been helped to the rear. The explosions were heavier than Brodrick had experienced so far and showered the occupants of his trench with sand.

"One-oh-fives," said a bombardier.

"Couple of one-fifties, too," added a sergeant.

There was a sound of running feet and Battery Sergeant-Major Miller jumped into the trench.

"Mr Brodrick, sir! Command post has taken a direct hit – I'm afraid the Major's dead. You're in command now, sir."

Brodrick found himself temporarily struck dumb. Suddenly, with no other officers present to turn to for advice, he had become responsible for the entire battery, and the thought terrified him. The Sergeant-Major read his mind.

"Just three serviceable guns left, sir – no more than you've been used to."

He steadied down, swallowed hard, and explained how Freeman had thought the battle would develop. As he spoke an idea began to develop.

"Send a runner to the nearest Rajput company. He's to tell them how things stand here and ask for as many men as they can spare, if possible with Brens. Make sure he gets there, and if he doesn't, keep sending blokes until someone gets through – it's that important!"

"Very good, sir."

The Sergeant-Major clambered out of the trench. As the enemy's shelling was restricted to the regiment's area, Brodrick calculated that once the runner was clear of battery lines he should have no trouble in covering the 400 yards to the Rajputs. He raised his binoculars, scanning the horizon from right to left. In the distance was a troop of three Mark IVs, shelling the Indians at extreme range, and several troop carriers. Opposite was a growing dust cloud, still beyond the skyline. To the left was another dust cloud, moving left. Freeman had been right. He switched his gaze back to the centre. Troop carriers had begun streaming over the crest but he did not attempt to count them as there was not a moment to lose.

"TAKE POST!"

The three detachments ran to their guns as the fire orders drummed into him reached the forefront of his mind.

"GEE EFF TARGET – EMPTY GUNS!"

The three guns banged simultaneously as the already loaded AP rounds were sent off into infinity.

"H.E. ONE-ONE-SEVEN – CHARGE TWO – BEARING-THREE-FIVE ZERO – ANGLE OF SIGHT ZERO - TWO THOUSAND – FIRE BY ORDER!"

The shelling had begun to slacken, indicating that the attack was about to commence. He watched as the ammunition numbers extracted shells from the limbers and ran forward with them while the rest of the detachments went about the business of re-aligning the guns. The enemy troop carriers were now hidden by the fold in the ground.

"How do you do, old chap? Busy sort of day you're having!"

He shook hands with the Rajput *jemadar*, who had brought some twenty men and, thankfully, three Brens, with him.

"We're about to be attacked by infantry. Can you look after our close defence? I can give you those of our chaps who aren't doing anything."

"That will be a pleasure – also you will find your Rajput comrades will assist you in other ways!"

"Sarn't Major!"

"Sir!" Miller was already at his elbow.

"Get everyone who isn't actually working with a detachment into the line with their personal weapons – the *jemadar* will tell you what's needed."

"Sir!"

The No 1s' hands were raised to indicate readiness.

"FIRE!"

The guns crashed out. He did not see the shells burst and suspected that they had landed in the hollow. He had left it too late, for the troop carriers had already started to appear. A radical correction was needed.

"ONE SIX HUNDRED!"

Again the No 1s' hands went up.

"FIRE!"

This time the bursts fountained some way ahead of the carriers. Three guns couldn't put down much of a barrage but it was the best they could do and he decided to maintain fire at this range. One of the enemy vehicles sustained a near miss and came to a standstill, its occupants leaping to the ground.

He dropped the range to 1,200 and saw another of the trucks overturn when a shell exploded beside it. There were plenty more but at 1,000 yards their drivers halted. The infantry tumbled out, continuing their advance in short, controlled rushes. He was surprised how many of them there were. They seemed to pass through his 800-yard line without difficulty. Glancing to his left he knew that no help could be expected from the rest of the regiment. Left Flank and Centre Batteries, with eight guns between them, were heavily engaged with a dozen or so tanks trying to work round their flank.

At 600 yards he began to doubt that the infantry attack could be held. Then four bursts that were not his own erupted among the enemy, followed by many more. He now knew what the *jemadar* had meant – the Rajputs' 3-in mortars were in action, and so were their Vickers machine-guns, maintaining steady oblique fire across the front of the enemy advance. Yet still the Germans came on. At 400 yards he heard the *jemadar* give the order to open fire. The splutter of rifles was punctuated by the short, hammering bursts of the Brens. Nevertheless, it was not until he had brought in the fire of his own guns to 200 yards that the attack started to break up, those at the back shredding away first. Brodrick had a sneaking sympathy for those who had come closest to pressing home the attack, for they were now pinned down and the Rajputs' tracked carriers were already racing out to pick them up.

The Germans' vehicles disappeared beyond the far crest. Leaving three more of their number burning, the tanks had also broken off their attack. The dust cloud gradually diminished to the west.

"By Jove, what a slogging match we've had!" said the *jemadar*. "Those fellows have had a damn good hiding! Should you require it, my men will be happy to assist you with the prisoners."

"Thanks – we're very grateful."

Brodrick sensed that the battle was over. The prisoners were herded in, carrying their own wounded. There were about a hundred of them, mixed infantry and tank crew. Stripped of their helmets and equipment, they seemed grubby, dishevelled and blank-faced. Guarded by the Rajputs, they started digging temporary graves for the battery's own dead.

Brodrick could hardly believe that he had survived. The battery position resembled some of the prints in his father's books about the Boer War. Everywhere one looked there were smashed guns, shattered limbers, a litter of brass cases, the dead sprawled in attitudes of abandon, and men with bandaged heads, arms or legs. The *jemadar*'s comment about a slogging match triggered something in his weary mind. After a game at school or The Shop you had tea in the pavilion with the opposition. He was suddenly struck by the absurd idea of sitting down to tea and sandwiches with the *Afrika Korps* and waving them off in their buses. He started to giggle, realised that he was on the edge of hysteria and checked himself. His hands had started to shake. Conscious that he must pull himself together, he walked towards the nearest gun, around which the detachment were sitting smoking. The previous day, or even that morning, they would have been indifferent to him, but now they welcomed him with grins. He realised that, for the moment at least, they were his men and he was proud of them.

"Yes, stand down," he said needlessly. "I wonder, can I scrounge a cigarette from someone?"

Several were offered and he was given a light. He had a raging thirst and was uncertain whether he liked the taste, but the nicotine had a calming, benevolent effect.

"Didn't know you smoked, sir," said the sergeant.

"I think I've just started."

"Same way as a lot of us, sir!" Everyone laughed.

He talked with them for a while then, realising that he had drawn strength from them, decided to visit the rest of the battery. He spoke to everyone and they seemed pleased that he had taken the trouble. He was struck that the men, normally rowdy among themselves, had become so quiet. There was little of the habitual cursing and bad language, only kindness and consideration for one another and especially the wounded.

All manner of things began to claim his attention. Several ambulances arrived and the Medical Officer swiftly categorised the non-walking wounded, British and German, into those who required immediate evacuation to field hospitals, those who could wait a little longer, and those who should be allowed to spend what little time remained to them in peace, their agony suppressed by morphia. Simultaneously, Brodrick toured the gun positions with the artificer sergeant who decided which guns could be repaired quickly, which could not, and which would have to be back-loaded. The senior NCOs had already started to tidy up, but as the ambulances began to leave he noticed how few men they had left. He walked across to the command post where a signaller looked up from the recently restored field telephone link.

"CO's Orders in thirty minutes, sir."

"Thank you."

Life goes on, he thought. He found the BSM with a small pile of identity discs and personal effects taken from the dead, and sat down beside him.

"Have to be sorted properly when we've more time," said Miller, and began to go through the Battery Roll. At length he handed it to the young officer.

"Battery state at 1745 is three guns, one officer and thirty other ranks, sir."

"Not a lot, is it?"

"Not a lot, sir."

Brodrick lapsed into silence, staring straight ahead. He had never imagined that comparative calm could be so luxurious, marred only by his raging thirst.

"Penny for 'em, sir," said Miller after a while.

"Tea, Sarn't Major – I was thinking about tea."

Miller chuckled.

"Scalding hot, strong and sweet, just what we all need. It's in hand, sir. Quartermaster-Sergeant is brewing round the back. Should be just about ready."

The BQMS was about to leave for the gun positions with a full dixie and he filled two of the many spare mugs in the command post for them. Never again in his life would Brodrick taste so wonderful a drink.

Students of the Desert War will recognise that this episode has been set during what became known as Rommel's Dash to the Wire. Having, as he thought, disposed of British XXX Corps, Rommel believed that by breaking into the British rear areas near the Egyptian frontier he would create such uncertainty in the mind of the Eighth Army's commander, Lieutenant-General Sir Alan Cunningham, that the latter would abandon Operation 'Crusader'. Such indeed were Cunningham's thoughts, despite the non-committal comment by the fictitious General Allan in the narrative. The Commander-in-Chief Middle East, General Sir Claude Auchinleck, promptly replaced Cunningham with Major-General Neil Ritchie. In the event, the German armour was badly mauled during actions such as the one described. When XIII Corps broke through to the Tobruk garrison during the night of

26/7 November, Rommel abandoned his operations on the frontier and hurried west to re-impose the siege. By now, however, he had been fatally weakened and was ultimately forced to abandon Cyrenaica to save his army from destruction. One of his few minor successes during the Dash to the Wire was the temporary elimination of 1st Army Tank Brigade's workshops at Sidi Azeiz, but even there he lost several tanks when the crews of Matildas under repair manned their vehicles and fought back until overwhelmed. There were no British survivors and there is evidence that the prisoners were shot; this was an uncharacteristic departure from the 'clean' war fought by both sides and is indicative of the German level of frustration.

The narrative is based on anti-tank actions fought by the 1st and 25th Field Regiments RA during this period and by the 107th Regiment RHA (South Nottinghamshire Hussars) the following year. Although the 25-pounder was a formidable weapon when used in the anti-tank role, it could not match the rate of fire produced by the enemy's tanks and its detachments had little protection. Casualties were therefore heavy, but the high courage and degree of professionalism displayed in each of these engagements made them all the more remarkable.

The expression 'cross-trumping' was sometimes used when neighbouring units were enabled by circumstances to take care of each other's anti-tank defence – if, for example, enemy tanks could only attack one unit by exposing their vulnerable side armour to fire from another, and vice versa. A notable example was provided by the epic defence of Outpost Snipe during the Second Battle of Alamein, discussed in greater detail in the author's book *Last Stand*.

PRIVATE AL HOGAN

US Marine Corps, Betio Island,
Tarawa Atoll, 20–23 November 1943

Alan Hogan had joined the Marine Corps on the advice of a veteran in his home town. The old man had served with the Marines in China and in France and, somewhere along the line, he had won the Medal of Honor. He didn't talk about it and rarely showed it to anyone, but he wore it alongside a string of others when he led the town's annual Memorial Day parade. When the Japanese attacked Pearl Harbor, Hogan had sought his advice about the service in which he should enlist. The reply had been uncompromising.

"Doesn't matter much who you hitch up with, son," the old man said. "What counts is that you're proud of it and your folks are proud of you. Me, I'd choose the Marine Corps every time. Fact is, everyone trains as a rifleman, and that's plenty tough enough for most. After that, well, you can specialise – mortars, artillery, tanks, signals, even fighters, but you'll still be a Marine and that'll earn you respect."

Hogan had found the training to be every bit as tough as the veteran had predicted. Stretched to the limits physically and mentally, he had it drummed into him that the Corps was the nation's élite and that it accepted only the best. Somehow, he passed through boot camp and squad training to emerge with the feeling that he had earned the right to his uniform. He had, therefore, been shocked to read on the postings list that while most of his buddies would be joining Marine infantry regiments, he was to report to something called an amphibian tractor detachment at Dunedin in Florida. Like everyone else, he had been subjected to minor hazing and, suspecting a joke, hurried to the office of the Gunnery Instructor who had been responsible for his intake.

The GI appeared to have been hewn out of granite. His hair was cropped to scalp level, his craggy face bore a permanently ferocious expression, and his massive fists looked capable of knocking your head off your shoulders. The dents in his lemon-squeezer hat were always precisely positioned, his uniform was pressed within an inch of its life and his boots gleamed like glass. Hogan had been terrified of him at first, but over a period of weeks he had learned that while he did not suffer fools gladly, and could make life hell for those who tried to challenge his authority, he was also fair, patient and understanding. He glanced up as Hogan knocked on his door.

"What is it, Hogan?"

"Sir, I think there's been a mistake with my posting."

Without speaking, the GI stood up and pulled Hogan's file from his cabinet. After studying it briefly he looked up again.

"You were a construction worker, right?"

"Yes, sir."

"And you drove a tractor, right?"

"Yes, sir."

"There's been no mistake. You drove a tractor, now we're giving you another one to drive – only this one floats!"

"Sir, I wanted to be assigned to an infantry unit – that's why I enlisted!"

"Forget it! You're more use to us this way!"

Dumbstruck, Hogan wondered whether all his efforts had been worth it when he could, with a lot less trouble, have volunteered for the Army's Engineer Corps and driven a tractor for them. He felt close to tears and must have shown it.

"Don't worry, Hogan, we've done you no favours," said the GI, not unkindly. "You'll get all the combat you can handle."

The big man rose and, to Hogan's surprise, his face cracked into something resembling a friendly smile as he shook hands.

"On your way, Marine – and good luck!"

Once he learned a little more about his new occupation he began to warm to it. The amphibious tractors were nothing like he imagined. They resembled a large bathtub mounted on a tracked chassis, the treads of which incorporated shaped vanes that provided propulsion when the vehicle was afloat, and they had a sort of cab forward for the driver and vehicle commander. The older hands called them Alligators as they had been developed from a rescue vehicle designed for use in the Everglades of Florida, but to the more officially minded they were Landing Vehicles (Tracked) or LVTs. Most people, however, simply called them amtracs. Afloat, they had a speed of approximately six knots, but ashore they could manage about 25mph. While Hogan was being instructed on how to drive and maintain the vehicle, he was warned to avoid hard ground whenever possible as this would cause excessive wear on the suspension and tracks, and told that such was the corrosive effect of sea water that the average operational life expectancy of an amtrac was estimated as being 200 hours' running time. The amtracs' role, he learned, was the transportation of supplies from ships lying offshore to the landing beaches and beyond, and in this capacity they had already given valuable service at Guadalcanal in the Solomon Islands, during the Allied landings in French North Africa, and at Attu in the Aleutian Islands. It sounded useful, but not particularly exciting, he thought.

His training complete, Hogan found himself aboard a troop transport, part of a heavily escorted convoy bound for New Zealand. On arrival he joined the 2nd Amphibian Tractor Battalion, which formed part of the 2nd Marine Division. The battalion's amtracs had already seen service on Guadalcanal and required much hard work to return them to operational condition. In some cases they were beyond repair, but at length 75 were considered capable of further use. These were being fitted with boiler plate armour as well as pintle mountings for four machine-guns. Naturally, the modified amtracs were heavier to handle than those Hogan had trained on, requiring him to adapt his technique. The battalion quickly reached the inescapable conclusion that its function was no longer seen as purely cargo-carrying and that, in some way it did not yet understand, it was to play an active combat role in future operations.

In due course this was made clear during a series of lectures. American strategy now involved an advance on Japan across the Central Pacific, supported by land-based airpower. This meant capturing tiny atolls on which the enemy had already built airstrips or on which airstrips could be constructed quickly. The problem was that the islands themselves were often surrounded by coral reefs which could not be crossed by conventional landing-craft because there was insufficient depth of water above them. The Marine Corps believed that the problem could be solved by landing the assault wave in amtracs, which could crawl over the reefs and cross the shallows beyond without the need to disembark the troops they would be carrying.

There was some interesting scuttlebutt on the subject, too. Inevitably, someone knew someone else who knew a mess boy, and mess boys were notoriously good at picking up the conversations of generals and admirals, especially when voices were raised in dispute. The Navy, it seemed, was confident that in certain tidal conditions there would be sufficient depth of water covering the reefs around the division's next objective, wherever that was, for landing-craft to be used. The Marines, and in particular Major General Holland M. Smith, commanding V Amphibious Corps, of which the division formed part, had taken specialist advice on the subject, and they did not agree. No one got in "Howling Mad" Smith's way when he was on the warpath and with his men's lives on the line he had apparently banged the table, shouting "No amtracs, no operation!" The Navy had changed its mind.

The division contained many veterans of the fighting on Guadalcanal who passed on their experience of the enemy to the new arrivals. The Japanese, they said, were adept at constructing layered sand and palm-log weapon pits and bunkers with interlocking arcs of fire, often connected by covered crawl trenches; there could be no guarantee, therefore, that because a position had apparently fallen silent it would remain so. Furthermore, the Japanese fought in a way that was unique to them. They would fight to the death in their trenches and when they attacked they would keep coming until the last of them was shot down. They worshipped their emperor and believed that dying in his service was the highest honour they could aspire to; the concept of surrender therefore had no meaning for them.

"Don't you go helping no wounded Jap," said a grizzled First Sergeant. "He'll kill you, first chance he gets, 'cos that's part of his religion. I lost a good buddy that way."

The sergeant watched his audience as the full implications of what he had said sank in.

"Okay, so it's rough, but the Japs don't think like us, so play it their way and stay alive. Remember that!"

Much training took place at a rocky inlet called Hawkes Bay, where the surf was dangerously heavy and lives were lost. During these exercises the amtracs practised embarking fully laden squads from the troop transports and ferrying them to the beach in formation. On 1 November 1943 the 2nd Marine Division embarked at Wellington for what seemed to be another landing exercise at Hawkes Bay, but on this occasion the transports and their escorts kept heading steadily north until, a week later, they dropped anchor in Mele Bay, off the island of Efate. Here further exercises took place and the division learned that its landing would be directly supported by a company of Sherman medium tanks, as well as its own tank battalion, which was equipped with Stuarts. The amtrac battalion was reinforced with 50 brand-new vehicles of a more advanced design incorporating integral armour, but as these had been shipped direct from the United States there was no opportunity to test them afloat.

When the task force resumed its northwards passage on 13 November it was joined by the naval units which would provide the preparatory bombardment for the operation. Hogan had never seen so many warships. In the distance were the huge shapes of battleships and aircraft carriers, while closer to hand there were cruisers, destroyers and minesweepers, too numerous to count.

Next day the details of the operation, code-named 'Galvanic', were communicated to the troops. Its objective was Tarawa Atoll, part of the Gilbert Islands, a British possession in the Central Pacific, and specifically an island called Betio on which the enemy had constructed an airstrip. Shaped like a tadpole, Betio was just 4,000 yards long and only 500 yards across at its widest point. It had been heavily fortified with the usual palm-log bunkers, supplemented by several large concrete structures containing coastal artillery or command posts. For its size, it was held in strength, but the Navy was confident that their weight of bombardment, supplemented by carrier air strikes, would pulverise any opposition.

As far as the detailed planning was concerned, the assault wave would board their amtracs some four miles out. The assault force would then pass through the entrance of the atoll's lagoon, fan out and head for the shore. Hogan learned that his company would be responsible for landing the II/2nd Marines on a beach designated Red 2, the eastern boundary of which was marked by a pier some 500 yards long, reaching out to the edge of the reef. It all seemed very simple.

Hogan was kept busy checking over every mechanical detail of his amtrac while the gunners, Dale and Svensen on the heavy .50s forward and Lefebre and Zimmerman on the medium .30s aft, stripped down their weapons, cleaned them and stowed ammunition. A Lieutenant Willard, responsible for maintaining direction towards their sector of the invasion beach, would be riding with them.

Late in the evening of 19 November they were summoned to the mess deck for what many laughingly called their 'last breakfast'. It consisted of steak and eggs but Hogan was not interested, partly because it was not a regular meal time but mainly because anticipation had tied his stomach in a knot, destroying his appetite. The scuttlebutt was that it would be a walkover. The divisional commander, Major General Julian Smith, had told them so, and the Navy had promised to obliterate the opposition. The general view was that a sledge-hammer was being used to crack a nut. Even so, most men retained private reservations and there was little conversation as they lay on their bunks to catch a few hours' rest. It was almost a relief when, at 0230, the amtrac crews were piped to their launching stations on the vehicle deck.

The launch was made into a level sea with just a hint of swell running. To Hogan's satisfaction, the old amtrac's engine was running smoothly. At 0355 the company came alongside its designated troop transport and heavily laden infantrymen began dropping aboard from the disembarkation nets hanging down the ship's side. The amtracs then moved away to circle until the moment for the assault came. Hogan quickly became disoriented in the darkness, having no idea in which direction Betio lay. Some thirty minutes later they received a signal to proceed north slowly as they had been carried away from their departure line by a two-knot current. Just as Hogan was told to start circling again a red star shell burst, illuminating the entire scene.

Minutes later the Japanese coast defence guns opened fire. Shell splashes mushroomed near the transports and the warships replied, belching huge flashes of light, smoke and shockwaves rather than audible sound. After several salvos there was a major explosion ashore, following which the Japanese guns fell silent, although the warships continued to batter the island.

Once the light began to strengthen, however, the Japanese were able to identify their targets and opened fire again. Near misses fountained near the transports, still engaged in disembarking the fourth assault wave which, because there were insufficient amtracs, would go in aboard conventional landing-craft. As soon as the craft were clear, the transports withdrew out of range.

Shortly after six the invasion fleet's bombardment group ceased firing to allow the first of the air strikes to go in. The amtracs were now heading for the entrance to the lagoon, still some 3½ miles distant, and Hogan could see through his visor that the entire island seemed to be covered with explosions amid which fires glowed sullenly beneath a pall of smoke and sand. Aware that the amtracs were pushing their way into a steady current, he glanced at his watch and realised that they would not be making the planned 0830 touchdown. It did not seem to matter as the bombardment group was continuing its work. Now that they were closer, Betio seemed to erupting in one long continuous explosion, its shattered palms barely visible above the drifting smoke. It seemed impossible that anyone could survive in that inferno.

They passed through the entrance to the lagoon and, swinging to starboard, began to form up on the departure line. Hogan's watch told him that it was 0823. The amtracs had been escorted thus far by minesweepers and destroyers, but only two of the latter accompanied them into the lagoon itself. While the lines forming the various assault waves sorted themselves out, Hogan found himself sweating; this final delay was the hardest of all to bear. He saw several gigantic eruptions of sand and sea water blasted skywards in the space between the island's reef and its shoreline. One, at least, of the battleships was firing short, he guessed. The submerged craters left by the huge shells might cause problems if the amtracs were running with their tracks grounded.

They received orders to commence the final run in. As they began to forge forward the bombardment lifted to permit another air strike. Freed of the adverse current, the amtracs made good progress, although they still had a long way to go when the last of the aircraft banked away. There was a moment of comparative calm during which only the two destroyers continued firing. Then, quite suddenly, the entire shoreline began to sparkle with the fire of automatic weapons and the flash of guns. Shells burst overhead or blasted waterspouts nearby while the surface of the sea was flayed by bullets. Hogan was aware of metallic strikes against the vehicle's hull. Next to him, Lieutenant Willard turned to shout at the gunners.

"Let 'em have it! Give 'em everything you've got!"

The Brownings hammered out, their tracers curving away towards the distant enemy emplacements. Away to the left, Hogan could see a landing-craft some way ahead of his line, approaching the head of the long pier. It grappled and marines swarmed on to the structure to engage the defenders. The scene passed out of his line of vision. He was now closing in on the reef and eased to the right to avoid the wreck of a small coastal steamer, run aground on the far side. As the tracks began grating on the coral he gunned the motor. The vehicle's nose began to rise as it crawled over the obstacle, then dropped to re-enter the water beyond. There was less depth under the tracks than Hogan had been led to expect. He read the name on the wreck's bow – *Niminoa*.

He calculated that he was about 600 yards from the shoreline, from which the volume of fire was undiminished. The amtrac was running flat out but its guns were now silent. He looked across at Willard and saw to his horror that the officer had slumped forward, a line of reddening bullet holes in his back. Closing the throttle, he glanced round into the interior of the vehicle. Svensen, the port .50 gunner, was dead, and so too was Lefebre, both with similar wounds. Dale, the starboard .50 gunner, had abandoned his weapon and was crouching as low as he could get, as was the rifle squad. Someone was applying a field dressing to Zimmerman's shoulder.

"The Japs – they got machine-gun teams on the wreck!" shouted Dale. "They're shootin' into us from behind!"

Hogan eased himself upwards and peered back at the *Niminoa*. Machine-gun fire was indeed flickering from the wreck, but the Japanese, believing they had dealt with the amtrac's crew, had found themselves other targets.

"Come on, buddy – whaddya waitin' for?" yelled the furious squad leader. "Let's get the hell outta here!"

Returning to the controls, Hogan accelerated towards the shore. He had fallen behind the leading wave which for some reason had begun to veer to the right. As the volume of fire from ahead was truly terrifying, he gladly conformed. He felt the tracks bite into the sand and the vehicle began to emerge from the water. Through the visor slit he could see that the beach was backed by a palm-log sea wall. Marines were vaulting over the sides of their amtracs and attempting to fight their way over the wall, but many were being killed in the attempt.

He pulled up just short of the obstacle. In a trice the rifle squad vanished. He reversed the vehicle, turned it in the shallows and headed back out to sea, his instructions being to await further orders at a designated rendezvous point; he had, besides, a badly wounded man aboard and wanted to transfer him. He was shocked to see the wide scattering of apparently lifeless amtracs in the space between the shore and the reef, some of them apparently resting on the bottom. Shortly after the tracks lifted clear of the sand there was a heavy explosion alongside.

"She's making water!" shouted Dale. "Side's bin blown in!"

The controls did not respond. Hogan felt the vehicle begin to list, then the port track touched bottom again and the amtrac slid into a submerged crater, coming to rest at a sharp angle. Dale dragged the bandaged Zimmerman over the side into waist-deep water but the wounded man was only semi-conscious and could barely stand.

"Gimme a hand with him, willya? He can't make it on his own!"

Before Hogan was clear of the driving compartment there came the brief scream of a second shell, followed by another explosion along-side. When he looked the water was stained red and there were pieces of uniformed flesh floating in it, but nothing that could be identified as Dale or Zimmerman. He began wading back towards the shore. Bullets were flaying the water but he did not seem to be anyone's special target. Rather, the Japanese seemed to be concentrating on the amtracs of the second wave, which he had seen crossing the reef. As they churned their way past, he found himself gripped by submerged barbed wire. By the time he had torn himself free and worked his way round the obstacle the third wave was coming in. With the sea-bed now shelving steadily, he tried to thumb a lift from returning amtracs but they passed by with no indication they had seen him.

When he reached the shore it was apparent that the second and third waves had fared no better than the first. The entire beach was covered with men seeking cover in the lee of the palm-log sea wall or scraping holes for themselves in the coral sand. The dead lay every-where, mainly in the shallows, and the wounded were being carried to an improvised aid post where Navy corpsmen were working with desperate urgency.

There were several amtracs lying on the beach or in the shallows. Seeking his own kind, he made for them. All were abandoned, some with dead crewmen still aboard and others obviously damaged. Sud-denly he felt very alone and frightened. He picked his way along the beach, looking for someone to report to, but no one seemed to be in command. The men of the II/2nd seemed to be hopelessly mixed up with those of the III/2nd. Platoon and squad leaders were searching for their men and men were looking for their leaders. He was deafened by the noise. There was no slackening in the volume of rifle, automatic weapon and artillery fire cracking overhead from beyond the sea wall. At length he came upon a captain and a signaller in a shallow scrape, struggling to get a response from their radio. Hogan saluted, feeling a little foolish.

"Sir, my amtrac has been knocked out – can you reassign me?"

"Don't bother me, son," said the captain impatiently. "Right now, this is any man's battle, so join in where you want. Where's your personal arm, Private?"

Hogan explained that his carbine had been lost when the amtrac went down.

"Okay, get yourself kitted out – this is no place to be naked!"

Hogan picked up a bayonetted Garand lying near a dead marine, then rolled the man over to remove his belt, pouches and water-bottle. The corpse grunted as the last air was expelled from its lungs and blood ran out of its mouth.

A swarthy man was sitting with his back to the log wall, cradling a Browning Automatic Rifle, his sleeves bearing the imprint of a staff sergeant's stripes recently removed. Hogan sat down beside him, suddenly hungry and thirsty. He took a pull on the water-bottle, then broke a chocolate bar, handing half to the former non-com. The man began to chew, eyeing Hogan speculatively.

"First timer?" he asked at length.

"Yes."

"Thought so. You learn to hang on to what you got an' take what you can get."

The man had a strong Brooklyn accent.

"Is it always like this?" asked Hogan.

"Nope. You t'ink we got it bad? Those guys out there are bein' moidered!"

He pointed to the lagoon. As had been forecast, there was not enough water above the reef for the fourth wave's landing-craft to cross it. The ramps were down and the troops within were having to wade the 600 yards to the shore. The deeper water offered some protection from the enemy fire, but once they reached the shallows the men were being decimated. Those killed were pulled to the bottom by the weight of their equipment, as were the wounded unless comrades came to their assistance quickly. The disorganised survivors straggled up the narrow beach to collapse in a state of complete exhaustion. Hogan was horrified by the sight.

"We can't just let this happen! We've got to do something!"

"You wanna do sumpn, go right ahead!" said his companion sardonically. "Graveyard's full of guys who did t'ings – you wanna join 'em?"

"We can't just sit this out!" said Hogan, but he knew the other was right. He had no idea what was happening elsewhere, but on their sector at least one Japanese machine-gun opened fire whenever a man exposed himself briefly above the sea wall, showering those below with flying sand.

"Let de officers figure it out – dat's what dey get paid for. When we get orders, we'll obey 'em – until then, just cool your ass!"

By degrees, Hogan learned a little about his companion. His name was Juan Lopez and his family had arrived in New York from Puerto Rico twenty years earlier. He had seen action on Guadalcanal, but said little about it. Hogan thought he was about thirty, forming the impression that he was a regular and something of a hard case who had been up and down the promotion ladder several times. Still, someone had thought enough of him once to give him stripes. He had noticed several little platforms protruding into the sea and asked Lopez if he knew what they were.

"Sure, dey're Jap johns. No room for 'em ashore on a little island like this."

"Are you saying what I think you're saying?"

"You got it – we bin wadin' through Jap crap!"

They both laughed. The naval guns had opened fire again and there were periodic air strikes by dive-bombers against centres of enemy resistance. The Japanese quietened down but any party that tried to cross the wall was immediately met by a storm of fire. Lopez pointed to the reef, where Sherman tanks had begun to emerge from the bows of landing-craft. They slid off the reef and began to forge their way towards the shore.

"Waddya know – the brass have finally got their brains in gear! Now mebbe we'll get some place! If they'd given you amtrac guys some kinda gun, this whole t'ing coulda bin wrapped up by now."

Hogan could see five of the tanks heading for Red 1 to his left; they disappeared behind the point. Four tanks were ploughing through the water towards Red 2. One plunged into a submerged crater and stayed there, its motor drowned. The turret roof remained above water but the hatches stayed shut and, for a while, huge bubbles broke the surface. The remaining three Shermans touched down some 200 yards to Hogan's right, crawled up the beach and disappeared inland. For a few minutes there was the sound of gunfire and then one of the tanks returned to the beach, crabbed round, and continued firing over the sea wall. He felt his heart sink.

"What happens now?" he asked.

"Waddya t'ink happens now?" replied Lopez bitterly. "We wait for the goddam Japs to run out of ammo!"

For a while nothing happened, then a small squad under a sergeant appeared, crouching as it picked its way along the crowded shoreline. The sergeant spotted them.

"Lopez, you lollygaggin' sonofabitch – I bin lookin' for you!"

"Hi, Judd!" said Lopez in the familiar tones of one who had once held the same rank. "Where the Lootenant?"

The sergeant shrugged and pointed to the lagoon.

"Out there someplace, mebbe – who knows? Listen, I figured a way to get us off this stinkin' beach."

"Sure you have, Judd. You feel gung ho, that's fine by me – I'm passin' this one up!"

"No you're not, Lopez, cos you an' that BAR are part of it – that is if you ever want to see those stripes of yours again! Now move your ass!"

"Yeah, yeah, Semper Fi," said Lopez, lumbering to his feet. "Let's all be heroes!"

The sergeant glanced at Hogan.

"What outfit you from, soldier?"

"Amtracs, sergeant."

"So now you're a rifleman again. Collect all the grenades you can an' tag along."

Hogan collected a dozen grenades from the nearest casualties, tucking them into his jacket. He caught up the squad, which was crouching near a breach in the sea wall, and handed them round. He noticed that several of the men were also carrying satchel demolition charges.

The sergeant, whose name he learned was Mossman, was explaining his plan. A heavy shell, probably from a battleship, had exploded just beyond the sea wall, blowing out the palm logs. It was possible to crawl unobserved under the logs into the crater beyond, and from there into a second overlapping crater. Ten yards to the right of this was a machine-gun post; thirty yards to the left was another, while midway between and thirty yards inland was a third, covering the approaches to the other two. The squad would crawl into the second crater and, at a given signal, open fire on all three bunkers simultaneously. The third and potentially most dangerous bunker would be tackled first, using the demolition charges. Once it had been neutralised, the remaining pair would be attacked from the rear, using grenades.

They squeezed under the logs and wriggled into the second crater. Sporadic bursts of automatic weapon fire could be heard coming from all three bunkers. Mossman raised his head briefly.

"Now!" he shouted.

The squad lined the edge of the crater and opened fire on the bunker slits. For a critical instant the enemy seemed disconcerted. Covered by Lopez with the BAR, Mossman and two more men with demolition charges began sprinting for the inland bunker. One of the men went down but someone from the crater raced out to take his place. Mossman flung his charge and the group flattened itself. The charge exploded just short of the nearest fire slit but the blast and flying sand temporarily silenced the enemy machine-gunners. By the time they had recovered, Mossman's companions were running hard for the bunker. Jumping on to its roof, they primed their charges and posted them through the slits below. The muffled explosions were accompanied by screams, then there was silence.

"Get the other two!" yelled Mossman.

The rest of the squad scrambled out of the crater and approached the flanking bunkers from behind, tossing in grenades then raking the interiors through the smoking fire slits. Hogan noticed that the palm-log and sand structures had been left largely untouched by the naval bombardment and air attacks. More men began to emerge from the breach in the sea wall until the squad had become a small platoon.

"C'mon, you guys, let's move it inland!" shouted Mossman.

They moved forward warily across a landscape of craters, unidentified structures and shattered palms through which Hogan could see the cleared airstrip and, beyond, the gleam of the sea on the far shore. He spotted an enemy light tank moving west across the airstrip, but it paid them no attention and continued on its way. Otherwise, there was little sign of the enemy although elsewhere the sounds of heavy fighting continued and once there was an enormous explosion. By degrees, he became conscious that other small parties had also broken through the defences until an approximation of a firing line had been formed among the trees. The advance halted while officers and senior NCOs organised them into provisional platoons. Hogan estimated that there were maybe 150 men present, which did not seem a great number with which to cut the island in two. Glancing at his watch he saw that it had stopped long since, evidently ruined by sea water, but sensed that it was mid-afternoon.

The thin line began to move forward, pausing when it reached the trees at the edge of the taxiway.

"LET'S GO! C'MON – MOVE IT!"

The whole line raced across the open space into the wooded area in the centre of the airstrip. Too late, the enemy machine-gunners opened a grazing fire along the length of the taxiway. Breathless, Hogan flopped down with the rest. They were now about halfway across the island.

"DIG IN – AN' MAKE IT GOOD!"

Using whatever tools were available, or even bare hands, the line began turning shell craters into trenches with low parapets. Hogan, working alongside Lopez and Mossman, saw a Japanese soldier lying some twenty feet beyond their trench. The khaki uniform was stained with blood and the figure lay perfectly still, its rifle some yards away. Seeing the enemy face to face for the first time, Hogan looked at him closely and decided that he must have been caught in an earlier shell-burst. He indicated the small anchor painted on the man's helmet.

"Reckon he's a marine like us?"

"Who cares?" said Lopez off-handedly. "Just dig, willya!"

A few minutes later Hogan glanced at the figure again. The head had moved slightly and seemed to be regarding them. Lopez and Mossman were engaged in regimental gossip, paying little attention. He carried on digging, then noticed that the man's right arm was moving very slowly. He knelt down, reaching for his rifle. Quite suddenly, the figure came to life. The right arm was flung back and in the hand was a grenade. Hogan shot him through the chest. The man was bowled over backwards, the grenade exploding behind him.

"What the ...?" snarled Lopez.

"He had a grenade."

"Jeez! An' dere was me t'inkin' I was lookin' after you!"

Mossman chuckled and extracted a tin of chicken from his equipment.

"Let's eat while we got the chance."

The tin was opened with a bayonet and the contents were shared out. Hogan was surprised how hungry he was, hoping that someone would manage to get rations up to them soon. Dusk came quickly. Their nerves became tense as they stared into darkness which seemed full of unseen movement. From time to time voices called eerily to them from the shadowy gloom.

"Maline, you die! We come soon! We kill you all!"

"Go boil your balls!"

"All Yankees die!"

"Suits me, boy," shouted a voice with a Southern accent. "Ah'm a Johnny Reb from Augusta, Georgia!"

Discomfited by the laughter, the Japanese fell silent, only to return shortly after with a more sinister ploy.

"Al, gimme a hand – I can't move!"

The voice was American and there was a desperate urgency to the request that unsettled Hogan. He tried to crawl over the parapet but was pulled back by Lopez.

"Not you, buster – you ain't goin' no place!"

"For Chrissake, Al, they're all round me! You gotta help me – please!"

"But someone's in real trouble out there!"

"No one's in trouble, kid – dat's a Jap talkin'. Some o' dem lived Stateside, speak good American, an' lotsa guys are called Al."

"They got me! No, please don't – please!"

A scream ripped through the night. Hogan tried to break free but Lopez had him in an iron grip.

"D'you hear that? That was real – we've got to help him!"

"Yeah, dey'd like dat real good – den we'd be de ones doin' de screamin'! It's a trick – dey tried it on Guadalcanal. Some guys got suckered, but it don't woik no more!"

Hogan relaxed but he was consumed by a blazing hatred for the voice in the blackness beyond the trenches and snatched up his rifle.

"Why don't we just blow his stinkin' head off?"

Before he could fire Lopez grabbed the weapon.

"Cos dey'd like dat, too. You give away our position, next ting we're sharin' out a grenade, see. Take it easy, kid – just enjoy de midnight sights an' sounds of lovely Betio Island!"

Hogan did as he was bidden and slid down into the trench. He felt ashamed that he had let himself go, although neither of his companions referred to the matter. As the night wore on, Lopez, too, began to show signs of tension.

"For Chrissake, why don't dey counter-attack?" he asked. "What are dey, stoopid or sumpn?"

"Mebbe," said Mossman. "They got the men, they got the firepower, so why don't they just roll over us? You never can figure 'em out."

No counter-attack was ever mounted and with dawn came an indefinable feeling that not only would they survive, but also that in some subtle way the tide had turned. Ostensibly nothing had changed, for from all around came the sound of renewed fighting, naval gunfire support and air strikes, yet somehow the battle seemed more controlled. Most of the men in the triangle formed by the airstrip's taxiways and main runway belonged to the I/2nd Marines, and their opinion was confirmed when they were unexpectedly reinforced by a party from the regiment's 2nd Battalion. The Japanese reacted quickly by opening a heavy fire along the taxiway with automatic weapons to prevent further reinforcements crossing. Despite this, the new arrivals were able to tell the weary, red-eyed men in the foxholes that the division's artillery and other heavy weapons had started coming ashore, and that some of the damaged Shermans had been recovered and repaired. Orders were that those in the triangle should continue the previous day's attack towards the island's southern shore. In preparation for this waves of carrier aircraft roared in to bomb and strafe the enemy defences beyond the main runway. In the event, the air strikes were too close for comfort, causing the marines to crouch low in their trenches as bomb splinters and bullets cracked overhead.

"Goddam fly boys!" said Lopez. "Someone should tell 'em go play some place else!"

At 1300 the officers' orders were passed down the line.

"We're moving out – c'mon, let's go!"

Hogan did not want to move. He was more frightened than he had been the previous day and there was a hard knot in his stomach. Nevertheless, he clambered to his feet. Again, the line halted at the edge of the trees. The main runway was 200 feet across but seemed far wider. He felt his legs start to shake. Then, without warning, the whole line broke into a mad dash. Enemy fire scoured the runway from both ends, bowling over several men. He did not expect to reach the other side but did so. More slowly now, the line pushed through the tangle of broken trees and craters, without meeting further opposition. As they began to emerge into the open the word was passed to stay off the shore, which was almost certainly mined. From his position on the left Hogan could see marines appearing from the trees on a frontage approximately 200 yards wide. They had finally cut the island's defences in two.

"We made it!" he shouted.

"Not yet we didn't!" said Mossman.

As he spoke machine-guns in strongpoints to the right and left of the penetration opened fire. The marines dived into a series of abandoned enemy trenches. Simultaneously, yelling Japanese infantry seemed to boil out of the ground near the eastern strongpoint, coming on at a run with fixed bayonets.

"TO YOUR LEFT! FOR GOD'S SAKE WATCH YOUR LEFT!" shouted Mossman.

Hogan was only able to remember disjointed flashes of the next few minutes. They usually recurred in his nightmares with horrible, slow motion, brightly coloured clarity. He remembered grenades arching through the air from both sides, explosions and screams; Lopez rattling away with the BAR at a group heading straight for them and dropping several; bringing down one himself and shooting at another who still came on, diving into the trench with levelled bayonet; trying to side step in the confined space and thrusting upwards himself; feeling his bayonet penetrate the man's belly and the latter's scream as his inertia carried him, still impaled like hay on a pitchfork, in an arc above the trench, to finally collapse on top of him; a rush of hot blood drenching his uniform and pain in his left arm; the sounds of shooting, fighting and screams above; then the dead man being dragged off by Mossman and Lopez, the latter holding a bloodstained Bowie knife.

"You okay, kid?" asked Lopez

"Yeah – yeah, I think so." Hand-to-hand fighting was horrible, he thought. It just wasn't like what they showed in the films, with all sorts of fancy moves – it was animal, over in seconds, and you were either dead or you weren't. He shuddered.

"The hell you are!" said Mossman. "Take a look at him."

With difficulty he took off his blood soaked-jacket and flung it as far from him as he could. The Japanese bayonet had slashed his left upper arm. As Lopez applied a dressing he looked round. There was not a live Japanese to be seen, but there were dead marines, too, and a number of men were receiving medical attention.

"It's gonna get stiff real soon," said Lopez, tying off the dressing. "Get it seen to when you can. You tink you can use your rifle?"

"Yes, I think so."

Mossman returned from touring the squad. He handed Hogan a jacket.

"Put this on – yeah, I know, it's off a dead man, but what else you gonna wear?"

"Anyone we know, Judd?" asked Lopez.

"Gianelli – straight through the head. Clean an' quick."

"Too bad."

"Yeah. All round, we had about thirty guys killed or wounded. We can't stand that kinda loss. Ammo's nearly gone, we've no rations and no water. It's not lookin' good."

There was nothing to do but sweat it out. Towards evening the sound of engines and the squeal of tracks coming from inland suggested that the Japanese were about to counter-attack again, this time with tanks. Hogan gripped his rifle as best he could, convinced that he had little time left to live. What emerged from the trees, however, were several amtracs, to be greeted by cheers. They had brought all the supplies the desperately tired marines needed and they were to take back the more seriously wounded.

"Best get aboard," said Mossman, jerking his thumb at the vehicles.

"I'm staying put," Hogan responded stubbornly.

"Quit playin' the wounded tough guy an' scram!"

"What for? With this arm I couldn't handle an amtrac if there was one. Anyway, the rations are here and I'm not missing out."

"He's learnin' fast!" chuckled Lopez.

"Yeah. Okay, you wanna stick around, that's fine, but remember you had your chance."

The night was comparatively quiet. From dawn onwards reinforcements began to arrive, confirming that the enemy positions covering the airstrip had finally been neutralised. In a series of local attacks the tight little perimeter was extended to the east and west, and at 1100 a battalion of the 6th Marines broke through to them from the west. The battalion passed through towards the eastern end of the island, where the sounds of fighting suggested that most of the Japanese were now confined.

It took Hogan some time to realise that the battle had passed over them. Many of those who had been separated from their units during its chaotic early stages came in, enabling the Second's battalions to reorganise their hard-hit companies. Hogan was able to get his wound properly dressed and enjoy the luxury of several hours' sleep.

Shortly after 1300 the following day the guns finally fell silent. Mossman was talking to a major who glanced in his direction and then walked over.

"You Private Hogan, Divisional Amtrac Battalion?"

"Yes, sir."

"Right."

The major scribbled on a message pad, tore out a leaf and handed it to him.

"Following the destruction of his vehicle by enemy action on November 20, Private A. J. Hogan served in a combat role with the 2nd Marines for the remainder of the operation. Further communication will follow.

K. N. Deverson, Major,

USMC,

November 23 1943"

"Hand this to your commanding officer," said Deverson. "He'll want to know where you've been for the last four days."

"Yes, sir. But I don't understand what you mean by further communication will follow."

"Don't worry, son, no one's going to accuse you of going AWOL and you've done nothing to be ashamed of. Now, report back to your unit."

Hogan wasn't quite sure how to take his leave of Lopez and Moss-man. When he shook their hands and wished them good luck they stared impassively at him from under their helmets.

"Get outta here!" said Mossman with the ghost of a twinkle in his eye.

Feeling slightly hurt, Hogan began walking away, but he had only taken a few steps when he heard Lopez calling after him.

"Hey, Amtrac!"

He turned and saw that they were both grinning from ear to ear.

"You did okay!" said Lopez.

He gave them a cheery wave and carried on. His arm hurt but he felt on top of the world. Their good opinion mattered a lot to him.

The 4,836-strong Japanese garrison on Betio fought to the death; only 146 prisoners were taken, of whom all but seventeen were Korean labourers. The 2nd Marine Division's casualties amounted to 51 officers and 853 men killed during the fighting; nine officers and 84 men mortally wounded; 109 officers and 2,124 men wounded; and 88 men missing. Naval casualties amounted to two officers and 28 men killed and two officers and 57 men wounded.

The officer commanding the divisional amtrac battalion was killed leading the first assault wave; by the time the operation ended 323 of his 500 crewmen were dead or wounded. During the assault, 35 amtracs were sunk and 26 were disabled by gunfire; because of this and other causes, including mines, damage ashore and breakdown, only 35 amtracs were still operational when Betio fell.

Understandably, the American public was inclined to wonder whether so apparently insignificant an objective was worth so terrible a price. The lessons, however, were quickly acted upon, one of the most important results being the rapid introduction of amtracs that were not only better armoured but which were also armed with heavy weapons that enabled them to deal with the enemy's beach defences on the spot.

Although the characters in this chapter are fictional, the incidents in which they took part are all based on fact.

LANCE-CORPORAL
TOM WOOD

7th Royal Barset Rifles, Normandy, July 1944

The weather in the Channel was atrocious. The steamer, which in summer usually carried day-trippers and holiday-makers between Liverpool and the Isle of Man, pitched and rolled horribly. Aboard her, most of the 7th Battalion The Royal Barset Rifles were violently seasick. Quickly overwhelmed, the heads ceased to function and the troop decks became foul with acrid-smelling vomit. Most of the men, praying for the ordeal to end, had ceased to worry about what lay ahead and longed only to set foot on the firm ground of Normandy, even if they had to share it with the German Army.

It took some twelve hours to complete the passage from Newhaven to the anchorage off the beachhead. As the pre-fabricated Mulberry piers were unable to accommodate the steamer, the troops would disembark into landing-craft which, for the moment, were unable to come alongside because of the gale. Their misery was, therefore, prolonged until the high winds and heavy swell abated to safe levels, some three days later.

Having recovered sufficiently, Lance-Corporal Tom Wood decided to leave the foetid atmosphere and seek some fresh air on deck.

"You coming, Mike? Do you good to get out of this rat hole."

Corporal Mike Holt, his section commander, rolled slowly off his bunk, buttoning up his battledress blouse.

"Why not? Anything's better than this."

The scene from the deck had a remarkable sense of permanence. Hundreds of ships of every type were anchored as far as the eye could see, some of them flying barrage balloons. Further out to sea a large warship, firing at some unseen target inland, blasted out periodic salvos of smoke and flame. From time to time formations of bombers, fighter-bombers and fighters appeared from the direction of England and vanished over the French hinterland. The beach itself was a hive of activity but at this distance, apart from a few ruined houses, there was little to suggest that, just three weeks earlier, the greatest amphibious invasion in history had fought its way across it. A gaggle of landing-craft appeared from nowhere and began nosing in towards the steamer. Unexpectedly the Tannoy blared.

"D'ye hear there! All troops return to troop decks in preparation for disembarkation!"

They went below and collected their kit, waiting their turn to be called to the entry port, from which they had to jump into the waiting LCI, rising and falling a few feet below. The landing-craft pitched horribly as it butted its way towards the beach, but at least the air was fresh and untainted by hot engine room smells. Then the ramp went down and they waded ashore to be greeted by the battalion's advance party, unbearably smug because they had already been in Normandy for almost a week, having sailed from another port with its transport and heavy weapons.

"Where've you lot been? Take a wrong turning, did you? We've got people out looking for you!"

At close quarters, evidence of the invasion lay all around – a smashed concrete gun emplacement covering the beach, exit gaps blasted in the sea wall, steel obstacles protruding from the water and wired-off areas with warnings of uncleared mines. A number of burned-out tanks and assault engineer vehicles had been neatly parked together, mute witnesses to the ferocity of the fighting. Now, stores were piled high, awaiting transport inland, and troops from every branch of the Army generated a scene of continuous activity as they bustled about their business. Unshaven prisoners, bareheaded or wearing peaked forage caps, sat disconsolately in a wire cage guarded by Military Police, waiting for transport to camps in England. Ominously, a long procession of stretcher cases and heavily bandaged wounded were filing aboard a landing-craft that would take them out to a white-painted hospital ship.

The battalion's transport was waiting on a track beyond the sea wall. They had not far to go but on the way they passed supply dumps, the harbour area of an armoured regiment, an engineer field park and a battery of 5.5in medium guns in action, all of which emphasised that the beachhead itself was still only a few miles deep. The convoy wound up a narrow line, dropping the companies off beside small fields in which they were told to dig in, not because of the immediate prospect of an attack, but as a defence against the enemy's heavy artillery which periodically opened a harassing fire on the Allied rear areas.

It seemed at first that they had simply exchanged one unpleasant stink for another. The local variety was heavy, clinging and sickly. Wood pointed over the hedge.

"That's where it's coming from – not much we can do about it!"

In the next field lay half-a-dozen dead cows, the victims of shellfire. They were crawling with maggots and were bloated by the gases of corruption to an immense size, their legs sticking straight up in the air. The sight did much to explain the ambivalent attitude of the dour Norman population; they were glad to be free of German occupation but understandably hated having their farms fought over.

Wood had joined the battalion shortly after the outbreak of war. It was still in England when the Dunkirk evacuation took place and had remained there ever since, brigaded with a battalion each from the Rutland and Pembrokeshire Regiments. In due course divisions had left for the Mediterranean or Far Eastern theatres of war, but that of which the brigade formed part was told that it was ear-marked first for home defence and then for the opening of the Second Front in western Europe. Year after year training had continued. There had been repeated exercises at company, battalion, brigade and divisional level in attack and defence, exercises with armour, artillery and engineers, until the men felt capable of dealing with every situation. Yet still there was no indication that the prospect of active service was any nearer. This, together with routine garrison duties and changes of station that were not always welcome, made them feel that the war was passing them by. Sometimes their frustration had boiled over.

"We know none of us will be going home until it's finished, so why don't they just get on with it?" Wood had said one day. "We're trained within an inch of our lives, so what more do they want?"

Holt, one of a small cadre of experienced officers and NCOs posted to the battalion at the end of 1943, had seen active service in Tunisia, Sicily and Salerno.

"Don't be in such a hurry," he had replied quietly. "When your turn comes it'll seem soon enough. Besides, training can only teach you so much – only the real thing will tell you the rest."

During the early months of 1944 the preparation for war acquired a new and purposeful urgency. By now, although some of the older faces had been replaced, the battalion had been together so long that it had acquired a sense of family with internal strengths and weaknesses understood and allowed for. Collectively, it possessed the will to give a good account of itself and the confidence that it could, tempered by the knowledge that not all of those who embarked would be coming back.

The slit trenches had been completed by the time Lieutenant Latimer, the platoon commander, returned from the company briefing. He signalled the men to gather round.

"The situation is this," he said. "For the moment the brigade will remain in divisional reserve while fresh operations are planned. So far, our progress has been unexpectedly slow because, as you can see for yourselves, this type of country, which is known locally as *bocage*, is ideal for defensive fighting and the Germans have taken full advantage of the fact."

That much was immediately apparent. They were surrounded by a patchwork of small fields separated by hedges planted in steep earthen banks. Here, machine-gunners, riflemen and snipers could remain undetected until the last minute, then open up with devastating effect.

"It also happens to be very bad tank country," continued Latimer. "Once we have fought our way out of it, however, the going gets easier and hopefully the tanks will be able to crack on ahead. That remains some way off. In the meantime, each company will be sending one platoon in rotation to units holding a quiet sector of the front so that when the time comes we shall all be at least partially acclimatised."

The platoons went up at dusk, were absorbed by their host battalions, and returned two nights later. Little of note happened, but Wood assimilated the tensions of daily routine at the front. He learned, too, to distinguish between the sound of outgoing and incoming artillery fire and the distinctive noise made by the enemy's weapons, notably the rip of the Spandau light machine-gun, which had a much higher rate of fire than their own Bren, and the strange howl of the German heavy mortar bombs known as Moaning Minnies. Once, the battalion was moved forward in anticipation of being used in the counter-attack role, but was then stood down. It began to feel that, as ever, it was to play no part in events.

A week later they were briefed for a brigade operation. Blocking the division's exit from the *bocage* was a ridge known as Mont-St-Gérard. It was not a particularly impressive feature, but it did possess commanding views of the countryside for miles around. Possession of the ridge was being bitterly contested by both sides, with heavy casualties. It was now proposed to outflank the feature by breaking through the enemy line where a low spur descending from its north-eastern slopes fell away gently to the valley of the River Odon. The brigade plan consisted of two phases. In the first the Pembrokes would capture the Château Landru, a large country house with extensive farm buildings, lying at the top of the spur, while the Rutlands took the village of Esqueville, at the bottom. The second phase required the Rifles to pass between the two and take the village of Molay beyond, which would serve as the base for a planned armoured thrust into the more open country of the enemy hinterland.

It sounded simple and straightforward enough and, looking at Lieutenant Latimer's map, the section agreed that if it succeeded the enemy holding Mont-St-Gérard would have to pull out or risk encirclement. Holt, however, had strong reservations which he communicated privately to Len Rawnsley, the platoon sergeant, another veteran of Tunisia and Italy.

"Jerry won't wear this, Len – not for a minute. As soon as he sees what we're up to he'll be down on us like a ton o' bricks!"

"Yeah, it looks like we've drawn the short straw and there's not a thing we can do about it. Just keep it to yourself, right?"

The battalion's mail caught up with them the same day. One of Wood's letters from his wife contained a photograph of their seven-year-old son. He showed it to Holt.

"Here, Mike, that's young Jimmy. Took it on embarkation leave. He's just started cricket, so guess how we spent most of our time!"

"Going to be a big lad, isn't he?"

"Looks that way. Pity I missed so much of his growing up. He seemed just a toddler the leave before that, now he's a boy growing out of his clothes faster than his mother can replace them."

Holt fished in his breast pocket, producing a photo of his own.

"Know what you mean, mate. These are my two – they're twins. The wife says they're my alibi."

"Why's that?"

"Always wanted a train set when I was little, but we couldn't afford it. When they were born I started putting together bits of Hornby Dublo electric so that we'd have a layout when they were older – as much for my benefit as theirs, you understand!"

He chuckled to himself.

"Anyway, I asked the wife to add to it while I was away. Trouble is, you can't get it new because of the war, and what you can get second hand is pricey. At the rate we're going we'll all be old men before we've got it properly set up!"

Abruptly, his good humour died and he fell silent. In quick succession, dark expressions of bewilderment, fear and an infinite sadness crossed his face, followed by mute resignation. When he spoke again it was quietly, as though to himself.

"Somehow, I don't think I'll be there. I've got a bad feeling about this one."

Shocked, Wood tried to talk his companion out of his black mood.

"Don't talk so wet! You've not been up the sharp end for a bit and you don't fancy going back – that's all it is!"

Holt shook his head.

"No, it's not that. When we were relieved at Salerno there were only seven of us left out of the original platoon that landed in Algeria. The rest ..." He shrugged. "Well, maybe I've had my share of luck."

"D'you want to know something? You're going to feel really bloody stupid when you come out of this the other end!"

"I read a story once. Bloke in Baghdad saw Death walking down the street towards him. Death grinned and said, 'You and I have an appointment,' so he legged it out of town to Samarra. When he got there Death was waiting for him. 'And this is where we are to meet,' he said. You can't duck it, mate, not when your name's down. Seen it happen to other blokes, but don't ask me why."

The next day was spent in preparing for battle and in being briefed on the battalion and company plans. The battalion would advance on a two-company frontage, with A Company on the right and B Company on the left, followed respectively by C and D Companies. A tank squadron would accompany them to the objective and remain with them until their own anti-tank guns and other heavy weapons could be brought up and emplaced. A Company would deploy with No 1

Platoon on the right, Latimer's No 2 Platoon on the left and No 3 Platoon behind, Company HQ being in the centre with its three PIAT anti-tank weapons. Within No 2 Platoon, Holt's No 1 Section would be on the right, No 2 Section on the left and 3 Section behind; Platoon HQ, consisting of Latimer, Sergeant Rawnsley, the signaller, the 2in mortar team and Latimer's runner, would be located between the three.

As second in command of the section, Wood's responsibility was for the Bren light machine-gun group, which consisted of himself and Riflemen Salter and Millard. Apart from Holt himself, the rest of the section included Riflemen Jenkins, Spears, Lister, Wilson, Archer and Bray. They were a fairly representative group whose occupations included farm labourers, factory workers, a barman, a printer, a post office clerk, and a dance band drummer. Wood thought that, on balance, they were a good lot but harboured some doubts about Wilson and Bray. The former was a spiv caught by the conscription net, a man who had angles on everything and Black Market contacts everywhere but performed well enough under supervision; the latter a whining teenage ne'er-do-well with convictions for theft, who performed as little as possible; still, Holt seemed to have the measure of them both. Jenkins and Spears were detached to the company's Left Out Of Battle party, which Bray also volunteered to join on the grounds that he was suffering from hay fever; his offer was sharply refused.

During the afternoon the Padre held a Communion service for those who wanted it. Holt attended and later wrote at length to his wife. In due course Lieutenant Latimer, whose responsibilities included censoring the platoon's letters, came across and the two spoke quietly.

"Anything new?" asked Wood when the officer had gone.

"Offered me Left Out Of Battle. I said it wasn't on."

"You alright?

"Yes – just forget what I said, will you!" the other replied shortly.

The operation was to commence at first light the following day, 10 July. At dusk the men paraded in battle order consisting of steel helmet, webbing belt, cross-straps supporting ammunition pouches and small pack, full canteen, and either an entrenching tool or a pick tucked in behind the pack. Section leaders fussed round, verifying the distribution of small-arms ammunition, grenades and mortar bombs.

At midnight the signallers shrugged on their heavy manpack sets and the battalion marched off along the narrow lanes to the brigade assembly area.

The opening phase of the operation had been sub-divided, with the Château Landru being the first objective. As the battalion moved forward to its forming-up point the scream of shells was followed by explosions around the château. The bombardment was sustained and heavy. Small fires spread rapidly until the target area was illuminated by burning buildings.

The surrounding darkness became grey with the approach of dawn. From the right squealing tracks and the roar of engines indicated that the Pembrokes were moving forward. Then the black bulk of Churchill tanks, machine-gunning steadily, began to stand out, followed by lines of trudging infantry. Now the tanks were using their main armament as defensive fire flickered around the château. The enemy's counter-barrage came down, bursting among the Pembrokes. Here and there men fell singly or in groups but the lines never wavered. Wood knew that among buildings and in woodland tanks were vulnerable to the enemy's *Panzerfausts* and was not surprised when, just as the supporting bombardment ended, the Churchills halted short of the objective. Cheering, the Pembrokes swept past them.

For the next hour there was the sound of small-arms fire and bursting grenades as the Welshmen fought their way through the house, its farm buildings, walled garden, orchard and adjoining woodland. The area was more extensive than Wood had imagined. Once the infantry had secured lodgements, the tanks moved forward to join them, sometimes battering their way through walls to do so, their guns adding to the sounds of battle. A steady stream of walking wounded and stretcher cases began making their way to the rear. Finally, the din died away and the Pembrokes' tracked carriers moved up to the captured position with their anti-tank guns and mortars.

A file of helmetless prisoners under escort passed nearby. They were very young and wore their hair long in the German fashion. Wood noted the SS rune collar patches and the *Hitlerjügend* cuff titles.

"What you got there, Taff?" shouted Rawnsley.

"Bunch o' vicious little bastards!" responded the corporal commanding the escort. "Like a bit o' killin' they do, especially hidin' an' shootin' you in the back when you've passed by, see. Or two o' them will pretend to surrender, then the third pops up with a Schmeisser an' lets fly. Well, they don't do it twice, I can tell you!"

Rawnsley wandered across and looked over the prisoners. One, taller than the rest, returned his level stare with a look of sneering contempt.

"What are you laughing at? Yes, you, the friggin' boy sergeant!"

The youth spat, swept back his long blond hair and pointedly looked away.

"I don't like this one," said Rawnsley. "Mind if I kick his arse, Taff?"

His boot connected with the base of the German's spine, dropping him in a writhing, gasping heap on the ground. Two of the prisoners were ordered to pull him to his feet. There were tears of pain and humiliation in the youth's eyes.

"There now, you've really got something to laugh at, haven't you, boyo?" said the Welshman. "You mind your manners, see, 'cos there's plenty more where that came from." The corporal set the line in motion again, giving a cheery wave. "Best o' luck, boys – I reckon this just about finishes me for the day!"

Their own supporting armour, nine Shermans backed by three tracked tank destroyers for use in the long-range anti-tank role, had now arrived and was marrying up with the companies it was to support. Holt seemed ill at ease.

"That's a pity," he muttered.

"Why's that?" asked Wood.

"Shermans can't take the sort of punishment Jerry will hand out. This is a job for Churchills. They may not have much of a gun and they're slower, but they've got twice the armour."

The attack on Esqueville had already begun. At first it seemed to duplicate that on the château, but there were many more Churchills present and Wood noticed that several of them seemed to be towing trailers. When the latter were just 100 yards short of the village they emitted huge tongues of flame which clung to the nearest houses, giving off dense clouds of black, oily smoke. Methodically, the tanks and the Rutlands worked their way up the village street and across the gardens until half the buildings were burning fiercely. Resistance was evidently not as fanatical as it had been at the château, for already the remnant of the defenders could be seen streaming in headlong flight for the safety of a belt of trees beside the river. Shortly after, the tanks with the trailers emerged and made their way to the rear.

"Phew, I'm glad we weren't on the receiving end of that!" said Wood.

"That's a new one on me," commented Holt. "A couple of those would have made all the difference at Salerno."

As Phase One of the operation had now been completed they expected to be ordered to advance immediately. Instead, they remained where they were. The tension rose and at length Rawnsley visited the sections in turn.

"What's the hold-up, Sarge?" asked Wood.

"We're ahead of ourselves. Timed artillery programme doesn't start for another seven minutes."

Holt exploded with rage.

"Then why don't they bring it forward, for Chrissake? We should be in among Jerry by now, not giving him the chance to sort himself out!"

"They'll learn – in time," said Rawnsley as he walked off.

"Yeah, and it'll be us who pay the bloody price!" responded Holt bitterly.

Exactly at the designated moment the shells of their own artillery support screamed overhead. Holt, glancing over his shoulder, saw Latimer's hand signal waving them forward.

"On your feet!"

Ahead of them, the three Shermans allocated to the company expelled clouds of blue exhaust smoke as they moved off.

Once they had crossed the crest of the spur the whole panorama of the battlefield unfolded below them. Here, indeed, the country opened out into broad vistas. The forward slope of the spur consisted of a huge cornfield dropping gently towards a series of mounds marked on the map as the site of a Norman motte and bailey castle. Beyond lay Molay, its church steeple protruding above the roofs of the village, with, some distance beyond, a large wood. To the right, the spur spread upwards to the château and the higher slopes of Mont-St-Gérard; to the left it descended to still-burning Esqueville and the river, lined by a thickening belt of trees that eventually merged with the wood beyond Molay.

Somewhere, someone with a bugle was blowing the light infantry *Advance*. Such things had little place in modern war but many of the men were stirred by the sound and began cheering. Wood, unexpectedly, felt glad to be there. It was a beautiful summer morning, there were pipits twittering and poppies growing among the corn. It was strange, but it was the poppies his father remembered most vividly, pinned down among them on another lovely July morning all those years ago, when most of his classmates had died on the Somme. Ahead, the rolling barrage's curtain of bursting shells lifted to each new bound with precise timing and the Shermans carved lanes through the standing crop. Then they were trampling through the corn themselves, maintaining the intervals between men and moving steadily forward. Wood glanced round. The companies and their supporting tanks were advancing in perfect formation while, on the crest behind, the tank destroyers had snugged down into fire positions. Apart from the continual scream and crash of the barrage, the scene differed little from any of the numerous exercises they had taken part in during the past few years.

There was a flash of gunfire on the edge of the distant wood, followed by others. One of the Shermans lurched to a standstill. Its hatches flew open and four of the crew jumped clear, taking cover in the lee of the vehicle. Seconds later the tank was engulfed in flames from stem to stern. The fire began to spread to the corn, creating waves of acrid grey smoke. Wood was horrified that, in so short a space of time, an apparently impregnable steel monster had been reduced to flaming wreckage.

The two other Shermans halted briefly to return the fire and he heard the tank destroyers going into action behind him. There were blazes now on the edge of the wood. The noise of the tank guns at close quarters was mind-numbing. The second Sherman began to erupt smoke and flame. Two men scrambled out, dragging a third whose overalls and hair were alight. The third tank had barely covered another fifty yards when it, too, was brought to a standstill; it was shaken by an internal explosion and this time no one got out.

Wood looked round again. Shermans were being picked off everywhere and, to the left, the edge of the woodland beside the river glittered with the sustained flashes of machine-gun fire. Men were flinging up their arms and disappearing into the corn as B and C Companies were raked from the flank. The neatly ordered scene from the tactical manual had vanished but order itself had not been lost. Instead, the lines had begun sweeping forward at a run.

"Come on, move yourselves!" shouted Holt. "Our best bet is to keep as close to the barrage as possible!"

The section doubled past the tank where the burned crewman was receiving treatment from his comrades.

"All the best, lads!" called one, looking up as he cut away the smouldering overalls.

"Give 'em hell!" shouted the other, about to administer a morphine ampoule.

"I wouldn't do their job for twice the pay," thought Wood.

Breathless, they reached the mounds marking the site of the old castle, pausing to get their second wind. Wood was vaguely aware of enemy artillery fire passing overhead. The outlying houses of Molay lay just 300 yards down the slope. Perhaps twice that distance beyond the village a considerable number of half-tracked vehicles were approaching across country from the opposite direction. Some twenty Panther and Pz Kpfw IV tanks were emerging from the wood to join them.

"Counter-attack!" shouted Holt. "We've run straight into a bloody counter-attack!"

Wood suspected that when the enemy planned their counter-stroke they had the recapture of the château and Esqueville in mind rather than Molay, which now lay in the newly created No Man's Land. The battalion's advance had therefore upset their calculations. The village had become a stumbling-block and would have to be fought for by both sides. The same thought seemed to have occurred to everyone else for, urged on by shouted orders, the wave of khaki swept on down the slope at a headlong run.

The barrage combed its way through the village, then ceased. At first they thought they had won the race, but as they reached the small square the first of the Panzergrenadiers appeared at a bend beyond. They had evidently left their vehicles on the outskirts and were coming on at a run down both sides of the road. Apart from prisoners, this was the first time Wood had seen a live enemy ready and willing to kill him. The sheer menace generated by the bobbing coal-scuttle helmets, thudding jackboots and cradled submachine-guns of those in the lead caused him to pull up sharply. To his astonishment the Germans did likewise and for a brief, frozen second each stared at the other in surprise.

Simultaneously, both sides opened fire and headed for the cover of the houses. Archer, the battalion cricket team's fastest pace bowler, had been among the first to react. His grenade, hurled with tremendous force, bounced and skittered across the *pavé* to explode among the nearest Germans, several of whom were felled. Wood saw Lister spin round and fall, but dashed through the nearest door and up the stairs with his Bren group, where Holt joined them.

Unearthly shrieks came from the street outside. Wood peered out and, to his horror, saw that Lister's chest was engulfed in flames and white smoke. Evidently a bullet had penetrated his ammunition pouch, exploding a phosphorous grenade within, and the result was burning its way deep into his body. He was writhing uncontrollably and screaming for someone to kill him. Holt leaned out of the window and fired a short burst from his Sten. Lister lay still but continued to burn.

Not one of them who survived the battle would ever shake off the experience, but its immediate effects on Holt were the most shattering of all. He slumped to the floor with his back against a wall. Unseeing, he stared blankly ahead.

"One of us would have done it if you hadn't – he'd have thanked you for it," said Wood quietly.

Still unfocused, Holt looked up at him.

"I warned 'em about carrying phosphorous grenades in their pouches. I should have checked, but I didn't, so some of it's down to me."

"It's down to Jerry, and that's all there is to it. Leave things to me for a bit."

Firing had broken out again. The windows suddenly splintered and bullet holes ripped across the plaster. A religious picture clattered on to the bed, its glass shattered. The Bren, firing obliquely upwards from a window, stuttered a short burst.

"That's you sorted out, matey!" said Salter, the gunner. "Ambitious gent with a Schmeisser on the roof opposite, Corp. Thought chimney pots were bullet proof – landed head first in the street."

Having toured the house, Wood was able to form a better impression of the overall situation. The house itself stood on a corner where a lane joined the square from the right. Opposite was the gable end of the house from which Salter had toppled the German; there were no windows in the gable but the garden did provide the enemy with a covered approach. Across the square to the left was the church and its walled graveyard. At the rear of their own row of houses the rest of the company was starting to dig in. From shouted conversations he knew that platoon headquarters was next door.

Firing had become more widespread as the enemy extended his own front and probed the defences. Holt resumed command, restricting the section's reply to visible targets. Latimer entered by the back door, accompanied by Rawnsley, and climbed the stairs.

"Right, you know the score. We've got half the village and Jerry's got the rest. We seem to have messed up his counter-attack plans but he's present in strength and sooner or later he'll try something. I need two men to beef up Number Three Section by the hedge at the back, Corporal Holt."

"Bray and Wilson, sir. They're downstairs doing nothing in particular."

They found the two carving up a ham Wilson had discovered hidden in a chimney breast.

"Why me?" said Bray truculently.

"Because I say so," said Holt, "Now get moving!"

Snatching up his rifle, Bray headed angrily for the back door. Wilson was less confrontational in his reluctance.

"Quite right, Corp, quite right. I'll just finish slicing this and see all the lads get their fair share."

"Leave it! I'll tell you when I want some slicing!"

Latimer returned to the platoon command post. Shortly after, their half of the village came under mortar and artillery fire. Simultaneously, their own artillery began to land shells among the enemy-held houses. Explosions mingled with the sound of falling masonry and shattering glass.

"Any minute now," said Rawnsley. "Looks like our Gunner bloke has spotted them forming up."

Wood knew that the battalion's attached Forward Observation Officer, an artilleryman, would require a good vantage-point from which to direct the fire of his supporting guns, and the probability was that he and his signallers had set up shop in the church steeple, which offered the only view across the entire village. Evidently the Germans had reached the same conclusion for when he glanced in that direction he could see the steeple being methodically knocked to pieces as one shell after another burst against it. The precision of the shooting indicated that the enemy tanks had taken it under direct gunfire. Suddenly, with a deep rumble, the weakened structure collapsed into the interior of the tower below, sending up a huge cloud of dust. The British artillery fire slowly faded away.

"Here they come!" yelled Holt. "Let 'em have it!"

There were Germans everywhere, charging down the road and across the square from doorways and alleys. Slater and Millard went into action at once, their stuttering Bren breaking up the attack on the road. Wood directed them to fire obliquely into the running figures on the square. The German line faltered then turned and ran whence it had come, leaving a dozen or so bodies on the cobbles. Holt appeared in the doorway.

"Back of the house, Tom – quick as you can! Archer and I can handle this side."

From one of the rear windows Wood could see that the enemy had made much better progress. Grenades were crossing in the air between their own garden and that of the house opposite. Several men in the platoon's incomplete slit trenches had been hit, but those not immediately engaged in the grenade duel were firing at groups of the enemy swarming across the lane some way beyond the bottom of the garden. At his direction the Bren raked the enemy hedge with several magazines, slicing through the foliage and branches to reveal a number of inert field-grey forms. He then switched his fire to those crossing the lane, taking particular satisfaction in the elimination of a Spandau light machine-gun team. Bullets shattered the remaining glass, smacking into the wall behind. At an adjacent window Rawnsley was firing methodically, counting slowly as he did so. The joy of battle was on him and he was smiling savagely.

"You really hate Jerries, don't you, Sarge?" said Wood.

"No," replied Rawnsley, squeezing off another round. "That's four. Your average Jerry's just a bloke like you and me. It's the friggin' SS I hate. Want to know why?"

He crouched beside the window, inserting two fresh clips of ammunition into his rifle as he spoke.

"I'll tell you. I had a brother in the First Battalion. Got wounded about a week before Dunkirk. Had to be left behind when his company were pushed out of a farm they were holding. Well, they took it back and what did they find? All our wounded had been shot through the back of the head. The SS did it right enough – there were plenty of them lying about. Now it's my turn."

He returned to the aim.

"Five. If you've no more questions, Corporal Wood, I suggest you get on with the battle."

There was a tremendous explosion overhead. Part of the ceiling came down, showering them with plaster, and tiles rained into the garden below. Seconds later the house shuddered as another shell struck. This was followed by several more which did little more than dislodge facing blocks from the immensely thick stone walls. Something unseen flashed by Wood's head, passed through the bedroom's thin partition wall and exploded in the stairwell, starting a fire. Wood could hear Holt and Archer dealing with it. He glanced upwards through the hole in the ceiling. The ancient beam against which the first shell had exploded was smouldering and there was daylight above.

"Give me a bunk-up," said Rawnsley. He peered briefly through the hole in the roof then dropped to the floor.

"Jerry's pushing tanks and more troops round both sides of the village," he said. "He's dropped off a few tanks to give the houses a hammering. They're in a hollow about five hundred yards out – too far for us to do anything about them."

Latimer entered the house by the rear door, shouting for Rawnsley. The sergeant ran down the stairs and the two could be heard talking urgently. Rawnsley returned, his face stony.

"Right, you lot, listen. The Colonel's been badly wounded and Major Dacres has taken over the battalion. Mr Latimer's taking over the company in his place. That means I'm commanding the platoon. We've been ordered to pull back through C Company and keep going until we're told otherwise. The signal will be two long blasts on the whistle. When you hear that use your smoke grenades while the mortars build up a screen. Once it's thick enough you go like hell. Any questions?"

"Why should we pull out when we're holding them off?" asked Wood.

"Fair enough, but we don't know what's going on elsewhere, do we? Right, I'm off to brief the sections in the garden."

Together, Holt and Wood discussed the best way to leave the house. They opened the front door but it was immediately apparent that the enemy had the main street covered with at least one machine-gun firing from the bend beyond the crossroads. Any movement immediately attracted a rip of bullets that struck sparks as they whined off cobbles and walls. Lister was staring at them from the roadway; above the smoking torso the eyes were open and the lips were drawn back from the teeth in a ghastly smile. Holt closed the door.

"Hobson's choice," he said, checking the magazine of his Sten. "Use the back. I'll cover you."

"What d'you mean – you're coming with us, aren't you?"

"I said I'd cover you. The section's my responsibility, so don't argue."

A whistle shrilled twice. They flung smoke grenades from every window, thickening the white fog already rising from the rain of whispering 2in mortar bombs. Gradually it built up until the entire company position was submerged.

"Now! Get moving!" shouted Holt.

Half blind, they joined those in the garden in a mad steeplechase over fences and hedges. Behind them they could hear shouts and the rattle of Holt's Sten. The enemy, too, was firing into the smoke. Archer went down heavily. Two rounds had struck him obliquely near the right shoulder-blade; one had emerged cleanly through the armpit but the second had glanced upwards off the bone, causing extensive damage to the shoulder. As yet there was no pain although he seemed stunned and barely conscious.

"Give me a hand, someone!" shouted Wood.

To his surprise Bray appeared, helping him to lift the wounded man to his feet. They were now alone and, together, they half-dragged, half-lifted him across the gardens until they reached C Company's position.

"Are you the last?" asked the company commander impatiently.

"No, sir – my section leader's still to come."

"I'm sorry, but I can't wait any longer," said the officer. "Make smoke and commence firing!"

They emerged from the village to find Latimer talking to Major Dacres. Latimer directed them up the slope to the old earthworks, in which both their own men and B Company were already taking up position. Rawnsley reorganised the platoon, arranging for two men to escort Archer to the Aid Post on the reverse slope of the feature. Shortly after, the two remaining rifle companies emerged from the smoke and came running in.

Wood knew that the battalion as a whole had sustained casualties but he was shocked to see how few unwounded men remained in each of the companies. He might, too, have been demoralised by their apparent failure had not Rawnsley returned from a company orders group and briefed the sections. The withdrawal, it seemed, was part of a plan agreed with brigade. It gave little away, as the enemy would still have to deal with the battalion before he could mount his counter-attacks on the Château Landru and Esqueville. What Dacres intended was to lure them into the open and inflict crippling loss before mounting a counter-attack of his own that would recapture the village. To this end a new FOO had been sent forward and he had many more guns at his disposal. Furthermore, a heavy air strike would be available on call.

"Told Mr Latimer that Jerry will wish he'd never been born by the time we've finished with him!" said Rawnsley, chuckling.

Wood felt better. Dacres was a quiet, self-contained man who spoke little but always meant what he said; he also had the reputation of being the best tactician in the battalion.

Their sudden withdrawal had certainly taken the enemy by surprise. They could be seen filtering forward through the village while their tanks conformed on either flank in preparation for an attack, pausing from time to time to give covering fire. The German artillery had already begun its preparatory bombardment but the shells were falling across a wide area, their effect further reduced by the protection of the old fortification's ditches and banks. The British guns were replying, firing concentrations against the enemy's probable forming-up points. Wood wondered what the Normans, who had clearly understood the principles of all-round defence, would have made of the modern soldiers using them.

"Here they come!" shouted someone.

The Panzergrenadiers were streaming out of the village – several waves of them. The section lined the bank, firing steadily. The enemy began falling but still came on in controlled rushes. Wood saw that the FOO had pulled in his defensive barrage to within 100 yards of their position then, to his horror, saw it lift altogether. Encouraged, the enemy swarmed forward. Teeth bared, their young faces, flushed with the anticipation of victory, began to come into focus. Wood began to doubt whether they could be held.

Incredibly fast smoke trails flashed across the battlefield from left to right, terminating in tremendous explosions among the attackers. With a roar of powerful engines, flight after flight of rocket-firing Typhoons swept past. Each rocket, Wood had been told, was the equivalent of an 8in shell, and as each Typhoon carried eight a full salvo was comparable to the broadside of a heavy cruiser. The attack disintegrated in flame, smoke and flying earth amid which men were blown apart or flung high into the air. The rest threw themselves flat as the aircraft banked away to the right to come in for a second pass, using their four 20mm cannon. The enemy tanks had already begun backing off, leaving two or three of their number behind. As the Typhoons droned away the surviving Panzergrenadiers broke and ran. Dacres was standing on the outer bank, waving his revolver and shouting at the top of his voice.

"What the hell are you waiting for? Get after them! Give them the bayonet – I don't want half measures from any of you!"

Battle-maddened and cheering hoarsely, the battalion swept down the slope past the still-smouldering craters and debris of the failed attack, then on into the village. Some of the enemy were shot as they ran. The rest were given no chance to rally or make anything more than the briefest of stands, being hounded from house to house and garden to garden before being swamped by the momentum of the charge. Within thirty minutes the complexion of the battle had changed. The entire village was in the battalion's hands and frightened prisoners were being herded together in the square.

In retrospect, Wood was shocked by the degree to which the collective blood lust had taken possession of him. As he fought the section through the village, they had entered the garden of the house they had defended. Holt was lying dead, face down across his Sten; between him and the hedge lay the bodies of three SS men.

"You could have got clear, but you didn't want to, did you?" said Wood. "Had to keep your bloody appointment in Samarra, didn't you?"

"You say something, Corp?" asked Salter.

Wood undid the dead man's breast-pocket and took out the family photographs.

"His folks will want these. Come on, we've a job to finish."

By dusk a defensive perimeter had been established around the village. At midnight, however, Rawnsley appeared.

"Get your blokes ready to move in five minutes," he said. "We're pulling back."

"You mean we're being relieved?" Wood asked.

"I mean we're pulling back – going into brigade reserve."

"So all this has been for nothing?"

"I'm not saying that. There'll be a reason, always is. Five minutes, and keep the noise down."

They filed along the ruined, rubble-strewn street, bewildered but philosophical. The wounded had been cleared but the dead of both sides lay among the shattered houses, some of which were still burning sullenly. They passed through the company checkpoint in the square. At the end of the street the company was met by battalion guides and led up the crater-pitted slopes, past the old earthworks and over the spur to a wood on the reverse slope. Here their Colour-Sergeant doled out hot tea and stew from his dixies. He seemed shocked that there were so few of them.

"Help yourselves to more, lads!" he said quietly when the last man had filed past. "There's plenty left."

They were given a blanket each and told to rest. Some seemed to drop easily into an exhausted sleep, but Wood's mind refused to release the images of the day. The section had been luckier than some which had been reduced to two or three men apiece. What could he tell his wife when he wrote? That half the battalion had been killed or wounded in a single day, including a majority of the officers? No, that would never do, even if it got past the censor; and he would never mention some of the things he had seen, like Lister's horrible death. He might tell her that Archer had got a Blighty one and would probably be discharged, although the chances of his ever bowling again seemed remote. It was odd how Wilson and Bray had buckled-to when it came to serious business. Perhaps Mike had ridden them too hard, particularly the latter. Mike. He would write to his widow and tell her how proud she should be of him. Maybe his own wife would visit her, perhaps contribute an item or two to the train set he had been collecting, or even buy it if she looked like needing the money ...

Sleep came, but the dreams consisted of rushing sounds, urgent voices, sudden movement, flames and unspeakable violence. Like many men for years to come, he would talk incoherently in his restless slumbers, striving to break free from the images projected by the retentive mirrors of his sub-conscious, and awake sweating in a saner world.

Because the Normandy Campaign was comparatively short and ended in a crushing victory for the Allies, it is sometimes forgotten that there were times when casualties among the infantry reached levels approximating to some phases of the Battle of the Somme. For some battalions, the saying was true that they had been five years in the making and a day in the destroying. During later phases of the war in northwest Europe it became necessary to break up some units and formations to provide reinforcements for others.

Students of the campaign will recognise that this chapter has been set in the area of Hill 112, where some of the bitterest fighting took place. It is based on the experiences of the 4th Somerset Light Infantry, 7th Hampshire Regiment and 4th and 5th Dorsetshire Regiment. In this context it should be remembered that the overall Allied strategy was to attract the German armour to the British sector of the beachhead with sustained attacks while the Americans prepared for the breakout operation which eventually saw the German armies destroyed in the Falaise pocket. As part of this strategy a series of heavy raids were mounted against villages in the area of Hill 112, provoking fierce counter-attacks which reduced the German armoured formations. That which I have described is based on one delivered at Maltot on 10 July, involving the surviving 30 tanks of a panzer regiment, several Tigers, the armoured battalion of a Panzergrenadier regiment and an armoured reconnaissance battalion. At the time, it must have been difficult for the British troops involved to understand why their hard-won gains had to be given up; only later did they learn of the good that came of their efforts.

For their part, the Germans were handicapped by Hitler's insane 'no withdrawal' order. This meant that they were forced to remain within range of the overwhelming and flexibly handled Allied artillery and tactical air support, and as a result their formations were bled white. The Waffen SS were responsible for the massacre of British prisoners in the days prior to Dunkirk, and at Hill 112 there were times when their vicious methods resulted in quarter being neither asked nor given.

CORPORAL KEN BURMAN

Armoured Car Commander,
Cavalry Reconnaissance, The Ardennes,
15–17 December 1944

Dusk came early in December. This winter, they said, was nearly the coldest in living memory. There was snow on the ground, still hardened to ice crystals by the previous night's frost where it had not been turned to dirty brown slush by the passage of vehicles. Heavy cloud masked the sunset, suggesting that there would be more snow that night.

Sergeant Tate Emerson kicked open the door of the farmhouse occupied by his platoon and emptied the sack on the kitchen table.

"Mail call!"

There was the usual scramble for packages and letters, following which the men squatted down around the fire to read in silence.

Corporal Ken Burman busied himself examining the contents of a battered package. It contained an equally battered iced cake which the enclosed note hoped would arrive in time for Christmas, still ten days off, some of his mother's cookies, mostly crushed to crumbs, some candy bars in reasonable condition, together with six pairs of socks, two sweaters and a scarf, a present from the ladies of the town's knitting circle. There were also a number of Christmas cards, some of them showing snow-covered hills and trees remarkably similar to the chill Ardennes landscape outside the window. The reality, he thought wryly to himself, was not so darn festive. Having read through several letters from his family and friends, he turned to his neighbour, Private First Class Ray Kramer.

"Remember Al Hogan – worked for Maguire's Construction Plant then joined the Marines? They've given him some kind of medal for Tarawa."

"No kidding!"

"Yeah. Won't talk about it, though. Says he got it just for being there, but his old man's got hold of the citation. Seems when his amtrac got knocked out he joined the nearest infantry, saved two guys' lives, killed a Jap in hand to hand combat, got wounded but refused evacuation."

"This the same Al Hogan? He used to be a quiet kind of guy – they say they're the ones you've got to watch."

"Yeah, he's doin' okay. He's a sergeant now, got his own amtrac platoon, been in all kinds of shindigs out there."

"I guess he's seen more action than we ever will. Brass reckon the Krauts are licked – I heard someone say the war won't last beyond Christmas."

In some ways, Burman welcomed the prospect, but in others he did not. In particular, though the thought of combat worried him, he did not want to return home without ever having seen it. Long, long ago, one of his remote ancestors had scouted for the cavalry on the frontier. The family had a framed picture of him taken by a travelling photographer somewhere out West. Impassively, the old timer's pale eyes, given a piercing quality by the photographer's flash powder, watched them from above a wide moustache every time they ate. He wore a buckskin vest over a check shirt, corduroy pants tucked into high boots, a gunbelt slung low and, for effect, was holding a Winchester rifle. As to his achievements, fact had become entangled with legend with the passage of time, but the story was inspiring enough for young Ken to decide that, if ever he went to war, he too would like to scout for the cavalry. Following Pearl Harbor, he had, therefore, headed for the nearest National Guard cavalry unit, taking Ray with him, and the two had enlisted.

Months of disillusion had followed. The regiment was already partially mechanised and its remaining horses were retired. It was then broken up to form separate armoured reconnaissance squadrons. This suited Burman very well as he would still be performing the role for which he had enlisted. The problem was that although the armaments industry had geared up for mass production the Army was expanding at a terrific rate and equipment had to be sent where it was needed most. His squadron therefore received just sufficient M8 armoured cars and M3 light tanks to carry out crew training.

He had qualified as a gunner on the 37mm, which was the principal armament of the M8 and the M3, been selected for a vehicle commander's course and at length been promoted to corporal. Ray Kramer had specialised as a radio operator but had acquired some driving experience as well. They both liked the six-wheeled M8, which could be wound up to 56 miles per hour on good going, touching 60 at times on downhill stretches. Its secondary armament consisted of a .30 calibre machine-gun mounted coaxially with the 37mm, and a .50 calibre machine-gun in an anti-aircraft mounting above the open-topped turret. Fighting, however, was not what armoured reconnaissance was about, they were told during their tactical training. Their function was the acquisition of information about the enemy and terrain features which could be put to operational use, and in that context the radio was the car's real weapon. Its guns, backed by those of the M3 light tanks, were there simply to get it out of trouble, should the need arise.

By degrees the squadron had become fully equipped and trained, but still there seemed no prospect of it being posted overseas. Many of its personnel, on the other hand, were despatched to units in active war zones, their replacements being draftees who had received only basic training. The North Africa and Sicilian campaigns slid into history, followed by the landings in Italy, still without any hint that the squadron would have an active role. In an attempt to raise morale the then commanding officer had decreed that each of the cars and light tanks should be named after the girlfriend or film star of the crew's choice, with her likeness portrayed in miniature on the turret side, a prize being awarded for the best effort. Some of the results enhanced nature in accordance with the artist's fancy, Burman's *Betty* having legs the length of which might have suited a giraffe.

Shortly after D-Day the squadron was told that it would be serving in the European Theatre of Operations. Even so, by the time it sailed from New York the Allies had already broken out of their Normandy beachheads and pursued the beaten remnant of the enemy across France to the German frontier. When it disembarked in late November the front had stabilised again but the general opinion was that Nazi Germany, under pressure from east and west and under continuous air attack, would not survive another winter.

In early December the squadron made a two-day road march through France and Belgium to find itself in the Ardennes. This, they were told, was a sector of the line so quiet that it was known as The Ghost Front and used not only to rest tired formations but also to acclimatise completely raw divisions just arrived from the United States.

The squadron's function would be to form part of a cavalry reconnaissance screen covering the gap between one such division, the 106th Infantry, positioned on a ridge called the Schnee Eifel, to the south, and the 99th Infantry Division to the north. The countryside was deep in the grip of winter and the lines were static with only limited patrol activity between them. As there was no prospect of mounted action the squadron's commander decided that his troops would occupy forward outposts in a dismounted role with one platoon each held back as a mobile reserve in the event of trouble.

In Burman's troop the 1st and 2nd Platoons were detailed to occupy two hamlets, Karlsdorf and Oberkarlsdorf, lying on the front line, while troop headquarters and the 3rd Platoon, of which Burman was a member, were based at Jägerstein, another hamlet equidistant between the two and about two miles back.

Burman thought that the country was pretty but did not like its inhabitants who, for all that they were Belgian citizens, were mostly ethnic Germans. They were sullen, disinclined to speak unless spoken to, clearly did not regard the Americans as liberators and pointedly discussed them among themselves in German. To make matters worse, the Belgian civil authorities regarded them as potential if not actual traitors and declined to feed them. When the Americans, trying to be friendly, offered some of their own rations, these were received with surly grace.

The platoon's nearest friendly neighbours were the reserve and rear echelon elements of the 106th Infantry Division, known as the Golden Lions because of their shoulder patches. Taken as a whole, the division seemed to consist of very young soldiers, the reason being, Burman was told, that it had recently been brought up to strength with large numbers of recently joined draftees. It had relieved a resting veteran division whose attitude had been condescending, but its first few days in the line had been uneventful and, as far Burman could tell, it seemed to be settling down.

Most of the platoon set out their Christmas cards around the farmhouse kitchen, giving the room a seasonal feel. Having built up the fire, they disappeared into their sleeping-bags, save for those on guard duty. Burman drew the middle shift, lasting from one until three, which he hated as it involved the interruption of a deep sleep to which he seemed unable to return afterwards. When the time came he put on his new scarf and was immediately grateful for it when he stepped out into a bitterly cold night. His breath hung in clouds and there were occasional snow flurries. A light shone through the window of a downstairs room occupied by the troop command post. Within he could see the duty signaller reading a lurid paperback. Occasionally he answered a jangling field telephone and sometimes spoke on the radio. Burman could not hear what he said and continued to walk around the yard. Looking up, he saw several stars twinkling through a gap in the clouds but they soon vanished. It was surprising, he thought, how quickly the eyes became accustomed to the dark, even when there were so few sources of light, for he could see most details of the snow-covered landscape. The Ghost Front slept on. At 0300 he shook his relief and turned in.

He must have slept for at 0530 he suddenly found himself sitting bolt upright, as was everyone else. There was a distant thunder of guns accompanied by a flickering light from the east. Then came a sustained eruption of shells up on the Schnee Eifel, in the 106th Division's rear areas, and from the direction of the front. After a few minutes it became evident that the farm was not a target. Puzzled and nervous, they went out into the yard. Captain Dick Schuman, the troop commander, emerged from his command post and Burman overheard him talking to 3rd Platoon's commander, Lieutenant Fred Lucas.

"Phone lines are cut and some bastard is jamming our radio frequency!" said Schuman. "What in hell's name is going on around here, Fred?"

"Search me," replied Lucas. "Those are Kraut shells right enough – maybe they're not as whipped as we thought. Want me to go take a look how the boys are getting on up front?"

"In the dark – are you crazy? No, maybe squadron have a better idea what's going on. Once I know something I'll put you in where you'll do most good. Just the same, we'd better be ready. What have you got, Sergeant Emerson?"

"Two M8s, *Rita* and *Betty*, and one M3, *Rhonda*. Like you said, sir, the rest needed attention after we got in from France. I've two replacement clutches, a new gearbox and a fuel pump promised for today."

"Right, get 'em warmed up."

Because of the intense cold, two heavy powder cartridges were need-ed to start the M3's air-cooled radial engine, which spluttered irritably until the driver placed it under load. Burman knew that the M8s' sump oil would have thickened to the consistency of treacle, but their bat-teries were well charged and after the carburettors of the 110hp Her-cules engines had been primed they fired fairly quickly, belching clouds of steam into the night air. The longer they were left the better, he thought, as until the oil thinned and the cooling system's thermostat opened they would barely be capable of ten miles per hour.

At about 0600 the bombardment slackened. Suddenly, the whole scene was bathed in a eerie glow as the light from hundreds of Ger-man searchlights was reflected off the low cloud on to the gleaming, snow-covered landscape beneath.

"Jeez, this is some weird place!" said Kramer.

The effect became less dramatic as dawn approached and finally faded altogether. From their own outposts and the Schnee Eifel came the sounds of small-arms and automatic weapon fire, punctuated by the thump of mortars and other heavy weapons, muffled by distance. The signaller emerged from the command post.

"Sir, all the telephone lines are out but I think I just got Lieutenant Baker. All I got was 'under heavy attack', then the jamming closed in."

"Hell! Any contact with squadron?"

"No, sir."

"Okay, I'll send a jeep back – maybe they know what's going on."

It took an hour for the jeep to return. The driver told Schuman that the roads were becoming increasingly congested with traffic heading for the rear.

"They don't know anything more than us, but they think some-thing big is coming off. They want you to send Three Platoon up and verify the situation, then report the enemy's progress. If communica-tions don't improve, information is to be routed personally through you and relayed by jeep messenger."

"Alright, Fred, you heard the man!" said Schuman. "Get your peo-ple mounted!"

Before they moved off, Lucas, Emerson and Burman conferred with their maps. It was decided that they would use farm tracks and minor roads to bring them on to a stretch of high ground from which both the outpost villages could be seen.

"Corporal Burman, take the point!" said Lucas, clambering aboard the M3. Burman, being the junior and most expendable, had expected the order. He eased into *Betty*'s turret, stowed his machine-carbine, shortened his binocular strap and placed his map in a convenient position. To the right his gunner, a young, recently joined draftee named Follett, looked pale and was swallowing hard.

"You okay?"

"Yeah, I – I think so."

"Don't worry – it's the first time for all of us." He ducked down into the turret. "Okay, you guys?"

Below him, John Evans nodded and grinned. Evans was the workhorse of the crew, the driver, who said little but would cheerfully drive and maintain the M8 day and night. Kramer, in the co-driver's seat to the right, tapped the radio in disgust.

"Nix – they're jamming solid right round the dial."

The squealing mush in his headphones had already told Burman as much and he reduced the volume. When he bobbed up Emerson was yelling at him from *Rita*.

"You got some kinda card game goin' in there? C'mon, move out!"

"Let's go!" said Burman into the intercom.

They led off out of the farmyard and across a broad field where furrows indicated a track under the snow. At the far side the track passed through a gate at which Evans halted, as they had during training, waiting for someone to open it.

"Go straight through!" shouted Burman. "There's a war on!"

The sound of splintering wood did much to dampen his annoyance. The farmer was a surly, sour-faced, grasping individual who took everything he could get and still charged extortionate prices for his milk and eggs. The track led down a sloping field into a narrow valley between rolling hills, along which they turned left on a minor road, then right on to another, climbing the wooded eastern slope until they reached a crossroads. Straight ahead, the road passed over an open crest to Oberkarlsdorf; to the left it joined a better road leading down into Karlsdorf; to the right, it passed round the shoulder of the Schnee Eifel. The three commanders left their vehicles and began walking up to the crest. Perhaps it was some instinct inherited from his great-uncle Jethro, the scout, for at the crossroads Burman dropped on one knee to examine some tracks. A number of vehicles had come from the direction of Oberkarlsdorf and turned left, pushing the snow into an untidy brown heap of slush at the outer edge of the turn but leaving marks on the hard surface of the road below.

"Just what in hell's name d'you think you're doing, Corporal?" asked Lucas irritably.

"Take a look at these marks, sir. That pile of slush has been pushed out by tracked vehicles. Marks aren't deep enough for tanks, so they must be half-tracks. Our half-tracks don't leave tread marks like this, so they must be theirs. My guess is they're pushing a force of armoured infantry round behind the 106th Infantry up on the Schnee Eifel."

Lucas looked at him speculatively. He did not want to believe what he was being told, but Burman was steady enough and not given to flights of fancy. He put forward a counter-argument.

"Your idea would be fine, but for one thing – we're holding Oberkarlsdorf, and that's where these tracks are coming from."

They left the road short of the crest and crawled to a hummock beside it. Oberkarlsdorf came into focus in their binoculars. Several of the houses were on fire. There were troops in white, snow overalls and unfamiliar vehicles in the hamlet's main street, with more approaching. A small group of men were sitting under a statue in the tiny square. One of their guards evidently gave a command, for they rose to their feet and began filing to the east, their hands raised.

"Those are our guys," said Emerson. "That's all that's left of Second Platoon – I recognised Grout, Swindelhurst and maybe a few more."

"Looks like you were right, Corporal Burman," said Lucas. "Let's take a look at Karlsdorf."

They swung their binoculars to the left. The village lay in a hollow but the church and the roofs of the houses, some of them burning, were clearly visible. What caught their attention, however, was taking place some distance beyond, where in a firebreak between two wooded features, a long convoy of tanks could be seen heading slowly but steadily to the north-west.

"This is big – really big!" said Emerson. "They were supposed to be licked – so how come they can do this?"

No one had any answers. Shells began to burst in Karlsdorf, starting more fires. From a belt of trees to the east of the village three low-slung assault guns appeared, firing as they advanced. They were followed by a wave of white-clad infantry. As the attack progressed it passed through an area apparently littered with humps. Burman guessed that these were casualties from earlier attacks and some of them did indeed rise and join this fresh assault. One of the assault guns stopped and began to burn. The attackers disappeared as they entered the hollow. The sound of small-arms fire and grenades continued for several minutes, then ceased.

For a while, no one spoke. When Lucas broke the silence there was anger in his voice.

"Whoever decided this goddam gap could be held by cavalry outposts has got one helluva lot to answer for! Right, now listen. Everything we've seen has got to be reported immediately, so if the radios are still jammed Sergeant Emerson will hightail it straight back to the farm."

He jammed the map with his finger.

"I'm going to hang around on this piece of ground overlooking Karlsdorf. Could be some of First Platoon got clear – if so, they'll need help. After that, I'll follow on."

"What about me?" asked Burman.

"I'd like you to check out that hunch of yours, Corporal Burman. Don't go too far along that road, though – you could get boxed in once that bunch in Oberkarlsdorf start following up. If that happens, join us by any route you can."

"Yes, sir."

Burman didn't like his orders, which sounded too much like a one-way ticket, but they were legitimate and had to be obeyed. The finality of armoured reconnaissance work struck him. If he got back having confirmed his suspicions the result would be fed into the overall intelligence picture; yet if he failed to return someone would draw the appropriate conclusions and the result would be the same.

"Radio still jammed?" he asked as he walked back towards the car. Kramer's head was poking out of the co-driver's hatch.

"'Fraid so. What gives?"

"Don't ask – you wouldn't like it."

Burman climbed aboard.

"Move it!" he said into the intercom. "Turn right at the junction."

He knew he was in a foul mood, but at least Evans didn't ask questions. He selected a canister round from the ammunition rack, opened the 37mm breech and slid it inside. The breech closed with a well-oiled click.

Follett looked at him nervously.

"Are we expecting trouble? An ambush, maybe?"

"No, we're going to meet Santa Claus and his reindeer round the next bend! Now keep your finger on that trigger – we're relying on you!"

Follett lapsed into miserable silence. Burman knew he was being hard on the boy, but so far he had done nothing to inspire confidence. The last thing he needed now was a bag of nerves across the turret. He concentrated on the suspicious tracks, which continued to follow the road along the tree-covered hillside.

Rounding a bend, they were confronted by a dozen American soldiers sitting on a bank. They said they belonged to the supply echelon of one of the 106th's battalions and were returning from a drop when they had been halted by a jeep containing four military policemen. They were told that their trucks had been commandeered for some sort of reinforcement operation and instructed to walk towards Oberkarlsdorf, where they would be picked up. The men seemed genuine enough, but there was something wrong with their story.

"There's nothing but Krauts behind us," said Burman. "You're heading straight for prison camp. Where d'you meet these MPs?"

"We bin walkin' for an hour, so maybe it was two, three miles back down the road," said a coloured corporal.

"See anything on the way?" Burman could feel his temper rising again. "Maybe like a convoy of half-tracks with big black crosses on the side, full of Heinie soldiers?"

"We aint seen nothin' like that," said the corporal, obviously stung. "'Bout a mile further on there's a turnoff – looked like plenty o' traffic bin usin' that, though."

"Alright." Burman showed the corporal where he was on the map.

"The front's busted wide open – you want to get back to our own people, keep heading north-west and stay off the roads."

"Thanks."

"C'mon, let's go!"

As the supply corporal had said, there was a turnoff to the left about a mile further on. It was a forest road that continued to lead round the rear of the Schnee Eifel, from which the sounds of battle had intensified. Burman dismounted to examine the tracks. They confirmed that the enemy had taken this route. The question arose in his mind, should he follow them? The answer came almost at once. He had obtained the information he sought, now he must find a means of communicating it as quickly as possible. What was more, the enemy would be sending up reinforcements from Oberkarlsdorf and they could not be far behind now. He looked at his map. If they continued, in due course they would reach a secondary road which led towards St-Vith and passed the entrance to the farm where the troop was based.

"Straight ahead," he said, clambering aboard. His discovery had pushed what the supply men had told him to the back of his thoughts, so that when the car rounded a bend it was a shock to see their 2½-ton trucks still parked at the roadside, about 100 yards away, with the MP jeep beyond. The four MPs seemed equally startled, for the car, like all of its type, was a quiet runner and they had received no warning of its approach.

"Halt!" The car came to a standstill. "Traverse to the rear," he said to Follett, who began swinging the turret round until the 37mm lay over the engine, the usual position when re-entering friendly lines. The MPs seemed to relax. They spread out across the road, but still maintained a purposeful grip on their machine-carbines. One, wearing a sergeant's stripes, grinned broadly and beckoned them to come on.

Burman sensed that something was wrong. MPs didn't usually grin, though that proved nothing. But what were they doing here, waiting around in the middle of nowhere, and what did they need with six empty trucks when they should have been controlling traffic behind the lines?

"Are you guys the rearguard?" shouted the sergeant. "How many of you are there? We have transport here for anyone who needs it!"

His English had a slight American accent but it was too precise to be genuine. What was more, his story bore no resemblance to that told by the supply men. The chill realisation struck him – they were Germans in American uniforms, intending to pull some stroke behind American lines, using American vehicles to transport troops already marching up from Oberkarlsdorf. He was about to take a terrible risk, with dire consequences if he was wrong. He looked at them closely. The painted white strip above the helmet rim seemed real enough, as did the MP letters above and the brassards, but the divisional shoulder patches were unfamiliar.

"Off you go," he said to Evans. "Speed up – we're going straight through!"

The sergeant, still smiling, was flagging them down. Suddenly, his expression changed to one of alarm as Burman's intention became clear.

"RUN 'EM DOWN!"

Frantically the MPs dived for the roadside. One of them, too slow, gave a scream as the car passed over his leg with a barely perceptible jolt.

"Let 'em have it! Fire, for Chrissake!"

"But they're our guys!" protested Follett.

"They're Krauts! NOW FIRE OR I'LL BLOW YOUR GODDAM HEAD OFF!"

The 37mm went off with its ear-splitting bang. Its elevation, however, was too high. All that the blast of canister achieved was to bring down a shower of snow and branches, shatter a truck's windscreen and rip part of its canopy to shreds. Slugs from the enemy's machine-carbines continued to tonk off the armour until the car rounded the next bend.

Kramer eased himself back from the co-driver's seat.

"You nuts or what? You just declared war on the Provost Marshal!"

"They were Krauts, I tell you!"

"Don't tell me – tell the court martial! Boy, are you having some kind of a day!"

"So what else d'you expect? I've got a gunner who can't shoot and an operator who can't operate!"

His face dark with anger, Kramer withdrew from view. Burman regretted his outburst at once, knowing that it was unfair of him to vent his spleen on them. They reached the junction to find that the secondary road was filled with 106th Division's transport, being driven recklessly and at speed. There was no apparent order, with empty 2½-tonners mixed with crane trucks, artillery prime movers, some of them towing guns, and jeeps driven by officers. No one was inclined to let the armoured car in. Horn blaring, the wild-eyed driver of a ¼-tonner tried to overtake. He cut in too sharply ahead of a water tanker and in the resulting collision the two vehicles locked together, slewing across the road. More horns began to blare as the column came to a stand-still. While frantic efforts were made to clear the tangle, Burman walked across to a communications truck with Signal Corps markings.

"What gives?" he asked the sergeant in the co-driver's seat.

"Search me, bud. We just got orders to bug out – keep going till you're through Saint Vith, they said. Something real bad is going down, but I don't know what it is."

"You in contact with anyone?" Burman indicated the radio. The sergeant shook his head.

"We've been jammed solid on every frequency all day. How about you?"

"The same. Listen, Sarge, I've got some really important informa-tion I've just got to get through. How about letting us in?"

"Fine by me. Watch yourself, though. There are MPs all over the place, directing traffic every which way. Don't seem to know what they're doing."

"Thanks, we've met some – they're phonies, Krauts dressed in GI uniforms."

The crashed trucks had been roughly shunted or manhandled off the highway. The sergeant waved the M8 out into the traffic stream and they made good progress. After a mile or so they swung right up the lane leading to the farm. It was like coming home and Burman felt the weight of responsibility lift immediately from his shoulders. Sec-onds later came the sickening realisation that the farm was deserted. The non-runners were still in the barn but otherwise there were few signs that the troop had ever been there. At length, in answer to his shouts, a figure appeared in the cowshed door. It was Winckler, the farmer, whom Schuman allowed back twice a day to attend to his live-stock. Burman spoke no German but he guessed that as a Belgian cit-izen Winckler would also speak French. He dredged through his own half-forgotten lessons.

"*Où sont les Americains?*"

"*Ils sont partis*," replied Winckler, adding maliciously, "*Au pas gym-nastique!*"

"*Oh! Quand?*"

Winckler shrugged and, laughing unpleasantly, disappeared into the cowshed. Burman would dearly have loved to punch him in the mouth.

To his surprise, it was beginning to get dark. The crew had dis-mounted and were obviously awaiting a decision from him. There were still sounds of fighting from the Schnee Eifel but the traffic con-tinued to stream past the end of the lane, indicating that for the pre-sent the immediate area would remain quiet enough.

"Everyone seems to have bugged out but us," he said. "I guess there's not much we can do but keep pulling back until we meet someone who knows what's going on. Follett, before we move out, why don't you and Evans fix us some chow?"

"The radio jamming has stopped, Corporal," said Kramer with flat formality. "Not that you can make any sense of what's going on."

Burman had no wish to quarrel with his old school friend and offered an olive branch.

"Look, I shouldn't have said what I did earlier – it was out of line and I didn't mean it. Can we forget it?"

"Yeah, what the hell! Aint much fun being in charge, I guess."

They shook hands. The earphones were now full of voices, most of them wildly excited. Procedure had been overtaken by panic and neighbouring frequencies were intruding on their own, producing a chaotic cacophony. If the Germans had ceased jamming in order to monitor American reactions they were wasting their time. He tried using their own call sign for several minutes without result, then gave up.

"We'll move to high ground and extend the antenna," he said.

Evans, stirring a can of coffee, was a calm eye in the centre of the storm. Not gifted with too much imagination, he thought very slow-ly. When he spoke, which was rarely, it was at the same measured pace, and in a mid-Western drawl. Now, he was chuckling to himself.

"Well, if that didn't beat all!"

"What did?"

"Why, runnin' down those MPs! They don't seem to like me, an' I sure don't like them. We just don't darn well get on."

He paused to reflect.

"Hear that feller holler when I ran over his leg? Must have hurt him a lot. Reckon we'll be in trouble?"

"No, they were Krauts!"

"Who cares? I bet Kraut MPs are no different!"

They all laughed and felt the better for it. At last light they left the farm, rejoining the now-thinning stream of traffic. Two miles back down the valley Burman directed Evans to leave the road and head for a belt of trees on a ridge to their right. While he satisfied himself that he had a good overview of the enemy's probable line of advance, Kramer added extra lengths to the antenna. There were still gun flashes on the Schnee Eifel and elsewhere, but it was impossible to get any clear idea of what was happening.

Radio operating at night was more difficult because of increased static. However, the flow of transmissions diminished and at about midnight Kramer suddenly looked up.

"Hey, I think we've got someone!"

"This is Charlie Three Charlie, over," said Burman.

"Come in, Charlie Three Charlie," answered a faint voice.

"Long sitrep follows, over."

"Send, over."

As concisely as possible, Burman detailed the loss of the outposts, the enemy's outflanking move around the north of the Schnee Eifel, and his opinion that the Germans were using infiltration parties in American uniforms.

"Sitrep ends, Roger so far, over," he said when he had finished.

"Roger so far. Position, over," replied the voice.

He had already encoded their position and gave it.

"Roger, wait, over and out," came the response.

For some minutes the headphones remained silent save for mush and some distant, distorted artillery chatter.

"Charlie Three Charlie, Sunray on set, orders, over."

"Charlie Three Charlie, send, over."

Normally, Sunray would mean Schuman, but the voice was unmistakably that of Major John Callender, the squadron commander. Burman assumed that so little remained of the three troops that he had consolidated the remnant and was controlling it personally. Callender's voice was steady and reassuring.

"Move to Boxcar. Take your own time. Report everything you see, but don't get involved. Then head directly for Tombstone, over."

Burman looked at the code-words on his map. 'Boxcar' meant the River Our, and 'Tombstone' was St-Vith, where the squadron command post was located alongside that of 106th Division.

"Wilco, over."

"You're doing a good job and we don't want to lose you, so keep your non-mobile transmissions short – you know why. Good luck, over and out."

Callender's warning made sense. The word was that the German intercept operators were hot stuff who could define the position of an observation post from just four minutes' transmitting time, after which an artillery strike could be expected.

The night passed uneasily. In the distance something, a building or a vehicle, was burning, but this was obscured when a mist descended. Suggestions of movement filtered up from the valley below. From time to time there was shooting, accompanied by shouts in German. The mist played tricks with sound, giving the impression they were surrounded. It cleared slowly after first light, enabling Burman to see what was happening.

On the lower slopes of the ridge a number of Panzergrenadier half-tracks were grouped, their occupants unconcernedly cooking breakfast or performing maintenance tasks. As he watched, a file of American prisoners was marched away. In the middle distance a column of tanks was approaching along the road. He was able to identify Panthers and Pz Kpfw IVs. He expected them to continue in the direction of St-Vith, but instead they turned off on a side road leading south and he reached the conclusion that their intention was to by-pass the town. His binoculars swept further out and the Winckler farm came into focus. A staff car and several command and radio vehicles were parked in the yard. He could imagine Winckler joyfully handing out free milk, eggs, butter and cheese to his liberators. It was a very annoying thought.

He transmitted a long contact report, describing the local situation and giving the Winckler farm as a possible formation headquarters. After this was acknowledged he continued to observe. Having no intention of staying any longer than necessary, he told Follett to tie down the extended antenna to prevent it whipping on the move and thereby damaging its base leads to the radio. Simultaneously, in anticipation of a move, Evans was priming the cold engine.

At the sound of far-off explosions, Burman lifted his binoculars again. Shellbursts were mushrooming around the Winckler farm. The yard resembled a disturbed anthill with figures running for cover and vehicles dispersing in all directions. Some of the buildings started to burn. He had expected to be asked for corrections but the gunners were evidently firing off the map.

His deep sense of satisfaction was short-lived. There was a brief screaming and several shells burst just short of the tree line. The car was showered with clods of frozen earth.

"Crank her up – they're on to us!"

It seemed an age before the sluggishly turning engine caught. The Panzergrenadiers, now alerted to their presence, opened fire with their machine-guns, clipping branches off the trees all around. Another salvo of shells landed.

"Reverse!"

He guided Evans back out of the trees, then had him swing the car over the open crest into dead ground.

"Turn left – keep going across the slope!"

The terrain was broken up by rocky outcrops and here and there dead bracken showed through the covering of snow. Evans was a good driver who could be trusted to pick his own route. Nevertheless, the going was painfully slow and at one stage the car began to slide downhill on the icy surface. Burman thought it would overturn, with probably fatal consequences, but Evans accelerated gently and steered into the skid, losing some height before he regained full control. At length they reached the butt end of the ridge, re-entered the trees and began to descend into a shallow valley with a track in the bottom.

Burman halted the car in cover. Two hundred yards to the left the track crossed the main road. He pulled out his map and pinpointed their position. The main road wound up the hill opposite and then traversed a rolling plateau before dropping down into the valley of the Our at St-Bernard, where a bridge was marked. He explained to the others that he intended setting up one last observation post at the top of hill then retiring as instructed. Their relief was obvious.

He was about to give the order to move off when Follett drew his attention to the sound of squealing tracks and a powerful engine, misfiring badly, approaching from the east along the main road. It could only be an enemy tank and it was using their only apparent line of retreat. His heart sank. The tank halted straddling the crossroads. The Tiger's huge gun and slab-sided armour were unmistakable.

The tank commander, evidently lost, was consulting his map. Burman conjectured that, struggling to catch up because of his sick engine, he had missed the turnoff taken by the rest of the column and was trying to get back to his designated route. The car, concealed as it was among snow-laden trees, was clearly invisible to him.

The German decided to turn left. Snarling and shuffling back and forth, the massive vehicle at length managed to insert itself into the narrow lane, filling it entirely with its bulk. The wide steel tracks began to accelerate away.

"Get after him!" said Burman tersely. The car moved out into the lane in pursuit. Burman flipped open the 37mm, inserted an armour-piercing round and extracted two more from the rack in readiness.

"You aim for his stern plate," he told Follett. "That's where his armour's thinnest. I'll get you as close as I can. You fire when I tell you and you keep firing, got it?"

Follett swallowed, nodding dumbly.

"Right, now get your eye on that gunsight."

They were approaching the crossroads when the German commander glanced round. For a second he stared at them in disbelief, then dropped from view. The Tiger halted and its turret began to turn.

"Speed up, for Chrissake!" yelled Burman

The great gun was swinging ponderously but inexorably towards them. It reached two o'clock, three o'clock, then four o'clock. Just 25 yards separated them from the Tiger.

"Halt!" cried Burman. Evans hit the brakes hard. The car rocked on its front suspension. The gun had reached five o'clock and was still turning.

"FIRE!"

The 37mm banged and there was a red flash as the projectile penetrated the enemy's stern plate. Burman slid another round into the breech. Again the gun banged, with identical result. At the third round there came the sound of a muffled explosion, the Tiger seemed to shudder and flames belched out of every aperture in the hull and turret. None of the crew got out.

"Reverse!" He had no wish to be caught in the blast from a terminal explosion.

"Nice shooting, kid!" shouted Kramer from below. "Seemed to me you put 'em all through the same hole!"

Seeing Follett looking hopefully at him, Burman grinned. He had given the boy a rough ride and now he deserved a word of praise, even if he could hardly have missed.

"Yeah, nice shooting. Tell your folks about it, something like, 'Dear Mom, today I knocked out my first Tiger – my corporal, who is normally a bad-tempered bastard, is real pleased with me!'"

Follett grinned diffidently, flushing with pleasure.

At the crossroads Burman directed Evans to take the St-Vith road. The timber thinned out halfway up the hill but at the top he pulled in behind an abandoned house. Satisfied that he could keep the crossroads under observation from the upper storey, he transmitted a contact report regarding the Tiger. The weary disbelief evident in the control operator's acknowledgement was followed by a warning.

"Boxcar will be closing down in three zero minutes, over."

He examined his map, verifying the code-name for St-Bernard.

"Charlie Three Charlie, Roger. Will move through Albany soonest, over."

"Roger, wait, out," said the voice unexpectedly. A minute or so later it was back.

"Charlie Three Charlie, message from Sunray. You are to exercise extreme, repeat extreme, caution approaching Albany. Move now, over."

"Roger, over and out."

The bridges over the Our were to be blown in 30 minutes. That was clear enough, but Callender was trying to tell him something else, something of benefit which could not be openly disclosed. Was the enemy in St-Bernard? No, he would have been told directly if they were. Then what? Had a rearguard been formed in the village, covering the engineers while they worked on their demolition charges? That seemed possible, and after the events of the past 24 hours they would be extremely wary of anything approaching from the direction of the enemy, even if it were carrying American markings. He was about to give the order to go when movement down at the crossroads caught his eye.

A jeep followed by six 2½-ton trucks had pulled up. One of the trucks had a smashed windscreen and a torn canopy. Behind them a line of Panzergrenadier half-tracks was coming to a halt. There were only three MPs in the jeep now. The burning Tiger, from which smoke was billowing across the landscape, had made them nervous. Apparently satisfied that the danger no longer existed, one of them walked back along the column to talk to an officer in a half-track.

Burman got off a contact report suggesting that the enemy infiltration party, with Panzergrenadier support, had the bridge at St-Bernard as their objective.

"Roger, over and out," was the laconic response.

The American vehicles were moving. They climbed the hill and drove past the house without spotting the M8 parked in its lee. The trucks, sheeted down, were driven by Germans. They disappeared round a bend, gathering speed as they headed for St-Bernard. The half-tracks remained where they were. Burman suspected that, to allay doubt, they would hang back until the infiltration party had secured the bridge, then reinforce them rapidly. He communicated his suspicions to the radio.

"Roger," said the voice. "Move now and watch yourself. Out!"

The half-tracks were moving. He ran down to the car.

"Get the gun over the tail!" he snapped at Follett as he clambered aboard. Evans was dozing in his seat. "Come on, move it! Out on to the road and turn right – give it all you've got!"

He loaded AP. As the car swung out he saw that the leading half-track was already approaching rapidly.

"Let him have it!"

Follett's shot was low but it took off one of the front wheels. The vehicle swerved off the road to crash into a tree. The next in line steered round it and came on. Their second shot glanced off the laid-back armour of the half-track's engine cover, flew along it to strike the front of the driving compartment and ricocheted upwards, smashing the commander's machine-gun mounting. Then they were round the bend and accelerating along an undulating road between wide fields. As the car was much faster than its opponents, Burman halted from time to time to get off further shots at their pursuers. The Germans had now opened up with their machine-guns and although they frequently blocked one another's line of fire they had begun hitting the car.

"Misfire!" shouted Follett during their third pause.

Burman ejected the round, tossing it over the side, and inserted another, reflecting on the wrath this would have provoked in his gunnery instructor.

"Misfire!" shouted Follett again. The fault must lie in the gun and this was certainly not the time to deal with it.

"Okay, use the coax and keep firing!" said Burman. The .30 machine-gun began to stutter bursts. In dead ground he manned the big .50, watching the traces curve towards the enemy and the sparkle of strikes. This, he thought, was too much like old Jethro Burman firing his Winchester over his shoulder as he out-galloped pursuing Apaches, but now the image was neither romantic nor comfortable.

Unexpectedly, the leading half-track jerked to a standstill and burst into flames. Those behind scattered into hollows on both sides of the road. As he realised that the pursuit was over he felt a hand tugging at his ankle.

"Village ahead!" shouted Kramer. "Looks like trouble!"

With his attention fully occupied with what had been going on behind, Burman had forgotten that they were approaching St-Bernard.

"Halt!"

They were just beyond the outskirts of the village, which straggled down the hill towards the river. He could see several armoured vehicles among the houses, but what drew his attention lay in the main street. There, a jeep and six trucks, one of the latter burning, lay riddled where they had been brought to a standstill. Around them, in their white, snow smocks and helmets, lay the bodies of their German occupants. A smaller number carrying their wounded were being pushed into a group at gunpoint.

"Some ambush!" he said, easing himself up on to the turret roof. "Let's go, but keep it real slow."

A tracked tank destroyer emerged from between two houses to block their path, its gun swinging menacingly towards them.

"Move another foot and I'll blow your ass back down the road!" shouted the commander.

Men swarmed from nowhere over the car, their guns at the ready. For several minutes they questioned each member of the crew about different aspects of American life and sport. At length someone attracted the attention of an officer down the street.

"These guys are alright, Cap'n – let 'em through?"

The officer beckoned the car forward. He wore the orange flash of the Tank Destroyer Force, showing a panther crunching a tank in its jaws.

"What's your unit, corporal?"

"Third Platoon, Troop C, 222nd Cavalr, Reconnaissance Squadron, sir."

"We were warned to expect you, but as you probably know better than the rest of us, we can't be too careful. I'm really glad you fellows made it back."

Burman guessed that he was the rearguard commander, noting that most of his men were rallied troops from the 106th Division.

"Step over here a minute, will you?"

Burman dismounted and followed the officer to where one of the MPs was standing under armed guard, a little apart from the German prisoners. His two companions were lying dead by their jeep.

"Have you seen this man before, corporal?"

Burman remembered the thin features and rimless glasses well. He described their previous encounters.

"That does it – I'm giving you one minute to say a prayer," said the captain to the prisoner.

"I am a German officer and I demand to be treated as such within the terms of the Geneva and Hague Conventions," replied the man confidently.

"You don't demand anything. You knew you forfeited those rights when you put on an American uniform. You'll get a firing squad and that's all."

The prisoners watched impassively as the man was stood against a wall and executed. Then they were marched under escort down the street towards the bridge. The captain turned towards Burman again.

"You can get on your way, corporal. We're pulling out now and I'd be glad if you'd tell the engineers at the bridge that my tank destroyers will be last across."

"Yes, sir." Burman saluted and returned to the car. Crossing the bridge, he passed the message to the engineer lieutenant in charge, who simply nodded. The infantry, covered by the tank destroyers, were already filing down the street.

There were just a few miles left for them to travel. A dull explosion told them that the bridge had gone up. There was now a river and a rearguard between them and the enemy. It was a different world here, reflected Burman. At last someone was in charge and, whoever it was, he was determined to make a stand. They passed tanks moving forward and, once, an artillery battery in action. As they neared the town he saw more and more troops wearing the flash of the 7th Armored Division.

Once again, it was a snowy dusk. It was at this time of day, long, long ago it seemed, he had received a battered Christmas cake. He wondered what had happened to it, and suddenly wanted a piece more than anything else in the world.

The Battle of the Bulge was the greatest pitched battle to be fought by the US Army in Europe during the Second World War. Like every such strategic battle it included a number of smaller actions bitterly contested at the operative and tactical levels, of which the epic defence of Bastogne by the 101st Airborne Division and attached units, and the loss of two of 106th Infantry Division's regiments, isolated on the Schnee Eifel by a pincer movement, have naturally attracted most attention.

These dramatic events have tended to eclipse what was taking place elsewhere. In particular, the few hundred cavalrymen screening the Losheim Gap, hopelessly outnumbered, did all that could have been expected of them, holding their outposts until overwhelmed, reporting the enemy's progress and imposing such delay as was within their power. These delays enabled reinforcements from the 7th Armored Division to reach St-Vith, a communications centre as important to the northern sector of the front as Bastogne was to the southern. The German time-table demanded that General Hasso von Manteuffel's Fifth Panzer Army should capture St-Vith by the evening of 17 December; in fact, the last American defenders did not withdraw from the area until 23 December. The following day Manteuffel, seeing no future in Hitler's planned advance on Antwerp, recommended that the German Army should abandon its offensive and withdraw behind the Siegfried Line. His advice was ignored and a month later St-Vith was back in American hands.

The strategic surprise achieved by the Germans on the first day of the battle did indeed cause the sort of confusion I have attempted to describe. Infiltration parties wearing American uniforms aggravated the situation; some were caught and executed. Despite these disadvantages, small *ad hoc* groups of locally-led Americans, consisting of a few tanks, armoured cars, tank destroyers and rallied infantrymen, succeeded in inflicting unacceptable loss and delay on the advancing enemy. If the reader has found difficulty in accepting that a small M8 armoured car could destroy a mighty Tiger tank, the US Army Armor School's paper *The Battle at St-Vith 17–23 December 1944* describes an engagement in very similar circumstances, the victor being an M8 of Troop B, 87th Cavalry Reconnaissance Squadron.

RIFLEMAN JAMES WOOD,

Royal Barset Rifles, Malaya, 1956

Jim Wood had never wanted to be a soldier, but he accepted that it was just something you did. His grandfather and father had served respectively in what they called the Great War and the Second World War, and now, aged eighteen, he was required to perform his National Service.

Four years earlier he had left school and become apprenticed to a printer. He felt bitter that just when all his work and study were about to pay off, the state demanded that he spend two years of his life in a totally alien environment. On the other hand, the experience would place him on a level footing with the older men of his family, whose general conversation made it clear that those who had never served in uniform were not quite their equals. On the Sunday before he reported for duty the family held a birthday tea for him, but it was not a festive occasion.

"You'll make some grand mates," his father said by way of encouragement. "Be a man before you know it!"

"How would you know?" asked his grandfather. "All you had was a boys' war!"

"Teach your lot a thing or two!" retorted his father, who had fought his way from Normandy to the Baltic. "Just better organised, that's all!"

Incomprehensibly, they both roared with laughter.

"Anyway, Jim," said his grandfather, "You'll be the third generation of us to join the Rifles – they're a good lot, take my word for it."

"Pity they're in Malaya." Until now his mother had sat silently at the end of the table. "Means we won't see much of you."

Her husband knew exactly what she meant.

"Well, not for a while, maybe. Still, they seem to have got the situation under control out there. Why, there's blokes coming home now who never saw a commie in their whole tour of duty!"

Nevertheless, though no one spoke of it, the enemy remained capable of mounting ambushes and every few weeks *The Barchester Chronicle* would report that a local man had been killed or wounded.

Jim had walked past Minden Barracks, the Depot of the Royal Barset Rifles, countless times without giving a thought to what went on inside. On the following Thursday he reported for duty there and, although he had been warned what to expect, the reality of his basic training was still a shock. Most of his hair was removed by the regimental barber and he was subjected to numerous injections by the medical staff. Then, day by day and week by week, he was chased by sergeants and corporals through an apparently endless routine of drill, weapon training, physical training, lectures, assault courses, map reading, boot polishing, brass shining and blancoing of webbing. Finding himself in the company of young men from every conceivable walk and condition of life, he suddenly discovered that he needed their help to get by, that the reverse also applied, and so a sense of comradeship began to grow. The constant exercise gave him a voracious appetite so that he filled out. His recruit intake was divided into two platoons which competed against each other in every field, the result being that even the most reluctant of the new arrivals was forced to give of his best or face the wrath of his comrades. Gradually, the civilian was replaced by the young soldier as he began to think and act in the Army's way. Some of the recruits were Regulars whose pay was twice that of the conscripts' 28 shillings per week. A few of the latter, unable to manage, enlisted on a three-year engagement and others, finding the life agreed with them after all, did likewise.

The end of the recruits' basic training was marked by a passing-out parade attended by their families. Conscious that they had just emerged from one of the most testing times of their lives, they swung past the saluting-base with a real sense of pride, their turnout now immaculate. After the parade there was tea, sandwiches and cake for everyone in the cookhouse. Suddenly, Jim's parents were confronted with a young man who was somehow bigger, fitter and more self-confident than the nervous youth who had left home weeks earlier.

"You'll do!" said his grandfather.

"Oh, he'll do alright!" said his father, and they both shook his hand as though welcoming him to an exclusive club. Even his mother said that uniform suited him and his younger brother and sister basked in reflected glory beside him when his photograph was taken.

Forty-eight hours' leave followed, during which he felt strangely adrift between two worlds, not wanting to go back yet missing the comradeship and the shared experience. On the Saturday he went to a dance. There were several other members of the intake there and they greeted each other like long-lost relatives, spending their pay on large quantities of beer. Later he walked a girl home and promised to see her on his next leave. As he turned in for the night he heard his parents talking in the next room.

"What now?" asked his mother.

"Well, I was talking to his sergeant and he says there'll be some sort of course. After that, he'll get embarkation leave then he's off to Malaya to join the First Battalion."

"They send them out too young – he's hardly more than a boy."

"No, he's not a boy any more, Sal. He'll take it in his stride, you'll see – and he's got a good home and job to come back to."

The course was designed to provide preparation for what might be expected in Malaya. It included lectures which described how the communist terrorists, referred to as CTs, were almost exclusively Chinese and how they had been placed on the defensive in recent years. This had been achieved by isolating them from their supporters among the numerous Chinese squatters who had been living in camps on the edge of the jungle since the economic recession of the 1930s. The squatters had been moved into New Villages, where they had been given construction materials, the title to their property and 100 dollars. Each village had a school, a clinic and shops, and was protected by a perimeter fence and a police post. Food was allowed in but none was allowed out. At a stroke, the measure dealt with many Chinese grievances and support for the CTs dwindled to the extent that many of their gangs were forced to disperse into smaller units in order to feed themselves. Furthermore, many CTs, half-starved, their resolve weakened by dropped leaflets and broadcasts from low-flying aircraft that promised amnesty and reward, began to desert. Many were only too glad to talk, with the result that the remaining communist sympathisers in the New Villages suddenly found themselves rounded-up. Some were sent back into the jungle to talk erstwhile comrades round, and others guided security force patrols to their former bases. The result was that the CTs were forced even deeper into the jungle, where they had begun to grow some of their own food. That did not mean they were beaten, for those that remained were the hard core. They were, it was stressed, still capable of mounting ambushes and would take full advantage of any sign of weakness to resume their campaign of terror.

There was also further intensive training with the weapons most favoured in this type of warfare – the FN Self-Loading Rifle, generally referred to as the SLR, the Bren light machine-gun, the Australian Owen gun, the American M2 carbine, the Lanchester carbine, the 9mm Browning pistol, shotguns and the No 36 grenade. The intake drew tropical greens and received preliminary instruction on how to live in the jungle. They were surprised to learn, for example, that in many places it was impossible to sleep on the ground, so they practised what the instructors called 'bashing up' in pairs. This involved slinging hammocks between trees with parachute cord and rigging waterproof ponchos to keep off the rain, as well as pooling their mess tins to cook compo rations.

At the end of the course they were sent on embarkation leave. Jim saw something of the girl he had met at the dance. She was affectionate enough, gave him her photograph and promised to write, but after two weeks he lost interest in her. As his leave drew to a close he began to feel curiously alone, wanting to get on with whatever lay ahead of him. He asked his family not to accompany him to the barracks, for he had already seen too many mothers smiling brightly, then dissolve in tears once the transport had driven off, and he wished to spare his own that ordeal. Even so, his departure from home was bad enough.

Because of the Suez Crisis the troopship took the long route via the Cape, Mombasa, Aden and Colombo. The strange sights and sounds were interesting, taking his mind off home, what his friends might be doing and the lads at the printshop. There were daily runs around the deck and constant physical training periods intended to preserve the level of fitness. During daylight hours there was the regular rattle of small arms fired at floating balloons trailed over the stern.

Six weeks after leaving Southampton, the troopship docked at Singapore. After a short spell at Nee Soon transit camp, Jim's draft, together with those for other regiments, were transported to the Jungle Warfare Training Centre at Kota Tinggi in Johore. There they learned of the different environments in which they might find themselves – swamp, rubber plantations, secondary jungle, which was cleared land that had been allowed to revert and was now covered in dense undergrowth teeming with red ants, and primary jungle in which huge trees reached skywards, their canopies blotting out the sun so that the dappled ground below always remained wet. They learned how to live and move in these conditions and how to cope with the frightening sense of disorientation which the jungle produced; how to set up platoon bases and ambush sites and how to patrol; how to read animal and bird behaviour that betrayed the near presence of other humans; and how to rely on the senses of sight, hearing and smell for their own survival. They learned how to employ the same stratagem as bird watchers entering a hide, noisily inserting a platoon into a suspect area and then ostentatiously withdrawing it a day or so later, leaving behind an ambush section that would lie beside a trail until its prey returned. They learned that if ambushed themselves they must respond with every weapon at their disposal and win back the initiative. They learned, too, the cruel fact of jungle warfare that wounding could produce better results than killing, for a wounded man needed the support of two or possibly four of his comrades to carry him to safety, and that the blood slicks he left might lead to a terrorist hideout. On this point they were assured that their own wounded would be picked up by ambulance on the nearest road or lifted out by helicopter from a suitable clearing.

The course lasted four weeks, culminating in a four-day exercise during which the various skills acquired were tested. The drafts then dispersed to their regiments, Jim and several others from his intake being sent to their C Company in Selangor. There, they were issued with regimental and divisional flashes to sew on their uniforms, and razor-sharp, locally-made parangs that were considered superior to the standard machete and had endless uses.

Three days later he went out on his first patrol, which was made in platoon strength. The course at Kota Tinggi had taught him what to expect, and although CTs had been encountered on the training area in the past, the presence of the instructors had given him a feeling of security. Now, for the first time, he was acting in deadly earnest. After passing through some rubber plantations and cutting their way through a belt of dense secondary growth, the patrol entered the jungle proper. He had been thoroughly briefed, but once the trees closed round he had no idea where he was or where he was going. The smell of decaying vegetation was intensified by heat and humidity. His greens were soon soaked with sweat and his equipment chafed. Birds shrieked and monkeys chattered as they crashed about in the canopy far above. Small things rustled in the undergrowth which he knew might conceal men waiting in ambush. His mouth became dry and his limbs heavy. For a few moments he came close to panic, then instinctively recognised that he was safer where he was. The rest of the patrol, their faces expressionless, seemed to know exactly what they were doing. Weapons loaded, they moved slowly and softly, looking alternately to left and right, forward, above and behind. In single file, they traversed the narrow trail in total silence, orders being communicated by hand signal passed down the line.

After an hour the platoon commander ordered a halt and, having posted sentries, allowed the men to smoke. It was during this break that Jim felt his sanity returning. The others, he discovered, were far from being unfriendly. Over half of them were National Servicemen like himself, and some had only a little time left to do. Talking in low voices, they asked where he came from and what his job was. Soon it was apparent that they knew many of the same people and places and did many of the same things. He began to look forward to these hourly halts, suddenly glad that if he had to do this at least he was among his own people.

During these breaks he noticed a surprising number of pipes protruding from young faces. Pipes, he was told, were more trouble, but they were better than cigarettes for keeping the clouds of flying insects at bay. Cigarettes also became soggy unless one took special precautions. They were, however, the only effective means of persuading leeches to release their grip, as he discovered that evening when the platoon established its base. To his disgust, he found two of them, apparently picked up when the platoon had forded a short stretch of swamp, firmly fastened to his legs. The little ones were the most dangerous, warned the old hands. Given the chance, they said, they would make themselves at home inside a penis; some blokes were so worried about it that they wore a condom on patrol. Less dangerous but equally startling were the huge variety of ground insects, some of which were enormous. Known collectively as 'weirdies', many were of such strange shapes that Jim wondered for what purpose the Almighty had intended them. Still, they seemed oblivious of the humans and bustled about their business without bothering anyone.

The platoon was out for ten days during which it was supplied by air. Having established its base, it split into smaller patrols which combed the surrounding area and manned ambush sites on trails known to be used by the CTs. During these there were times when whoever was commanding the patrol prohibited smoking. Jim found this hard, but during his fourth day he discovered why it was essential. His patrol, commanded by the platoon sergeant, was proceeding along a trail when the smell of tobacco brought it to a standstill. The source could only be a CT and, after deciding from which direction it was coming, the sergeant silently ordered the men to form an assault line on both sides of the trail. Weapons levelled, the line advanced stealthily. At the critical moment, however, the signaller's radio crackled into life with a routine check. There was the sound of frantic scrambling in the undergrowth ahead. Cursing, the sergeant fired several rounds from his carbine, but no blood slicks or any other trace of the smoker could be found. This was the platoon's only direct contact with the enemy, although one day a patrol was sent to a CT cultivation patch detected by an Auster light observation aircraft in a small clearing, destroying the crop with its parangs.

Accompanying the platoon was an Iban tracker from Borneo who wore a corporal's stripes. The jungle was his natural element and Jim was fascinated by his ability to make a meal out of whatever was to hand, including the occasional snake. He would laugh uproariously at almost anything, but the old hands respected his tracking ability and said he was viciously efficient in a scrap. Naturally, he spent much time with the platoon commander. One day towards the end of the operation Jim was close enough to hear their conversation as they discussed some faint marks at a trail junction.

"How many?" asked the officer.

The Iban examined the tracks more closely, held up three fingers, then one finger.

"Three feller, one woman belong."

"Little bit long time gone?"

The Iban examined the surface of the tracks, then felt the depth of the heel marks.

"Plenty long time gone. Three, four days, maybe."

"Plenty carry?"

The tracker nodded. "Plenty."

So that was it. They had stumbled on the trail of a CT food-carrying party. This was further investigated for some distance in both directions and the matter was reported by radio. As a result, they learned later, a clandestine supply of rice had been seized in a tapper's hut and the tapper was given a prison sentence.

It was the rain which Jim disliked most. It fell in torrents unimaginable at home, drowning every other sound and making speech almost impossible. Long after it had stopped, huge drops continued to thud down from the canopy above. Jim had entertained vague hopes that he might march in from his first patrol like a conquering hero; instead, he returned to camp unshaven and looking like a drowned rat.

Three days later he was out again. Thereafter, the weeks began to blur into a series of long patrols, short patrols and manning ambush sites, all without incident. He was never as afraid of the jungle again as he had been during that first terrible hour, but he retained a healthy respect for it. On balance, he preferred to be out and doing rather than in camp, even if it simply meant manning the checkpoints where the bags of anyone leaving the local New Village were searched for food or other items which might be useful to the CTs.

Throughout, the Company had no hard contact with the enemy. Rumour had it that the battalion's commanding officer, and the company commander, too, were getting restive about this. The CTs were certainly out there, for only recently a patrol from the Cumberland Fusiliers had been ambushed with the loss of two killed and three wounded, while a night attack on a jungle base held by a platoon from the brigade's Gurkha battalion had been foiled when one of the enemy blundered into a trip grenade. In return, both the Fusiliers and

Gurkhas were producing a slow but steady score of kills and captures. The members of C Company could only shrug and comment that if the CTs had gone elsewhere it was hardly their fault.

Jim had been with the Company for about six weeks when he received a letter in the unformed, childish hand of his girlfriend. Usually her letters covered a single page with difficulty and described the latest acquisition in her range of make-up. The content of this, however, was different and he read it with a sense of relief.

'My Dearest Jim,
This is a very difficult letter for me to write as you see I have met someone else who I love and think a lot of. So you see we cannot go on as we are. I know you are doing your bit and want to help so will write again if you want as I know you like getting my letters. Try to forgive me and write soon.
    Yours faithfully,
    Celeste XXX'

"Well, that's that then," he said, removing her photograph from his bedside locker.

"What's this?" asked Andy Fowler from the next bed. "You had a Dear John?"

Jim and Andy had been together since their basic training.

"Read it," said Jim, "and before you ask, the answer's No I won't be writing back."

Andy read the letter and burst out laughing.

"Oh dear, oh dear, you're well out o' that, mate! Tell you what, I'll get my sister Susan to write to you. She's seventeen and I reckon you two would really get on."

During their first period of Rest and Recuperation they went into Kuala Lumpur. Jim had his photograph taken, sending one copy to his parents and giving another to Andy to pass on to his sister. A month later he received a letter enclosing a picture of a fair-haired girl with a pretty, open, smiling face.

"She's nice," he said.

"Course she's nice – she's my sister, isn't she?" retorted Andy. "You mind what you say to her, now!"

Susan wrote long, interesting letters, telling him about herself, what she was doing and what was happening in Barchester. Jim found her easy to reply to and wrote equally long letters whenever he could.

One morning his platoon had just come in from a long patrol when a grey car drew up outside Company Headquarters. It belonged to Inspector Butler, the Special Branch officer at the local police post, a regular visitor, and therefore attracted little attention. Half an hour later, however, as the men were showering, shaving and changing into clean greens, the Company Sergeant-Major appeared in the basha's doorway.

"Alright, Seven Platoon, don't make yourselves too comfortable – you're going out again!"

There were howls of protest but the CSM was adamant.

"Sorry, lads, but there's no one else – Eight Platoon are out, Nine Platoon are getting ready to go out and you're needed. Outside in fifteen minutes, short patrol order, two days' rations! And make it *jaldi!*"

They were briefed by the platoon commander.

"Last night a female CT named Ah Min gave herself up to the police. She was the long-term mistress of the local District Secretary, Lu Chan, who we know is a very nasty piece of work. Recently, he's taken up with another female CT, Soo Chong, who is an even nastier piece of work. Ah Min now hates his guts and is willing to lead us to his camp. It seems that he's got seven or eight CTs with him and apparently he's been trying to set up a new District Headquarters in our area, which may explain why we've been left alone for a while. Before we move off, are there any questions?"

"Could this be a set-up, sir?" asked the platoon sergeant.

"The police don't think so. Anyway, we've got to take that chance before the lady cools down."

A truck dropped them five miles from the camp at a point where the road was joined by a secondary track leading into a rubber plantation. Inspector Butler was waiting for them with two Malay policemen and a Chinese woman of indeterminate age in a ragged khaki uniform.

"My, but she's ugly," said Andy. "Can't blame old Lu Chan for kicking her out of bed!"

"Have to take what you can get in the jungle, I suppose."

The Inspector walked across to the platoon.

"Just in case you're worried we're going to walk into something, our informant has been told she'll be the first to die – that's why my constables are here. I think this is on the level, though, and we'll get a result."

They marched for two miles along the secondary track until they reached a stream flowing through a culvert. They turned up the right bank of the stream and soon the jungle closed round them. For two hours they trudged on in total silence. Then, at about 1400, they halted where a smaller tributary joined the main stream from the left, running down a long re-entrant between two spurs. Very quietly, the platoon commander briefed each of the sections in turn. Ah Min had indicated that the CT camp lay beyond the head of the re-entrant and warned that there was a sentry post at the top of the right-hand spur. The sergeant and several riflemen would seal off the bottom of the re-entrant; No 1 Section was to line the right-hand spur at 20-yard intervals, taking care not to alert the sentry post; No 2 Section would similarly line the left-hand spur; the assault party, consisting of himself, the Inspector and No 3 Section, which included Jim and Andy, would be guided by Ah Min to a point beyond the CT camp. The idea was that the assault would drive the occupants of the camp down into the natural killing-ground formed by the re-entrant. He had allowed two hours for everyone to get into position and the assault would go in at 1600. They synchronised their watches.

The going was far harder than anything Jim had experienced. The slope was extremely steep but it was its surface, still slimy from the previous night's rain, that caused most of the trouble. Jungle boots scrabbled ineffectively, sliding back two feet for every yard gained. Normally, one could have hauled oneself upward with the aid of saplings, but any disturbance of the foliage above would have been seen by the watchful occupant of the sentry post. Here and there one of the panting men fell heavily. Jim thought that the noise they were making would long since have scared off their prey. Luck was with them, however, for it began to rain, drowning every other sound. Once they were level with the head of the re-entrant they made much better progress, guided by Ah Min with a police pistol at her head. When they had covered a further 300 yards the informant indicated that they should swing to the right, then told them to halt when they were approximately level with the re-entrant.

They lay down in their assault line while the platoon commander disappeared stealthily into the undergrowth. Five minutes later he was back, holding his thumb up and then five fingers to indicate that they were in the correct position and that the perimeter of the enemy camp was fifty yards away.

Jim's watch told him that there were fifteen minutes to go. His stomach began to flutter with apprehension. Time seemed to drag, yet every time he looked at his watch it seemed to have leapt forward. The rain continued to batter down and, uncaring, the weirdies got on with whatever they were doing.

At 1557 the platoon commander rose to his feet. The assault line did likewise, moving forward at his signal. Once again, Jim felt the terrible heaviness in his legs. He was conscious of vines clawing at his equipment as he fought a powerful desire to hang back. He wondered if Andy and the others were as frightened as he was. Glancing along the slowly moving line, he saw only determined faces and levelled weapons and knew there could be no turning back if he wanted to live with himself. There was a glimpse of daylight ahead and then they were in the camp itself.

"CHARGE!" yelled the platoon commander.

Firing as they went, they broke into a run. They must have taken the enemy completely by surprise, for all Jim could see was a man stirring a pot under a waterproof sheet and several makeshift bashas in which the CTs were obviously sheltering from the rain. The same thought clearly occurred to others, for even as the cook went down, shot through the chest while reaching for his weapon, there was a shout of "Hit the bashas!"

The flimsy structures were raked with fire. A man with a Sten raced from one but was dropped before he could use it. Another, carrying a Lee-Enfield, emerged and was shot dead. Two more appeared with their hands raised.

"Dickens, Warner and Doyle, secure the prisoners!" shouted the platoon commander. "The rest of you, keep moving – follow through and clear the bashas on the way!"

Another CT, badly wounded, was found writhing in agony on his bedding. As they neared the far side of the clearing Jim had a momentary impression of a small, khaki-clad figure darting across the few yards separating the last of the bashas from the jungle. By the time he entered the trees it had gone, but it had seemed to be running in the direction of the sentry post.

What happened next took only seconds, but he was always to remember it in horrifying slow motion. There was a rattle of fire to his left front, which he took to be No 1 Section eliminating the sentry. Then, the khaki figure reappeared, just twenty yards away, running hard. It was wearing a sort of floppy cap with a red star on the front. Seeing him, it swerved, stumbled and lost its footing. The cap fell off and long black hair cascaded around a woman's shoulders. Teeth bared and eyes projecting a murderous hatred, her expression remained with him as a mask of evil incarnate. He got off one round from his SLR but, agile as a cat, she had already rolled and had a pistol levelled at him. He saw its muzzle flash then fired again as she scrambled to her feet. The round hit her in the left shoulder and she went over backwards with a yelp of pain. He closed in, saw the pistol flash once more, and fired six rounds into her, hearing the succession of thuds as they struck home. From his left there came the sound of running feet. His nerves tightened to breaking-point, he instinctively swung the rifle round to meet his new assailant.

"It's me, Jim! Easy lad, for Christ's sake!"

The shock of what he had done left him temporarily speechless, but he was glad Andy was there. They stared down at the woman. Blood was soaking into the rain-sodden khaki drill from wounds in her stomach, chest, shoulder and throat. The snarl had become the sardonic smile of death, but her eyes remained open and fixed Jim's with their unwinking, malevolent stare. The platoon commander and the inspector arrived, bringing Ah Min with them.

"You all right, Wood?" asked the officer.

"Yessir," he replied mechanically.

The inspector pushed Ah Min forward and pointed to the corpse.

"Soo Chong?"

"Yes, Soo Chong!"

The woman smiled happily and spat on the body of her rival.

"Charming!" said Andy. Jim, unspeaking, continued to stare down at the dead face, still conveying its message of hatred.

"You've done us all a favour, lad – well done," said the inspector. He seemed to understand what was troubling Jim and bent down, closing the eyes. That seemed to break the spell.

The attack had yielded six CTs killed, including one who died from his wounds shortly after, and two prisoners. Ah Min said that Lu Chan was not among them. The police collected numerous documents and maps from the bashas, giving full details of CTs' district organisation. While the platoon commander spent some time on the radio, the rest of the men cooked themselves a compo meal.

"Looked at you on the way in," said Andy. "Knew you were spoiling for a scrap – ferocious bastard!"

"I was scared stiff, if you really want to know," said Jim.

"That makes two of us, mate!"

At length the platoon commander called them together.

"There'll be a Gurkha platoon from Brigade Reserve along to relieve us presently – if Lu Chan hasn't turned up by then they'll lay on a welcome home party for him. We're to march out with the prisoners. A Home Guard carrying party will bring out the bodies."

Two days later, back in camp, they were told that the Gurkhas had picked up Lu Chan, who had offered no resistance. The operation, therefore, had been a complete success. Jim was ordered to report to Company HQ, where the major told him that he had he would be receiving a Mention in Despatches. The news did not altogether please him.

"Will this get in the papers, sir?"

"Sure to."

"Then if it's all the same to you, sir, I'd rather do without it."

"Why?"

"Well, sir, I shot a woman and I'm not proud of it. I don't want people at home reading about it."

"I respect your feelings, Wood, but this isn't a gentleman's war. The late Soo Chan had fifteen murders to her credit and she tortured her own people, women as well as men, without mercy. We've a file on her that would freeze your blood. In her eyes, she was a soldier, so let's leave it at that, shall we?"

"I don't know, sir. It just seems wrong, somehow."

"I understand how you feel, because that's the way we were brought up. We've allowed for it in the report and you may feel better once you've read it."

Jim looked through the report and found that the only reference to himself was contained in a single sentence.

"The senior terrorist in the camp, a prominent member of the communist district organisation suspected of several murders, attempted to escape into the jungle but was pursued by Private J. R. Wood and killed during an exchange of fire."

"That's what happened, wasn't it?" asked the major. "As far as everyone here is concerned the fact that Soo Chan was a woman just doesn't come into it."

"Yes, sir. Well, I suppose put like that it's alright."

It would take some time for the Mention to be posted on orders and Jim did not speak of it. However, three weeks later he entered the basha to be greeted by a hail of boots and yells of good-natured banter.

"Who's a bloody hero, then?" shouted Andy, handing him an airmailed copy of *The Barchester Chronicle*. On the front page was an article, illustrated with the photograph he had sent to his parents.

"BARSETS' MALAYAN SUCCESS

"TERRORIST GANG WIPED OUT

"BARCHESTER MAN KILLS CHIEF

"Acting upon information received, a patrol of C Company Royal Barset Rifles, led by Lieutenant Nigel Egerton, executed a well-planned attack on the jungle base of a ruthless terrorist gang a fortnight ago. Most of the terrorists were killed and two were taken prisoner. The elimination of the gang has effectively destroyed communist influence throughout the area. No casualties were sustained by the Barsets.

"During the fighting the senior terrorist in the camp attempted to escape into the jungle but was pursued by 18-year-old Rifleman James Wood and killed in single combat. Rifleman Wood, a National Serviceman, lives with his parents at 20 Station Road, Barchester and is a printer with one of the city's oldest established firms, Holt & Company."

Although he took part in countless more patrols and setting of ambushes, Jim Wood never saw another terrorist. As the months passed and the platoon's personnel turned over he acquired a lance-corporal's stripe and sometimes led his section on operations. Life assumed a rhythm, then, quite suddenly it seemed, his intake became due for release. It surprised them all that the Regulars were genuinely sorry to see them go.

"Civvy Street's the real jungle, lads – you're better off here with your mates! You'll be back!"

Once again, the troopship took the long route and because of this it was announced that National Servicemen due for discharge would, immediately on landing, proceed on disembarkation leave. At the end of this they would report to their depots, hand in their kit and receive Discharge papers formally ending the Regular phase of their service.

"Reckon you'll miss it?" asked Andy as they entered Southampton Water.

"You mean the leeches and lying out all night in the rain? Shouldn't think so. I'll miss the lads, though – they were a great bunch."

"We got three and a half years with the Territorials to do yet, so we'll keep up with some of them. You get a twenty quid bounty if you go in for four, so I'll do that, I think."

"Makes sense."

Tugs were fussing round the ship, nudging her into the same quay from which they had left all those months before. It was crowded with families and friends, all waving wildly, and a band was playing 'When Johnny Comes Home From War'.

"Great welcome!" said Jim. Then he saw his own family. It was strange, but his parents and grandfather seemed smaller than he remembered them. Perhaps it was because he was looking down at them – no, that couldn't be right, because his brother and sister seemed taller.

The band changed to a jerky version of 'Walkin' My Baby Back Home', which was more in keeping with the men's mood and was greeted with cheers. They were called to disembark and proceed through Customs by draft numbers. The Customs men were unsmiling but seemed little interested in the presents Jim had bought and thumbed him through. After he had drawn pay and ration allowance from the temporary Pay Corps office, he joined his family in the other half of the shed. They hugged him and wrung his hand and said how brown he was and how he'd grown and his mother said she'd got his favourite sausages for tea and they plucked at his stripe and fingered the Mention oakleaf on his General Service (Malaya) medal ribbon. They were still all talking at once when he felt a hand on his shoulder.

"There's someone here who wants a word with you, mate!" said Andy.

He found himself looking at blue eyes and the nicest smile he'd ever seen.

"Hello, Jim."

"Hello, Susan."

For a moment he couldn't think of a single sensible thing to say, so came out with what had already firmly impressed itself on his mind.

"You're much better looking than your picture."

"So are you," she said.

Jim Wood was typical of the young National Servicemen who saw active service not only in Malaya, but also in Korea, Kenya, Cyprus, Egypt and other trouble spots around the world. Their attitude was understandably ambivalent. They resented the fact that the Army was taking two years of their lives, but welcomed the chance to prove they were their fathers' sons. They were often irreverent of the Army's ways, but, for all their youth, they were extremely good soldiers and on active service they displayed qualities that earned them the sincere admiration of senior officers. When conscription finally ended, the Army was saddened to see them go.

The operational background to this chapter is based on that of the Royal Hampshire Regiment, which earned an enviable reputation during the Malayan Emergency. In February 1956 one of the regiment's platoons eliminated a terrorist gang in a manner very similar to that described.

The character of Soo Chong is based upon that of a real terrorist, Sieu Choy, otherwise known as the Bitch of Bentong. Originally a schoolmistress, she began her terrorist career as a member of the Li Ton Ten, enforcing the Party's discipline on the Chinese civilian population. Simple murder, however, was never enough for her; a natural sadist, she liked to emasculate her victims or slit their bellies as well. Her superiors thoroughly approved of the terrifying grip she had on the Chinese community, but when things became too hot for her she was forced to take to the jungle. Many regiments would dearly have loved to put paid to her account and at one stage a Royal West Kent patrol believed that it had put a round or two into her rump. Several Hampshire patrols came close to cornering her, but she always managed to slip away. Rumour had it that she was sent straight to hell by a patrol of the Somerset Light

Infantry; that her name does not appear among the regiment's list of female terrorists killed is not conclusive evidence either way. Like many another failed communist, she simply vanished into one of history's black holes.

PRIVATE JOE LUBNIK

US Artillery, Vietnam, 1968–1969

Private Joe Lubnik did not like Vietnam. It was hot, humid and dangerous, the people were unfriendly, their language unintelligible, and all the place names sounded the same. Nor did he like his own lifestyle. He had never wanted to be a soldier, the fire support base was claustrophobic, he was performing a boring mechanical function, and even when he was allowed local leave to Saigon everyone seemed to have an angle designed to rip him off. Nor was he interested in the war he was supposed to be fighting, believing it to be a local quarrel best left to the Vietnamese to settle among themselves. He was halfway through his tour in the country and couldn't get the next six months over quickly enough.

His parents had come to the United States from Yugoslavia shortly after the end of the Second World War and still spoke English with a strong Slovenian accent. As his father, a carpenter, had never experienced difficulty in finding work, the family enjoyed a standard of living that would have been impossible in the old country. They moved around for a while but now they had settled in a pleasant small town, like many another across the country. Joe was interested in art and hoped to develop his skills at university with a view to a career in graphic design.

Like all such towns, it had its senior citizens, some of whom were the more respected for having fought in foreign wars. Two of the most prominent of them used to spend the summer evenings on the verandah of one or other of their homes, re-fighting the Second World War and conversing with passing neighbours. One, he knew, had served with the Marine Corps in the Pacific and the other, it was said, had been awarded a battlefield commission while serving with an armoured cavalry outfit during the Battle of the Bulge. One evening, the latter had hailed him as he walked back from the drugstore.

"Hey, Joe, why don't you step up here and join us? Reckon he's old enough for a beer, Al?"

"Sure do, Ken. Why, he'll be off for his military service in a month or two. That's right, isn't it, Joe?"

"That's right, Mr Hogan," said Joe. "I guess there's no way round it."

The former cavalryman handed him a can. On occasion he could look very stern, as he did now.

"Well, maybe that's how it should be. If folks come to America to work hard and get themselves a decent life, then it's only right they be prepared to defend it. Isn't that fair?"

"Yes, Mr Burman, that's fair."

That wasn't quite how some of his contemporaries saw things at High School or in the drugstore. Their view was that the United States was wrong to impose its immense strength settling quarrels among foreigners, and that the government had no right to spend American lives in this way. As the involvement in Vietnam escalated into a full-scale war opinions polarised and began to harden. One or two declared that they would resist the draft and even go into hiding in Canada, but Joe did not support their extreme views.

During the next few weeks he joined the two veterans for a beer on several occasions. They bickered constantly but were obviously the best of friends.

"Pay no attention to what this tin can soldier says," said Al Hogan. "You join the Marine Corps and you'll have the best buddies a man can want."

"Hell, don't you do that!" retorted Ken Burman. "One leatherneck in town is enough! Take my advice and go for the Armor Corps – that's where you'll find the really intelligent people."

"Then how come you got mixed up with them?" asked Hogan.

And so it went on. Not wishing to offend either of them, Joe had opted for the artillery during the draft induction process, and been accepted. It was a decision he began to regret when his drill sergeant at boot camp had taken a dislike to him. Though good at his job in a bullying sort of way, Sergeant Harris's intellect and imagination were limited and he had clearly reached the upper limit of his promotion prospects. Realising this, he resented anyone with a brighter future. In particular, he resented conscripts, especially the better educated, hippies, immigrants, long hair, and The Beatles.

"Move your ass, Polack!" was his particular taunt for Lubnik.

"I'm not a Polack," Lubnik would reply at first.

"Yeah? You got a Polack name, you act like a Polack, I say you're a Polack! And you address me by rank, soldier!"

"Yes, sir, Sergeant Harris, sir!" responded Lubnik, standing rigidly to attention but feeling nothing but contempt for the man.

"You're insolent, Lubnik. I don't like insolence – most of all I don't like dumb insolence. You just earned yourself a week's extra duties in the mess hall!"

Harris all but killed whatever interest Lubnik may have had. He deliberately held him back, recommending him as an ammunition number on the M101 105mm howitzer when others were sent off to more demanding training. At length, when the time for posting came, Lubnik was summoned to the company commander's office, where Harris was standing beside the officer's desk, millboard in hand. Lubnik saluted, giving his name, rank and number.

"Yeah, Lubnik," said Harris, chuckling. "You're going to 'Nam, Lubnik!"

Lubnik felt his heart sink, but he said nothing.

"Nothing you wanna say?" Harris was gloating. "No questions you wanna ask?"

"I was just wondering, if I do really well, d'you think they'll make me a sergeant like you?"

Harris's face became suffused with rage and for a moment Lubnik thought that the NCO would strike him. The company commander's expression remained impassive.

"That will be all, Lubnik!"

"Yes, sir!"

Before flying out, the reinforcement draft underwent a short but intensive course of instruction. This included periods on orientation, very necessary in so heavily forested a country, jungle survival, field sanitation, perimeter defence of outposts and sentry duties. Significantly, half the course was devoted to ambush and counter-ambush drill.

In due course Lubnik was delivered to Fire Support Base Diamond, close to the Cambodian border. There he found the atmosphere more relaxed, friendly and helpful than he had expected. The officers and NCOs, in fact, tended to steer him out of trouble rather than into it. He began to take a more active interest in his surroundings. The fire support base, he learned, provided the answer to numerous tactical problems in a campaign where the terms front, rear and flank held no meaning whatever. It not only gave prompt and efficient all-weather fire support to troops operating in the surrounding terrain, but also enjoyed the mutual support of neighbouring FSBs if it came under attack, and vice versa. The two closest FSBs in their own complex were Ruby and Pearl, located within easy range of the M101 howitzers with which they were all armed. Each of the three FSBs deployed a battery and was protected by its own infantry company.

The base was laid out in a circle about 200 yards across. In the middle were the command post, the fire support co-ordination, communications and ground surveillance centres, aid post, administration offices and mess hall, all dug-in and sandbagged, an observation tower and a helicopter pad. Five of the six howitzers were emplaced in a five-pointed star with the sixth in its centre; each sandbagged emplacement contained ammunition racks, living quarters for the gun crew and a powder pit. Around the guns and command structures the infantry company was deployed in a series of small bunkers. Additional defence was provided by a pair of 81mm mortars, searchlights, trip-flares and Claymore anti-personnel mines, the last camouflaged in the area between the infantry and the outer perimeter, which consisted of triple-piled barbed wire.

"What happens if they break through?" Lubnik asked.

"Well, then we got a coupla surprises for them," said PFC Mitch Thompson, who had been deputed to see the new arrivals properly settled in. He pulled a projectile out of an ammunition rack.

"It's called Beehive. Contains eight thousand little darts. Turns just a few guys into a crowd – spreads 'em all over the place. Course, they don't like it and now they know what to expect they'll drop below the line of fire and crawl. That's when we start using Killer Junior."

"What's that?"

"Why that's just plain old-fashioned high explosive fused to air burst thirty feet above the ground. We can use it from as close in as two hundred yards way out to one thousand yards. It gets results, believe me."

"Say they get through that – what then?"

"Well, then it's down to you an' Old Faithful here." He slapped the butt of his M16 rifle.

Lubnik began to feel uneasy.

"Have you ever been attacked?"

"Once or twice in the last FSB. We been here a month now and nothing much has happened."

"Don't mean a thing," interjected Winston Ambrose, a big coloured soldier from Mississippi. "If Charlie does something, he's always got a reason – if he don't do something, then he's got a reason for that, too."

Charlie was the name given to their Viet Cong opponents, who usually belonged to locally recruited guerrilla groups. Most of the men in the base were respectful of Charlie, however small and scrawny he might be, because he had demonstrated his suicidal courage on numerous occasions.

"Charlie ain't really running things no more," commented Thompson. "Nowadays, it's the NVA, the North Vietnamese Army, who call the shots. In the end, it's all the same to us."

Hot and sweating, Lubnik made to remove his helmet and flak jacket until Thompson stopped him sharply.

"You leave 'em on – the Captain will kick your ass real hard if he sees you without 'em! Fact is, we may not have been attacked, but every so often we get incoming mortar shells and rockets. The guys without 'em are the ones we stretcher to the casevac whirlybird. Right, Winston?"

"Right on, man."

Gradually, Lubnik got to know the other members of the battery. Many were conscripts like himself serving a one-year tour in the theatre, so the comings and goings were constant. Some, he discovered, had also been through the bullying hands of Sergeant Harris and suffered far worse humiliations than he had himself, even physical violence, carefully administered so that it did not show. Harris had generated a store of hatred for himself and, thought Lubnik, in future it would be wise if he avoided some downtown areas of New York, Detroit, San Francisco and other cities.

The guns were in action some part of each day. He was told they were producing good results, but had no idea what they were firing at. Helicopter activity was constant as troops from their division were inserted into the jungle for specific operations, then lifted out. The number of kills recorded after each operation were posted regularly; they were sufficiently numerous for some to question who was doing all the fighting. After a while, the routine of passing ammunition and intoning fire orders with the others had a mesmeric effect. Daily, infantry patrols left the perimeter and disappeared into the jungle. Sometimes the rattle of small-arms fire would be heard, and sometimes they would return carrying a casualty or two of their own; more often than not these were caused by booby-traps such as sharpened bamboo stakes, known as *panjis*, hidden in a camouflaged pit on a trail, or by trip-wire grenades. It was reassuring that the injured men were so quickly evacuated by helicopter, but such incidents proved that hidden eyes were always watching the base. Once, the infantry brought in a wounded Charlie, who was promptly flown out for interrogation; he was wearing the black pyjamas Lubnik had heard so much about, and he looked impossibly young. Again, as Thompson had predicted, salvos of three or four mortar bombs would land in the base from time to time. Although they caused little damage and only minor casualties, they kept people on edge, as the enemy intended.

The base soon began to feel like a prison bounded by the jungle with its own strange animal noises and the known but hidden menace of the enemy presence. Once a week a heavily escorted truck went to the nearest village to purchase supplies of fresh vegetables, a duty which Lubnik drew from time to time. Although the village had been declared 'friendly' he thought the description inaccurate. The villagers were glad enough of the money but that was as far as it went. Every attempt to strike up a conversation with the girls, some of whom he thought were remarkably pretty, was met with flat, expressionless stares. Around the village there were plenty of people working in the fields under their conical straw hats; few bothered so much as to glance up as the Americans drove by.

"Lotta those guys are VC," Thompson told him. "Work on the farm during the day, then at night it's on with the old pyjamas and off for a spot of back shooting and murder. Can't prove anything and, like you saw, nobody's talking."

The officers did their best to maintain morale with organised sports, supplemented by nightly film shows and other activities in the mess hall. There was also a rota for two-day local leave in Saigon. Once it had obviously been a beautiful French colonial city, but now it was a place of flaring neon signs, hookers, over-priced drinks and tacky souvenirs where everyone was willing to do anything, for a price.

Quite soon after his arrival Lubnik had realised that the boredom would rot his mind unless he did something about it. At his request his parents sent him a set of water-colours and paper. He was, therefore, able to spend much of his off-duty time sketching the various aspects of life in the base, becoming a popular figure as people began to recognise themselves. He sold most of his work at modest prices; the battery commander, Captain Holder, bought several, commenting that in days to come he could boast of having an original, signed Lubnik over his mantelpiece.

Five months into his tour there were two developments. First, the old M101 howitzer, which had served the Army well since the Second World War, was replaced by the M102. The older hands, who had grown up with the weapon, were sorry to see it go but were forced to concede that the new howitzer was lower, lighter and could be traversed on its carriage across a far wider arc without the need to shift the trail. Against this, the M102's breech was much lower, which meant that serving it over a protracted period was back-breaking. During such engagements the usual breech number would be relieved from time to time by other members of the detachment.

"Y'all goin' up in the world!" said Ambrose to Lubnik the first time he performed the duty.

The second development was the unexpected arrival of Harris to replace one of the administration sergeants whose tour was up. The atmosphere within the battery changed suddenly as he proceeded to make his presence felt. He seemed unable to grasp that there was a real difference between life at boot camp and life on active service, laying about him with extra duty awards and formal charges for minor infringements to which a blind eye had previously been turned. The officers, aware of the situation, were unable to do much about it as he always acted within the law, which he often quoted to them.

Lubnik was sitting at a table in the mess hall when Harris, turning out of the chow line with his tray, spotted him. Leering, the sergeant walked across.

"Well, if it isn't Lubnik, the little Polack with the big mouth!"
Lubnik did not reply.

"You got nothing to say, Polack? That's wise, real wise – 'cos I got some things I wanna say to you! Know what I mean?"

At that moment Lubnik's gun commander, Sergeant Gus Lane, left his table across the aisle and strolled over. He was a lot bigger, fitter and younger than Harris and there was an unpleasant look in his eye.

"Harris, you listen, because I'm going to tell you something," he said, prodding the other in the chest. "You stay right away from my boys or you get a bust in the mouth, understand? Now, if you don't like that, just say so – then we'll step outside and sort it out."

"What's the big deal?" asked Harris innocently. "The kid and I go way back. I was just funnin' – he knows that!"

"That so? I like fun, too. I think this is funny."

He tipped Harris's tray so that meat, vegetables, gravy and ice cream cascaded down his immaculate combat fatigues. Cursing vilely, Harris flung down the tray and strode out of the mess hall, pursued by laughter.

"Thanks, Sarge, but that was my fight," said Lubnik.

"You couldn't win," replied Lane. "Stay out of his way. Now finish your chow, you've got fuses to count."

Harris did not forget this incident. He made life as difficult as he could for the section, which found itself doing more than its share of battery duties, although he always had a plausible explanation. It also found that some of its mail from home had been tampered with or mysteriously gone astray. Rumours began circulating that Harris would arrange favours in exchange for payment, and that he was trading stores with the villagers during the vegetable run, though nothing could be proved.

During the next month enemy activity around the base increased steadily. Intelligence sources suggested the probability of an attack on the base. Additional Claymore mines were emplaced around the perimeter and security was tightened. The atmosphere grew tense. Lubnik remembered that the old soldiers back home had said that war was ninety-nine per cent utter boredom and one per cent sheer terror, reflecting that waiting around for something to happen wasn't too pleasant either.

When it did happen, it was without warning. At about midnight the base was hit by mortar fire, accompanied by rockets whose fiery trails converged from different points in the jungle. There were explosions all over the interior of the base. As the gun crew tumbled out of their accommodation bunker they could hear the infantry opening fire on the north-east sector of the perimeter. The searchlight snapped on and was promptly shot out. Seconds later there came the coughing of the base's own mortars as they put up illuminating rounds, followed by the battery's own No 6 howitzer. The whole scene was bathed in eerie, flickering light. The sound of firing died away.

"Sounds like we held 'em," said Lubnik hopefully.

"No," Lane replied flatly. "That was the diversion. The big one could come in anywhere, just about now."

It came in on their own southern sector. The Claymores were suddenly activated, blasting thousands of ball bearings in spreading cones towards the perimeter wire, from which came the sound of screams. Simultaneously, the nearest infantry bunkers opened fire. Once again, the illuminating rounds soared aloft, revealing what seemed to be hundreds of men cutting their way through the wire. In some places there were explosions in the entanglement; later Lubnik learned that the enemy sappers had used Bangalore torpedoes, that is, long tubes filled with explosives, to blast gaps through the piled coils. Lieutenant Crombie, the section commander, rushed into the emplacement.

"One round Beehive – now!"

"We got authorisation, Lieutenant?" asked Lane. This was important as the tempest of metal darts would pass straight through the infantry position, killing everyone above ground. There was, however, no one visible and Lubnik knew that the reverse of their bunkers had been specially strengthened for such an eventuality.

"Yes – immediate! Come on, move it, for Chrissake!"

The round was withdrawn from the embrasure and loaded. Lubnik had not expected the tremendous muzzle flash as it was fired. When his night vision returned he saw that the enemy at the wire had dissolved into heaps, parts of which continued to move convulsively.

"Killer Junior – fuse two hundred! Come on, let's go!" yelled Crombie.

"Fuse two hundred!" repeated the ammunition numbers mechanically as the setting was checked.

The howitzer fired. Seconds later there was a flash near the edge of the trees and something trailing fire impacted just below the parapet, its explosion showering them with earth. The howitzer had just fired again when there was an explosion against the front of the weapon. The crew were felled and the right-hand tyre began to burn redly, giving off pungent black smoke. Some of the men were hit by shards of flying metal, but their flak jackets protected them from the worst effects; others were simply stunned for a moment or two.

"Recoilless rifle, sir!" said Lane, pointing. "There, at the edge of the jungle – spotted his backblast last time he fired!"

Crombie peered through his night vision binoculars.

"You're right. Okay, those sonsabitches have just fired their last shot. I'll lay this one myself – fuse for impact!"

"Gun's damaged, Lieutenant!" warned Lane.

Crombie carefully laid for line and elevation, then fired. The damaged recoil mechanism was unable to absorb the force generated and the howitzer bounded backwards, knocking the officer to the ground. He tried to climb to his feet but collapsed beside the weapon.

"Did we get him?" he asked.

"Yes, sir, you got him," said Lane. "Sort of tripod mounting – you blasted it and the crew are down, too."

"Fine." Crombie winced as he tried to move again. "Looks as though we've fired our last shot, too, but you can man the parapet when they come in, Sergeant Lane. I think my leg's broken, so I need a shoulder to get me to Number two Gun."

With Petersen, one of the ammunition numbers, serving as a crutch, the officer hopped off towards the section's second gun. Once more the infantry bunkers had begun spitting rifle and machine-gun fire towards the jungle.

"Close off the entrance!" shouted Lane.

They dragged the wrecked howitzer back into the entrance of the emplacement and began piling sandbags from the parapet around it to form a barricade.

"Check your weapons!"

They grabbed their M16s from the crew ready room and lined the parapet. Training and discipline had helped Lubnik cope with his fear while he had something to do, but now, knowing that the enemy was coming out of the darkness for him, he was seized by blind terror.

This time, there would be no Claymores, no Beehive and no Killer Junior to stop them. Eyes fixed, he could see what seemed to be huge numbers of enemy charging towards the now partially flattened entanglement. At the wire the enemy halted briefly. A rush of fiery trails streaked towards the infantry bunkers and their own emplacement, exploding against the sandbags or flashing just overhead with a roar.

"RPG-7s," commented Thompson laconically. "Anti-tank rockets – real wild, but you're okay behind layered sandbags."

Suddenly the enemy were charging forward again in a human wave that reminded Lubnik of a football crowd surging on to the pitch after an important game. Small-arms fire began to crack past. He later admitted to himself that he would have run but for the fact that his shaking legs would not have obeyed him and the realisation that there was nowhere to run to. The infantry were abandoning their bunkers and running as fast as they could go to rally near the headquarters complex in the centre of the base. One or two of them fell and remained motionless.

"There go the grunts!" shouted Lane. "Cover them!"

They opened a ragged fire which brought several of the enemy down. The muzzle of Lubnik's M16 waved about as the contents of his magazine vanished into thin air. He was conscious that Lane was shaking him violently.

"You're on automatic – switch to single shot and aim, boy, aim like they taught you. You want to live? Then pretend all of those goddam gooks are called Harris!"

It worked. Steadied down, Lubnik began picking his targets. After he had put the first one down the rest weren't too difficult. Then the enemy was there, face to face. For Lubnik he appeared in the form of an NVA officer wearing a solar topee. He had sprinted up the sandbags fronting the parapet, waving on his men with a pistol. For a second their eyes locked, then Lubnik shot him twice and he fell backwards. Looking round, Lubnik saw several more dead North Vietnamese sprawled across the parapet. Winston Ambrose, his white teeth bared in a snarl, was battering in the head of a youth with the butt of his M16.

Two grenades sailed across the parapet. One bounced under the trail of the gun and exploded without harming anyone. The second landed at Lane's feet. The sergeant was on the point of hurling it back when it exploded in his hand. He stared in disbelief at the mess of blood and fragmented bone that had replaced his wrist, then Thompson thrust him into the crew ready room to apply a tourniquet and field dressing. The rest of them kept firing.

The main weight of the assault had swept past, leaving them isolated like an off-shore rock surrounded by the incoming tide. Lubnik could see that their No 2 Gun was similarly isolated. A vicious shootout was taking place around the central bunker complex in which the infantry and headquarters personnel were being slowly pushed back by the attackers. About one-third of the base seemed to be in enemy hands. He was calmer now, but did not really expect to survive the night.

During the next few minutes several things happened. Although the sounds of fighting drowned the noise of its engines, there was clearly an aircraft overhead for suddenly the scene was as brilliantly illuminated as if it had been floodlit; looking up, Lubnik saw a series of huge white flares, each of immense candlepower, drifting down from a great height. Shortly after, there was the sound of tearing cloth and six shells burst in a line across the point where the enemy had broken through the perimeter. Lubnik guessed that one of the other FSBs had prevented the enemy's reinforcements entering the fight and had interdicted his line of withdrawal.

At this point he noticed that the battery's No 3 Gun had been swung round and was now pointing across the line of the enemy attack. The implications were terrifying and he yelled for Thompson. The latter took one brief look and dived for cover.

"Get down! For Chrissake get down! He's gonna use Beehive!"

"Without authorisation? What about us?"

"The way things are he doesn't need it – besides, his is the only gun that will bear into Charlie's flank without hitting our own people. Chances are he doesn't even know we're here, and if he did it would make no difference."

There was a belching roar as the gun fired. Something like a tempest swept past, ripping the sandbags to shreds at the rear of the emplacement. From beyond came a brief but high-pitched collective scream.

"Stay down!" shouted Thompson.

Again the gun blasted its hail of death across the interior of the base, and again came the screaming, though this time it was muted. Then there was comparative silence, punctuated by the continuing rattle of small-arms fire.

They peered over the parapet into the interior of the base. The enemy dead lay scattered over a wide area. Some of the survivors were firing their AK-47s and submachine-guns as they pulled back, pressed by the infantry; others were carrying or dragging their wounded with them. At Thompson's urging, the crew sniped at them as they went. More fell as they passed through the barrage on their way back to the jungle. As the firing ceased Lieutenant Crombie hobbled in with the assistance of his human crutch.

"You guys okay?"

"Sergeant Lane's hurt real bad, sir," said Thompson. "Reckon he'll lose his forearm. Otherwise, we're okay."

"Get Lane to the aid post as fast as you can. You did well, all of you."

Lubnik did not know whether he had done well or not. All he knew at the time was that he had been fighting for his survival, but now he was awed by Lane's sacrifice and conscious how much he and his comrades had depended upon each other.

The gruesome task of tidying up began shortly after dawn. The enemy dead, many of them horribly mangled, had to be sorted from the wounded. Lubnik recognised several faces he had seen in the village during the vegetable run. He overheard the Captain interrogating a wounded NVA officer whose legs were so smashed up that he would never walk again. The man had an intelligent face and spoke excellent English.

"You keep trying this and every time you get whipped," said the battery commander. "Don't you people have any regard for your men's lives?"

"You do not understand us," replied the prisoner. "The fact that we lose battles is not relevant. We shall go on fighting for ten, twenty, fifty years if necessary. In the end, it will be you who tire of the struggle."

Holder shrugged wearily.

"That's your General Giap talking and I've heard it all before. Try thinking for yourself once in a while."

When the final accounting was made there were 96 known enemy dead, a dozen wounded prisoners and a large quantity of captured arms. The infantry company had five killed and 21 wounded, while the battery's loss came to three killed, fifteen wounded and one howitzer put out of action. Two of the artillerymen were killed defending No 2 Gun's emplacement. The third, Sergeant Harris, was found riddled with grenade fragments outside the entrance to his bunker. This did not lie in the direct path of the enemy assault, but there were no witnesses to his death and, in view of the confused nature of the night action, further investigation would have proved pointless.

During what remained of Lubnik's tour the battery was lifted to a new FSB, but was not attacked again. He tried painting the enemy assault to get it out of his system. He was only partially successful, for although his pictures contained much vivid, accurate detail and were eagerly sought after, he knew they lacked integrity. He could never, he knew, convey his own terror during those hours; perhaps there were artists who could, but his own brush was unequal to the task.

When he left Vietnam he still did not approve of the war, although he understood its nature a little better. He had, however, learned much about himself. Most of all, he understood what the poet meant when he had said 'no man is an Island, entire of itself'. Good men had relied on him for their survival, and he on them. You could not be half a soldier, but you would have to have been there to know that. He chuckled as he looked out of the aircraft window, watching the Vietnamese coast recede. The two old guys back home would understand.

Once the tactical concept had been accepted, the Fire Support Base became a constant thorn in the communists' side. Repeated attempts were made to eliminate FSBs regardless of the cost involved. During these battles the Viet Cong and the North Vietnamese Army displayed suicidal courage in pressing their attacks to close quarters, only to be foiled by an equally courageous American defence; safe in Hanoi, the communist hierarchy remained completely indifferent to the horrific losses sustained by its soldiers.

In some cases the supreme courage shown by individuals in defence of FSBs resulted in their being awarded their country's highest decoration, the Medal of Honor. Some such episodes have formed the basis of this chapter, notably the awards made to Staff Sergeant Webster Anderson and PFC Sammy L. Davis for their actions at, respectively, an un-named FSB during Operation 'Wheeler', and the defence of FSB Cudgel.

The average age of the Americans serving in Vietnam was 19, considerably younger than their counterparts who had fought in the Second World War or the Korean War. As the Vietnam involvement was less than popular at home, the conscripts were conscious of pressures from a vocal peace movement which had the support of large sections of the media and the academic world; simultaneously, they belonged to a generation inclined to challenge the established social canons at every level. Having said that, it is a matter of record that the US Army was not defeated on any battlefield, a fact readily acknowledged by its former enemies.

CORPORAL
GARY SHANKLAND

Light Infantry attached 1st Cumberland Fusiliers,
Saudi Arabia and Kuwait, February 1991

The major called the company to attention and saluted. The grey-haired, bespectacled man wearing a light sweater and open-necked shirt waved cheerfully as he climbed aboard his Land Rover.

"Good luck, everyone!" he called in his quiet, modulated voice.

The men dispersed as the numerous vehicles of the Prime Minister's entourage disappeared into the distance, leaving the dust to settle in their wake.

"Seems like a decent enough bloke," commented Corporal Gary Shankland to his fellow section commander, Tom Gill.

"Oh aye, an' on his best behaviour, too!"

Gill was a tough Tynesider, inclined to be forthright and sometimes bitter in his opinions.

"But then he would be, wouldn't he?" he continued. "All he's doin' is askin' us to put it on the line for him before he gives us the chop! He's got a lot o' brass neck, I'll give him that!"

Shortly before the war the government had produced a defence review entitled *Options for Change*. Ever since the collapse of the Soviet Union everyone had regarded some reduction in the size of the armed services as inevitable, but the proposed cuts were deep and dangerous, involving the abolition or amalgamation of numerous regiments and the redundancy at a time of high unemployment of some 40,000 men. Gill's bitterness was understandable as his chances of finding a job at home were particularly slim. Shankland was sympathetic as Gill, who had a growing family, was older and his regiment, the Cumberland Fusiliers, was one of those expected to disappear.

"Maybe they'll think again," he said. "They were caught with their pants down over the Falklands and the same has happened this time. It might just have sunk in that wars come out of nowhere."

"Aye, an' pigs might fly. They're politicians, man – they need the money for deadbeats, scroungers an' foreigners who want to live off our social. What chance has the squaddie got against competition like that?"

"Come off it, Tom. Most people aren't on benefit because they want to be, and you know it."

"I'll name you a dozen who do, straight off, an' that's just in our street! See you."

He wandered off to join his own section. Shankland pulled a bottle from the water box and sat down with his back against the Warrior. His men had started a kickabout but he was too hot to join them, so he read through his post again.

There was, of course, something in what Gill had said. Ever since the 1950s political expediency had seen the Army progressively reduced in size until, even before the latest proposals were published, it was having difficulty in meeting its commitments. Shankland himself hailed from Barchester and would have joined his county regiment, had it still existed. As it was, the independent life of the Royal Barset Rifles had ended twenty years earlier when it was absorbed into the Light Infantry, one of the new 'big' regiments with several battalions, any one of which could be axed by the government of the day, safe in the knowledge that there would be no political repercussions within the original counties. Now, all that remained of the Royal Barset Rifles was the Light Infantry office where he had enlisted, a fine regimental museum covering more than two centuries of history, and the Old Comrades in their blazers and shiny shoes, marching proudly to the Cathedral every Armistice Sunday. Of course you couldn't blame blokes for not signing on when they knew their careers could be ended prematurely. The result was often under-recruiting, so that battalions going on active service sometimes had to be temporarily brought up to strength by borrowing men from other units. Because of this he had done a couple of extra tours in Ulster and, for the same reason, he and a dozen riflemen had been attached to the Cumberland Fusiliers.

He opened a copy of his own regimental journal which had arrived with the day's mail. There was a full-page photograph entitled 'The Road to Mons'. It showed part of the 1st Battalion Royal Barset Rifles fallen out beside a Belgian road. In the foreground, apparently oblivious to the photographer, two sergeants were sitting smoking. The caption said that one, Sergeant Dick Platt, had been killed the following day and that the other, Sergeant John Brodrick, had risen to commissioned rank by the end of the war, occupied the post of Regimental Secretary for several years, and died in 1965. The ranks of stolid, moustached faces stared belligerently at him across nearly eighty years from under their peaked caps; hard men used to hard soldiering all over the world for a pittance. He compared them in his mind with the modern soldier who, thanks to social changes, was bigger, healthier, fitter, better educated and thought for himself as a matter of course. Furthermore, he was selectively recruited. From personal experience of weekends held for potential recruits Shankland knew that some, shocked by the discipline and need for self-reliance, would proceed no further; others, who displayed some aptitude but were unfit because they did not take regular exercise or were unable to march far because their feet had been softened by years of wearing trainers, might be told to come back once they had got themselves into some sort of order; some did and others didn't. On balance, from every ten potential recruits, two would be considered suitable for further training. That he thought fair in a professional army, for unlike the men of Mons, who were simply required to march and fight, the demands on the technical skills of the modern infantryman were heavy. He might, for example, in addition to becoming expert in using the entire range of infantry weapons, drive and maintain the Warrior Infantry Fighting Vehicle or operate a variety of radio sets and night vision devices. In some respects, Shankland reflected, the almost universal possession of family cars and early acquaintance with computers balanced the drag on recruiting caused by soft living as those under instruction experienced little difficulty with technical training, much of which was carried out with simulators.

The footballers finished their game and, sweating profusely, converged on the bottled water box.

"Take your salt tablets," said Shankland. "Do it now, before you forget."

In the desert failure to counter dehydration with salt as well as water could result in heat-stroke.

An Egyptian convoy drove past. The section cheered, waved its bottles, began walking jerkily and started singing 'Walk Like an Egyptian'. Uncomprehending, the Egyptians grinned and waved back. Someone on high, more than likely a politically correct civil servant from the Ministry of Defence or the Foreign Office, had tried to prohibit the song on the grounds that it might offend some Arab members of the Coalition army. Consequently, the soldiers sang it on every possible occasion. Shankland chuckled to himself. Who in his right mind was going to submit a charge sheet reading: "Conduct to prejudice of good order and military discipline in that he, having been ordered not to do so, did sing 'Walk Like an Egyptian'?"

Lieutenant Mason, the platoon commander, strolled past, feigning ignorance.

"What *is* that song they're singing, Corporal Shankland?"

"Wouldn't know, sir. Terrible racket. Ought not to be allowed!"

A Humvee drove up and four Americans tumbled out.

"Hi, guys! Wanna trade?"

British and American troops always seemed to prefer the other's diet. Soon a brisk trade was being done on a democratic basis as British compo tins were exchanged for American K rations. This was followed by an equally brisk exchange of pornographic magazines, accompanied by exclamations of appreciation and amazement.

"We just got our shots this morning," said the American sergeant. "You guys had shots?"

"Yes, we've had shots and more shots, then pills on top of that."

"Hope the eggheads know what they're doing. Still, you never know what kinda stroke Big Bad Saddam is gonna pull. They say he's real big in the biological and chemical warfare department – even gasses his own people if he's a mind. This your version of our Bradley?"

He pointed to the Warrior.

"That's right," said Shankland. "Fancy a look around?"

He led the way aboard, pointing out the various features of the vehicle.

"Seats for four riflemen on the right and three on the left, all with seat belts. They can stow their kit under the seats or in the sponsons. Enter and exit by double doors in the rear wall. The vehicle commander sits on the right of the turret but dismounts to lead the section whenever it's necessary to fight on foot. The gunner's on my left and the driver sits down there with the engine on his right."

"Uh-huh. Layout's a little different but it's pretty much the same as ours. What's your armament?"

"30mm Rarden cannon and coaxial 7.62mm machine-gun. The Rarden will take out any of his personnel carriers at above a thousand metres – his tanks as well, if we get a flank or rear shot. Pretty accurate, too – at that range we can get a metre grouping with six shots. Cases are ejected forward and we don't get fumes in the turret."

"Sounds good to me. Say, you got a set of combat fatigues you wanna trade, mebbe two for one?"

The Americans seemed to like the British pattern of camouflage-dyed khaki drill.

"It's a good offer but you'll get me shot."

"Too bad. We'll be on our way – take it easy, you guys."

The Americans had barely left when a long Land Rover arrived, bringing a civilian television crew and their minder, an RAF flight lieutenant. The occupants were hot, sweaty and ill-tempered.

"You C Company, Cumberland Fusiliers?" shouted the driver.

"That's right, mate."

A woman of about 35 with long blonde hair jumped out. She might have been attractive had it not been for her feral expression and angry, darting eyes. Shankland recognised Paula Newton, a harsh, abrasive interviewer. She was sufficiently prized within her industry for her to be able to name her own salary. He had come across her once or twice in Ulster and her style was definitely not soldier-friendly. This, he reflected, was not something the men of Mons had needed to worry about.

"I've been all over the pissing desert looking for you!" she yelled. "Where the **** have you been? Anyway, I've got permission to interview you, so I'll start now."

"You'd better speak to Major Grantly first – let him know you've arrived, Miss."

"Mizz!" she bridled. "Alright, where the **** is he, then? I haven't time to waste!"

Shankland pointed to a Warrior in the centre of the leaguer.

"You'll find him by that vehicle with the pennon on the aerial, Miss Mizz."

She glared at him and stalked off with her minder in tow.

"You got straight up her nose," said Lance-Corporal George Douglas, the section's second in command. "She's got a right cob on, hasn't she?"

"She can get on with it – earns a lot more than the divisional commander, I can tell you," Shankland replied. "Too big a fish for the correspondents' pools. Likes to make her own news."

Five minutes later she was back, accompanied by Lieutenant Mason and Frank Barraclough, the platoon sergeant.

"Time for you to shine," said Mason while the platoon gathered round. "Paula Newton is representing several Northern independent television companies. She wants some material on the regiment and we've been selected to give it to her. By tomorrow night your ugly mugs could be glaring out of the screen all over Cumbria."

"I'll just do a short introduction then get round to talking to you personally," said Paula Newton, smiling broadly. In this mode she really looked rather nice. She began.

"Since I last spoke to you from the front the British First Armoured Division has moved far to the west ..."

"Cut!" interjected her RAF minder sharply. "That's not on and you know it! It will have to come out."

The virago was suddenly back, her face a mask of fury as she rounded on him with a torrent of obscene language. Shankland could see that the men didn't like it. By now they were used to girls who wanted to be one of the boys, but most of them came from decent homes and, however they talked among themselves, they still had little time for a foul-mouthed woman.

"The sooner I'm clear of you, you utter ponce, the better!" she concluded before starting again.

"These are the men who are shortly to tackle Saddam Hussein's battle-hardened army ..."

"Crap!" said Tom Gill. "The air force have been battering them for weeks – have you seen the state o' their deserters?"

"Cut!" said the sound recordist. "Afraid I picked that up."

She started again. "These are the men who are shortly to tackle Saddam Hussein's battle-hardened army, and not least of their worries will be his crack Republican Guard ..."

"Crack!" commented Fusilier Braithwaite. "They couldn't crack a broken window – they've never had to fight anyone who fights back!"

"Cut!" said the sound recordist.

"I think we'll do the introduction in long shot," said Paula Newton coldly.

"Give her a chance, lads," said Barraclough when the camera crew had moved off into the distance. "She's only doing what she sees as her job."

When it came to the personal interviews Shankland had to admit that, although she pointedly ignored him, she was very good indeed. With surprising ease she got the men to talk about themselves, nodding as though in complete agreement with what they said. However, when it came to asking them how they felt about going to war, he sensed that she was uncomfortable with their replies.

"It's my job," said one. "It's what you pay me for."

"This is what it's about," said another. "I knew that when I signed on – I'm a professional."

"This isn't what she wants to use," thought Shankland. "She wants something with an angle more in line with her own opinions. She's picking her victim, then she'll bowl him a googly."

She picked Fusilier Norman Cranthorpe, the biggest man in the platoon, and pounced suddenly.

"Some people are suggesting the war is being fought for the benefit of the oil companies," she said. "Do you agree with them?"

"Cut!" said the minder. "The question has political implications and I won't allow it!"

Cranthorpe might seem slow but he was as intelligent as any of them and could be very plainspoken in his opinions when annoyed, as he clearly was now. Though the camera had stopped running, he squared up to the interviewer, towering over her.

"She asked me a question and I'll give her a fair answer if you don't mind, sir. I say bugger the oil companies. When you get down to it, Saddam's in Kuwait, he's no business there, and we're going to throw him out – it's as simple as that. What do you think of most of the world's oil supplies being controlled by a nutter like that? Think on that, woman!"

Her jaw dropped and there was a moment of silent tension.

"Alright, Cranthorpe," said Shankland. "Now that the two of you have got that sorted, why don't you ask her to marry you? The two of you would get on like a house on fire!"

She joined in the good-natured laughter.

"Don't you think I've got troubles enough without taking on a great brute like you?" she said to the grinning Cranthorpe. Then, looking round at the rest of them, she revealed an unexpected side of her character. "I don't think I'll see you again before the ground offensive starts – look after yourselves."

She turned to her minder.

"I think I've just learned something," she said. "Honesty can be plain bloody devastating when you're not used to it! Come on, you, I owe you an apology – yet again!"

"Turned out to be almost human after all," said Gill as they watched the Land Rover drive off.

"It was Cranthorpe who got under her skin. No one's dared to speak to her like that for years. Touched a nerve and for some reason she couldn't handle it."

"Ay, well, man, if she likes that sort o' thing she should spend more time in Geordieland – we talk like that all day long!"

"Weapon inspection in thirty minutes!" shouted Sergeant Barraclough.

In the desert weapons were kept oil-free and remained wrapped for as long as possible to keep grit from penetrating the moving parts. Shankland stripped down his SA80 assault rifle, wiping each part with care. He hadn't liked the weapon when it replaced the SLR, just as the old hands had not welcomed the latter when it replaced the old Lee-Enfield which had seen the Army through two world wars. It was not, however, just his soldier's innate conservatism, as at first there had been problems with the weapon, most of which stemmed from the manufacturing process. Once these had been eliminated he began to like the little bullpup rifle in which the designers had managed to maintain the barrel length yet still produce a weapon that was handy to carry and shoot. In particular he liked the optical sight, which gave very accurate results. He checked his two ready-use magazines, each loaded with thirty 5.56mm rounds and taped securely together upside down for speed of changeover, satisfying himself that they were free of grit. Finally, he gave a wipe to the short bayonet, the business end of which was viciously shaped like a Bowie knife. It may have seemed strange to some that in this age of massive firepower the bayonet was still issued, but the fact remained that it had been used in the Falklands and, as it was the infantryman's weapon of last resort in close-quarter combat, it still could not be ignored. Nearby, Douglas and Braithwaite were stripping down the section's light support weapon.

This was very similar to the SA80 but was equipped with a heavy-duty sustained fire barrel and bipod. It was, he reflected, a much handier piece of kit than the old General Purpose Machine-Gun when it came to scrambling in and out of the Warrior; furthermore, it had a theoretical output of over 700 rounds per minute.

"Strike the bivouacs and start stowing your kit," said Mason when the weapons inspection was over. "We're moving an hour after last light. You've got time for a brew and a hot meal if you're quick about it."

The move took them westwards again. They were used to night marches, for such was the firepower available on the battlefield that it had long been obvious during their years of training in Germany for the possible war against the Warsaw Pact that most movement and fighting would take place during the hours of darkness. In the troop compartment most of the riflemen dozed, their heads nodding in response to the Warrior's movements. Towards first light the company was met by guides and led into its new leaguer. Nearby, the last tanks of the Dragoon Guard regiment they would support were coming off their transporters. By dawn the battlegroup was concealed under its camouflage nets.

A keen sense of anticipation began to build up. The Coalition's air offensive against Iraq had been running for more than five weeks and had become a part of daily life; now, few even bothered to glance up at the aircraft passing overhead and even the distant rumble as the giant B52s unloaded hundreds of tons of bombs generated little interest. It had been established beyond reasonable doubt not only that the enemy's command and control structure had been neutralised but also that his lines of communication had been so severely disrupted that the Iraqi army in Kuwait was on the verge of starvation and short of supplies of every kind. For weeks now that same army had been pounded from the air as had no other in history. In recent days Shankland had noticed that the self-propelled guns and multiple rocket-launchers of the divisional artillery had been engaging in 'shoot-and-scoot' fire missions to destroy whatever remained. Looking around the thousands of fighting and support vehicles spread over the desert he knew that the curtain was about to rise on the last act of the drama and wondered how he would react if he were a starving, nerve-shattered Iraqi soldier required to face such an onslaught.

Against this, he knew that nothing could be taken for granted. The Iraqis had been in Kuwait long enough for them to have constructed extensive defences, the nature of which had been revealed by detailed air reconnaissance. Along the frontier they had raised a sand wall, filled ditches with oil ready to be set ablaze, and laid minefields. Beyond lay their infantry divisions in triangular keeps, sited in depth, each containing mortar and machine-gun positions, bunkers and dug-in tanks or APCs. Behind the infantry lay the bulk of the Iraqi armour, including the Republican Guard, apparently ready to counter-attack.

Shankland was under the impression that their own principal task would be fighting through the keeps once the tanks had neutralised the armour within. To this end they had endlessly practised their trench and bunker clearing drill, developing a speed and aggression which he felt would have terrified him had he been on the other side. As to the degree of resistance they might expect he had no idea. If the Iraqis were as demoralised as they were said to be, well and good; on the other hand, there were plenty of examples throughout military history confirming that even second-rate troops could fight well behind prepared defences.

Within the leaguer area the day was spent in a bustle of purposeful activity. Drivers checked over their vehicles, calling in the fitters to rectify a fault where necessary. Commanders and radio operators pored over newly issued signals instructions. Fuel was replenished and ammunition supplies augmented. Each vehicle received rations and water for several days. Towards evening Lieutenant Mason briefed the platoon.

"Alright, the waiting is over. The ground offensive starts before first light tomorrow. The overall situation is as follows. The Arab contingents and the US Marines will attack across the southern frontier of Kuwait and advance on Kuwait City. As you know, since we moved west, our division has become part of the US VII Corps. The division's task is to advance north across the Saudi/Iraqi frontier, then swing east into Kuwait. This will have two objects. Firstly, it will get us behind the enemy's forward defences and he won't like it. Secondly, when the enemy armour counter-attacks, the division will act as an anvil; the hammer will be provided by two American armoured divisions which will make an even wider left hook and enter Kuwait behind them. On the left of VII Corps is the US XVIII Airborne Corps."

"What will they be doing while all this is going on, sir?" asked Fusilier Dyson, a member of Tom Gill's section with a reputation for questioning his orders.

"What's it to you, lad?" said Gill, thumping him in a hard but friendly manner. "Maybe you'd like a word with Stormin' Norman on the subject? Just mind your own bloody business!"

When the laughter had died down Mason responded.

"The short answer is I don't know because I haven't been told – deliberately, I suspect. But you can depend on their being kept pretty busy and as they've got airborne and airmobile assets and a French armoured division you can use your imaginations.

"Right, as far as Phase One is concerned, the US 1st Infantry Division will be responsible for clearing lanes through the enemy minefields, neutralising the oil trenches and breaching the sand berm. The British 1st Armoured Division will then pass through the gaps created. Our own battlegroup, that is, the Dragoon Guards, ourselves, our supporting artillery and engineers, will not be the first through and no move is anticipated before noon tomorrow."

At the end of the briefing Mason urged them to get a good night's sleep as it was unlikely they would get another for several days. Shankland experienced no difficulty in dropping off but was woken before first light by the artillery opening fire. Poking his head out of the bivouac he saw that it was raining.

The section washed, shaved, cooked breakfast, donned battle order and stowed the Warrior. They were unusually quiet and Shankland knew that they were as keyed up as he was. The hours of waiting that followed did not help. At length they were called forward in the wake of the Dragoon Guards' huge Challenger tanks. Abruptly the column came to a standstill as orders were passed down the radio net. It seemed that the battlegroup commander had decided that if Saddam was going to use his biological and chemical weapons, now was as good a time as any. Shankland, though inclined to agree, felt an unreasonable annoyance.

"Close down!" he shouted, flicking on the overpressure system when all the hatches were shut. "Get your Noddy suits and gas masks on!"

The air within the troop compartment was blue with cursing. It was no easy matter pulling on the disposable NBC suits in the confines of the vehicle and the addition of gas masks under helmets made the already hot and humid interior unbearable. The column began moving forward again. Shankland could see that the Americans waving them through the gap were wearing goggled anti-gas hoods. No doubt this had influenced the battlegroup commander's decision. He glanced at his watch. They had crossed into enemy territory at about 1430 but there was little sign of fighting.

For the next three hours they drove slowly but steadily on, catching up with the supply and support echelons of the previous battlegroup. The column then halted and the removal of NBC clothing was authorised as the fuel replenishment trucks arrived. Some of the men, stepping gratefully out into the heavy rain, were seriously alarmed by the thick, greasy drops which left black smears on skin and clothing.

"Are you sure this is alright, sir?" Shankland asked Mason as the latter walked down the platoon's line of vehicles.

"Yes, it's unpleasant but it's alright. I've just heard that as soon as the attack started Saddam gave orders for every oil well in Kuwait to be torched. The prevailing wind is bringing the smoke across from the coast. It's a case of 'If I can't have it, then neither can you!'"

They had now reached the startline for the wheel eastwards towards the Kuwaiti frontier. At 1930 the battlegroup shook out into tactical formation and moved off. From his cupola Shankland could see the Dragoon Guards were advancing with two of their tank squadrons forward while the third covered the right flank. Their own company was some distance behind, in the centre, while the self-propelled guns paused from time to time to fire concentrations at likely targets ahead.

The rain ceased, for which Shankland was grateful as he had begun to feel as though he had taken a bath in diesel oil. Otherwise, little happened until about 2230 when one of the Challengers was illuminated by an infra-red searchlight. Both forward tank squadrons halted and opened fire immediately. The searchlight suddenly died. Shankland, peering through his night vision scanner, was forced to provide a running commentary on the engagement for the others.

"Looks like several T55s, dug in facing south. The nearest's got his turret traversed this way but he's started to burn. He's masking the fire of the others ... One's trying to reverse out of his scrape ... they've blown his turret right off! Now it's ten yards away, upside down ... The rest of them don't like it. They're bailing out ... Hang on, the position's bigger than I thought ... They've started machine-gunning our tanks ... about four different posts as far as I can see ... and there's some personnel carriers on the left ... BTR60s and MTBLS, half a dozen of them ... make that five, four, no three, minus crews running like hell ... bit of mortaring, too, all directed at the tanks, but it's wild ... they don't seem to know we're here ... we're probably too far out in the dark ... our blokes seem to have switched to HESH ... jeez, what a wallop! I've never seen so many blokes airborne at once! ... and there goes one of his mortars – that won't pass inspection next time around! ... hello, they seem to be packing it in ... standing up in their trenches with their hands up."

Major Grantly's voice came through incisively in the headphones.

"All stations India Three advance behind our friends and clear the position. Seven right, Eight left, Nine follow through. Out."

The artillery had begun firing illuminating shells. The tanks could be seen moving slowly forward, headlights blazing and guns traversing with infinite menace as they closed in on the trenches.

"Put your foot down, we're going in!" said Shankland to the driver, Fusilier Ted Roberts. "Right, lads, now's your chance! They look cowed, but don't take any risks!"

The line of Warriors surged forward, roaring through the intervals between the tanks to halt on the edge of the position with their own guns covering the Iraqis. Bayonets glinting wickedly, the section boiled out of the rear doors and tore across the trench while the other platoons methodically cleared the rest of the position. They began the business of separating the prisoners from their arms, frisking them, shoving them into groups and making them sit down. The Iraqis were grubby, needed haircuts, were unshaven and very frightened. One of them, babbling, abased himself before Shankland, banging his forehead on the ground as he seized the corporal's ankles in a grip of iron.

"Someone get rid of this creep!" said Shankland in disgust.

Cranthorpe lifted the weeping man effortlessly and flung him among his fellows.

"Aye, you're all very brave when it comes to gang-banging the Kuwaiti girls, but it's different when it comes to men's work, isn't it?"

"Anyone speak English?" Mason asked.

One of prisoners came forward, smiling ingratiatingly.

"I speak good English. I work for oil company."

Mason took out a grenade and showed it to him.

"Anyone in the bunkers? You tell them they've got ten seconds to get up here. Understand?"

The man nodded and began shouting into the bunker entrances. Two or three more frightened figures appeared.

"That it?" said Mason. "Alright, they've had their chance."

Muffled explosions came from all over the position as the bunkers were cleared. Company Sergeant-Major Fisher and a squad of riflemen were already marshalling the prisoners. Sergeant-Majors seemed to speak some kind of international language, reflected Shankland, for as a result of Fisher's bellowing the Iraqis, several hundred of them, were quickly herded into an inwards-facing circle and made to sit down, there to await the arrival of the transport that would take them to the prisoner-of-war compound.

From start to finish the engagement had taken about an hour. Then they were off again, trundling along behind the Dragoon Guards. At 0330 the Challengers again halted and began exchanging fire with dug-in enemy tanks. Once more, these had been emplaced to meet an attack from the south and were at a severe disadvantage, being quickly set ablaze as they traversed their turrets to meet the unexpected threat from the west.

When the Fusiliers were committed to clearing the position on foot most of the Iraqis surrendered willingly enough, but others made a run for it and Shankland's section was among those involved in the exchange of fire, dropping several before the rest vanished into the darkness. One man in Gill's section received a flesh wound in the arm but declined evacuation.

First light was slow in coming because the eastern sky was blackened by the huge curtain of smoke rising from Kuwait. After a while it revealed a dismal panorama of burning tank hulks and wrecked vehicles. In the distance numerous Iraqis could be seen wandering about singly or in groups. Mason's platoon was sent out to round them up while the Challengers refuelled and re-ammunitioned; all were happy to begin the trudge into captivity. Shankland received the surrender of a brigadier and his staff. The brigadier said in excellent English that he was the commander of an armoured brigade that had been destroyed. Leaving the staff to make their own way, Shankland shoved him into the troop compartment. He was short, fat, sleek, gave off an all-pervading smell of middle-eastern after-shave and was clearly disgruntled by having to sit on the floor.

"Do we have to have him in here?" protested Braithwaite. "Exhaust fumes and body odour we can take, but he stinks the place out!"

"I don't want him," said Major Grantly on their return. "He's your collar, so you can take him across to the battlegroup commander."

The lieutenant-colonel commanding the Dragoon Guards was sitting on his tank turret drinking tea from a tin mug. He remained where he was while Shankland extracted the brigadier from the back of the Warrior. Grinning, the rest of the section followed.

"Nice one, Corporal Shankland," said the colonel, reading his name tape. "Who is he?"

"Says he commanded an armoured brigade, sir."

"Does he?" The colonel looked askance at the prisoner who, despite his seniority, had assumed a deferential stance. "Speak English, does he?"

"I speak English, Colonel," said the prisoner. "My expectation, of course, is to be accorded the courtesy due to my rank."

The colonel took another pull at his mug and continued to regard him coldly from on high.

"I should have thought that the welfare of your men was your first consideration."

The brigadier spread his hands and shrugged.

"My men are dead, prisoners, scattered or fled. I have no men. I was on my way to summon help when I was captured."

"You know," said the colonel at length, "There's something else about you people I find difficult to understand. Tanks and APCs are offensive weapons, yet you waste them by digging them into the ground. Why is that?"

The brigadier suddenly became voluble.

"In our army the orders of the Revolutionary Command Council must be obeyed to the letter. Besides, the contest is not a fair one. For forty years you have been training to fight World War Three, whereas we have been forced to adopt the methods of World War Two. What is more, we have no air force to help us."

"And whose fault is all that?" asked the colonel. He turned to his adjutant. "Give him to the Intelligence Officer. When they've finished chatting you can send him back to division."

The battlegroup commander's frigid manner vanished as he grinned down at the section.

"Well done, you lot – they really are the pits, aren't they? You can tell everyone it's all going far better than we expected. The whole thing looks like being sorted very quickly."

The better weather meant that the day's advance was constantly overflown by tank-busting aircraft and helicopters that pounced on anything that moved in their path. As the desert dried out the Warriors were forced to pass through the dust clouds thrown up by the Dragoon Guards. Shankland lowered his goggles and covered his nose and mouth with a scarf which he tied behind his helmet. Despite this, the combination of unshaven stubble, the rain's greasy residue and particles of sand soon began to make his face sore. He longed for a wash but winced at the thought of shaving.

It was soon apparent that whatever remained of the Iraqis' will to fight had drained away into the sand, like the previous day's rain. Having abandoned their personal weapons, large groups of them regularly came forward to surrender, waving white articles of cloth. There were too many of them to administer so they were simply told to keep walking east until someone picked them up.

There were numerous abandoned positions, some of which contained smashed field guns and other weapons. Elsewhere, there were burning transport vehicles, self-propelled guns, armoured cars and personnel carriers that had been caught by the Coalition air force as they tried to escape. At the day's first major objective the Challengers halted to engage a line of emplaced T55s. There was no reply and the Fusiliers were quickly sent in. They found that two of the tanks had already been knocked out by air strikes and the rest had been abandoned by their crews, who were found cowering in nearby bunkers.

"Not much of a choice for them," commented Shankland as the section winkled them out. "If they move out into the open their tanks get wellied by aircraft while they're trying to escape, and if they stay here and fight they get a good clobbering off the Challengers."

"Shouldn't have joined if they can't take a laugh," said Braithwaite, unmoved.

After the Challengers had slammed a round into each of the captured tanks the battlegroup moved on. There were several similar encounters during the day, each of which confirmed that the Iraqi army had broken. After dark, however, the enemy took advantage of the reduced air activity to attempt the withdrawal of some at least of his units.

At about 2200 the leading Challenger squadrons had halted hull-down behind a low ridge that was barely more than a swelling in the desert. Their night-vision devices revealed a large convoy moving north across their front. Using their thermal image gunsights, they opened fire. Two T55 companies wheeled towards them in an attempt to protect their charges. While the gun flashes tore the darkness apart, the Fusiliers received orders to move on to the left flank of the engagement and shoot up the convoy with the Warriors' main armament.

Shankland's gunner, a taciturn Fusilier named Conron, had not until now been required to use his weapons. Shankland directed him to lay on a large articulated lorry that was labouring along near the front of the convoy. The Rarden banged and they watched the trace vanish into the target. The thunderclap explosion, accompanied by an enormous fireball, was audible inside the troop compartment.

"Magic!" said Conron, well pleased with his effort.

"Looks like you've taken out someone's ammo supply for the next three months!"

The explosion had wrecked or set fire to several neighbouring vehicles. The rest of the convoy came to a standstill, men piling out of trucks and personnel carriers with their hands raised. Several of the T55s were also burning and the rest tried to scuttle off into the darkness. Most of them were easily picked off. Sergeant Barraclough's gunner claimed one with a shot through the stern plate, this being hotly contested by Conron, who had taken the same point of aim. Mason decided they should share the kill.

After the prisoners had shuffled off and the remnant of the convoy destroyed, the battlegroup resumed its advance. This continued remorselessly throughout the night and the following day, its nature now set. The men were becoming tired and hungry, having been unable to snatch more than a quick brew and a bite during the brief halts.

At dusk the battlegroup halted to allow essential maintenance. The fuel, ammunition and water trucks arrived, followed by repaired breakdowns and the exhausted fitter teams who had worked without pause. Orders indicated that the battlegroup was operating on schedule and that there would be no move before first light. After their various tasks had been completed, Shankland's section cooked themselves a large communal curry and thankfully retired to their sleeping-bags, having drawn their turns for guard duty out of a hat.

At dawn on 28 February the battlegroup moved off again, crossing the shallow wadi which marked the western boundary of Kuwait. The morning was hazy with visibility reduced to about half a mile. There was no opposition, merely the usual abandoned positions and wrecked vehicles. By now they had become used to the heavy pall of smoke cast by the burning oil wells, but as the multiple raging fires came into view it began to seem as though they had entered hell itself. Major Grantly's voice in the headphones was flat and non-committal.

"All stations India Three. The enemy has agreed unconditionally to evacuate Kuwait. All Coalition forces have therefore been ordered to cease firing with effect from 0800. You will unload and clear guns at that time. Out."

The battlegroup went into leaguer thirty minutes later. There was general relief that their victory over the world's fourth largest army had been so easily achieved, that the fighting was over, that they had survived and that their casualties had been so trivial. The early elation, however, was soon replaced by a sense of anti-climax.

"The job's only half finished," was Shankland's comment to Gill. "Just a few more days and we'd have sorted that bastard in Baghdad once and for all."

"Aye, but what d'ye expect when it's politicians runnin' things? Maybe they think Saddam would pull up short if he was in our shoes? Some hopes! Why, he's laughin' at us fit to bust, man!"

The victory won by General Norman Schwarzkopf's Coalition army in just 100 hours resulted in between 40,000 and 60,000 Iraqi soldiers being killed, some 80,000 captured and the dispersion of a similar number; more than 3,000 tanks, 2,400 APCs and 3,000 artillery pieces were captured or destroyed. Coalition casualties amounted to 166 killed and 207 wounded; of the former, 28 died in a Scud missile strike against Dharhan air base and a high proportion of the remainder were killed in 'friendly fire' battlefield accidents.

President George Bush's imposition of a ceasefire on 28 February will remain one of history's questionable decisions. It not only enabled Saddam Hussein to use the remnant of his Republican Guard to put down local risings, killing thousands of his subjects in the process, but also ensured that his continued presence would provide a source of trouble for many years to come.

After the Gulf War the British government implemented its ill-considered Options for Change policy, reducing the Army to the size it had been during the early years of the 18th century; in some areas this was undoubtedly one of the contributory causes of its catastrophic defeat in the General Election of 1997.

Of its very nature, the relationship between the Armed Services and the media is ambivalent as each need the other yet both have differing priorities. This is particularly true of television, which has enormous power to influence. Controversial television coverage of the Vietnam War resulted in restraints being imposed during subsequent conflicts. Despite this, during the Gulf War the highly sensitive news that the British 1st Armoured Division had moved west was broadcast; had Saddam Hussein and his advisers possessed an average degree of strategic insight, this would have enabled them to divine some, at least, of General Schwarzkopf's intentions and act accordingly.

At the time of writing the so-called Gulf War Syndrome, apparently stemming from the complex use of drugs to combat the possible use of chemical and biological weapons, remains under investigation. All that can be said is that veterans of earlier wars do not appear to have suffered in this way.